need you NOW

AVA HUNTER

Need You Now
Nashville Star Series, #3
Copyright © 2022 Ava Hunter

ISBN: 978-1-7374743-3-3

Need You Now is a work of fiction. Characters, names, places, angst and incidents are a work of the author's imagination and are fictitious. Any resemblance to real life events or persons, living or dead, is entirely coincidental and not intended by the author.

Cover Design: Sarah Hansen/Okay Creations
Cover Image: © Regina Wamba
Editing: Eliza Dee of Clio Editing Services
Paperback formatting: Champagne Book Design

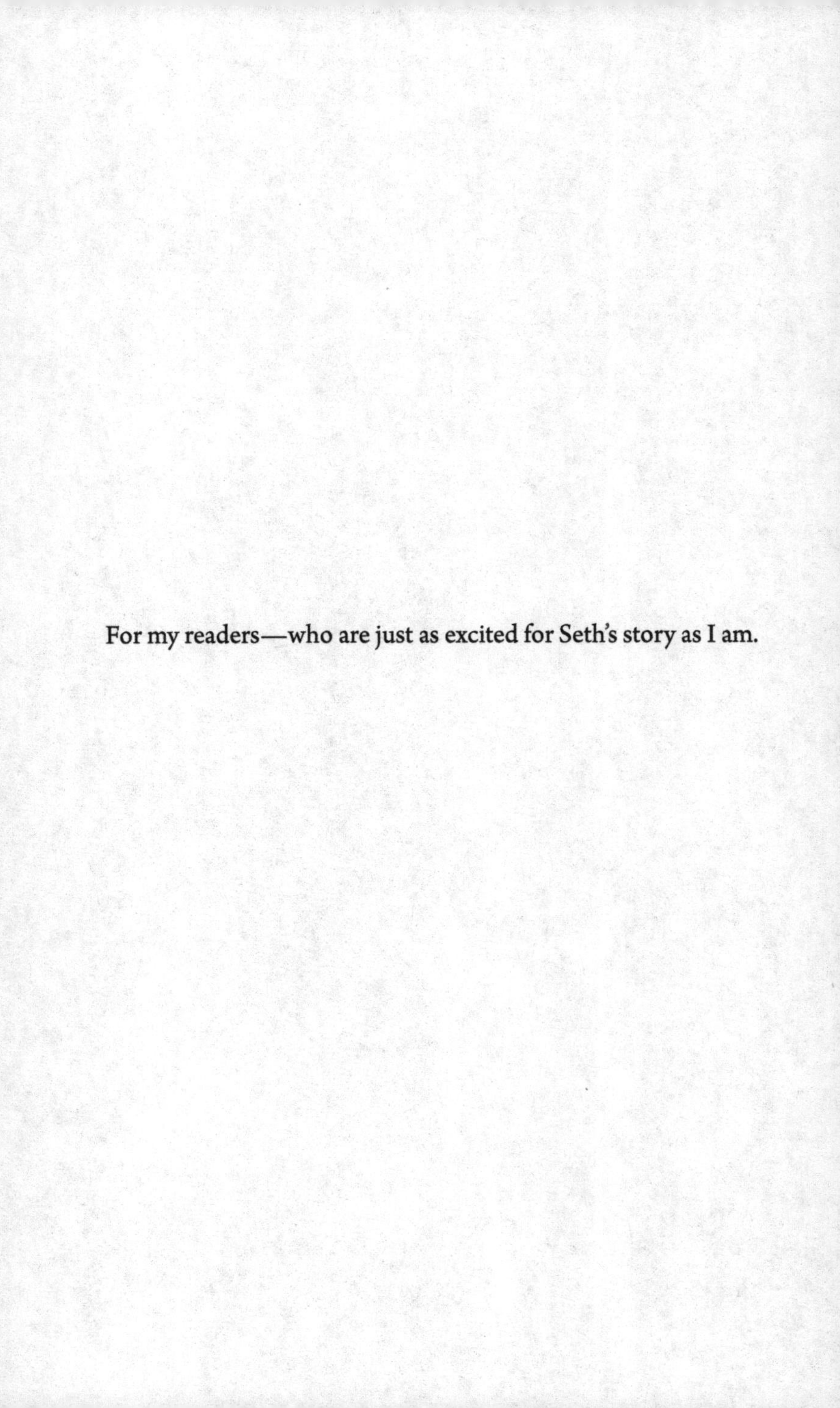

For my readers—who are just as excited for Seth's story as I am.

chapter
ONE

Throw it away. Just flush it down the fuckin' drain, man.

The voice inside Seth Kincaid's head is insistent, damn near on a tear. But he doesn't listen. He can't. Instead, he sits on his couch staring at the baggie of white powder, his vision blurry from alcohol, from tears, wondering if he's got anything left to live for anymore. Wondering if everyone back at the hospital hates his sorry, pathetic ass.

Because he sure as hell does.

Because if anything happens to his brother, he'll never forgive himself.

"Fuck," Seth says, shoving at the coffee table. He falls back against the couch and rips a hand through his hair. Contemplates a dangerous habit he hasn't touched in over ten years. Snorting down a reckless line of white powder, searching for that slow sink into numb oblivion.

That's all he wants to do.

Forget last night.

Forget the image of Jace and Griff practically carrying a grief-stricken Sal to Luke's hospital room.

Seth leans forward. He wants to make a mistake. Make the awful feeling in his heart go away.

The baggie's heavy in his hand. A distraction, a death wish, he doesn't know. But he could find out. He wants to find out. Wants to go back to ten years ago, make his OD permanent, make his dumbass-self null and void.

He squeezes his eyes shut.

Luke.

His brother's the glue that holds their family together. The backbone of the band. How can they live without Luke? It should have been him. Not Luke. Never.

A pounding on the door has him opening his eyes.

"Go away," Seth shouts, waving his arm in what he thinks is the direction of the sound.

But the knocking's insistent, grating.

Gritting his teeth, he shoves off the couch, wading through his drunken haze, stumbling for the door. When he gets there, he braces a hand on the door frame. Briefly, he watches the room spin. Then he squares his shoulders and yanks open the door.

The blast of icy air hits him hard, and he isn't talking about the chilly September night.

Lacey Sutton stands there, arms crossed, a scowl on her pretty face. Her golden-blond hair falls around her shoulders like corn silk.

"Go away," he repeats, though he doesn't know if she heard him the first time.

She lifts her chin, haughty. Not bothering with a hello, she says, "You left the hospital, Seth. You left Sal. And . . ." She sniffs the air, levels him with a decisive eye. Her nostrils flare. "You're drunk."

He damn sure is drunk. Earlier tonight, he fled the hospital for the nearest bar. He couldn't handle the conversation or the scene. Everyone sitting on hard plastic chairs, waiting for Luke to wake up, wondering, worrying about a brain bleed. Sal, holding hands with Jace, never looking at Seth, and it was killing him, not knowing if she blamed him.

When he returned, five strong drinks in, Lacey was there. He doesn't remember how he got back to the hospital. He could barely walk a straight line, let alone piece together what the doctors were saying about Luke's potential head injury. Finally, it was Griff, damn Griff Greyson, who had taken him aside. "Go home,

Seth, you're scarin' Sal," Griff commanded. But what Seth saw in his eyes wasn't the irritation they usually had for each other.

It was pity.

Seth moves to shut the door on Lacey, but she shoves a long, trim leg into the opening.

"Goddamnit," he swears, stopping the door in time from crushing her limb. "You ain't comin' in, Lacey."

"I am and I will."

With that, she elbows her way inside.

Seth watches blearily as she blows in like a hurricane, ready to thrash everything in her path, including him.

He groans, smearing a hand down his face. The click-clack of her high heels is like a miniature drill on his brainstem, but instead of leaving like he expects her to, she slams the door and locks it.

Seth hasn't seen Lacey in months. Now she's in Nashville, having flown a red-eye to be with her sister, Sal, during the torturous wait for Luke to wake up. She had arrived tonight and apparently followed him back to his apartment.

Lacey's accusing eyes land on him. "You should be at the hospital. You should be there with Sal, not here ready to sleep off a bender. Luke needs you, Seth."

He flinches. "I ain't in the mood, Lacey."

Lacey props her hands on her tapered waist. She knows where his mind has gone and it's nowhere good. "You know it's not your fault, right?"

"Did Sal say that?" he asks bitterly. "Or hell, maybe Jace asked you to come by, smack some sense into me."

She sighs. Her mouth turned down into an unhappy scowl. "*I* know what happened and *I'm* the one saying it's not your fault."

But it is his fault.

He nearly got his brother killed. Him and his big fat fucking mouth.

It's been years since Seth started a fight, let alone lost his temper at a gig. But two nights ago, down on Broadway, he did.

Seth braces himself against the memory, but he's helpless to stop it. It's a freight train approaching, and he's right in the god-damn way.

The Brothers Kincaid, plus Sal, were in the bar, grabbing a drink before their show. A couple of rednecks in a corner booth were talking shit about their band, about Sal. Luke wouldn't start a fight, especially with Sal there, but Seth didn't have the same high standards as his brother. He's a nice guy, but you fuck with his family and all bets are off.

So, he shot his mouth off about something he can't even re-member now. When the fight threatened to get physical, Luke stepped in, trying to defuse the situation, trying to talk everyone down. Arms up, hands out, he said to the redneck, "Hey, man, we don't want any trouble. Let's just forget it and go our sepa-rate ways."

They all agreed. But when Luke turned to walk away, the red-neck cracked him across the back of the head with a beer bottle.

His brother stood stunned, then he fell.

And Sal—

Sal screamed, her voice shredding on Luke's name, some awful, unearthly sound, as she collapsed to her knees. Her hands hovered around Luke's head. The blood on her hands as bright as a spotlight.

All Seth could do was stare at his brother's lifeless body lying in a pool of blood.

Then he snapped.

Fists flying, he was on the redneck so fast he could have killed him. He nearly did. "Motherfucker, you are a dead man," he hissed before Jace dragged him off the guy.

From there it was a blur. The ambulance, the hospital, the *Nashville Star*, the police and their questions, everyone gather-ing, coming for Luke.

If Seth would've listened to Luke and walked away, then his brother wouldn't be in a hospital bed right now, hurt, unconscious, God knows what else.

His fault. All his goddamned fault.

"Seth?"

Lacey's soft voice floats over him, pulling him from his memories.

Seth blinks, his mind foggy. When he looks up, all he sees is the light of the moon shining through the window and her thin silhouette.

He turns away from her, not wanting her to witness him at his lowest. "You gotta go, princess. Go on, get outta here."

She doesn't budge. Any other person he'd kick their ass out, but he knows he doesn't move Lacey.

He trudges to the couch and sits down. Time to make his mind a big blank slate.

Lacey opens her mouth to yell at him, but the snappish retort drops from her lips. Her green eyes light on the coffee table, the bag of powder.

Slowly, she crosses the room and lowers herself beside him on the couch.

"Oh my God, Seth. Where'd you get this?" Horrified, Lacey reaches over him, so close he can smell her lavender and sea salt scent. A scent that shouldn't be so familiar, shouldn't smell so damn good, but does. When she snags the bag from the coffee table, his stomach twists. The sight of her holding something so dangerous has him trembling.

He grabs her hand. "Don't."

She stares at him.

Instead of extricating her fingers, she twines them with his, the baggie caught between their palms like a kind of temporary jail. Her hands are warm, her touch a torch.

"You can't." Her whisper cuts the silence between them.

He swallows. "I have to."

"No, Seth. You don't."

He squeezes his eyes shut, hot tears burning his lids. His throat bobs. "I need you."

Those three simple words have her face softening.

"I know."

And then her hand, delicate, graceful, removes itself from his. The bag disappears, where he doesn't know, and then Lacey's cupping his scruffy cheek. Her face so damn beautiful, so kind, it has him choking up. "I'm here, Seth. Okay?"

It breaks him. Her words, her offer, like some heaven-sent angel.

"Oh God," Seth cries out, pressing a hand to his eyes. Every emotion spilling over inside of him. Guilt, love, pain. His greatest fear. Something happening to Luke. His best friend. His bandmate. His brother. His *fucking* brother.

"If Luke ain't okay—"

"He is, he will be," Lacey soothes. She holds Seth close, sweeping tears from his face.

Seth sobs.

Sal and Luke have been through so much. Luke just learned that he's going to be a father. Without Luke, without him singing beside Seth on that stage, it's all hollow. His life means nothing.

Lacey lowers herself to her knees beside him. Seth wraps his arms around her waist. He grips her tight and buries his head against her stomach. "It's my fault. It's all my fault."

Shushing him, she leans down. She kisses the back of his head softly, her palm making smooth, healing caresses over his spine.

He raises his face.

Caught by an impulse, that same impulse that keeps getting him in trouble, he kisses her. His lips meet hers for the first time in months, soft and sweet, damn near desperate. He clutches her to him. Better than any drug.

His escape, his release, his goddamn savior.

When he goes to stop himself, to end their kiss, to pull his hand from her long blond hair, it's too late. He can't. He never could.

But then Lacey pulls away with a small gasp, leaving the chalk outline of her kiss on his lips. Her slender hands cradle his face. Her breath a pulse against his. "We can't," she whispers. "Not like this."

Even as he shakes his head in protest, he knows she's right. Blearily, he wonders when it changed, when they've gone from a sometimes fling to this. When they keep saying *not anymore*, only *not anymore* keeps turning into *I need you now*.

"I'm sorry," he mumbles.

She presses her cheek against his. "Don't be."

With a quick sweep of her hand, she palms the drug, a drug he never should have touched, and then the girl he never should have kissed is standing, swishing down the hall, delicate footsteps, a flourish of silk, the flush of a toilet, and then Lacey's back, returning to him, no drug in sight, a glass of water in her hands.

Once again, she sits beside him.

In that moment, Seth's hit with a hot rush of shame at the thought of what he's done.

Ten years ago, after a near-fatal OD, he promised Luke he'd never touch the stuff again, and what did he do? He broke that promise to both him and Sal. He failed the people he loves most in this world.

"Fuck," he moans, burying his face in his hands. "You can't tell, Luke. You can't ever tell him."

"I won't." Lacey's eyes blaze with fire. With protection. "He'll never know, Seth."

He nods, dumbly. Alcohol clouds his vision, his thoughts. He smears a hand across his face, needing to pull himself together, but he can't think. Exhaustion has him.

Lacey takes his shoulder, gripping hard with her manicured nails, and pulls him against her. The two of them lay back on the couch, Lacey's arms wrapped tight around his chest.

"You'll be okay," she says, her voice as fierce as Seth's ever heard. "I won't let you be anything else. Do you hear me?"

"I don't care about me," he chokes out. "Tell me Luke will be okay."

"I care about you." Lacey kisses his brow. "And he'll be okay."

"Tell me until I believe, Lace."

"Luke will be okay. He will be okay."

She repeats it, like a vow, over and over again until her soft voice lulls Seth.

He closes his eyes at the feel of her thin fingers sweeping through his hair. He wants to tell her thank you, tell her he couldn't make it through tonight without her, but he's asleep before he finds the words to tell her what she means to him.

S ETH WAKES TO DAYLIGHT, TO COTTONMOUTH, TO HIS head resting in the cradle of Lacey's lap.

Shit.

Lacey.

Craning his neck, he blinks his eyes and stares up at her. She's asleep, sitting uncomfortably to accommodate Seth, her lashes dark against her tan skin. His chest strains. He reaches up a hand, barely grazing the tips of his fingers against the angular, cutting curve of her cheek, when her eyes snap open.

"What're you doing?"

He retracts his hand. "Nothin.'"

He ain't stupid enough to tell her the truth. That she looked beautiful. That he couldn't have survived last night without her.

That she saved him. Brought him back from the edge of too-far-gone.

With a groan, Seth eases himself up. Every bone in his body hurts, including his head.

Lacey suddenly starts like a bull with a red flag. She's let her guard down with Seth a second too long. She hops up, leaving the couch abruptly, and glides to the counter to check her phone. "How do you feel?" she asks after a minute, her eyes still on her phone.

He rubs his face. "Like shit."

"I have some ibuprofen," she offers. "If you want it."

"That'd be great. Thanks."

As she rifles through her purse, Seth watches her observant

eyes survey his apartment. Some kind of cross between the Grand Ole Opry and a bachelor pad. A brick accent wall. The white kitchen with a stack of songwriting notebooks on the counter. Seth's fiddle case nestled on a leather chair. Hatch Show concert posters. Enormous windows that overlook the same river Luke's farm does.

A little impressed murmur leaves her lips.

"What?" Seth asks.

"This is nice." Her mouth purses around the compliment like it's a lemon. "Your apartment." She runs a hand down her rumpled silk skirt, her green stare finding him over her shoulder. "I always pictured you living in a barn or something." Her eyes rove. "You have curtains, Seth. A blender."

He chuckles. "Blender's hard to come by these days?"

"You'd be surprised."

For a brief second, Lacey smiles. A real, gorgeous smile. And it's easy to pretend like last night's kiss was meant to be. Like she's made to be in this space with him. One where Lacey is in his house having sleepovers. But he can't pretend. At least not for long, because suddenly, the other side of last night all comes rushing back.

Luke. His drunken bender. How close he came to using again. To breaking his promise to Luke and Sal.

Seth clears his throat. "About last night."

She holds up a hand. "We don't have to discuss it."

Seth flinches at the look on her face. Impassive, shuttered, her eyes dodging his. As if she's regretting last night, how much she gave him. It's then he's reminded that Lacey knows nothing about his past. Sal never told her, so of course his idiot actions have knocked her for a loop.

He scared her. The thought has him cursing himself.

"It was a mistake," he admits, squeezing the back of his neck. "I don't know what I was thinkin.'"

He means the coke, but he doesn't know if he means the kiss. Because goddamn, if she asked him to kiss her again, he would.

He'd kiss her and this time, he'd hold on.

To his surprise, she meets his eyes. "We all make mistakes, Seth." A quick toss of her hair and then she's dropping her gaze. "Let's just agree not to do . . . whatever we've been doing anymore. Okay?"

Her desire to end things between them cuts like a knife to the chest. But before he can say anything—agree, argue—there's a buzz from his phone.

He groans, then scoots himself forward on the couch. He stiffens. His throat constricts as he stares at the name on the screen.

"It's Sal," he croaks out.

This is it. News about his brother. News that will make or break his entire world.

Quietly, Lacey crosses the room and sits beside him. She nudges his shoulder. "Answer it."

A quick glance tells him she isn't faring any better than he is. Her hands are clasped so tight together her knuckles are bloodless, her face pale.

Dread curling in his stomach, he picks up the phone with a shaky hand. "Sal?"

"Seth?" Her inhale is watery and ragged. "It's Luke. He's okay."

A ragged sob tears out of Seth. "Thank Christ."

"He's awake," Sal goes on, sounding awed. "He's talking, and he's fine. There's no brain damage, no brain bleed." She sniffles. "Will you come, Seth? He's asking for you."

Seth's boots sound loud down the hospital corridor. Lacey walks fast beside him, her stilettos keeping an in-sync clickety-clack. When he gets to the waiting room, he stops. Stares. It's cleared out, which means Luke really must be okay for everyone to up and leave.

After a quick shower and a cup of coffee, he's clearheaded and calm. At least on the outside. Inside, his nerves are hot-wired and frayed. He doesn't know what Luke will say when he sees him.

Will his brother forgive him? Is he pissed at him for leaving, for not doing enough to help Sal? Luke needed him and he fell apart. What would he say if he knew the truth about last night?

Fuck. He's a goddamn mess.

As if she's read his thoughts, Lacey puts a hand on his arm. Gives it a gentle squeeze of comfort. "It's going to be okay, Seth."

He turns to her, opening his mouth to respond, but before he can, Luke's hospital room door cracks open.

Sal hovers in the threshold, a tired smile on her face. A palm pressed against the small bud of her stomach. "Seth," she breathes.

His throat tightening painfully, he goes to her and pulls her into a fierce hug. As if he can tell her how damn sorry he is for being a shit excuse for a brother, a best friend.

"Where've you been?" Sal asks when she pulls out of his embrace. Her words hold no trace of anger, only a sad puzzlement. As her emerald eyes search his, he blanks out her unasked questions. Sal can read him better than most anyone, and the last thing he wants to do is upset her. "I was worried about you."

"Nah," he says, forcing a smile to reassure her. "You ain't got to."

She bites her lip. Hangs on to him a second too long. "Go see him."

Relief, instant relief, fills Seth when he steps inside the room. Chirping monitors. The cloying scent of antiseptic. And Luke.

His brother sits up in bed, his right pupil enormous, a bandage wrapped around his head. He looks a little pale, a lot tired, but alert.

Seeing Seth, Luke lifts his hands in greeting. "Hey, man, I missed ya."

Seth offers a casual smile as if he's not fucking dying inside at the sight of his brother whole and alive. "You look good, Luke. A little pale, but nothin' a beer won't fix."

Luke holds up a middle finger. "Yeah, maybe so, but I still ain't happy to be here." He scowls at his IV.

Seth rolls his eyes. Leave it to Luke to piss and moan about being in the hospital for less than forty-eight hours.

Sal steps around Seth to give Luke a look of reproof. "You touch those drugs," she warns, arching an eyebrow, "and I'm gonna whoop your ass, country boy."

Seth smiles at Sal's stern command of Luke. The only one who can boss his older brother around.

Luke chuckles, his eyes warming at the sight of his wife.

"How you feelin'?" Seth hovers by the side of his brother's bed, uncertain, undeserving, riddled with guilt. He shouldn't be here.

All of this—it's his own damn fault.

"Got a goddamn headache," Luke grouses. "But I'm okay." He stares up at Seth, his dark brown eyes clouded with painkillers and worry. "You?"

Seth shakes his head slowly, eyes filling with tears. He can't pretend anymore.

"I'm sorry," he says, his words choked by pain. Unable to bear Luke's concern.

His brother reaches out to squeeze Seth's arm. He might as well be pressing on Seth's throat because he can't talk, can't do anything except be grateful his brother is still around.

"Ain't nothin' to be sorry for," Luke says with an easy grin. "Next time just tell me to duck."

Seth rubs his wet eyes. He leans down, wrapping Luke in a hug the best he can. "Fuck you, man."

"I'm okay," Luke says quietly. Serious now. "I'm just glad you're here."

"Yeah." Seth clears his throat as he straightens up. "Same here."

Thank Christ for Lacey. His witness to his fuck-ups. His guardian angel in heels. He can't imagine getting the phone call Luke was okay and being half-goddamned-stoned out of his mind. She saved his ass.

He frowns. *Where is she anyway?*

When he glances over his shoulder to scan the room, Lacey's gone.

Lacey stays long enough to make sure Luke's okay, and then she's slipping out of the hospital room and walking hurriedly down the corridor.

The elevator. The elevator's her salvation.

A beacon of escape. Not from Luke, or Sal—she never minds helping her sister, wishes she could do more—but the last thing she wants is to be stuck with Seth Kincaid any longer than necessary.

She liked it too much. That sweet kiss from last night. When Seth swept his lips across hers, she felt a yank in her heart, and when she looked down a string was unraveling from somewhere deep in the pit of her soul. It was a feeling she'd never felt before with Seth. The slow burn of a kiss. Tender, reverent, like she was something else. Like she mattered. Like she *liked* him.

It sent her whirling. Knocked something loose in her. Maybe something blooming all along, maybe something just beginning, but either way, she doesn't want to know. Can't know. Won't know. Whatever they've been doing, they can't do it anymore. She's calling it quits.

While they've been together before, a few times now, more times than she'd like to remember, it wasn't like last night. It wasn't within reach. Honest. Vulnerable.

A side of Seth she had never seen before.

When she showed up at the hospital last night, she came to support Sal, but it looked like Seth needed it more. She saw him, swaying and slurring his words, being escorted out by that angry blond country singer, and she wanted to help him. Take away his pain. Keep him safe. So, she followed him back to his apartment. And a good thing too, because what he was about to do . . .

It shook her seeing Seth—cool, easygoing, sunny Seth—like that.

But she also understands it.

The only thing that could sink Seth that low was Luke. His brother. She went down that same destructive path when Sal went missing. Seth losing Luke, losing their fierce bond, losing their brotherhood, would kill him.

She can't judge him for what he was about to do, and she won't.

She knows all about mistakes. Bad habits.

And now that Luke's fine, she can go.

Lacey pauses in the hallway to call an Uber to the airport. All she wants to do is get back to LA. Never mind all that's waiting for her is an empty fridge and about a zillion emails from her boss. She needs to chase away that fluttery feeling Seth's kiss had churned up.

Emotions. They make her itch. They're a risk she can't take. The only one who gets her emotions is her sister. Sal's the only one she has space for in her life.

She's nearly to the elevators when a voice calls out, "Lacey, wait!"

Lacey groans. She's caught.

She turns, raising an amused brow at the sight of Sal hurrying down the hall, hands cradling her belly like she can keep the small bump in.

Lacey's lips curve. For a while Sal and Luke weren't sure they'd even be able to have a baby, so to see an adorably pregnant Sal hustling down the hall has her smiling.

"Where are you going?" Sal asks when she catches up with her. Sal's face is pale. Tired, dark circles beneath her eyes from the bedside vigil she's kept on Luke.

Lacey's heart twists. Too much pain. Sal and Luke have had too much pain. She could never do something like that. Have a love she could lose. It's an overrated risk that's not worth it, because in the end, no one stays. Not really.

"Home," Lacey says with a casual shrug. She lifts her chin. "Luke's okay. And I have a client who needs me."

Sal's face falls. "I need you."

"I'll be back for that baby," Lacey promises, clutching at Sal's hand. She's going to be the cool, fashionable aunt and can't wait to spoil that little baby senseless. "I have a go-bag ready to roll."

Sal smiles faintly, disappointment furrowing her brow. "That's too long."

It is. Waiting six more months to see her sister and meet her little niece or nephew is agonizing, but Sal will be just fine. Her sister has a life out here in Nashville and Lacey has hers in LA. Lacey is just a small piece of Sal's pie.

"It'll go super fast," Lacey says. "I'll be back before you know it."

Sal pulls Lacey into her arms. "I love you."

"I love *you*."

Lacey hugs her sister, rocks Sal in her arms. Even though Sal lost most of her memory in a horrific plane crash two years ago, it's as if nothing's changed between them. She smiles, glimpsing them in the elevator's reflection. Blond and tall. Dark and petite. Her better half. Her only half.

"Get Luke better, okay?" Lacey's eyes move to Sal's belly. "Don't operate any heavy machinery. And stay off horses. Oh! And no soft cheeses."

Sal laughs, tears in her eyes. "I will."

Inhaling a resolved breath, she turns on her heel and does what she does best when she finds herself getting too close to Seth Kincaid.

Run.

Three Months Later

"I DON'T CARE HOW YOU DO IT," LACEY SAYS INTO THE receiver, her chipper voice a clipped, no-nonsense rattle that wards off any arguments. "I need the cake changed."

She lets out a sigh of frustration, listening to the harried protest on the other end of the line. Her eyes do double duty as she glances at her computer screen, clicking through the link for alpacas. She squints. Or is it llamas? Either way, she bristles at the thought of getting them into a trailer. She turns her attention back to the phone call. "Yes, I am aware it is four days before the party. I understand we'll be fully charged for this cake. And yes, I understand squid ink–pomegranate is a combination that should only exist in the seventh circle of hell, but my client has had a change of heart and demands that the cake be changed."

Once again, she listens, adjusting a cuff on her gray blazer. "Right. That's what I thought." She smiles. "I'll send you the order over email. Remember, we want the cake to look like it's bleeding. Yes. Thank you."

Ending the call, Lacey swivels in her chair. Her eyes brush to the smog-filled skyline of LA. At least she has a view. Her cramped cubicle chafes her, but if she has her way, it won't be for long. She opens her desk drawer, finding it empty. Her stomach rumbles, disgruntled. A missed breakfast, a missed lunch, doesn't have it happy.

"Lacey."

Lacey lifts her eyes to Autumn, her boss's personal assistant and an associate event planner. Autumn's a pain in her ass, usually acting as Prentiss Scott's watchdog. Always on the hunt for mistakes. Lacey's mistakes especially.

She can never tell if Autumn wants to support or sabotage her. So, she keeps her distance. An icy distance.

She stares at Autumn. "What?"

Autumn's over-plucked brows nearly hit the ceiling. "Prentiss wants you in his office. Now."

Keeping her sigh inside, her face placid, Lacey pulls herself up and struts down the hall.

Prentiss Scott is the owner of Shock and Awe Events, a luxury event-planning firm that plans parties and weddings for Hollywood society and celebrities like Oprah, Taylor Swift, and Snoop Dog. They're the crème de la crème of Los Angeles event planners, always in demand, always on-call.

When she gets to Prentiss's obscenely large office, he's scrolling through Pandora, Beats draped around his neck like he wants them to catch him DJing.

She raps the door and enters. "Prentiss, hi. You wanted to see me?"

Prentiss's eye twitches behind his dark-framed glasses. The way his fingers dance across his phone tells her he's ready for his afternoon coffee and Xanax. "Give me a rundown on the Cane account."

She's ready, has it nailed by now. "Run of show is nearly done. Cake is being changed. Flowers will be picked up and arranged on Friday. Caterers are scheduled for noon on Saturday."

Autumn raises a hand. "What about the alpacas?"

Lacey shoots her a withering glare. "They are llamas, Autumn. And they are fabulous. And they're being delivered Saturday."

"Fantastic." Prentiss glances at Lacey, his slicked-back black hair so greasy he needs blotting papers. "It has to go off without a hitch, Sutton. I need you there. On the ground. In the shit. Anything Colin Cane needs, you do it."

Lacey blows out a breath, knowing she's expected to work

nonstop this week until the party's over. Only then can she collapse in an exhausted heap. "Where else would I be?"

"Nowhere but here, I'd hope." He checks his watch, closes his laptop. "Off with you, Sutton. I have a tee time at four."

His dismissive tone has Lacey wanting to set herself, or better yet him, on fire. But she plasters a sweet smile on her face. No pushback. All yes, sir. She reminds herself it will all be worth it. She's this close to a promotion. After five years of interning, five years of ordering coffees with obnoxious names like Smaug Fog and Dirty Chais and Red Eyes, five years of schlepping event decor down Hollywood Boulevard and sweating through her silk shirts, she's finally on top.

She has the Colin Cane account.

The man's a legend in Los Angeles high society. Socialite. Handsome. Rich. It's her only account, and she loves everything about it. She had better. Because she's a slave to it. For the last six months, she's been working twelve-hour days, six days a week, to get this holiday party off the ground. If it all comes together like it should, if Saturday's event is a success, she'll get that corner office next to Prentiss. Not Autumn. Not a woman who wears head-to-toe leopard print.

She flashes a frosty smile. "I'm out too."

Back in her cubicle, Lacey shuts down her computer and grabs the duffel bag she keeps stashed under her desk. When she glances over her shoulder, she sees Autumn hovering behind her, eyes narrowed. "Hot date?"

Lacey tosses her hair and straightens up. Anticipation curls her stomach. "Something like that."

The crash of the waves stops Lacey at the lip of the beach. Brushing wet hair from her eyes, she glances over her shoulder at the thrashing ocean. She's battered and bruised, but today the surf was perfect.

She needed this. Her heart, her soul, feel lighter than they have in days. She doesn't have time for much—friends, men, family—but she'll make time for the ocean.

Getting a grip on her surfboard, she lugs it back to where her things are.

She drops her surfboard to the sand and sits on top of it. Every single muscle in her body sings with exhaustion.

Exhaling, she stares out at the waves, glances around. Tuesday, midday, the beach is practically hers. She shivers in her wet suit but doesn't bother with a towel. It's December, and while most people would think the water cold as hell, she's been surfing so long she's conditioned to the icy temperatures.

Whenever she needs a refresh, a recharge, she comes back to the ocean.

Not only is it the one place she allows herself to be reckless, to take risks, it's where she feels close to her mother.

Her mother, Michelle, was a surfer. Some badass California chick with a VW bug and a smile that could light up the sky. Lacey was only six when her mother died of breast cancer. All she has are meager scraps of memories. And now Sal, with her memory loss, can barely remember their mother either. To Lacey, it feels like a really shitty deal. She always counted on Sal to tell her about their mother and their stories, and now they're both left with none.

She has one memory, though. The most precious.

How do you swim a wave if you're drowning, Lacey? her mother would always ask, pointing out at the waves, beaded bracelets dangling from a slender wrist. *You break through it. You break it.*

Lacey's always kept the words close. Advice she hears when she needs hope, a way out, a breakthrough. Her way of being like a woman she can't remember. Of taking the top of a wave and saying, *Hey, Mom, I'm here, I remember you.*

Anytime something bad happened, anytime she needed a safe place, a reassurance or a reset, Lacey went to the water.

Her savior more times than she can count.

After her mom died, after Sal moved to Nashville, after she

woke in the hospital with a drip in her arm, her stepmother telling her she had made a mess of everything, she always came back to the ocean.

Pulling a towel around herself, Lacey rifles through her straw bag for her phone.

"Shit," she swears, seeing a missed call from Colin Cane. Five texts asking her to run into downtown LA and pick up a rare book order from the Last Bookstore. It's an emergency. Apparently, everything's an emergency for Colin.

Fabulous.

Lacey sighs, seeing the night she planned for herself go up in smoke. Gone is the hope of a horror movie. The late dinner where she will drink. The bath where she will feel better. Still, she reminds herself why she's doing this.

It's her job. Literally.

Even though being Colin's personal assistant is not in her job description, she reminds herself that Prentiss won't care. He won't give her a pass either. He wants the client happy, and if the client's happy, Prentiss is happy. And if Prentiss is happy, she'll get that promotion. It's so close she can taste it. She needs it too. Financial freedom. A corner office. More shoes. Loads of vacations. A beach somewhere. Better, Paris. Even better, seeing Sal. Her sweet new niece or nephew.

Lacey absentmindedly fingers the delicate gold locket around her neck. Her and Sal's names inscribed inside. Another treasure from her mother. Another link to her she never takes off.

"I . . . am . . . on . . . it . . . ," Lacey singsongs, fingers typing out a reply. She hits send and immediately gets a heart emoji. She shakes her head in amusement. Despite Colin's current pain-in-the-ass status, she's never had more fun working with a client. Not to mention spending his money.

Exiting Colin's chat, Lacey scrolls through the texts her sister sent earlier. She smiles at the attached photo of Sal. Her sister propped up on the couch, her half-moon of a stomach in the frame.

Sal: *I am sooooo bored, Lace.*

Lacey: *Good. Stay bored. How long is ur couch vacation?*

Sal: *A week. Which means as long as Luke wants. Did you give any more thought to Christmas? Can you come to the cabin?*

The offer stares back at her from the screen like a tantalizing dangle of a carrot. Luke's taking Sal on some dreamy mountain getaway before the baby is born. Lacey wishes she could go. Spending Christmas in the Smoky Mountains with Sal sounds like a dream. But she has to save her vacation time. If she aces this event, she'll get bigger clients. Which means even more limited time.

She's twenty-eight. Only ten years younger than her mother was when she died. Her mother never had the life she wanted, married to a man who was gone all the time, who cheated while she was undergoing chemo all by herself. Is that what Lacey wants for her life? Planning vapid Botox parties and obnoxious conscious uncoupling celebrations? Turning into some risk-averse, single, type A, Rolaid-chewing woman?

Most times, she loves her job. Event planning is so much more than ordering and organizing. It's being there for the client, acting as therapist, confidante, and sometimes a groveling kiss-ass, but she's good at it and her clients love her.

She stares out at the setting sun. She doesn't know. But what she does know is it's what she has at the moment. This job. Her job.

A life she can control. A life that doesn't leave her.

Her eyes drift back to the text.

Sal: *You have to come. Everyone will be there. Please? Pretty please?*

Lacey bites her lip, the words like a dare. A cruel, tempting dare.

Everyone.

That means Seth included. She hasn't seen or spoken to him in three months. Not since Luke's accident. She almost called him a hundred times after she saw that awful article the *Nashville Star* put out last month. But to what? To say she was there and that she knew what happened. That if he needed her to, she'd speak up. But she never did reach out. Her and Seth—they're worlds apart. Coastlines. She barely even thinks of him.

Her fingers hover over the keypad. Wanting to give Sal an answer, but not knowing what it is.

A text from Colin bumps Lacey out of Sal's chat.

ETA, darling? TLB closes at nine.

She squares her shoulders. *On my way.*

Changed back into her skirt and blazer, Lacey keeps a quick pace as she teeters her way down Wilshire Boulevard, following the address on the text from Colin. Not only did she have to FedEx the books to France, but now she's getting dragged out to BFE to pick up a custom chef-created cupcake.

A freaking cupcake.

Still, it's not the most ridiculous request she's ever received. That honor goes to DeVorah DeVine and the guinea pig she planned a Viking funeral for.

What is ridiculous is the fact that she's starving. She barely had time to scarf down a chalky Luna Bar in the parking garage before getting pinged once again by Colin.

Lacey hangs a left, pausing in the lip of an alley, in a small sliver of silver moonlight. She blinks up at the different storefronts, trying to pick out the address. "I deserve a raise," she grumbles. She glances down at her phone and groans. She took a wrong turn somewhere. She's nowhere near where she needs to be.

Rolling out her shoulders, she tucks her phone in the pocket of her bubble skirt. Her eyes survey the desolate alley. It's not late, but it's December and it's dark, making six p.m. feel like ten. No one else exists on the street but her. The grating electric glow of a neon sign casts the alley in a hot pink glow. Lacey sighs, thinking about the sixteen-hour day that waits for her tomorrow. All she wants is her apartment, which is across town in Reseda. Not to mention her car, which is parked five blocks down. The unholy trek reminding her that Los Angeles is not meant for walking. Her heels aren't either.

Forget it. Colin can wait for the cupcake.

Lacey turns to leave, moving for the mouth of the alley when there's a rustling behind her. She pauses, listening. A rat, a cat, a something, she tells herself.

But she knows it's not.

It's the sound of footsteps.

She's sure of it.

She moves fast now, her high heels sure and swift on the rough cement, her brain alive and alert with flight.

Footsteps, faster. Behind her. Her body goes rigid, fear prickling her spine. She picks up the pace. Her pulse races. Milk-white moonlight casts eerie shadows on the brick wall, the trash cans, and for a second, she thinks her eyes are playing tricks on her, but then out of the corner of her eye, she sees a shadow move.

Stupid, stupid, she's so stupid.

A rough hand snakes around her stomach and slams her back against the brick wall.

The air's knocked from her lungs. Lacey's eyes fly open. Before she can scream, cold metal is pressed against her throat. A masked face, a rough voice in her ear. "Give me what you got or you're dead."

Lacey's brain fizzes, fast-forwards to the end.

This is it. This is where she dies. Where she's raped. Where's she's cut into little pieces like those damsels in distress in those gory horror movies she loves, movies she now regrets watching too many of.

The mugger tugs at her purse.

Lacey thrusts her hands out in front of her. "Take it," she says, flinging her purse across the alleyway. "Take it all."

She watches the mugger move for her purse. That stupid expensive purse she fell behind in rent payments for. Lacey flinches against the wall, wishing her nightmare over, but then like he's changed his mind, he forgets the purse. He's on her again.

"Little bitch," he hisses. His heavy body pins her against the brick wall. His meaty hands slip-slide over her skirt, holding her hips, his thigh creeping between her legs to spread them. The scent of motor oil and nicotine stings her nostrils.

Lacey squeezes her eyes shut and freezes at the rough hand curving around her throat. Her brain, her body shutting down, readying themselves for the worst, for something that is out of her control.

"This is pretty."

Lacey's eyes flash open. The mugger fingers the gold locket, his chapped lips pulling up into a cruel grin.

Her hand automatically flies to her throat, covering it protectively. The necklace she treasures with her life. "No."

And then her mother's voice in her ears, whispering to her: *How do you swim a wave if you're drowning, Lacey? You break through it. You break it.*

A fire lights in Lacey. Her body, her brain remembering how to move. How to fight. How to swim against an asshole tide. Because she's not dying here. Not tonight, not like this. She has too many things she still needs to do. Go shopping in Paris. Skinny-dip in the Pacific. Most importantly, hugging Sal, spoiling her new niece or nephew like crazy.

Lacey slams herself back against the brick wall, yelping as every muscle, every bone in her body is harshly jolted. Her right heel snaps. The backs of her elbows shredded.

With a growl, the mugger yanks the necklace from her neck. Lacey cries out in anger. She scratches, kicks, bucks her body, draws blood, puts up a fight no man would tangle with.

For a second, she thinks it's worked.

The mugger backs away, levels her with a look, and then his arm juts out.

It feels like a punch. But it's not. It's the slash of a knife. The hard suck into her stomach and then back out again.

Lacey sways, fawn-like, and then glances down to see blood. Warm and wet, it spills over her palms as she presses them against her tender stomach.

"Oh," she whispers, and her mouth is as dry as cotton.

The world around her goes blurry. There's the rustle of the mugger, the hiss of *bitch* and then she's tipping over onto cold cement.

She tries to scream out, but the words won't come.

She needs help. Someone. Anyone.

Seth.

She groans at the horrifying thought.

And then Lacey lets go. Lets her body go limp, her eyes rolling back as sweet, unconscious oblivion takes over.

chapter
FOUR

THE WARM LIGHTS OF THE FARMHOUSE TWINKLE AS Seth pulls into the dirt drive of Wild Antler Farm. He hops out of his vintage Bronco and swears at the cutting chill of the December night. Striding fast for the passenger side, he grabs the plastic bag of barbeque takeout and a six-pack of beer.

He pauses in the driveway and blows out a nervous breath. He's not just here for a beer with his brother. He knows what he's coming to say will piss Luke off something fierce, and if he's smart, he'll walk away now.

But he can't. Because he got the Brothers Kincaid into this mess and he's got to be the one to get them out.

Luke, his older brother and frontman of their country band, the Brothers Kincaid, is on the front porch, staring out into the night, a glass of whiskey in his hand. Although judging by the pained look on Luke's face, his brother's wishing for a cigarette right about now.

"Take a break." Seth lifts the six-pack in greeting. "I brought dinner."

"You brought yourself," Luke drawls. "'Bout damn time."

Seth ignores the comment and climbs the stairs. He sets the food on a rocking chair and breaks the six-pack. "How's Sal?" he asks, handing over a beer.

Luke nods his thanks and cracks open the can. "About ready to leave me."

Seth laughs. "You fuckin' love it, man."

"She's on the couch." Luke glances back toward the screen door and frowns. "She better be."

Seth hides a smirk. Luke's got Sal on lockdown.

"How you doin'?"

Luke gives him a tired smile. "Hangin' in."

Even in the harsh glow of the porch lights, Seth can see Luke's exhausted. What else is new? He's worrying. Worrying about Sal, who only last week was kicked in the stomach by a panicked patient during a routine hospital transfer. She started bleeding, and the doctor put her on two weeks of temporary bed rest just to be safe.

Luke ain't taking any chances. Not with Sal and sure as hell not with his kid.

Seth's over here to help, to do what he can to keep his brother sane.

It's as if after Luke's accident, life's put the Brothers Kincaid through the wringer with their share of bad luck. Rescheduling missed shows. Postponing working with famed producer Devlon Block. Pushing back the recording of their highly anticipated eighth album until after the new year so Luke can be with Sal. Seth knows it doesn't sit well with his brother. Disappointing the fans isn't an option for Luke, but then again, neither is leaving Sal's side.

Luke's brows sweep together. "Where've you been, Seth?"

Seth winces. The question loaded. Accusing.

He should've known his brother would see through him. Usually, he's over at the house so much Luke threatens to charge him rent. But for the last two weeks, he's been MIA. Almost like his shitty mistakes could infect everything he cares about in one fell swoop.

"Seen you at practice," Seth says, keeping his shrug easy. "You're busy."

Luke braces himself against the railing. "Not that busy."

Seth whisks his hands together, nerves getting the best of him. It's now or never. He licks his lips. His words roll out in a slow rumbling drawl. "Listen, Luke. I know it's a bad time, but I wanted to talk to you about somethin'."

Luke eyes him warily, like he knows what's coming. "What's the somethin'?"

Shit.

Seth inhales, gathering courage, pulling it the fuck together, then says, "I was thinkin' about takin' some time away from the band."

Immediately, Luke bristles. His eyes widen and then he curses viciously. "This is about that article, ain't it?"

Seth smears his face in his hands.

Of everything that's gone bad over the last few months, the *Nashville Star* article was the goddamn kick of a cherry on top.

Last month, it was the featured story in the Sunday tabloid and on its website. A big juicy story with a headline that read: *The Brothers COCAINE: Seth Kincaid a Druggie?*

It knocked Seth and the Brothers Kincaid for a loop. He thought it was over after Luke got out of the hospital. Thought he could forget, put it behind him. But then his mistake came back to bite him—and the band—in the ass all over again.

The story was bullshit. It came out three months too late, got a million facts wrong, but still, it was close. That hazy line between truth and rumor.

Luke went ballistic. With the help of their manager, Bobby, he promptly launched a blistering defense of Seth in the press. Their fans ate it up, and while the Brothers Kincaid took a beating, losing a tour sponsor, getting bumped from a handful of gigs, in the end, Nashville stood behind Seth and the Brothers Kincaid.

But the one who stood by Seth the most was his brother.

Jesus, Luke never even asked Seth if he was using again.

When he saw the article, all he said was, "Are you steady, Seth?" Seth had said yes, and that was it for Luke. That's how much fucking faith his brother had in him.

It made him feel like shit.

Seth doesn't deserve his brother's fierce defense. He's given Luke a lifetime of worry already.

Luke eyes him unhappily. "Is leavin' what you want?"

Hell no. Leaving the band is the last thing he wants to do. But maybe it's time. Time to walk away and work off this restless feeling that's settled in his soul.

Seth licks his lips and swallows down his guilt. His brother's staring at him, waiting for an explanation. "I don't wanna bring you and Jace down, man. That article could have done damage . . . we're lucky it didn't."

"I handled it," Luke growls, his expression fierce. "The *Star*'s gonna issue a retraction and if they don't, I'm gonna sue the hell out of those sons of bitches."

Fuck.

Anxiety balls Seth's stomach. That's the last thing he wants Luke doing—taking out some personal vendetta against the *Star*.

He shakes his head. "You got enough problems to deal with."

But Luke won't let it go. "It's my problem when it involves you. You're my brother and someone rippin' you in the press ain't happenin.'"

Seth swallows, the knot in his stomach growing larger.

Staring out into the dark night, Luke clenches his jaw for a fraction of an instant.

And Seth sees it. Luke's angry. His easygoing, steadfast brother is pissed as all hell. Overprotective, on the defense when it comes to his family. Which tells Seth all he needs to know. Has him shaking off any courage to tell his brother the truth. If Luke's this pissed about the story, how will he take the news that Seth almost fucked up again?

Jesus. He can't face that.

The past.

The memory of Luke sitting by his bedside after Seth overdosed, his eyes lined with tears, saying words that still haunt him. *I'll never forgive you if you do this again. Because I can't do this again. I won't.*

It's that fear, Luke's pain-filled words, that have him in a stranglehold.

Besides, Luke and Sal have enough to worry about. They don't need him stacking his bullshit to the pile. Sometimes he still feels like that young dumb kid, making idiot decisions, having Sal and Luke sweep his mistakes under the rug, letting down everyone he loves, damn near tanking the band all over again.

Shit, the *Nashville Star* headline may as well have read: *Seth Kincaid, Eternal Fuckup for Life.*

"You oughta talk to Jace," Seth says in a hoarse mumble, hoping their straight-arrow upright bassist, and Luke's best friend, Jace Taylor, will talk some sense into his brother. "Take a vote."

"I don't need to talk to Jace. You ain't quittin' and that's that." Luke's voice drops an octave, a sympathetic look crossing his face. "What you did—it was a long time ago, Seth. You got nothin' to be sorry for now."

Seth stands there, numb, guilt gripping him.

Luke grins, but all it does is make him feel worse. "If you think I'm makin' music without you, think again."

Luke's tone is final. Fucking loyal as hell.

Seth swallows the brick in his throat.

His brother's dark eyes evaluate him intently, his brow now furrowed in concern. Telling Seth he's this close to pulling out the overprotective big brother card. "Somethin' else on your mind?"

Luke's way of asking him what's really up.

If only Seth knew.

But he doesn't. All he knows is that these days, he always wants to hit something. A door. A mirror. His own damn self.

Because he feels fucking lost. Uncomfortable around his own family. Disconnected from the music. It's like he's burning inside now, all the time, ever since Luke got hurt. Overthinking, over-drinking, replaying that damn fight in his head, avoiding his brother and Sal like they can see through his bullshit.

And the one person who knows him the best, who's asking what's really wrong, he can't talk to.

No matter how hard he tries, he can't chase away this funk he's in. Sometimes it seems like all he's good for is letting people down and fucking things up.

"You okay, Seth?"

Seth looks up to see Luke staring hard at him.

"I'm gonna go say hi to Sal," he says, moving for the door before his brother can get into it further. He gives him a cocky grin. "Sounds like she needs some entertainment in her life."

Luke's snort follows him.

Inside the farmhouse, the fireplace crackles, chasing away the chill of the outside night. Seth shrugs off his flannel jacket and hangs it on the coat hook.

Sal's in the living room lying on the plush leather couch, looking small but mighty. She's propped up by about a million pillows. A book balances on her tiny swollen belly, the television on mute. Winston, her scruffy terrier, is curled up on the floor. Ever the loyal guard dog, he looks up when Seth approaches and lets out a low woof.

Seeing Seth, Sal's green eyes light up. "Oh, thank God," she says, wiggling into a sitting position and pulling her legs beneath her. "Someone to talk to."

"How's the bean?" Seth asks, slipping beside Sal and curling an arm around her shoulder.

Sal smiles. "Kicking." She palms her growing belly. Although you'd never know she was pregnant. She and Luke have been doing their damnedest to keep it out of the papers.

Before she can catch him worrying, Seth gives her a quick once-over.

Despite being stuck on the couch for the last week, Sal looks bright-eyed and happy. Which makes him goddamn ecstatic. This kid's coming in a couple of months and everyone's on pins and needles waiting for it to be born. Seth included.

Sal nudges him with her shoulder. "I missed you."

"I missed you too." He makes a disgusted face at the TV. The

Nashville Star's flashing pictures of the best CMA fashion mistakes. "Why are you watchin' this shit, anyway?"

Sal raises an eyebrow. "Making sure they don't say anything else about you."

He groans. "Sal, you're pregnant. You don't need to be worryin' about this." But his protest is useless. Sal's shaking her head. Her pretty face fierce, her eyes sparking with determination.

"You're our family, Seth. We're not just going to let the *Star* trash you." She squeezes his arm. "Besides, you'd do the same for us. You *have*."

At the slam of a door, the rustle of plastic, Seth glances over the back of the couch. Luke stands, the bag of food in his hands, an amused smile on his face.

"You were right," Seth says. "She ain't so good at relaxin.'"

"I'm tellin' you, she's gonna have me goin' gray before I'm forty," Luke jokes, tapping a finger against his temple.

Seth winces. The callback to where Luke got clocked by the beer bottle still stings.

The ringing of a phone has Sal gasping in delight.

"It's for me." Sal holds up a hand to Luke, who's made a move toward the phone. "And it's my only source of fun, Luke, so let me get it." She narrows her green eyes, sliding the bar to answer it. "I will bite your hand off, country boy."

Luke barks a laugh and settles into the corner recliner. He glances in Seth's direction. "You still on for Christmas?"

Seth nods. "Hell yeah. Barbeques. Bonfires. Freezin' lakeside. Sign me up."

He trails off when he realizes Luke isn't listening to him. His eyes are trained on Sal, who's suddenly gone still and pale. Sal, who's saying, "This is the sister of Lacey Sutton."

Her anxious eyes flick to Luke, who's already on his feet and moving for her.

Seth's mouth goes dry.

"What?" A small intake of breath. "Oh my God. Is she okay?"

Sal uncurls her legs, sliding to the edge of the couch. Then she softly asks, "What happened?"

Seth meets Luke's worried eyes.

"Okay," she says in a small voice. Her feet hit the floor, and she stands. Her brow furrows, deeper and deeper as she listens to the voice on the other end of the line. "I don't know . . . I don't—okay, yes, I will. I'll let you know. Thank you."

Sal disconnects and looks up at Seth and Luke. Her eyes glitter with unshed tears. Small parentheses of stress bracket her mouth.

Luke eyes Sal with concern. "Darlin'?"

"It's Lacey." A tear slips down Sal's cheek. "She was in an accident."

Fuck.

Seth's heart shuts off. Any rational thought in his head destroyed. He opens his mouth to ask what happened, but Luke beats him to it.

"She was mugged." Sal's lips tremble. "She's hurt."

Seth swallows. "How hurt?"

"She was stabbed in the stomach. The wound isn't deep but . . ." She stares down at her phone, her grip tight like she wants to strangle it. "That's all they gave me. I mean, what the hell kind of information is that?"

"I want you to take it easy, Sal. Right now." Luke edges close, his voice as stern as Seth's ever heard it. Winston barks, as if echoing Luke's sentiment.

Sal doesn't hear him. She takes a step away from Luke, lost in concern for her sister. She paces, her pretty face contorted in anger and pain. "They just left her there . . . they left her in an alley hurt and unconscious . . ."

Seth's fists clench. *Motherfucker.*

The thought has Seth's body physically responding to the news. He tries to rein in his emotions, rage, shock, emotions reflected on his brother's face, but he can't.

A swear blasts from his lips. "Fuck."

Luke's eyes move from him to Sal.

She holds her belly, swaying unsteadily on her feet.

"Darlin', sit down." Luke puts a hand out to catch her and pulls her close. Helps her settle on the couch. She sits, her expression dazed and far off.

"Lacey's all alone out there," Sal says suddenly, desperately turning her teary gaze to Luke. Her trembling hands make smooth circles over the orb of her stomach. "She needs someone to help her . . . I have to go, Luke. I have to go. She doesn't have anyone—"

"Sal . . ." Luke shakes his head, hating to be the asshole, to say no, but knowing she can't go to her sister. Not now. Not on bed rest. He brings her close, kisses her temple, runs a hand down the back of her head. Smooth, calming strokes. "You can't, darlin'. I'm so sorry, but you can't."

In Luke's arms, Sal begins to cry. Stark, silent sobs that have Seth slowly dying inside.

Luke, his own eyes wet, kisses the top of her dark head.

Flames leap from the fire, the crackle of wood.

"I'll go."

It's a blurt, a restart of Seth's heart, and then two pairs of eyes are swiveling to him.

The words are out of his mouth before he realizes what he's said. Before he realizes he has to go, won't let anyone else go but him. Gripped by some fucking ridiculous need to see for himself that Lacey's okay.

Hell, he owes it to her. She stopped him from making the biggest fucking mistake of his life. She came to him when he was at his lowest and didn't flinch. *I need you*, he said, and she helped him.

She saved him that night. He knows it in his soul.

"You will?" Sal asks, untangling from Luke.

"Yeah," he rasps out.

The look on Luke's face is one of relief. Relief he doesn't have to leave Sal. Relief Seth will take care of Lacey.

"Your gigs," Sal murmurs. Wiping her eyes, she looks between Seth and Luke. "Can he?"

Luke chuckles. "Bobby's gonna have a fuckin' aneurysm, but yeah." Determination roughens Luke's voice. "A day or two. We'll make it work. Whatever we got to do."

Sal embraces Seth, hugging him with ferocious strength. "Thank you," she says, her voice low and raw.

Seth tightens his grip on Sal.

Los Angeles. That's where he's going. It's where he needs to be. Out there with Lacey.

Even if she is gonna rip his goddamn balls off.

SUNLIGHT. LACEY HATES IT. NOT BECAUSE IT MEANS SHE'S awake, means she's alive, but it means she should be at work right now and she isn't. Instead, she's stuck in a dreary hospital bed, battered and bruised, hooked up to a tangle of cords and wearing a scratchy hospital gown that doesn't do a thing for her figure. She's already called Prentiss, who gave her the tongue-lashing of the century. Too embarrassed to fess up to the mugging, she lied, saying she had the flu. Nothing puts Prentiss off more than stomach issues. In return, Prentiss grudgingly granted her one day off. One day and then she has to be back in tip-top shape. It's bad enough he sent Autumn to fix her fuckup and save face with Colin.

Ugh. Bested by a cupcake. She'll never live it down.

Lacey lays in bed, staring at the ceiling, feeling numb. Numb about everything. About the cops, answering their stupid questions, listening to their stupid lecture about why she should have been more on guard in downtown LA. About the doctors who said she was a lucky girl, but she doesn't feel lucky. All she feels is stabbed.

The door cracks.

A sharp-eyed nurse blows into the room. She does her job fast, checking Lacey's vitals and changing her bandage. Then she props a hand on her round hip. Gives Lacey a no-nonsense look. "You're ready to be discharged, but you need a ride home."

"I'll call an Uber." Lacey wets her lips, forces a smile. "I promise."

The nurse laughs, loud and ball-busting. "Honey, if we ran on promises, I'd be out of a job." She wags a finger. "Find a ride."

Scowling, Lacey points at the cup of water just out of reach on the hospital tray. Her gaze drifts reluctantly to the nurse. Asking for help isn't in her vocabulary. "Can I have—"

But the nurse exits before she can voice her request.

With a deep sigh, Lacey rolls her head across the pillow. Beyond the window, the afternoon sky is grayer than gray, choked by smog and cotton-ball clouds.

This is pathetic.

She's pathetic. Stuck in this hospital bed with no one to call.

Lacey doesn't have close friends. She has acquaintances. And the thought of calling Autumn has her bristling. She'd rather swim in shark-infested waters.

Lacey blows out a breath. She can handle this. All on her own. She doesn't need anyone.

At least she has her cell phone. The mugger left her with one scrap of her dignity intact. She shifts in bed, wincing at the pain radiating through her body as she fumbles beneath the pillow for her phone.

She stares at the screen, lit up by frantic messages from Sal.

She should call her sister, but she can't. Can't bring herself to make Sal worry. Maybe the hospital bed will take Lacey, suck her down into the void and let the drugs dissolve her memory. Because that's all she wants to do—forget. Voicing what happened to her aloud will make it real, and all she wants to do is force last night down into a small box, duct tape it shut, stomp on it with a stiletto, and bury it six feet deep.

She was so stupid. Putting herself in that situation. Not paying attention. Freezing up like some dumb deer in the headlights.

Lacey puts a hand to her throat, her lower lip trembling at the absence of the gold lavaliere.

He took her necklace.

The only thing she had left of her mother.

Hot tears hit her, sharp and quick. She squeezes her eyes shut as agonizing memories of last night resurface. The mugger, his hands on her hips, across her throat, his hiss of *bitch* in her ear, the stench of cologne and motor oil, this twist of the knife in her—

Lacey gasps and slaps a trembling hand over her mouth.

Don't freak out. You absolutely cannot freak out right now.

But she absolutely is.

And worse, there isn't a thing she can do about any of it.

Seth stalks down the hall of Good Samaritan, looking for room 434, scrambled as all hell. The plane ride was a bitch, the traffic in Los Angeles a nightmare, and now he's in his own worst torment. Because if there's one thing Seth hates, it's a hospital.

They take him to the darkest place of his memories.

The hospital he checked into after his OD, before the Brothers Kincaid were big, back when they could keep it out of the papers. Luke after the plane crash, the bar fight. Finding Sal in Florida after her abduction from Roy Williams, when she had no memory of her life with Luke.

His entire fucking family's been in one and now Lacey.

Seth doesn't know what to expect when he sees her. It terrifies him. Because what if she's hurt bad? Really bad.

Christ.

He ain't so sure he can handle that. Not because he doesn't want to deal, but because when Lacey hurts, he hurts for her.

He damn near called her a hundred times to say thank you for that night, but he always chickened out, he always told himself *next time.* And now regret washes over him at a missed chance.

Seth takes a sharp corner, finds the room and enters.

The air rushes out of him.

"Fuck."

The sight of Lacey in the hospital bed hits him like a crowbar to the chest. All he can do is stare at the tubes and wires curling around her arm. Her eyes are closed, her typically sun-kissed face pale and bruised. Her long blond hair lays lank and tangled around her shoulders. She looks so helpless, her defenses down, and suddenly Seth wishes for the sight of the girl he knows. Lacey, haughty, nostrils flaring, her mouth on a tear, ready to rip him a new one.

The only other time he had seen her look this fragile, this vulnerable, was when Sal went missing.

It was the first time they slept together. But not the last.

Seth braces a hand on the wall, bracing himself against the memory.

Bursts of images cycle through his brain. The motel room in Florida. Red wine at the bar. A lot of goddamn red wine. Lacey coming to him later, half-dressed, a little buzzed, a lot crying. *I need you, Seth,* she whispered. The first time she had ever said it that way. A plaintive plea. A desperate entreaty. He should have said no. She was Sal's sister for Christsakes. But she looked so helpless, so distraught that he couldn't. And then she opened her mouth, spread her legs and Seth turned into one weak son of a bitch. The moment her lips hit his, he couldn't stop her. Didn't try.

The next morning, Lacey was on a plane back to Los Angeles. Four months later, she was calling him, demanding he tell Luke to declare Sal dead. He didn't understand her then. But he does now. He gets Lacey. Too much.

It scares the fuck out of him.

Clearing his mind, Seth takes a step inside the room and slings his duffel bag on a corner chair. He hisses a breath as it bangs against the wall.

Smooth move, dumbass.

Slowly, Lacey stirs. Her green eyes flutter open, land on him.

His chest expands.

He gives her a grin. "Hey, princess."

Her voice comes soft, confused. "Seth?" Then, eyes clearing, as if she remembers where she is and what's happened and why the hell is Seth Kincaid in Los Angeles, she jolts upright, cords yanking, tangling around her as she thrashes. "What—what are you doing here?"

Before Seth can react, she tears the IV from her hand with a sickening slurp.

He rushes across the room. "Jesus, easy," he says, grabbing her trembling hand and cupping it between his to stop the bleeding. "You're gonna hurt yourself."

"Too late," she shoots back, still on her best banter game, even with drugs and sleep coursing through her system.

That's when it hits him. He scared her. Of fucking course he did. He's a man who came tiptoeing into her room after she was mugged. Goddamn idiot.

"Hold still," he says softly, taking her hand. Gently, he works at untangling the cords wrapped around her wrist.

Her gaze skims over him, a frown on her face. "What are you doing here, Seth? Don't you have a hay bale to go roll?"

He lets the comment slide.

"I'm here because Sal asked me to come," he says, helping her settle back against the pillows. Resisting the urge to keep her hand in his. "To make sure you're okay."

Even as he says it, he feels like a fucking fraud. Hell, he's here because he wants to be here, not because Sal asked him. Because he cares. Because he can't stand the thought of her alone for even a damn second.

Still, the lie's well practiced, well lived in after all this time. A reminder. He doesn't care. He can't. She's Sal's sister.

Seth tries again. "Besides, you helped me. Now I'm helpin' you."

Lacey lifts her chin. "I don't want your pity."

He grinds his teeth. "Goddamnit, Lacey, it ain't—"

He breaks off, feeling like the biggest asshole yelling at her as she lies hurt in a hospital bed. He lowers his voice. "It ain't pity. It's a favor to Sal. I'm gonna take you home, get you settled, get out of your hair. How does that sound?"

She crosses her arms. "Fine."

He glances around the room, irritation chafing at him. It shouldn't matter that she wants him here or not. He's here, she's going to deal with it, and tomorrow he'll be on a plane back to Nashville.

He drops into a chair next to her bed.

His eyes scan her face, the up-close view of her. Wide-set green eyes, a full bottom lip, her pretty face scrubbed clean of makeup. He hasn't seen her, hasn't spoken to her in months. Three, to be exact. Not since she left the hospital in a blur, without a goodbye, her demand to end things ringing in his ears. He doesn't know what happened that night, but ever since then Lacey's been taking over his thoughts. Some haughty high-heeled dream stomping around his memories.

Seth fixes her with a look she can't outrun. "How are you doin'?"

"Fine."

"Try again."

She frowns his way. "What?"

"Try again." Hands on the thighs of his jeans, he leans into her. "You ain't fine. You were fuckin' stabbed. So give me the real answer. Or lie better."

Fear slams into her green eyes, long enough for Seth to catch a glimpse of it. Then her eyes shutter. She grimaces. "I hurt, Seth." A long exhale. A windup. A release— "I feel like shit. Like a crash test dummy. I have twenty stitches in my stomach, I look awful, I hate this gown, it itches, and in two weeks I can take a bath. There. Happy?"

"You're right," he says finally. "The gown definitely ain't your color."

That gets him a laugh. A pink blush that gives her pale face a pretty glow.

"But you don't look awful, Lace. You look—" Beautiful. Dangerous. Fragile. "Stabbed."

She rolls her eyes.

The room falls silent.

When he sees her gaze land on the hospital tray, he immediately stands. "You want a drink?"

She nods eagerly.

He grabs it up and brings it to her lips. Her slender hand closes over his, warm and shaky, as she gulps water. Seth takes in the tired planes of her beautiful face. She's thirsty, exhausted, and God knows what else. How she's keeping it together is a feat known only to Lacey.

When she's finished, he sits back down. He can't help it. He has to ask. "Your stomach, you said?"

"Yeah."

"Where?"

Her eyes, glazed with pain, drift downward. "In my side. Right above my hip bone. It was so quick . . . I didn't even realize at first . . ."

Anger hits Seth hard, curls his fists. Whoever did this left Lacey to die as if she never existed. What he wouldn't give to meet the son of a bitch in that same dark alley with a sock full of pennies.

"You talk to the cops?" Hot anger edges his voice.

"I did. You know how that goes," she says, and he does. Their minds both moving to Sal's ordeal. Lacey shrugs, running a hand through her blond tangles. "I gave them the best description I could. They'll get him or they won't."

"They'll find him, Lace."

They goddamn better.

The door cracks. "Oh good," the nurse says. "You have a ride." The nurse looks at Seth. Booms a laugh. "She's a fussy one."

He grins. "You're tellin' me."

Lacey scowls, but Seth doesn't miss the pain in her eyes. She looks as lost as he felt back in Nashville. All he wants to do is get her home and get her settled. Take her hand and tell her everything will be alright. Because it will be.

He'll make sure of it.

LACEY STARES OUT THE WINDOW WITH VACANT EYES, the pharmacy sign blinking red above her. Seth's left her in the rental car while he stopped to pick up her prescription for pain pills. She shivers and hugs her bandaged elbows, feeling groggy and unlike herself. Her body a train wreck of aches and pains.

She closes her eyes, trying to disengage from the memory of last night.

Tune everything out and focus. There's no missing necklace. No man with his hands over her mouth. And there's definitely no blood streaming out of her stomach like the warmest waterfall she's ever seen.

Lacey replays the surf in her head. A coping technique her therapist turned her onto years ago. *Picture the beach. The crash of waves, the swell. The crash. The swell. The—*

Hand on her forehead.

Stiffening in her seat, she opens her eyes.

Seth's back. Sitting in the driver's seat, staring at her with worry. "You okay?"

"I was asleep," she snaps, straightening up in her chair. The cell phone in her lap buzzes. She looks down and fires off a frantic text to Autumn about linens and llamas.

"You call your sister yet?" Seth asks in a low, rumbling drawl that has Lacey's belly flipping over multiple times. "She's worried."

Lacey keeps her eyes on the window. On the Jesus Saves sign standing tall in the distance. "I will."

"When?"

She turns to him, eyes flashing. "I will, Seth. Jesus, I didn't know we were on a schedule."

Leveling a dry look her way, Seth tosses her medication on the dash, on top of the police report she's been given, her hospital discharge paperwork listing instructions to change her bandage often and watch for infection.

Then they're in motion, Seth steering the car one-handed down the streets of Los Angeles.

Another ping on her phone. Lacey groans. The caterer sent over the wrong menu.

Seth side-eyes her. "That thing ever stop going off?"

"It's my job, Seth," she fires back. Fires off a text.

"Yeah, well, I already hate your job," he says, his voice cloudy. "Some dipshit sending you to downtown LA at night deserves to have his ass beat."

Without looking up, still typing, she says, "I'm in Reseda. Stay on this and then take the 101 to Spring Street."

"You got it, Your Highness."

Seth accelerates, then brakes, cursing at someone who doesn't let him through the intersection.

"Oh, you gotta be kiddin' me," he snaps and Lacey looks up. They're stopped again. Ducking her head, she smothers a smile watching him try to navigate around LA. She can already tell he hates it here. Good. Maybe he'll leave sooner than later.

Her eyes skim over Seth, who's staring at the traffic with an intense scowl. Her belly goes tight, a slow flush creeping over her.

He desperately needs a haircut. Its current state is boyish and floppy, but adorable in that way only Seth can pull off. He's like a colt. An eager, sandy-colored, long-legged colt. With boots.

He's irresponsibly attractive. Seth and his rock-and-roll T-shirts, his muscled arms, his country boy charm, his smug attitude. It's disgusting. Infuriatingly ridiculous.

Soon, she'll be stuck with him at her apartment for

twenty-four hours. Seth messing up her space. Her and him to-gether. Alone.

Her memory travels to earlier this afternoon. Seth strolling into her hospital room like some countrified Lancelot. She doesn't know how she feels about him flying to Los Angeles for her. Stunned, yes. Flattered, maybe. Happy, definitely not. He's only here for Sal, anyway. Settling debts he doesn't need to settle.

She came to him that night because she wanted to. Because he needed help.

She hopes he found it. Because all she came away with from that night has been a case of utter confusion and frustration.

Her heart hasn't stopped racing since that kiss. A kiss that bound them somehow. A kiss that told Lacey Seth could be hers in more ways than just their typical quick hookup. If she wanted him.

Which she doesn't. Most definitely not.

Her face heats. She turns her face to the window, not wanting Seth to see.

Stop it, she hisses at her reflection. *Stop swooning like some dumb, lovesick teenage girl.*

Which was exactly how she acted the very first time she met Seth, all those years ago. She was sixteen, Sal and Luke were engaged. When a twenty-year-old Seth came strolling in late to the engagement dinner, Lacey felt that flutter all the way in the pit of her stomach. He was wild, cute, funny and older. So sure, she had a crush on him. But when he promptly called her a princess and teased her for the big ball gown she had picked to wear to her sister's party, all crushing was off. Since then, he was always Luke's incredibly annoying younger brother. Sal's best friend and Lacey's competition.

And that's what he still is.

They can't do what they've been doing anymore. She told him that back in Nashville. Her only reassurance is that he leaves tomorrow. All temptation gone. All her focus on the Colin Cane party. The way it should be.

Twenty minutes later, they're in Reseda. Lacey taps a nail

against the window as Seth takes a right on Cooley Avenue. "This is mine," she says as they pull up to the Desert Wind apartment complex. With relief, she sees her car has been towed back thanks to her AAA membership. The one nice thing her father's ever done for her.

Seth pulls up to the curb and cuts the engine. He sits there for a long second, frowning at the crumbling stucco building.

He looks over at her. "Did he take your keys?"

She startles. "What?"

"Your keys," he repeats slowly. "Do I need to call a locksmith?"

Lacey bites her lip, grateful for Seth for thinking of that since all she's done is blank out the world around her. Grateful to him for taking it on with her.

She shakes her head. "No. Just my wallet." But as soon as she says it, her chest tightens with terror. She grabs his arm, making eye contact. "Seth. He knows where I live."

She can't stop it. The tremble in her voice. The icy chill seeping into her bones.

Seth's jaw goes tight. He looks over at her, covers her hand with his. His long fingers slide under hers, scooping them up in a tender clasp, and instantly, she's warmed. "It'll be okay, okay?"

She stares at him, wanting to believe. Seth's voice so confident, so determined, her entire body untenses as if it aches to lean into his words, his arms.

Lacey wets her lips. "Okay."

Then his hand leaves hers and Seth's out of the car, hustling over to her side, cracking the door. Lacey sucks in a breath as she tries to sit forward. Her stomach aches. Invisible wires tug at her sutures.

"Here." Seth leans in the doorway, offers her a hand. She takes it, and he grasps her elbow. Slowly, wincing right along with her, he pulls her out of the car and into a kind of hunched-over standing position.

"Shit," Lacey exhales, resting a hand on the car roof for

support. She gulps in a few sharp breaths of air. Growls a sound of frustration. "This hurts."

"C'mon," Seth urges, his eyes full of sympathy. "Lean on me."

She does, pressing her entire body up against him, the steadying warmth of him cloaking her like a blanket. Close enough that she can see the crystal blue of his eyes, his chiseled profile.

She stiffens as Seth wraps an arm around her waist to guide her up to the sidewalk path that leads to the apartment gate. Only then does she realize she's practically sniffing him, drinking in his familiar scent like she's trying to huff paint. Warm cedar and sawdust. *Holy shit, what is she doing?* Clearly, she's traumatized. Quickly, she jerks away from him, breaking their connection, and Seth steps back, an amused smile on his face.

"Which one is yours?" he asks, eyes scanning the complex. The boring sand colors with rotting palm trees. The garbage pails full of trash. Lacey feels her face flush with secondhand embarrassment.

"Upstairs. Third floor."

"Of course it is."

"There are elevators, Seth."

He smirks. "Lead the way. I'll tag along, while you hobble."

She ignores him. Gritting her teeth against the pain, she walks as fast as she can for the keypad, very much aware Seth's trailing behind her at a slow lope, letting her lead.

Never mind the razor-like pain in her side. The stabby pains that accompany her every footstep. All Lacey wants to do is get home and then get Seth out.

Bypassing the small overgrown courtyard, they take the elevator up to the third floor and follow the walkway to Lacey's apartment. She sticks her key in the lock, deftly positioning her body in front of the doorknob that sticks like a son of a bitch. Suddenly she's very aware of where she lives. In a run-down apartment in a very not-prime neighborhood of LA.

Seth peers around her, arching an eyebrow. "You need some help there, princess?"

"No. I don't." She wiggles the sticky knob. "Just . . . a . . . little . . . more . . ." She puts her shoulder into it and the door flies open with a clattering bang.

Immediately, they're in the kitchen.

Seth whistles as he follows her inside, his normally sunny face sober as he sets his duffel bag on the kitchen floor.

He looks at her. "I thought you had a job." The edges of his mouth twitch and she can't tell if he wants to laugh or frown.

"I do have a job and a good one." She shuts the door behind them, says, "It's LA, Seth. I'm lucky I can afford a car."

But she's suddenly self-conscious, noticing Seth's scrutinizing gaze, the way his eyes rove the place, his dark scowl.

She's proud of the little apartment she decorated and bought herself. She can't do much about the surroundings, but she's still made it her cozy, safe space. There's no sadness here, no stepmother. Everything, she controls. It's her space. One she's tried to make as cheerful as she can.

The scuffed-up walls are a warm gray. A plush pink rug covers the stained shag carpet. Potted plants add color to the living room. Brass hooks on the wall for jackets. Small photos of her and Sal hung across the back of the couch. No photos of her father; the photo of her mother lives in her bedroom, pinned to her bathroom mirror.

Seth swaggers around, peering out the kitchen window to be met with a direct view of another kitchen window. "Christ." His blue-eyed gaze sweeps to her. "It's like Attica meets Shawshank."

"Shut it, Seth."

"This ain't no life, Lace," he says, kicking his boot against a loose baseboard.

"Sorry we can't all have spacious digs by the river."

The beach. Think of the beach. Not killing Seth Kincaid and dumping his remains in the Pacific.

He steps close to her and her heart dips. Only Seth moves to the door instead, his face tight as he fingers the broken safety chain. "This is pretty damn important, don't you think?"

Her gut churns, not wanting to think about the mugger.

Lifting her chin, she strides past him, not touching him, not once, to the living room, where she gingerly lowers her leaden body on the couch. Seth's gaze is intense, his eyes won't leave hers and because it's too much, because his kindness, his worry is palpable, Lacey closes her eyes.

"I'm tired, Seth. Can we not do this right now?"

All she wants is to change her clothes, pour a glass of wine and pull out her laptop. Seth being in her apartment has her antsy. She's never been this still. She's never not worked.

Seth's rumble of a drawl washes over her. "When's the last time you ate somethin'?"

Unable to help it, she flinches at the talk of food. A bad habit, a bad past that still creeps around the edges of her put-together life.

She opens her eyes, watching as Seth steps into the postage-stamp-sized kitchen. She sighs, already knowing what he's going to see, but too tired to do anything about it.

He yanks the fridge open and swears. He stands, staring into the void of fluorescent light, like he's trying to gather himself, and then says through gritted teeth, "Lace. You ain't got no food here." He turns to look at her over his shoulder. "You eat, don't ya?"

"Only on a full moon and standing over the kitchen sink."

Seth blinks, unsure if she's joking or not. "There a store around here?"

It's Lacey's turn to blink. "You're going shopping?"

"Hell, I think someone's got to."

She nods, sucks in a breath. Food would be nice. Something hot, melty and delicious. "Two blocks down. On the corner of Hershel."

He grunts, sweeping up the car keys.

At the door, he pauses. His blue eyes take in her slumped position on the couch. His forehead creases. "You'll be okay?"

She waves a dismissive hand, trying to ignore the hard pump

of her heart at the thought of being left alone. "Go, Seth. I'll be fine."

He rolls his eyes at the word, then fixes her with a look. "Stay here. Lock the door. Call Sal. I'll be back in twenty."

The slam of the door has her jumping. And then Lacey's up, moving as fast as she can, which, if she really wants to admit, is an embarrassing turtle-crawl.

The doctor said she'd be sore, but sore's an understatement.

She locks the door. Fires up her laptop. Slips into a chair at the small round table she uses more as a desk than a place to dine. As the laptop rouses from its slumber, Lacey eyes her phone. She groans, her sisterly duty telling her to suck it up, and then she calls Sal.

Her sister answers on the first ring. Breathless. "Oh, thank God. I've been so worried. Are you okay?"

"I'm fine," Lacey says. "I'm out of the hospital and I'm home."

"I'm so sorry I can't be there, Lacey." Sal makes a sound of frustration. "I'm just so, so mad."

Lacey smiles. "Everyone's just trying to be extra careful. Make sure that baby stays put."

"I know." Sal sighs. "Is Seth taking good care of you at least?"

He always takes good care of me.

The horrifying thought floats through her mind before she can stop it. Lacey fights the urge to gag, to barf the image right out of her brain.

Lacey needles her temple. "He's being his usual annoying self."

Sal laughs. "Well, I'm glad he went out there. You needed help."

Her expression pinches. *Never. She'll never admit it.*

Tucking the phone beneath her ear, Lacey clicks into her email, halfheartedly listening as Sal rambles on about bandages and infections and proper wound care.

Shit.

Lacey's eyes bug at the thirty unread emails. Mostly messages from the caterer and DJ asking about setup start times. All emails she needs to reply to and confirm details.

"I called Dad."

That takes Lacey from her thoughts. "You got a hold of him?" she asks, rubbing her pinched brow.

"I did."

Of course she did. He'd answer for Sal.

Lacey's face burns, fighting that hot wave of resentment, not directed at Sal, never at her sister, but at her father. When Sal went missing, she had to fight the military tooth and nail to make it through the channels to get a note to their overseas-based father. But when Sal calls, he answers. Like their relationship's always been the perfect father-daughter pair. Like Sal hasn't hated him for years for cheating on their mother while she was in chemo. But Sal can't remember, so their father can put on a show for Sal. Call her every few months, pretend he's a good father, while keeping that detached distance he was always so good at.

"I know Seth leaves tomorrow . . . ," Sal ventures. "Dad can't be there, but . . . he said to call Vivian if you need to."

Lacey's mind overheats at the mention of her stepmother. "I'll never call her."

Vivian, her overbearing tyrant of a stepmother—the Witch Woman is what she and Sal used to call her—is the reason she went to live with Sal and Luke right after they got married.

Lacey examines a long-faded white scar on her knuckle.

One reason at least.

"Okay," Sal says in that sad, bewildered tone she uses whenever their stepmother gets mentioned.

She doesn't understand because Lacey will never tell her, despite getting the go-ahead from Luke. Her sister has been through so much, was the only mother she knew, has always looked out for her. It's Lacey's turn to protect Sal. Her sister doesn't need the burden of Lacey's bad memories. Bad memories Lacey wishes she herself could forget.

She closes her eyes, not wanting to think about the past. But it's coming in hot, like smoke from a flame.

Food. How she'd eat everything she could and then kneel in front of a toilet bowl to purge. How she kept going until she felt empty. Until she got control.

Stop.

Hospitals. The day her sister flew to San Diego in a rage, packed Lacey's bags and got her out of that house.

Stop it.

Sal. Her sister, weeping. Luke, in the doorway of Lacey's bedroom, his dark eyes so sad, telling her she could stay as long as she wanted.

Please stop.

"I know how you are, Lace," Sal says, breaking through her memories. There's concern in her voice. "You're not alone. Don't be afraid to ask for help."

Lacey bites her lip. "I won't."

After a few more minutes of reassuring Sal she's okay, Lacey says goodbye and hangs up.

She sits back in her chair. Hot tears spring to her eyes.

She shakes her head, chasing away the emotion. She doesn't have time to deal with her old, sad memories; with what happened last night.

With a sigh, Lacey opens her laptop and rubs her hands over her face. What she needs to do is dig into work, stay distracted, feel invincible.

Even if the only thing she feels is all alone.

chapter
SEVEN

S ETH EXITS THE HARDWARE STORE, STICKING THE PLASTIC
sack containing a new lock and a screwdriver into the inside
pocket of his jacket as he hustles across the street to the
grocery store. Hell, he should have just gotten Lacey a toolbox for
all the work she needs done around that dump of an apartment.

He grimaces, thinking about his reaction. He didn't hide his
surprise. Hell, he couldn't have acted more like an asshole if he
tried.

He's not sure where he pictured Lacey living, but it wasn't
some run-down shithole apartment the size of a fruit stand. She
always put up an act that she had the good life, could afford fancy
things. Maybe it wasn't an act—maybe he pegged her wrong,
maybe she was trying her best.

Even though he doesn't have any say in it, her living there
doesn't make him happy. He wants her safe, and thinking about
her being anything but safe makes his chest ache.

Seth pauses at the entrance of the grocery store. He pulls out
his phone and stares at it.

Sal and Luke are waiting for him to call back home and report, but what's he got to tell them? That Lacey's a mess, but she
ain't caving, not yet, not by a long shot.

One thing he's learned about Lacey: she'll either fake it until
she makes it, or she'll break. Both options he isn't a fan of. He saw
it on her face, every emotion she's trying to hide. She's traumatized. Fucking exhausted. In agonizing pain, but still too damn
proud to admit how hurt she is.

And she ain't gonna show it until she cracks. Like she did that night at Tonk's when she unleashed. Her tears still haunt him. He always knew Sal was tough, but Lacey could go toe-to-toe with her sister. She's closed off like Fort fucking Knox. A PhD in *I'm fine*.

It's only a matter of time before she implodes, and he wants to be there for her when she does. He doesn't trust anyone else to know what she needs. He understands her. Even if she wishes he'd drop dead.

Seth sends a quick text to Luke that he'll call him tomorrow.

Inside the grocery store, he grabs a cart, ready to get in and get out. He hates leaving Lacey at home alone, especially after what she's been through, but she needs food and rest. What she doesn't need is to be running all over Los Angeles. That's his job.

Blowing out a long breath, Seth scans the unfamiliar surroundings. It's strange to be in a city other than Nashville. Hell, he hasn't traveled in years without the band. Without Luke.

A sharp pang of regret hits him at the thought of his brother. Their last conversation they had left unfinished. But he was the one who ended it, wasn't he? He's the one who can't pull it the fuck together.

Seth navigates his way down the aisles, steering the rickety cart. He has no idea what he's looking for, what Lacey likes. He doesn't shop. Lunches out, takeout, dinner at Sal and Luke's is all he's good for.

Bread.

Girls like bread, right? He tosses a loaf in the cart. White, then wheat. *Milk*, he thinks when he hits the dairy aisle. Organic. That coconut yogurt with that weird fruit jam on the bottom.

In goes cheese. Fancy cheeses, cheeses with names he can't pronounce. Deli meats. Magazines. Tylenol. Butter. Eggs.

"Fuck," he says, picking out the grapefruit he just added to the cart. Lacey's allergic. An allergy as fussy as she is.

Seth's eyes snag on dark chocolate peanut butter cups. He grabs a pack and, after a second thought, grabs another. They're Lacey's favorite. Next, Gatorade, Pedialyte and broth. Chicken, veggie, bone, all the goddamn broths. Healthy shit to get her better.

He swears as he's slammed hard in the shoulder by a woman in yoga pants and a hoodie walking fast like if she goes one more minute without organic oat milk she'll die.

"You're fuckin' excused," he mutters to her retreating figure.

Fucking LA.

At least in Nashville people have manners. He could never live in this damn city. It's like living in the mouth of a nightmare. Especially the traffic. Still, despite the smog-choked hellhole that is LA, he hates to admit it, he's breathing easier. A day away from Nashville, dealing with someone else's problems, has him forgetting his own. Although this is the last place he should be. Out in LA with Lacey Sutton, a girl who thrashes his heart like a goddamn hurricane.

After adding a bottle of wine and a six-pack of PBR for himself, Seth settles in line to check out. "Shit," he says when he sees the time.

He's been gone longer than he wanted.

Seth knocks, triple knocks, calls out to make sure Lacey knows it's him, but when he swings open the door, empty silence greets him. He scans the living room. Sets the bags of groceries on the chipped countertop. As he passes through the kitchen, he palms the top of the closed laptop sitting on the kitchen table.

It's warm.

Goddamnit.

"Lace?" he calls out, louder than necessary.

A heartbeat later, her clipped voice. "What?"

"I'm back."

"And?"

Hands in his pockets, Seth walks down the hall and stops in

front of the closed bathroom door. He raps twice, earning an exaggerated sigh from Lacey.

He smirks. He can practically feel her glare through the door. "What're you doin'?"

"Changing my bandage."

"You need some help?"

"No."

"Don't forget to wash your hands. And no pullin' at the stitches either."

Silence.

Seth waits, crossing his arms to lean against the wall.

Another sigh.

"Are you going to hover outside my bathroom door for the next twenty minutes, micromanaging every little thing?"

Seth smiles. "I hadn't planned on it, but now that you mention it . . ."

The door swings open. Lacey pins him with a scowl. "Fine, get in here and help me if you think you can do it better."

Seth steps through the threshold and freezes. "Good Christ, Lacey," he says, staring in horror at the hellscape that is her bathroom.

She purses her lips, following his gaze. "I know. It's so small."

"It ain't the damn size." He gestures at the counter. Her beauty products spread everywhere like a goddamn tornado ripped through the cosmetics aisle.

She crosses her arms, her glare slicing his way. "I need all this, Seth."

He picks up a tube of something beige. "For what? Spackle?"

"Just help me," she snaps, snatching away the tube.

After clearing a space in the bathroom and washing his hands, Seth steps up, his eyes tracking over Lacey. She's changed out of scrubs into a light purple knit top and linen lounge pants. Her hair waves around her shoulders, and her bored gaze tells him she's waiting for him to get on with it.

Without a word, he slowly lifts her top, revealing a taut and toned abdomen. Her bandage is already off. An angry red incision stares back at Seth. He sucks in a breath. "Jesus."

His thoughts turn black. Whoever did this, they could have killed her. Someone hurt Lacey. Someone hurt his—

Friend. *Wrong.* Best friend's sister. *Better.* Sal's sister. *Perfect.*

"I know," she says, her voice sad, not understanding Seth's reaction. "It looks so ugly."

Lacey stares up at him, her blond hair in her face, her green eyes so forlorn, he can't help himself. He cups her cheek, feathering a thumb across the arc of her cheekbone. "It don't look ugly, Lace."

Her eyes widen slightly, and then she glances down, her lower lip pulled between her teeth. Like she's trying to chase away the emotion, his touch.

With careful hands, Seth cleans her wound. Lacey shivers as his fingertips graze her skin. Though his focus is changing her bandage, he can't help but take in every part of her. Her bronze skin, the curve of her hip, the smattering of light freckles arcing around her belly button like a constellation.

Lacey stands robot-stiff, slightly angled into him, her eyes closed. So still, he can't be sure she's breathing.

After he finishes taping on a new bandage, he says, "There. That feel okay?"

She nods, running a finger across the tape, and raises her eyes to him. Seth blinks. He never noticed the color. A light turquoise, like blue-green sea glass, not the deep emerald of her sister's. So damn different from Sal's. So damn beautiful.

He clears his throat, too many emotions all at once, and moves out of her space.

Christ, what's wrong with him?

"You wanna eat?" he asks, dragging a hand through his hair to mask his discomfort. "I'll fix us up somethin'. You gotta be starved."

"You cook?" she asks, following him out of the bathroom, genuine curiosity in her tone. She turns on the lights as they make their way to the kitchen. City noise from the street filters through the thin walls. Outside, the sun is setting in a blue-winter glow.

"Ain't so sure." Seth flashes her a crooked grin over his shoulder. "We'll see."

After finding the frying pan, directed by Lacey with a point of her manicured nail, he rustles through a grocery bag. Pulls out what he wants. Bread, butter, cheese and pepperoni. An easy meal he and Luke used to make when they were living on tips from their guitars.

Over his shoulder, Lacey peeks into the bags, her expression turning from amused to stunned all in the span of five seconds.

He points with the spatula as he turns on a burner. "I got you Tylenol and Pedialyte and that weird yogurt you liked. I wasn't sure if you had bone broth, so I got a few different brands. I tossed in some magazines in case you're bored. They ain't the best quality, but I thought . . ."

Seth trails off.

Lacey's staring. Her head tilted at a strange, quizzical angle.

Suddenly he's clamming up.

Fuck.

He knows too much about her.

Only she saves him by asking, a small smirk on her face, "How much do I owe you?"

He grunts. "Don't be dumb."

Her nostrils flare.

But she unpacks, saying nothing for once, leaving the ball-busting alone, a smile on her face at his obvious stammering.

His jaw flexing, Seth turns to the stove, focusing on the food, focusing on reining in his scrambled brain. What is it with Lacey? How does she do that? Have him in a million little pieces with that damn scowly smile of hers?

A gasp has him looking over.

Lacey's eyes glow as she tears into the bag of peanut butter cups he's bought. "These are my favorite." Her pretty face pulled into a wince, an expression that has Seth hurting, she gingerly seats herself at the kitchen table.

Seth busies himself with slathering bread with butter. He slaps a piece of bread into the heated frying pan, butter side down, then tops it with cheese and pepperoni before covering the toppings with another slice of bread. The sizzle of hot grease and melted cheese has his stomach rumbling. If he's hungry, Lacey must be starved.

"Seth?"

He glances over his shoulder.

Lacey's stacking a peanut butter cup cairn on the table. Wrappers scattered around her. She eyes him beneath her long lashes. "Thanks." Her mouth purses. "For . . . everything."

He chuckles. "Wow. How hard was that thank-you?"

A lift of her chin. A hint of a smile. "Only slightly agonizing."

With a quick turn of the wrist, he flips the sandwiches over. "You're welcome," he says, his eyes holding hers. "I'm glad I could help."

Then the sandwiches are on a plate, the napkins in his hands, and he joins Lacey at the table.

The ping of Lacey's phone. Instantly, she jumps to attention.

Seth snags her arm. The contact like a spark. "Forget the phone," he says to her wide-eyed gaze. "Leave it and eat. It's been a goddamn day and you ain't workin'." He gives her a look. "Not anymore at least."

Lacey blushes at being caught. She takes a sandwich, tearing it in half, and pops a bit of crust and gooey cheese in her mouth. As she chews, she lets out a groan of satisfaction. "Oh my God, Seth, this is so good."

Seth can't keep from smiling, because he can see her trying to act all prim and proper but then giving in and devouring the sandwich like she damn well should.

"Luke and I used to make these all the time back when we were on the road," he volunteers after a bite of sandwich. "Prime bachelor food. Drunk-as-hell-after-the-bar food."

Lacey laughs. She pops another piece of sandwich in her mouth and sits back in her chair. Her eyes on Seth. "Are you okay to be away?" She arches a brow. "You're not missing a show or anything?"

"Nah," he says with an amiable smile. "Thinkin' of takin' a break, anyway."

She frowns. "From the Brothers Kincaid?" She lowers her voice dramatically. "Like quitting?"

Seth shifts uncomfortably, a lump in his throat. He searches for the words. An explanation he can't seem to figure out himself. "I wanted to, but I ain't so sure Luke will let me."

"But why would you leave?" Her frown, her question, is genuine. Her green eyes wide and shocked.

"You saw the article?"

"I saw it," she says slowly. "But it wasn't true, Seth." She leans in and clutches his hand with surprising ferocity. Her contact like an anchor. "I was there."

Seth stares. Something electric passing between them. A familiarity, a friendship. But it's more than that. It's the notion she cares, she's listening, she's not shying away from what happened that night. She's not shying away from *him*.

"Yeah, well, I didn't tell Luke," he admits.

Her lips thin out, but not from judgment. From sympathy. Understanding. "Why?"

"I ain't so sure he'll forgive me."

She frowns, hesitates, then says, "You're his brother, Seth. He might be mad, but he'll forgive you."

Seth shakes his head, trying not to look at her hand wrapped up in his. "I don't want Luke or Sal anywhere near it. Luke's tryin' to help, but I don't deserve that. He's got enough on his plate with the baby and Sal." Lacey sits, waiting for him to say more, so he does. "I made a mess of everything. And steppin' away from the band is the only way I can think to fix it."

Fire leaps into Lacey's eyes. "You didn't make a mess. You

made a *mistake*, Seth, and you still didn't do what that stupid newspaper is saying."

His face feels hot, guilt and memories wreaking havoc. Hell, if Lacey knew about his past, would she be saying the same thing? What would she think if she learned he fucked up back then?

Lacey lets out a growl. "It makes me so mad." Seth watches in amusement as frustration creases her pretty features. "I should call the *Star* and give them a piece of my mind."

Seth laughs. "Easy, princess. I appreciate it, I do, but that ain't how it works. It's what the *Star* does. The story'll be in the dust once somethin' else comes along."

Lacey leans back in her chair, her hand pulling away from his. The loss of her contact like a kick to the stomach. She props her chin in her palm, looks at him with a sad gaze that seems to see right through him. "Are you okay, Seth? Are you really, really, really okay?"

He doesn't get the question, but he does. He understands what she's asking.

Slowly, Seth shakes his head. "Hell if I know." He sighs. "I get back to Nashville tomorrow, I got some shit to figure out."

She drops her eyes to her empty plate. "Right. Tomorrow."

His heart gives a jerk and Seth finds himself wishing he could stay longer. It doesn't feel right leaving her.

As Seth surveys Lacey, the lump in his throat grows. She looks tired and delicate, like she could fall asleep where she sits.

"How you feelin'?" He peers at her. "You look ready for bed."

"I feel ready for bed," she admits.

And then as if it's suddenly dawned on her that she's been opening up, being nicer than normal, Lacey goes rigid in her chair and wraps her thin arms around herself.

"I don't suppose you booked a hotel," she asks, her tone clipped. Any familiarity they shared gone.

Seth crosses his arms and arches a brow. "Do I need to?"

"I only have one bedroom."

He lifts a palm. "Hey, it's fine. I sleep in a bus. I can survive a couch."

She smiles. But it's nervous. Uncomfortable.

Seth wonders how they got here. Something changed at their last encounter. In him and in Lacey. There was no sex, and yet it was still intimate. And he's the one wanting to give in, goddamn, does he want to give in, while Lacey's got a pitchfork between them sharpened to the hilt.

"Relax, Lace," Seth says, stretching out where he sits. "Ain't gonna cramp your style. Just gonna change that lock you got there and then settle in for the night. Won't even take off my boots."

"Okay." She stands, slipping her phone into her palm. "I'll set out a pillow and some blankets."

With that, she gives him a tight smile and then turns and walks down the hall without looking back.

Lacey sits on the edge of her bed, trying to muster up the energy to reply to one of Prentiss's twenty emails. Only her mind is on her conversation with Seth. She can't believe he's talking about leaving the Brothers Kincaid. Luke would go ballistic. Sal, too. He's their family, and his leaving would hurt all the way around. It would be unfathomable.

But she understands what he was trying to do. Get out before they got hurt. She could see the pain in his eyes. Wondering where he belongs, worrying over his mistakes. She yearned to tell him he's a good person. That Luke's proud of him, loves him, but when she went to say that, she clammed up instead.

Lacey rubs her hands over her face. God, why does she pull away from everything? Why can't she be more like Sal? Not surviving life, but *living* it. Open and loving with friends and family. Enjoying her time on this earth and not working herself into a frenzy.

Because who knows how much time she has left?

It's her greatest fear. Dying alone, dying young, dying of cancer like her mother. Without time. Without someone by her side to hold her hand. To tell her they love her. But having all that requires getting close to someone, and having a relationship is like a grab bag of awful possibilities. Never knowing what she'll get. A serial cheater like her father? Or heartbreak like Sal? Her sister and Luke are soulmates who have come so close to losing each other too many times. Lacey couldn't bear it. Never.

Which is why she's steered clear of long-term relationships.

There were a few boyfriends years ago, but Lacey always called it quits before they could. Jumped ship before it got too serious. Men, like friends, are scarce.

Still, sometimes she wishes she could love things without worrying, without wondering when her heart would break. When they'd leave.

Which is what Seth needs to do.

Leave.

She's done a good job at controlling her relationship with Seth. Enemies. Then friends until sex. But now he's in her space, and her emotions are all over the place. She knows she told him no more, but those warm feelings from Nashville have dug in their claws and aren't letting loose. Seth being so nice to her doesn't help either. Earlier tonight, his expression so fierce, hands so gentle as he changed her bandage. The loads of food he brought home from the grocery store, like he had never shopped a day in his life, but he was glad to do it. For her.

Lacey groans, shaking her head to chase away thoughts of Seth Kincaid.

She needs him out of here. Stat.

She has too much baggage for Seth, anyway. A long-term, serious relationship would mean she has to show him the real her. Her eyes close. God. What would he think about her past? All her bad habits. He'd be disgusted, wouldn't he? He wouldn't understand. Sometimes she barely does herself.

Setting her phone on her nightstand, Lacey climbs into bed, leaving the lamp on.

She isn't ready for the dark. To relive last night. A shudder ripples through her body as the mugger's face edges into her brain space.

Needing comfort, calm, Lacey reaches up for her necklace.

Only it's gone.

Her eyes fill with hot tears.

A sob erupts and she presses both hands to her mouth, last night closing in around her like a scream.

She buries her face in a pillow and sobs, not wanting Seth to hear, to have a front-row seat to her unraveling.

Stop.

Please stop.

Seth lies on the couch, staring at the cracked ceiling, unable to sleep. The sandwich has settled heavily in his stomach. He's coming down with something. Man, if he gets sick out here in the land of sunshine and bullshit, Luke will never let him live it down.

But he doesn't think that's the reason he's feeling so horrible. He thinks it's Lacey.

His thoughts move to tonight. Lacey's hand in his. That slow curl of his stomach. That girl's a goddamn hurricane, driving him fucking nuts, and even though he tells himself he doesn't like her like that, he's not so sure he believes himself anymore.

Now he's paying the price. Being here in LA with her, close quarters, has him thinking about her in a different way. In a *he wants to be around her all the time* kind of way.

Before the night of that kiss, he never even entertained the notion of them being something more, of getting together. For a variety of reasons. Because she was Sal's sister. Because Lacey lived in LA. Because he was lying to himself. But now, now . . .

Hell, he doesn't fucking know.

It's bullshit is what it is. He's a grown man agonizing over an incredibly hot, incredibly dangerous, sharp-tongued woman. Not to mention, she was mugged. His priority is keeping her safe, not wondering whether she's been thinking about him as much as he's been thinking about her.

Jesus. He smears his face in his hands. He needs to pull it together. Get back to Nashville and start singing again.

He ain't good at this. He doesn't date. At least not long-term.

Sal's theory was that he never found the right girl, and she was right, but only because he never *tried* to find the right girl.

Seth kept his life free and easy. Tried not to take anything in it too serious, because if he did, he usually fucked it up.

He could count the things he cared about on one hand. Luke. Sal. The music. Bars on Saturday nights. Sunday Supper.

It's not that he doesn't want to settle down. Hell, he wants what Luke and Sal have—that real, honest friendship and love— he just doesn't know what love is because he never had it, never worked hard for it.

And with Lacey, he doesn't have to try. He doesn't mean that in a lazy way. He means it in an easy way. She's always been in the periphery. Sal's lanky baby sister, who he teased mercilessly. Someone he saw every holiday, every summer, someone he had a foe-to-friendship with first, someone he's realizing he now knows better than anyone he's ever dated. No one can match her for banter, wit, ice-cold glares, and goddamn gorgeous looks.

He don't got a clue how to act around her anymore.

Besides, who's to say she even feels the same way he does? They agreed to call it quits back in Nashville. And Lacey's clearly keeping her distance. But still, what if she—

Christ, he's overthinkin' it. What would Luke say? Not like his brother knows anything about him and Lacey, but still, what would he do?

Shit.

Seth chuckles.

He'd say write her a song.

Luke's MO since the dawn of time.

The way Luke even got Sal to go on a second date with him after she realized he smoked. He sang her a love song in that bar on his third beer of the night, and two months later they were getting an apartment.

He could. What if he did?

Seth smears a hand down his face.

Sal's sister, he thinks. *Sal's sister. Sal's sister. She's Sal's goddamn sister.*

And that's when he hears it.

Crying.

Soft, sniffling sobs trickling out from beneath Lacey's closed bedroom door.

His stomach flips over. "Fuck," he whispers to the ceiling. "Fuck. Fuck. *Fuck.*"

Seth resists the urge to smother himself with his pillow. A girl crying is his kryptonite. It threatens to detonate everything inside of him. He feels so fucking helpless.

He weighs his options. Go in there and get his ass chewed out, or sit out here and listen to the worst sound he's ever heard in his life.

Finally, he can't take it anymore. He shoves up from the couch, pounds down the hall, and, without knocking, enters the room.

The curve of her thin hip. Her golden-blond hair tangled around her. Lacey, her face tear-stained, her eyes red, lifts her head from the mound of throw pillows she's nestled in.

"You're cryin'," he states like an idiot.

Her face clouds, her red-rimmed eyes glistening. "So?"

"So . . ." He strides across the room and sits on the edge of her bed. "You wanna tell me what's wrong so I can fix it?"

"You can't fix this."

Like the snap of an old guitar string, Seth watches her break. Lacey's face scrunches up and she's sobbing into the pillows again and all he can do is sit there and make a fist. Her pain pries open his heart like a rusty crowbar.

The words that come next are a whisper. "He took my necklace."

Seth strains to hear. "What?"

She lifts her face, tears spilling from her eyes. "The mugger took my necklace." Her hand moves to her throat. "My mother's."

Seth swears. He knew how special that necklace was to Lacey. That delicate gold locket she always wore, the lavalier that puddled in the hollow of her throat when they lay in bed together, naked, gulping air after one of their frantic hookups.

"Damn. I'm so sorry, Lace."

Her lower lip quivers. "I should have let Sal have it. She would have taken better care of it." Seth shakes his head, but before he can say anything, she goes on. "I fought back. I made him mad." She closes her eyes, her brow creased in pain. "I should have been paying attention. I wasn't—"

She begins to weep and Seth does the only thing he knows how to do. He gathers her into his arms, cradling her against his chest. He waits for resistance, for a defiant slap, maybe a hard right to his face, but instead, she grips his shirt and cries.

"Don't do that," he says hoarsely. "Don't you fuckin' dare blame yourself." He kisses the top of her golden head. "You were doin' your job and someone decided they were gonna wreck your entire world. That ain't okay, Lace. And that ain't your fault."

He holds her close as silent sobs wrack her body.

He knows this will be a hell of a thing for Lacey to get over. He's seen how Luke handled Sal's trauma, and it won't go away overnight. It'll stick with her. She'll break a thousand times over. She'll break and Seth will be there. He won't be anywhere else.

And that's when he knows. He can't leave her.

Lacey grips his shirt tighter, burrowing into his chest. "I thought he was going to kill me," she whispers.

Seth swears darkly and pulls her deeper into his arms like he can shield her. Lacey's voice rises, fever-pitched, distraught. "I thought it was over. I thought I was going to die, Seth."

"Oh, Lace." He hugs her close and then pulls back to stare into her eyes. "Well, you ain't dead. You're here, right?" He smooths a hand down the back of her head, her golden hair sifting through his fingers like silk. "You're here and I got you."

Tears roll down her cheeks. "I can't get him out of my head. The way he came out of the shadows like a ghost. The way he smelled." Her eyes close, her body a violent shudder. "The way he touched me."

Seth's heart stops. Just fucking flatlines.

He clears his throat. "Did he . . . ?"

He can't bring himself to say it. *What did he fucking do to you?* Because he'll find the bastard, track him down like a hound and hurt him tenfold. Whatever he did to Lacey, Seth aches to make him pay. To hurt him as much as he hurt her.

"No," she says to his unasked question. She shakes her head, again and again. "No."

A combination of relief and rage has Seth going weak. Relief that Lacey didn't experience the worst thing a woman could experience, but still rage that she was made to feel unsafe. Violated. Hurt.

He closes his eyes. "Thank Christ."

For a few long minutes, they stay like that, Seth holding her, letting Lacey's emotions, her breaths, come down to calm, knowing it won't be the last time she crumples. When her sobs have ebbed, Seth unfurls her from his arms. He cups her face, a strand of hair tangling between his fingers, and stares into her eyes. "You're safe, Lace. I ain't gonna let anything happen to you. Never again, do you hear me?"

He hopes she does. He wants her to know she won't go through this alone. That he's here with her.

Lacey shivers at his words, the tilt of her face leaving their lips only inches apart.

It's instinct to comfort her and he leans in, brushing a soft kiss against her brow. Not a kiss of trying to take it further or get her in bed. A kiss to show here he is here. That whatever she wants, she's got it.

And then, without a word, his lips are meeting hers. She whimpers, then kisses him back just as hard. Breathless. Desperate.

"Fuck, I'm sorry," he says when she breaks the kiss with a gasp. Guilt crowds him and he curses himself. He should be caring for her, not kissing her. "I should go." Before he can stand to leave, she grabs his shirt.

"No." She bites her lip, clings tighter. Tears sparkle on her lashes. "Can you . . . can you stay with me tonight? I don't want to be alone."

He hesitates.

Say no. Walk away. Keep your hands to your fuckin' self.

But he can't.

No matter what he does, he can't let her go. Not when she's looking at him like that, her expression so needy, so damn beautiful it carves up his heart.

"Please, Seth?"

In answer, he eases down onto the bed next to her. Slowly, Lacey curls up against his chest and snuggles down beside him. Like it's habit.

Like this is how it should be.

Seth closes his eyes.

Like she's his.

chapter
NINE

P ING.

Ping. Ping. Ping.

Lacey smiles, ignoring her phone, and stretches out in bed. Warmth beside her. A hard body. She's never been so relaxed, never had such a glorious night of sleep. She sighs, snuggling deeper into the covers, into the silk sheets, into a lean, muscled—

Seth.

Shit.

No.

Her eyes flash open.

She groans inwardly, her gaze taking in Seth's sleeping form. He's curled up beside her, one arm tossed over his messy head of hair, the other draped protectively on her hip.

She resists the urge to be mortified. Embarrassed. After all, they did nothing last night. They just shared a bed. A kiss. Never mind the fact that she completely broke down in front of him, like some hot mess of blubbering baby. Never mind the fact that she's never felt so cared for in her entire life.

Seth was something else. He showed her a side of him she had never seen before. Caring, tender. The fury in his eyes as he told her it wasn't her fault. She appreciated that. There was no *I told you so*, no blame. He didn't shy away from her tears, her distress. Instead, he took it as his own, holding her, catching her as she fell apart.

Somehow, he understood.

Annoyed with her sappy thoughts, Lacey scowls. Slowly, she

inches away from Seth, determined to make it out of bed without waking him. Uncomfortable conversations are not on her agenda this morning. Not with her phone blowing up. No doubt it's Prentiss telling her to get her ass out of bed and get to work.

Still, she can't help her eyes drifting to Seth. His long, tan body. His lean build, muscles like corded leather. Hesitantly, she reaches out, brushing a lock of hair from his brow.

He reminds her of the beach. With his sandy-blond hair and his eyes as blue as the Pacific, a sunny smile that continuously has her melting—

Holy shit, what's wrong with her?

This line of thinking is completely bonkers. She and Seth, they'd never work.

For thousands of reasons. He's reckless, wild. She's type A, thrives on order. She has her dream job in Los Angeles, and Seth, he's in Nashville, a country superstar singing all over the world, girls climbing on his pant leg every night.

Plus, the most important reason: he's her sister's best friend. She's ashamed to admit it, but she never really gave any thought to Sal the first time she and Seth slept together. And why would she? Her sister was presumed dead. And Lacey needed something, needed someone to help her ward away bad habits. To help her forget her sister was missing, possibly gone forever. Just for a night.

And then it was every time she came to Nashville.

The time after Tonk's.

When he drove her to her bed-and-breakfast after Roy Williams attacked Sal.

At the Hermitage, putting that hotel room to good use, after Sal went back to Luke.

Last Christmas when she came out for a show in North Carolina.

She always said it was the last time. Until it wasn't. Every time they were together, she fell for him more and more.

She doesn't know what Sal would say about them. She's not

sure she wants to know. She loves her sister more than anything, and if she found out . . .

But why would she?

Seth is a good thing that's temporary. There is nothing between them that will last. Besides, he's leaving today. Why bother?

Ping.

At the insistence of her phone, she sits up, vowing to put last night behind her. She cannot go down this path. She was vulnerable, like some dumb damsel in distress, clinging to anything that would help her feel better.

Lacey shoves off the covers and grabs her phone. She's about to crawl out of bed when a hand snags her wrist. "Where you skulkin' off to?"

She glances down at the mound of covers. Seth's sleepy blue eyes stare back at her.

She sniffs. "I do not skulk, Seth."

"Mind tellin' me where you're goin', then?"

"To work."

He grins a lazy grin. "Don't suppose you wanna cook me breakfast first?"

"You're a Neanderthal."

Disentangling from his touch, she stands and slips on a flowered robe. Grabs her laptop off the dresser. Realizing she's serious, Seth sits up and scowls. "No way. You're stayin' in bed today."

In response, a flip of her hair. She exits the room.

She hears him scramble up. There's a bang, a curse, and then he's limping out of the bedroom.

Swiftly, she seats herself at the table, opening her laptop and depressing the ON button. "What time's your flight?"

He grimaces, rubbing his knee. "Noon, but—"

She bangs loudly on the keyboard. "Great. That means you have about two hours before you leave. You should get there early. LAX has some great restaurants."

She clicks between an email from Prentiss and the run of show schedule. Her saving grace is she's lucky. Lucky she's mostly needed for phone calls. Lucky she has interns she can boss around. If she can get through the next two days working from home, she'll be healed up by Saturday in time to be on the ground the day of the party.

Easy.

It's all easy.

Seth stands extremely still, as if he's having some kind of internal fight. Finally, he lifts his arms and lets them drop to his side. "Okay, you know there's no way in hell I'm leavin', right?"

Her eyes tear from the screen. "What?" Panic tightens her ribs at the thought of Seth sticking around to monitor her every little move. "You have to."

Ping.

He gives her a hard look. "I leave, you ain't gonna take a break, are you?"

Lacey fights the scream in her throat, deciding to try calm and rational. Try the truth.

"Work is crazy," she says in a breezy tone. "I can't stop until this party happens."

Ping.

"Which is?"

"Saturday."

Ping.

"Lacey." He smears his face in his hands. "You oughta be on that couch—"

Ping. Ping. Ping.

"For fuck's sake." He stalks close to her and snatches up her phone. His face strained and irritated.

She's up, out of the chair, scrambling after him. "What're you doing? That's private."

"Oh, I know it's private," Seth drawls, striding across the living room. "I'm just tossin' your damn phone out the window."

She grabs his shoulder, yelping as her stomach pulls. "You can't do that, Seth. That's my job." She stands on tiptoes beside him, cursing his tallness as he holds the phone up and out of reach.

"Yeah, it is, and you don't need this shit right now." He thumbs through the messages. "Pick up linens? Buckets of flowers? Stuff gift bags?" Concern etches itself across his handsome features. "This is heavy liftin'. You can't do any of this. What did your boss say when you told him you were mugged?"

Propping her hands on her hips, she meets his eyes. "I didn't."

"Didn't . . ." He inhales, shakes his head. "Lacey."

"Prentiss won't understand. He doesn't take breaks."

"Sounds like a swell guy." Seth frowns down at her. "What would Sal say if she knew what you were doin'?"

She glares. "Don't you dare use my sister against me."

Without a word, Seth cracks the window.

The phone pings in his hand.

Lacey sets her jaw. "Do it, and I'll scream, Seth."

They stare at each other, defiant. Stubborn.

A knock on the door has her stiffening. Seth, surprised, turns, the phone bobbing in his hand. Smoothly, she inches forward and snatches it away. Seth sighs. In response, she sticks out her tongue.

"Real mature," he says, not hiding his irritation.

"You started it," she snaps, heading for the door.

What Lacey sees when she peers through the peephole has her swearing.

It's Autumn. Autumn with her over-plucked eyebrows and extremely tinsled Christmas sweater.

Of course, Prentiss sent his crony to check up on her. She glances at Seth over her shoulder. "Get in the bedroom," she hisses.

Seth scowls but trudges off, muttering something about hard-headed women being the death of him.

When Seth's disappeared, she runs a hand through her hair, hopefully combing it into something presentable. She wishes she were in anything but pajamas. Like a power skirt with big 1980s polka dots.

Inhaling a steeling breath, Lacey swings the door open, a smile plastered on her face. "Autumn, hi," she says brightly.

"Lacey." Autumn raises a salty brow. "Poor thing. You look so tired."

Lacey lets the comment slide. Decorum, too. "What do you want, Autumn?"

"Prentiss sent me over to let you know that I handled Colin's errand. I take it you're feeling better?"

"Right as rain," Lacey chirps. "The whole stomach issue's a thing of the past."

"Good. Because we have a problem you need to handle." Autumn stoops and drags an enormous cardboard box out of the hallway through Lacey's doorway.

"What's this?" Lacey blurts, her chest constricting.

"The linens for Saturday night."

Oh God. She stares in horror.

Already she sees the problem. A very big problem.

Lacey closes her eyes.

This is worse than she thought. She's out of commission for twenty-four hours and already a thousand things have gone wrong. She's panicking. Spiraling. Seeing all her hard work, all those wasted hours she's skipped dinners, dates, virtual move nights with Sal, going down the drain called *was it worth it*?

"Do you see the issue, Lacey?"

Lacey finds her voice. "I see it," she says through her teeth, forcing herself not to scream. Typically, she has a calm head under pressure. But this. This. She can't focus. She's freaking out. "Why didn't you call the manufacturer?"

"I have my own accounts," Autumn says. "I can't cover for you."

"Yes, I know that." She gives Autumn a sharp look. "What did you tell Prentiss?"

Autumn shrugs. "Nothing. Not until his uppers and laxatives kick in."

Great. She still has time to fix this.

Lacey sinks down to inspect the linens, instantly wishing

she hadn't. A sharp pain slices through her stomach, the stitches pulling tight.

"Something wrong?" Autumn asks.

Besides her life? The crippling pain in her abdomen? Losing her dignity in front of Autumn? The very fact that she's unable to stand back up on her own?

Lacey chokes down a whimper. "No. Nothing." Black dots blink in her vision, a cold wave of clamminess washing over her.

"Are you sure? You look like you're going to barf."

Lacey closes her eyes. She feels like she's going to barf.

But Autumn keeps going on, oblivious, her shrill voice like needles in Lacey's temple. "Are you still sick? Because Prentiss will flip. You remember what happened at the Horatio Duke party, when Prentiss sprayed Mary with bleach because she coughed on the juice bar." She lowers her voice. "She walked funny for a week."

Lacey lifts her head, rallying a scoff. A lie. "Of course I'm not still sick. I'm fine, Autumn. I'm perfectly—"

There's movement beside her, and then there's Seth. He's squatting down, pretending to peer into the box of linens. "Huh. This looks dubious."

Lacey looks at Seth, and he stares at her, his eyes telling her to take the damn help he's offering. A palm covertly extended between them. Lacey makes a fist, pressing the hard ball into his palm and using his leverage, his strength to push herself up into a standing position.

She grips the doorway, sweat beading her brow as she straightens up to face Autumn.

But Autumn's not looking at Lacey. She's looking at Seth. A predatory smile spreads across her face. "Who's this?"

Lacey digs her nails into her palms. Autumn's staring at Seth like she just stumbled upon some holy grail of hotness.

"He's, uh . . ."

As her eyes drift to Seth, who's watching her with a schoolboy smirk, her mind lights on an idea.

Lacey waves a palm over Seth like she's presenting an Oscar. "This is Seth. My assistant."

"What?" Seth and Autumn ask in unison.

Autumn stares in suspicion. "He's too cute to be an assistant."

"He is the exact opposite of cute," Lacey snaps, flustered. She takes a breath, aware she's being stared at like she's nuts, and exhales. "Thank you for bringing this shitshow to my attention, Autumn. I'll take care of it."

Autumn opens her mouth.

"Goodbye," Lacey says and slams the door in Autumn's over-powdered face.

For a few long seconds, Lacey stays at the door, waiting until the click-clack of Autumn's heels fades, and then she whirls around.

So much for getting Seth Kincaid out of LA.

Seth blinks at Lacey, her hands clasped to her chest, her face full of hope. Hope and what looks suspiciously like an idea he wants no part of.

He draws back distrustfully. "What?"

"You have to help me with the party."

He scowls, the request landing like a grenade. "No fuckin' way."

She tilts her blond head. "You said you were staying."

"Yeah, but not as your damn personal assistant."

She harrumphs. With a flick of her hair, she turns her back on him and stalks to the door. "Fine. I'll do it myself, then."

Seth sighs, watching as Lacey bends at the waist, gripping the sides of the box. She wobbles and struggles like a newborn fawn as she tries to move the heavy box further into the apartment with an almost comical exaggeration of defiance.

He stands still, jaw clenching. Trying to resist. Trying not to help her stubborn, idiot self. But when she winces, letting out a little whimper of pain, he caves so damn fast it's embarrassing.

"Goddamnit," he says, hurrying to Lacey to gently move her out of the way. He lifts the box of linens with ease, setting them on top of the kitchen counter. He turns to her, quickly running his eyes over her to check for any injury. "You're gonna hurt yourself."

"That's why I need you."

He groans. "Get someone else to help. That winter girl."

"I can't. No one at work can know I'm not one hundred percent." She pounds a fist into her palm. "I need this account; anyone will pounce on it the moment I look weak."

"Weak? It's a party, Lacey, not brain surgery."

Her lower lip pushes out.

Shit.

He's an asshole. If anyone came along spouting shit about the Brothers Kincaid, he'd tell them to fuck right off.

Lacey's gaze slides away from his. She rests a hand on top of the box of linens. "It's Beverly Hills and it's my job, Seth. It's important. I've been working so hard for this promotion. This could derail my entire career. I can be replaced like that. And Autumn . . ." She scowls. "That little bitch is just waiting for me to fuck up."

"Whoa." He stares. Impressed. Terrified. "Damn, tiger."

"Please, Seth. It's only for two days and then—" She sucks in a breath and doubles over in pain. Her hands clutch at her side. "Ow, ow, ow."

Seth swears under his breath. He moves toward her, sliding a hand over her shoulder. "Easy. Just relax," he says, not wanting her to get worked up, but it's too late. Her face is pale, her eyes bright and sparkling, but determined. And that's when he gets it. Really gets it.

With or without him, she'll do the party. She's Sal sister. Strong as hell. Of goddamn course she won't quit.

Seth sighs in resignation. "Lacey, take a breath. I'll help you."

"You will?"

"I will." His eyes drop to the box of linens. "So, what am I lookin' at here?"

She inhales a breath, gathering speed, details. "It's the wrong color. It has to be black. Pantone Color 19-4010, specifically. My Soul."

He squints. "Looks black to me."

"Well, it's not, it's blue."

"Can't we just use it?"

"Oh my God." She rubs her temple. Gives him a withering look. "He'll notice. Colin Cane notices everything."

Seth rolls his eyes. "Is that what a party planner does? Help incredibly rich assholes fulfill their dumbass demands?"

Lacey crosses her arms. "Colin Cane is high society. A mover and shaker of LA. He has *galas*, Seth."

"Yeah, but he hires you to throw the party." Seth laughs at the ridiculous notion. "So you're tellin' me you do all the work and he takes all the credit?"

Her lips twitch. "Something like that."

He rubs his hands together, deciding to just go with it. The sooner he helps her out, the sooner she'll rest and fucking relax. "Okay, so tell me about this party."

"It's on Saturday night. The vibe is Death meets Disney. The Once Upon a Dark Night party."

Seth wrinkles his nose. "Isn't that the same thing? Or is that Batman?"

She closes her eyes, pained. "Seth . . . can you just help me?"

He coughs, trying to smother a smirk. The vein in her temple looks like it's on her last nerve. "Sure, princess. What do you need me to do?"

Her expression remains stern, but he sees a flicker of relief in her eyes. "Return the linens to the address on the box. Find the new ones and have them delivered to Colin's house. I'll text you the address."

"Fine. But if I do that, you're doin' this . . ."

With a quick step, Seth scoops Lacey up in his arms. Ignoring her yelp of protest, he carries her to the living room, depositing her gently on the couch. If Lacey isn't going to do it herself, he's damn sure going to make her listen. He grabs her laptop off the counter, resisting the urge to toss it into the sink, and hands it to her. "If you're gonna work, you rest too. I'll do the runnin' around."

Her cheeks color, something stirring in her eyes. "Okay. I will."

The heavy-lidded look she's giving him is like a hook in his sternum. Dry-mouthed, he turns on his heel, picks up the linens and strides for the door.

He's gotta go. Now. Before he takes her impossibly beautiful face in his hands and kisses her senseless.

This is not what he needs right now.

This is not what he needs at all.

chapter
TEN

SETH PARKS THE RENTAL CAR ALONG THE CURB AND EXITS. The late-morning sunlight shines brightly overhead, a crisp chill in the air, but still warmer than Nashville. Hands in his pockets, he walks down the street. Headed to an address he's memorized by now.

Only it's not Lacey's address.

That errand's already handled. Easier than he thought, too. The rental company didn't order the wrong linens, just sent over the wrong ones. Seth waited while they found them and made sure they sent them to the address provided.

He never thought he'd see the day when he'd be Lacey Sutton's errand boy, but he'll do it if it means keeping her healthy, happy, sane. He could see her, during her conversation with Autumn, about to crack.

Lacey needs him. And he ain't about to let her down.

At the entrance of the alley, Seth hesitates and then steps inside. He drags in a pained breath, feeling like someone's punched him in the stomach. He got the address where Lacey was mugged off the copy of the police report, and being here where she was hurt, left for dead, is about ready to wreck him.

He wants to find the guy. Hunt him down and annihilate every bone in his body.

Steadying himself against his dark thoughts, Seth scans the surroundings. Two dumpsters at the back, brick walls on either side, graffiti, tall windows. He turns in a circle, then crouches, his eyes on the dirty ground, searching for gold, for that necklace Lacey loved.

He hunts for a good twenty minutes, then stands and swears. It's not here. He had hoped maybe the mugger dropped it in the scuffle, but no such luck.

Seth exits the alley, slapping his pockets for the keys, when his eyes drift. Across the street is a drab strip mall, as only LA can do. The type with an unimpressive appearance, but behind-the-scenes good bars, hip restaurants, hell, even churches, but in Seth's case, a pawnshop.

Quickly, he crosses the street and enters the shop. Above him blinks a screaming neon PAWN PAWN PAWN sign. The front desk is empty, a small TV scrolling through black-and-white images. Guitars on the walls. Ancient VHS tapes in a cardboard box on the floor.

Seth moves to the front desk, his eyes on the glass jewelry case.

He knows the deal with pawnshops. Way back in the day when he was deep into his addiction, he pawned his fiddle to get the money to score another hit. After Luke learned what he was doing, saw that Seth was playing on some shit cheapie, he went and bought his fiddle back for him, spending hard-earned money from his own pocket. Money they didn't have back then.

Just another goddamn time he let his brother down.

Another goddamn reason he doesn't deserve Luke.

Seth forces the memory from his mind and clears his throat, glancing around the pawnshop. "Hello?"

From behind the wall comes the faint sound of music. Seth listens. Strings.

A rail-thin kid appears from out of the back room, wearing a Yoda T-shirt, tugging earbuds out of his ears. "Hey, man. Help you?"

"Yeah, I'm lookin' for a necklace."

"Aren't we all." The guy settles into his chair. "What kind? Diamond. Emerald. Opal."

"One sec . . ." Seth pulls out his cell phone and finds Lacey's Instagram account. He chooses an image of her from last Christmas. Zooms in on the necklace. "See this?" He shows the kid his phone.

"How can you miss her?" the kid says, giving Seth a sly smile like they're here to ogle Lacey.

"Not her," Seth bites out, zooming in even further so the kid can't see Lacey's face. "The necklace. Have you seen it? Had it in here?"

To his credit, the kid gives it a careful look. He shakes his head. "Sorry. Haven't seen it."

"Would you call me?" Seth asks, reaching for a pen and one of the business cards that are on the counter. "If you get it in? It's important."

The kid takes the card. Examines the chicken scratch scrawl with Seth's phone number. "Sure thing, Seth."

"Thanks." He turns to go, pauses, eyes the kid. "You work with that noise goin' all day?" He points to the wall behind the row of guitars where a faint warble of a banjo sounds.

The kid grins. "It's not so bad. Even if it is country."

Seth rolls his eyes.

He exits the pawnshop, stepping into the parking lot to take in the neighboring sign above. The Blue Cowboy. The name sounds familiar. He frowns, trying to place it.

He doesn't know. But someone would.

He pulls out his phone, his stomach clenching in hesitation. He's got to call Luke anyway. They don't know he's staying. He's not sure how his brother will react to the news, but he can't dance around it any longer.

The video call cuts out quick and then it's back. Seth grins. His brother's on hands and knees, putting together an olive-colored crib. "Look at you," Seth drawls.

"Yeah." Luke wipes his brow, his face flushed and happy. "Look at me."

"How's Sal?"

"Countin' down the days." Luke sits back against the wall, dropping a wrench on the wood floor. "She ain't bleedin' no more. The doctor gave us the okay, so it looks like we're still on for Christmas."

"That's great, man." Seth lets out a breath of relief, happy Sal and Luke got cut one damn break with this pregnancy. "So, listen, who do we know in LA?"

Luke thinks on it. "Graham Watts."

Seth blinks. "Oh, no shit. Greasy Graham."

Graham Watts was a musician the Brothers Kincaid met in Nashville when they were busking on the corner of Broadway. They were down to their last dollar when Graham found them. Old, weathered, a legend in Nashville, he had criticized the way Seth played his fiddle. But a few days later, they got an invite to play at MerleFest, which was where they met Mort, their first manager. Graham saw their potential, despite their scrappy youth, and was key in giving the Brothers Kincaid their jump start.

"He's gotta be at least a hundred years old by now," Seth says.

Luke laughs. "Think he owns a bar or somethin' in LA."

Seth glances up at the sign. "Think I'm lookin' at it."

Luke frowns, realizing where Seth is. "You ain't at the airport."

"No, I ain't." Seth meets Luke's confused gaze and sighs. "I gotta stay, man. Lacey's a mess. She's actin' okay, but you know how that goes."

Luke nods. "Yeah. Shit." He gives him a droll look. "Way to bury the lede, Seth."

Seth thrusts a hand through his hair. "Sorry."

"How much longer you thinkin'?"

His throat tightens, guilt washing through him. "Through the weekend. But I know we got gigs we can't cancel . . ." Seth lets his words hang in the air between them. Feeling like an asshole. Giving Luke just another thing to fix.

Luke smears a hand across his grizzled jaw, the muscles flexing. "We'll get someone to fill in. I'll ask Greyson. He knows some musicians we can use."

Seth nods. "Cool. Thanks."

"Listen," Luke says. "I know Sal will appreciate you helpin' Lacey. But . . ." Luke stares at him, worried shadows darkening his eyes. "Are you stayin' out there for Lacey or are you just tryin' not to come back to Nashville?"

Seth's stomach clenches. He hears the confusion, the worry in Luke's words—where they stand, what's going on with him.

But what does he tell him? That out here in LA he feels like all his problems are solved? Like he can be less of an idiotic fuckup? Which is a goddamn dumbass notion. He can't hide. He owes Luke the truth. Because his brother knows something's wrong and keeps trying to fix it.

But Seth wants to tell Luke he can't.

He can't be fixed.

Doing his best to hide a grimace, Seth flashes a crooked grin, says easily, "Hell, Luke, relax. I'll be back."

But it's a halfhearted answer, and his brother doesn't buy it.

Luke nods and lifts his eyes to Seth's. "I sure as hell hope so. I'm worried about you, Seth. I want you home."

Home.

He's got to get back there.

Somehow.

Seth steps into the bar, the smell of whiskey hitting him like a memory. The space is dim, grungy. A lesson in dive bar. Frosted windows. Horseshoe booths line both sides of the belt buckle–decorated wall. A jukebox sputters Eric Church. A large stage takes up the entire back half of the room. Behind the bar, the bartender preps for her shift. A gray-haired old man, the lone customer, sits on a barstool nursing a beer and a cup of coffee.

Seth peers closer, realization dawning. "Graham?"

At the sound of his name, the familiar drawl, the old man

swivels around on his barstool. "Seth Kincaid?" His bushy brows quirk together as he stares, owl-eyed. "Kid, that you?"

Seth grins, swaggers. "One and only."

"Well, I'll be good and goddamned." To the bartender, he says, "This kid is insane on the fiddle." Graham crooks a finger toward the stool next to him. "Stop standin' there gawkin like an idiot and sit down and have a beer."

Seth chuckles. It's the same old Graham he remembers. A little more weathered and gnarled, but still ornery and kicking.

Seth takes a seat at the bar. The bartender slides him a beer and smiles. "Loved your last album," she says with the effortless cool of a pro who interacts with big acts.

Nodding his thanks, Seth whistles as his eyes scour the bar. "Man, never thought I'd see you in LA." He turns his attention to Graham. "How's country music farin' out here?"

"We get some good acts." Graham gives a proud nod. "Gets rough and rowdy on a Saturday night like it should be." He sucks the tobacco in his lip. "This place has been in my mind for the last twenty years. Finally got it out and up a few years ago." He appraises Seth. "Brothers Kincaid ain't doin' so shabby themselves."

"Hell, we owe you, man. Pulled us out of the gutter."

A highlight of Seth's career was performing with Graham when the Brothers Kincaid were just beginning. Even now, even as famous as they are, he can't help but get starstruck by Graham. The guy's a legend.

Graham barks a smoker's laugh. "You kids would have got there, eventually. I just gave you a boost in the ass."

"Best boost in the business," Seth drawls and Graham snorts. "How's Becky doin'?"

Graham's mustache twitches. "Passed last year."

"Shit. I'm sorry, man."

"Nothin' to be sorry for. She was a damn good woman. Lived a damn good life."

"Damn straight."

They lift their beers and clink, each of them taking long sips in honor of Graham's late wife.

"What brings you out to this neck of the woods?" Graham spits tobacco into his coffee cup. "You finally leave Guitar Town?"

Seth laughs. "Nah. Just helpin' out a friend."

The words are hard to get out. They seem like a disservice to Lacey. Like a lie.

Graham arches a bushy brow. "Long way to come for a friend."

Seth shakes his head ruefully as his thoughts shift from the present to the past. That kiss from last night. Sleeping next to Lacey like he didn't have a care in the world. Lacey ain't just a friend. Or a fling. After last night, he knows that now. Being out here with her has him feeling like himself again. Some semblance of the old Seth Kincaid. Not so lost, a little more found.

Graham lets out a grunt, breaking him from his pensive thoughts. "You runnin' away from that trouble in the paper?"

Seth sighs at Graham's take-no-prisoners approach to the conversation and scrubs a hand over his face. The last thing he wants to do is talk about the *Nashville Star* article. Leave it to Graham to hit the nail on the goddamn head.

Seth finds his voice, the truth sticking like glass in his throat. "Gettin' away from everything," he admits. "But I don't know if runnin' away's gonna do it."

To his surprise, Graham doesn't push. Instead, he says, "Let me tell you somethin', kid. You can't get far followin' that lost highway. There ain't no shame takin' a beat to figure out what you want." Graham's milky eyes stare him down. "Sometimes if you ain't sure where you're goin', you stand there. You stay in one goddamn place and when you figure that shit out, that's when you move. You understand?"

Seth nods and grips his beer, considering it. "Yeah. I do."

"You oughta bring her by."

Seth looks up. "Who?"

"That girl you're thinkin' about. Bring her by, or bring me a song." Stretching, Graham slips off the barstool. "It's the only way you're gettin' back in here, kid."

Seth snorts, watching in amusement as the old man hobbles across the bar. "I don't know what the hell you're talkin' about."

Graham cackles. "Listen to your elders, kid. We know all the good country lies."

chapter

ELEVEN

Lacey fires off the run of show to Prentiss, her last email of the day, and then sinks into the kitchen chair with a tired sigh.

Coffins, check.

Flower delivery scheduled, check.

Seating chart seated, check.

She's done. Finally finished.

For tonight, at least.

She smiles, content. She worked hard today. If this doesn't seal her promotion, nothing will.

Everything requiring heavy lifting has been assigned to her team of assistants. Normally, she'd hate delegating. Giving someone else control. But as Seth's reminded her, not to mention the pain in her side, she has to.

He's saved her by staying. There's no way she'd be able to do her job, get this party finished without him.

She scowls.

Damn Seth Kincaid. Why does he have to be such a good guy? Couldn't he be like the hundreds of other losers she's dated? Guys who think she's too uptight, a pain in their ass, but a pretty pain in their ass. Guys who want her for a quick hookup and an even quicker goodbye.

Not like she's dating Seth. Not by a long shot.

Even if he is the only man she's been with in the last three years.

At the thought, her face goes hot.

She doesn't know what happens next between them. Seth staying completely changes the ball game. Their ball game. He was leaving, there was no time to talk about them. But what even is them?

She can't deny she likes having him around. The way he smells. The way he laughs. How he utterly shows up and then some.

They already kissed once. They could kiss more.

Lacey shakes her head and slips out of her chair, moving to the counter for a sip of water.

This can't happen.

He's here for Sal. A favor to his best friend. Not a favor to Lacey and her sorta-kinda desire to get naked. Besides, she told him no back in Nashville. And now she's telling herself no. She can't start this up again. She knows what she felt the last time they kissed, and it wasn't anything good. It meant trouble. It meant heartbreak and—

She closes her eyes, inhaling a deep breath to chase away the thoughts.

A wave, breaking on the beach, a wave, taking her out to sea, a wave—

"Hey, you okay?"

Lacey gasps, fear making her freeze up. Her eyes flash open.

Seth's standing at the front door, sacks hanging off his arms, his worried gaze on her.

"Sorry, I'm—"

"Jumpy," he finishes. "I get it. I shoulda knocked louder." His gaze shifts to her laptop. "You get your shit done?"

"Yes, Seth. My *shit* is finished." She props a hand on her hip. "How about you? Did the errand go okay?"

"Got it all fixed," he says, fishing a receipt out of his pocket. He sets it on the counter.

"Thanks. I appreciate it."

He holds her gaze, warmth lingering behind his blue eyes. "You're welcome." With a shrug, he strides to the living room. "I was tryin' to make it quick, but I made a few stops too. Figured I needed more than one pair of clothes."

Lacey perks up, her eyes zeroing in on the bags. "You went shopping?" She's impressed.

He laughs. "Next time, princess." Seth stops and stares at the made-up couch. Blankets folded. Pillows gone. No duffel bag to be seen. He turns and glances at her over his shoulder, confusion washing over his features. "Where's my stuff?"

"In the bedroom." She tosses her hair, trying for casual, but feeling the tips of her ears go pink. "It's silly sleeping on the couch. Especially if you're here for . . ."

He gives her a strange look. "Three days."

"Three days," she echoes. Then she shrugs. "Or don't. It doesn't matter."

She pushes herself off the counter and stalks into the bedroom. Seth follows at a slow lope. Perching on the edge of the bed, Lacey slips on her slippers while Seth transfers the clothes he's purchased—two T-shirts and a black Henley—to his duffel bag. When he steps into the bathroom, toiletry bag in his hands, he clears his throat and gives Lacey a pointed glance.

She stiffens. "I made room."

The bathroom counter is clean and clear. Lacey's makeup and hair supplies crammed beneath the sink. A barely acceptable solution, but she'll make it work.

A laugh escapes Seth. Baritone deep, happy as hell. Angry at the way her stomach flips, Lacey stands and jams a manicured nail in his chest. "This was hard, Seth. To make room. So use it, or don't."

Eyes widening, he holds his hands up in a *don't shoot* motion. "Hell, Lace, I'm touched."

As he turns away to set out his meager man-toiletries, Lacey digs her nails into her palm.

A warmth, familiar, unwelcome, floods her veins. Lacey eyes Seth, standing in her bathroom, and wishes he looked out of place. But he doesn't. In fact, he looks perfectly placed.

Finished, Seth looks up, bracing himself against the counter to face her. The lean muscles in his tan arms flex. "What now?" he asks.

What now, indeed?

Lacey crosses her arms and shifts her tense stance.

An awkward silence settles around them. If she can feel it, he can. It's strange to be stuck in LA, in her apartment with Seth Kincaid.

But they're not strangers. Not anymore.

In fact, the awkwardness comes from them *not* feeling like strangers. How she wishes for that return. Seth barely paying attention to her. Civilized, familial actions she can work with. But then she realizes that was over ten years ago, when they were both young and dumb. The last five years, they've been friends. Singing bad karaoke down on Broadway. Seth sneaking her backstage passes to a show. The two of them helping Sal when she came back to Nashville, scheming like villains to take down Mort, the Brothers Kincaid's slimy ex-manager, who set up Luke as a cheater and caused Sal's car accident. Sleeping together. Again and again and again.

Seth slaps his hands on his jeans. The sharp sound jolts her from her daze and she blinks.

He grins at her. "You still like those shitty movies?"

She glares at him. Hard.

He laughs. "C'mon, princess," he says, moving too close to her. He curls a hand around her shoulder and Lacey has to fight the urge to lean into him, to press herself into the warm solid comfort of his body, to never leave the orbit of adorable annoyance that is Seth Kincaid.

A squeeze of her shoulder. Then he's letting go. "You put a movie on, I'll order a pizza. Mushroom and sausage okay with you?"

She stares up at him. "Yeah."

Before she can say another word, he's exiting the bedroom, leaving Lacey frowning after him.

Pizza, yeah. That's what she wants.

Lacey buys a movie about a tribe of zombies living on a beach who need to collect enough bones as fuel so they can escape the island and come to America in search of more brains. She's a sucker for cheesy B horror movies. Old-school monsters that creep and chase and chill.

She curls up on the couch, waiting, while Seth bullshits with the pizza delivery guy, who's recognized him and asked for an autograph.

Ping.

Casting a furtive glance in Seth's direction, she slips her phone out from beneath a pillow.

Prentiss: *The run of show is late.*

Lacey swallows, a hot flush of embarrassment and anger flooding her cheeks.

Lacey: *By two minutes.*

Prentiss: *And? Perfection, Sutton.*

Tears prick Lacey's eyes. She worked her ass off today and that's what she gets?

Asshole.

"Everything okay?"

Seth, coming back to the couch, two beers balanced on top of the pizza box he carries, peers at her close.

"Fine."

Fuck it.

She tosses her phone on the coffee table, far, far away from her so she isn't tempted to reply. Seth's observant eyes flicker, but he says nothing and sits beside her.

He doles out slices of pizza, salty and gooey with cheese. Lacey's stomach burbles. She doesn't think she's eaten this well since before Seth came along.

Seth nudges her shoulder with his. "Think you can scoot your bony butt over?"

She scoffs. "The couch is small, Seth."

Her fingers find the remote and she presses play. Eerie music swells over the credits, blood dripping down the screen.

They settle into silence, watching a bloodthirsty zombie battle montage. As they watch, Lacey sneaks a glance at Seth. He sits, relaxed, his arm draped over the top of the couch. One smooth curl of her body and she could be in that arm. Under it.

"Oh, shit," Seth cackles, cracking his beer as a zombie uses a severed limb as a baseball bat. His eyes flick to hers, amusement there. "I don't know how you watch this stuff."

"You're watching it."

"Yeah, with you and no one—"

Whatever he was going to say drops off, and his eyes move back to the TV, his throat bobbing.

But Lacey hears the unsaid words.

No one else.

She takes a bite of pizza, chewing robotically.

Normally, it'd be her favorite, but it feels slimy going down, settling like a brick in her stomach.

Lacey sits unmoving, fuming. Hating that it's a compulsion to know where they stand. Hating that Seth has no right to be that attractive. Hating that she wants to talk about them when there is no *them*, hating that she's giving it more energy than she should, because in the end, no one stays, not really.

Still . . . she wonders what he wants and if that's her. If she's been misreading his signals. If he wants to kiss her just as bad as she wants to kiss him.

Maybe they could do this. Just for three days. A trial run of emotions they can opt out of at any time.

"Seth . . . ," she ventures. "What're we doing?"

He frowns, his eyes locked on the screen where a redheaded female zombie is decapitating her victim while exposing adequate amounts of rotting cleavage. "Watchin' a movie, ain't we?"

She scoots to the edge of the couch. Ready to get into it. Ready to be that girl saying she wants no strings but really ready to hog-tie herself with every Seth-string she can get her greedy little hands on. "Yeah, but . . ."

Her words choke off as the stabbiest of stabby pain wrenches her stomach. She sucks in a hiss, resting a hand on the throbbing wound. Clearly all her running around is coming back to bite her in the ass.

In an instant, Seth's hands land on hers, gently pulling up her shirt. "Let me see."

She shivers as his lean fingers frame her bandage, brushing over her bare waist. His expression fierce, his shrewd eyes scan her for injury. Then, satisfied she's okay, he looks up. Cups her cheek like it's the most natural gesture in the world. His eyes soften, search hers.

"Lace, I want you relaxin', you hear me?" Worry stains his drawl.

She juts her chin. "I am relaxed."

"No, you ain't. C'mere."

And then he's taking her in his arms and pulling her back against him. His solid body the perfect cradle, the perfect couch.

Lacey lets out a sigh. She doesn't know if it's joy or frustration. Seth's hold like the lull of a gentle rocking chair. She closes her eyes, oblivious to the screaming on TV, oblivious to everything but Seth's strong arms around her.

Lacey wakes to movement, to being carried. Blinking away sleep, she murmurs, "What happened?"

"With the movie or with you?" Seth's deep rumble comes from above her. His breath tickles her hair. "The zombies ate the brains, and you're damn exhausted."

Inside the bedroom, Seth sets her on the bed and turns on the nightstand lamp. "Does it hurt?" he asks quietly, catching her wince as she reclines against the pillows.

She gives him a tight smile. "Not too bad."

"Sorry," he says, slipping off her slippers. "I was tryin' to be careful." He pulls the sheet up around her, an amused expression crossing his face. "You snore, you know."

She narrows her eyes. "I do not."

Seth crosses to the other side of the room and sits on the edge of the bed. Lacey watches as he slips off his jeans and T-shirt, getting down to boxer briefs. Her stomach tumbles as she takes in the view of his tan, athletic frame. Tall, broad-shouldered, lean and muscular.

It's nothing she hasn't seen before, but somehow, Seth being here in her bedroom, with nothing sexual between them, makes it even more personal. Hotter.

Lacey chases away the thought, only to be hit by another. "Where's my phone?"

A sigh from Seth. He crawls into bed beside her, flipping on his shoulder to look at her. "Left it in the livin' room." A line appears between his brows. "Take a break, Lacey. You ain't workin' at midnight."

Lacey rolls onto her side, mimicking Seth's stance. Which she instantly regrets, because she meets those eyes. Searching, as blue as the sea, seeing right through her.

"I can't take a break," she says, sticking her hands under her cheek so she doesn't brush his unruly hair out of his eyes. "I'm on track for a promotion and we're busy. Prentiss isn't exactly big on time off. He expects us to be there for clients twenty-four seven. Weekends, weekdays, holidays."

"Emergency health situations," Seth adds in disgust.

She nods. "Pretty much."

"What about Christmas? You thinkin' of comin'?"

Guilt floods her and she groans. "Sal asked, and I want to, but . . . I have to save my vacation for the baby. I used up more than I could when Sal came back and I'm still making up for it."

"You should come," he says simply. "Sal wants you to."

She smiles, softening, always softening toward Seth when he talks about Sal. He's done so much for her sister. He's the one who found Sal in that Florida diner, who pulled her out of that terror, away from that monster who kept her, and brought her back to Luke.

Lacey lets out a long breath, the long-overdue words sticking in her throat. "You know, I don't think I ever thanked you for that."

He frowns, puzzled. Adorably earnest. "For what?"

Her mouth kicks up at the corner. "You found my sister, Seth. You brought her back to everyone. You brought her back to me. The only family I have."

He pushes her hair behind her ear. "You got a lot of people, Lace."

She lowers her eyes, overwhelmed by emotion. "Why are you so nice to me?"

He chuckles. "Because I like you."

His words, choked by something she can't place, have her breath stalling. "You do?"

"Yeah." He gathers the sheet, pulling it up around them. "I do."

She's quiet for a long moment, staring at him from beneath darkened eyelashes.

The confession's out before she can stop it.

"I'm glad you're here," she whispers. "I feel safe."

His face goes tight at her admission, then soft. Handsome in all the right places. He smiles. "Good," he says, his voice husky. "You deserve to feel safe."

He reaches for her, his eyes asking, and at her small nod, Seth takes her in his arms. He pulls her close, pressing a kiss to her forehead.

Lacey tenses at the contact, untenses. She might as well enjoy it. She's cold and he's warm. It makes perfect sense.

Ping.

Lacey sighs, not wanting to leave Seth's comforting hold but knowing she should get her phone. Prentiss is probably having an aneurysm, and at the thought, Lacey's mind runs through a checklist of all the remaining things she still needs to get done.

As if reading her thoughts, Seth tightens his grip. He sweeps a finger under her chin, bringing her gaze to his. "We'll get it all done. I promise."

Lacey closes her eyes, fighting the urge to mentally plan for tomorrow, to try to get it all done in her head, and instead quiets her mind. Seth's reassurances are like a salve. She trusts him.

They'll get it done. Her and Seth.

Together.

Perfectly professional.

chapter
TWELVE

S ETH HANGS BACK AGAINST THE COUNTER, WATCHING Lacey channel her inner party planner extraordinaire. This morning, she got a delivery from the LA flower truck, and now her small apartment is filled with flowers and fragrant scent. Lacey stands, wearing a messy braid and a fuzzy pink lounge set, her tongue quirked out of the side of her mouth while she hums and examines the bouquets on the table.

He nurses his coffee, eyes on her, happy she's doing at least one activity that isn't heavy lifting. He's seen her schedule of to-dos and thanks Christ he stuck around to help.

Although, he wonders if he's stuck around for more than that.

His jaw goes tight as he thinks about what happened last night. The way Lacey curled up in his arms like she belonged there. The way her soft thank-you damn near had him falling to pieces. The way he could have kissed her right then and there. Key idea being *could have*. Because Lacey's got to be the one to make the first move. That girl's been through some hell. The last thing she needs is Seth pawing at her.

If Lacey's idea of cruel and unusual punishment is having them share a bed, then he's a goddamn sucker. Sign him up, night after night. Anything to get her in his arms.

Seth pushes off the counter, moving toward her. She stands in front of a huge arrangement of black peonies, specially dyed for the occasion.

She looks up and smiles. "Colin adores a good monochromatic floral arrangement."

"I thought they had people for this," he says. "You know, professional flower arrangers."

"It's Colin's request. He . . ." Her eyes fall, an embarrassed flush coating her cheeks. "Wants my hands on them."

He draws back, wrinkling his brow in disgust. "Christ, like a kink?"

"No!" She laughs and slaps a hand against his chest. Seth's heart jumps, her very touch electric, and he has to fight the urge to cover her hand with his, keeping her there.

Her smile grows soft as she palms the blossom of a peony. "He thinks it's good luck." A shrug. "Maybe it is, maybe it isn't, but what he wants, he gets."

"Okay, slightly worried, but I'm into it." He leans in. "Do you need help?"

Her lips lift in an amused sneer. "You?"

"Hey, there's nothing I love better than flower arrangin'."

She laughs, relenting. "Sure. Hand me that pampas grass over there."

He squints. "The what now?"

With Lacey's instruction, he finds some of the strange grass that looks more like a weed than a flower. Together, the two of them arrange black peonies and pampas grass into a strange cylindrical shape. They work swift and quiet, the only sound traffic in the distance, Lacey's sweet hum. Seth can't help sneaking glances at her pretty profile. Her vivid green eyes bright and alert. The cute purse of her mouth telling him she's deep in concentration.

When they're finished, Lacey steps back to examine the arrangement. She laughs happily, the sparkling sound bubbling up deep inside her core. It's a sound that jump-starts his heart, has him coming alive. Making her laugh always feels like he won the lottery. She does it so rarely that earning a real, true laugh from Lacey means he did something right.

Lacey arches a brow, turns a wry eye his way. "Seth, it looks like Mr. Magoo arranged these flowers."

He can't disagree with that fact. He chuckles and lifts a brow. "Hey, I just sing."

"Mr. Cowboy in LA," Lacey teases.

She moves around him, evaluating the arrangement from every angle. As she brushes past Seth, he can't help it. His hands, magnetized, graze against the small of her back. She jerks away. Her nostrils flare. "What're you doing?"

Seth turns, facing her fully. Unable to keep the shit-eating smile off his face. "I don't bite, Lace."

She lifts her chin, haughty. "That's not what I remember."

Damn her, Seth thinks as his dick gives a jump in his pants. He stares, loving that fierce flash of fire in her brilliant green eyes. That flirty tone that has him coming unhinged. Banter as only Lacey can do. Banter that drives him goddamn crazy.

With a long sigh, she fluffs the pampas grass. "We agreed not to do this anymore."

He gives her a grin. It's either gonna set her off or make her kiss him. He isn't sure which one he wants more. Anything that'll shake a little more feistiness into her, he'll take it. "What's *this*?"

She stamps her foot. "You *know*, Seth."

"Why?" He can't help the question, the god-awful need to know, the agonizing wrench of his heart if she says yes. "You seein' someone?"

Her jaw drops. "No. I—that's—that's irrelevant."

"Because I ain't."

"What?"

"Seein' someone."

She flushes. "I didn't ask." She turns her back to him, snapping a leaf off a thin peony stem. "Or care."

Seth runs a hand through his hair. "What if I do?"

Her eyes widen, her expression going slightly stunned. Then she shakes her head, like she's trying to erase his words. "You're leaving. This can't be anything serious."

It's out of his mouth like a bullet. Fast. Searching. "Why not?" He steps closer, giving her a sheepish look. "I'm tryin' to be good here, Lace. And I'm admittin', it's hard. Real damn hard." He grips the curve of her hip and holds her face in his eyes. "I haven't been able to get you out of my head since that night."

Her lips go flat, wary. "That's because you see me as some manic pixie dream girl." She sniffs. "Don't worry, you'll get over it." But her voice is strained, like she doesn't believe what she's saying. Like she's feeling the same as Seth.

"No," he says, pulling her in closer. "That ain't it."

He doesn't know how to tell her that his feelings didn't happen overnight. Things have been changing between them for a damn long while. If anything, that night had him seeing it clear. Her clear.

There's so much more to Lacey than he ever imagined. Goodness. Gorgeousness. She's gold inside and out. There's a connection between them that he hasn't felt with anyone else.

Lacey wets her lips. "This isn't Nashville, Seth."

Seth hesitates.

Say it or not. Because he's on the edge of something he can't rewind. Admitting he wants more, wants her . . . is he fucking crazy? They live two thousand miles apart. She's Sal's sister. But still, hope swells in his chest. Maybe she wants it too. Wants them.

He reaches out, cupping her cheek. "Maybe I don't want it to be like Nashville."

She stares up at him, speechless. Her palm presses against his chest like she's planning to shove his sorry ass away from her. Or better, grip his shirt and haul him to her lips. The angle of her body, the heat coming off her, her scent, her long blond hair, has him delirious. Has him leaning down. Has him—

Lacey startles and jumps back from him. "You need to leave."

He shakes himself out of his daze, grimacing at the hard flex of his cock. "What?"

"I just remembered." She smooths her hair, her voice wobbly. "You need a tux. For the party tomorrow."

"Tuxes make me itch."

"It's a black-tie gala."

"So you're sayin' spurs and boots?"

She raises the pampas grass. "A tux, Seth. Now."

"Okay, okay," he grouses, ducking her swat. "Jesus, I'm goin.'"

At the door, he pauses, a sudden thought coming to him. He slides his eyes over Lacey, who looks pretty and flustered amid all the flowers and greenery.

"Hey, Lace."

She gives him a skeptical look. "What?"

"What's your favorite flower?" He grins. "For future reference."

Her face softens. All her sharp edges chased away. "Tulips."

Seth stares at her, and then he smiles. "Got it. Tulips."

Seth slings the black bag over his shoulder and hoofs it up Sunset. It's already late afternoon, and he's frustrated as all hell. It took him forever to find a goddamn suit last-minute. Not to mention getting around LA takes forever and a day, and all he wants to do is get back to Lacey.

She's an eternal pain in his ass, but one he can't get enough of. Their arguments used to drive him crazy, and now they just drive him crazy for her. Nothing turns him on more than their banter.

Seth lets out a frustrated breath at the thought of that almost-kiss. Lacey pressed close to him, the warmth of her palms against his chest, her lips sweeping against his.

Her reaction to his admission that maybe he wanted more wasn't what he expected. Hell, this whole thing wasn't what he expected. Lacey should be off-limits. But being here, with her, has all his feelings from the last few months coming to a head. Has Seth feeling like himself again. Not like Lacey needs a guy like him. Someone fucking up all the time, making bad mistakes when she's beautiful, professional and smart as hell.

And Christ, not to mention, his whole ballsy bravado when he asked if she was seeing someone. Because hell knows what he would've done if she'd said yes. The very thought has him sick to his stomach.

The buzz of his phone breaks through his thoughts. Pulling it from his back pocket, he glances down at the screen. Luke.

"Hey, man."

"Hey, how's it goin'?"

"Oh, it's goin'. Lacey's got me pickin' up a tux."

Luke laughs. "For what?"

"Some fancy party she's plannin'."

"Sounds like you're at her beck and call."

A smile quirks his lips. "Guess I am."

Luke sighs heavily. "So, listen, I wanted to tell you before you see it in the *Star*, we got ourselves a new fiddle player."

Seth's stomach dips.

He knows what he said to Luke about stepping away from the band. Knows he doesn't want to be in Nashville at the moment. Knows Luke doesn't have any choice. But the Brothers Kincaid replacing him, if only temporarily, stings.

"It's for a month," Luke says, sounding like he's chewing dirt, none too happy about his brother's replacement. "That's what we got for a contract. The guy's manager wouldn't have it any other way."

"Who is it?"

"Beau Dallas."

Seth frowns. He's heard of the guy. Some hillbilly rocker with a hard-on for trouble who used to pal around with Griff.

"Great," he mutters at the thought of another Griff Greyson clone. "Good luck."

Luke doesn't sound amused. "My band ain't here," he says, his tone taking on a serious edge. "Because you're not. I miss you, man."

A rock grows in his throat. "I miss you too."

The evening sun is gorgeous, warming the chill in the air as Lacey cracks the blinds and lets in the light. As she crosses to the stove, she smiles. Evaluates her kitchen, now cleared of flowers. She has that calm before a party. That crash before the high tomorrow. Everything's done. Every email answered. Prentiss reassured. Colin calm.

Because of her.

Because of Seth.

She'd never have been able to get through this without him. He's made the last few days fun, easy. That's what she loves about Seth. He keeps her calm. He makes her laugh. Which is why the thought of him leaving has her feeling not so together.

The only reason she's getting through the nights is because he's been there beside her.

And she wants to keep it that way.

She can't stop thinking about earlier. They both danced around the issue, but Lacey thinks she heard it clear. He wanted more than sex. Something different from what they had in Nashville. She thinks she wants that too. The last few days she's been trying to figure out her feelings, and they're more than just a warm clench down below. There's a clench in her heart.

Which means they're a bad idea. He's a superstar, charming, confident, hot; he doesn't have time for her. And she doesn't have time for heartbreak or more loss.

Still, she can be nice. She can ride this out until he leaves.

As if to prove her point, Lacey walks over to the stove and stirs the dish bubbling on a burner. She's making dinner for Seth. To thank him for everything he's done.

Even though every bone in her body is screaming at her to rest. She promises herself she will. After the party, a nice long nap is in order. A silencing of her phone. A binging of horror movies.

Two knuckle raps and a whistle sound at the door.

Lacey smiles at Seth's familiar knock. He's doing everything he can to make sure she's safe and comfortable. Her heart warms. She appreciates it so much.

"Smells good."

The low rumble has her glancing over. Seth's skirting through the door, a black garment bag slung over his shoulder. With a quick stride, he opens the coat closet, hangs up the tux and then glances her way.

"I cooked," she says awkwardly, jerking her hands to the stove.

"I can see that." Seth steps inside the cramped kitchen. He leans close to her, inspecting the dishes on the stove. His mouth turns up. "Catfish?"

"Yeah. I had it Instacarted over." She shrugs. "I thought . . . I mean, it's southern." Her eyes flit to his, suddenly self-conscious. Panic she read the room wrong. *Oh God.*

"You like catfish, right?"

"A lot, actually." His throat works, his eyes swerving to the made-up dinner table.

"It's dinner," Lacey offers. "I made you dinner. You know. To thank you for helping me."

He stares at her, his expression unreadable. Then he grins. "Kinda premature, don't ya think? We still got tomorrow. What if I botch setup?"

"Setup is my forte." With a flick of her wrist, Lacey snaps off the burner. She turns to pull down two bowls, but Seth's already there, setting them on the counter.

"What time do we got to be there?" he asks, stealing a taste of coleslaw.

She smiles at the *we.* Shakes the thought out of her dumb brain.

"Setup's at nine."

"Jesus. That's all damn day."

She scrapes the cornflake-crusted catfish into the bowls, returning the empty pan to the stove. The scent of butter and garlic wafts between them. "What?" she asks, adding a ladle of coleslaw to the bowl. She gives him a sly grin. "You have better things to do?"

Lacey freezes as Seth braces his hands on both sides on the counter, trapping her. His blue eyes stare into hers and her breath quickens. "I don't want you liftin' shit, you hear me?" His expression is so serious, so full of care, that for a second her heart ceases to beat.

"I won't," she breathes. "I have people for that."

His eyes grow soft. "You have me."

She exhales, twisting her body to grab a dish. "We should eat."

After a second, Seth lets her loose. Together, they carry the bowls to the table. They settle in, the awkward clink of utensils, the first few bites, and then Seth's laughing. "Holy shit," he says.

She frowns, worried. "What?"

"This is good."

"You sound surprised."

He quirks a grin. "Well, you are Sal's sister."

A choked laugh escapes her. "Oh my God, I know. That time she served that lasagna?" She shudders. "I still remember the crunch. Luke was so nice he actually ate the entire thing." She jabs the fork at Seth. "Do not tell Sal I said that."

"Kinda violent, ain't we?" Seth says, scooping up a bite of catfish. "Slappin' me with flowers. And now sharp utensils?"

Lacey shrugs, breaking off a piece of flaky fish. "The dangerous life of an event planner. Deal with it."

A brief silence falls as Seth digs into the food. Only Lacey doesn't eat; instead, her eyes take in the handsome planes of Seth's face. His crystal-blue eyes, his wide grin. The easy way he sits there, countrified and cool.

Lacey bites her lip and looks down at her food.

She likes this. Too much. A happy presence in her space. Conversation that's effortless. Like she and Seth are two people who've come home after a long, hard day at work and can't wait to download and dish.

"Talked to Luke today." Seth's rumble has her glancing up. "He got someone to fill in for me while I'm gone."

She tilts her head, hearing the bitter tone in his voice. "Are you okay with that?"

"I have to be." He shifts in his seat, his handsome face contorting. "Hell, it just has me seein' what it'd be like if I left and I ain't ready to do that."

"Good. You deserve to be there."

"I don't know." His Adam's apple bobs. "Sometimes I think Luke would be better off."

Her heart twists at the pain in his voice.

"That's stupid," she says hotly. She reaches out and grabs his hand. "You're being stupid, Seth. Luke needs you. You're half of the Brothers Kincaid." She glares at her fish. "Ugh, this is all my fault. If you weren't out here with me—"

She trails off. Seth's shaking his head, his expression fierce. "I wanna be out here. I wanna be with you."

The loaded words slip over her like a promise. A vow.

She lets out a long breath. Seth's staring at her in some ridiculous turn-her-knees-to-jelly hungry, hangdog way. He looks tortured.

"What're we doin', Lace?" His voice is a hoarse drawl. He slips his fingers through hers, linking them.

"I don't know." Butterflies fill her stomach. "Maybe we should just stay friends."

He frowns. "Is that what we are?"

"I don't know that either."

He opens his mouth, but before he can say anything, she leans forward, locking eyes.

"Can we not do this now?"

Though she aches to talk about it, talk about *them*, she's chickening out. Talking means decisions, means giving up control, means losing focus on the party, means she's one step closer to letting Seth Kincaid upend her entire world.

Upend her right into bed.

Oh God, she's slipping.

She's sunk.

Lacey squeezes his hand. "We'll talk. We will. I just . . . I have to get through tomorrow."

His eyes flicker, hurt there, but also understanding. "Yeah. Sure. Tomorrow."

THIRTEEN

THE NEXT MORNING, SETH LIFTS HIS DARK SUNGLASSES, stopping in his tracks to gawk at the glossy exterior of Colin Cane's Beverly Hills house. "Jesus Christ."

Lacey rolls her eyes and shuts her car door. "So, he's wealthy." She gives Seth a look, bumping him with her shoulder. "In case you've forgotten, you and Luke aren't exactly paupers."

"Yeah, but we ain't livin' like glitter puked all over us."

Fighting a smile, Lacey strides for the iron-gated entrance of the super-sized gothic cathedral mansion. Seth's right. The house is gaudy, but it's also all Colin.

Seth and Lacey walk up the circular driveway to the custom stone arches that allow entrance to the front of the house. They've come prepared to work, dressed down in jeans and T-shirts. While Seth carries Lacey's dress and his tux, she has a large mesh tote slung around her torso. Inside are items that come in handy during a pinch. Tape. Granola bars. Chalk. Walkie-talkies. Velcro. Zip ties.

When they reach the front door, Lacey flings it open like she owns the place. She smiles.

Already, the house is bustling with interns and associates. Spider cranes hang fluffy black clouds from the ceiling.

In the foyer, two majestic crystal chandeliers dangle from the vaulted ceiling. A grand imperial staircase is its main centerpiece with wrought-iron railings. Centered in the middle is a table with a sculpture of two men with knives embracing.

Seth whistles, his blue eyes sweeping over the madness in front of him. "Okay, how do you not get strong *American Psycho* vibes from this guy?" He leans close, his breath tickling her hair. "That statue . . . it looks like a butthole."

Lacey elbows him, trying to smother a laugh. "Seth!"

Seth looks her over, concern heavy on his face. "How you feelin'?"

"I'm fine." Which is both the truth and a lie. She's moving slow this morning, her stomach achy, but it's her own fault. She should have stayed off her feet yesterday. "I'm practically healed."

He gives her a doubtful look. "I mean it. You come get me if—"

"Ms. Sutton!"

The silvery voice has her turning, has her smiling. "Colin!" She extends an arm to the man sweeping down the staircase and immediately is swept up in his crushing hug. Colin pulls back, kisses her cheeks. He's dressed to the nines in a gold tracksuit that complements his brown skin and a spike neck choker.

"So good to see you," Lacey says, slipping into work mode. Charming. Professional. Ready to impress and amaze.

"You as well, my darling. Things are looking perfect. But . . ." He arches an inquisitive brow. "What about the llamas?"

"We have the llamas. And the flower crowns. And the coffins." She beams. Her chest swells with pride. "It's going to be whimsically sinister. You'll love it."

Beside her, Seth's silent, observing.

"You're a dream. An absolute dream," Colin crows. His eyes land on Seth and he presses a hand to his heart like Seth deserves his life story but will never get it. "She's a lifesaver. I'll never work with anyone else." His black eyes jump back to Lacey. "Tell me you're staying for the party."

"Wouldn't miss it." She smooths a hand down her tattered jeans. "I did bring a change of clothes."

"Use the guest suite on the second floor. I insist." His gaze jumps to Seth. "You and your . . ."

"Assistant," Lacey says quickly.

Missing nothing, Colin gives her a *yeah right* look, then a nod.

"I'm off. You work your prettiest magic and I will see you tonight. Save me a dance, darling."

"Absolutely."

After a frantic batch of air-kisses, Colin's gone, breezing through a second set of interns arriving for setup.

Lacey reaches into her bag, fumbling around for the next step of the process. When she glances up, Seth's staring.

She narrows her eyes. "What?" She can't read his expression.

"You're just . . ." He stares at her a long minute, then shakes his head. A sunny smile breaks out across his handsome face. "In your element."

She grins. Flattered. Touched.

She knows what he means, though. In the weeks leading up to the party, she's a mess. But the day of setup means they're almost there. It means she can shine. But it doesn't mean she's done. Despite her interns, she'd never dream of letting them handle the rest. If she's not down in the shit with them, how can she expect them to put in their best team effort?

"Watch this," Lacey says with a wild grin.

"Oh, Jesus." Seth groan-laughs as she pulls out a wireless microphone.

Recognizing her signal, the eager-eyed interns circle her.

She loves this part. She gets to take charge. Make her clients happy. Work her magic.

"Okay, everyone," she says into the mic. "Thank you for being here today. I know this can get stressful, but we'll get it done and we'll do it right. You understand me? I am here and you come to me if you need help."

A chorus of nods, even Seth's nodding, his blue eyes flickering with something she can't quite place. Pride? Awe?

She claps her hands together. "Let's put in your best effort. That's all that matters."

With that, the interns and workers disperse. Autumn, who's shown up, halfheartedly stands around watching with a bored stare.

Meeting Lacey's eyes briefly, Seth gives a grin and a lazy salute and lopes off to help.

She watches him go, then inhales a breath.

Pull it together and get to work, Sutton.

The day passes in a frenzied flurry. Lacey dealing with AV techs, the musicians, setting up the llama lounge in the stone motor court. Before she knows it, the morning sunlight has turned to cool-blue noon, then a golden almost-sunset glow.

Every so often, her eyes seek Seth, who's busting his ass like he's another one of the interns. But he's not. He's Seth Kincaid, country superstar. He left his band for her, is missing tonight's gig, and is instead schlepping around flower buckets. She bites her lip, trying to rein in her heart. She's never been so grateful to him.

Ugh. She's being ridiculous. He's had two dinners in her home and already she wants him to stay.

As she's giving the space one last walk-through before the party, she spies an errant feather loose at the top of the step-and-repeat. She grabs a ladder and climbs up, pulling a pin from her pocket.

Once again, her thoughts drift to Seth. To the talk that awaits tonight. She can't ignore it anymore. Seth appearing in LA stirred an ache in her, one she's been trying to ice over, deny.

She wants him.

Definitely sex, and maybe, possibly, more than that.

But they were friends first. If they go farther, will it ruin everything? Most importantly, will it hurt Sal? Because of her memory loss, of living a life with Roy Williams that was all a lie, Sal treasures the truth. Fiercely. If she finds out Lacey and Seth have been sneaking around for the last three years . . .

Stretching up to pin the feather, Lacey swears between clenched teeth as her stomach twinges. She glances down, placing a hand on her bandage. It's tender.

"Hey, hey, hey . . ."

Lacey blinks, startled by the urgent voice. By the warm palm gently pressing against the small of her back.

She looks down.

Seth stares up at her with an odd expression.

"What's wrong?" she asks.

"You're on a ladder, Lace."

"Oh," she says dumbly, realizing her mistake. Her face flushes, goes hotter than hot. For once, she doesn't have a snide retort. "Oops. Old habit."

"It's okay," he says softly, extending a hand to help her down. She leans against him, his palm still on her back, his eyes locked on hers. "You be careful."

Her heart's in her throat. The way he says it . . .

She licks her lips. "I will."

Seth reaches for a lock of her hair and she lets him take it. She holds her breath as he runs the long blond strand through his palm, like he's considering something. Then he tucks it behind her ear and lopes off toward the interns.

Lacey lets out a breath, a nervous excitement settling in her heart.

Tonight, she reminds herself, they'll figure this out tonight.

Whatever *this* is.

An hour later, setup is complete. The black carpet ready to be walked. The llamas humming in the courtyard. A pink neon sign screams GIVE ME DEATH OR GIVE ME A DRINK.

Seth hangs back and dusts off his hands. He watches Lacey hand out granola bars to hungry staffers as she sidles through the space, evaluating with a keen eye and making final adjustments.

The house looks amazing. *Lacey* is amazing. Today, he saw a person full of life. A machine. She's spent hours ironing linens, helping her interns, making sure the details on the cake match Colin's drawing.

At least she's finally on the ground.

He scowls. Damn girl. He saw her scaling that ladder and it

nearly gave him a heart attack. He doesn't know why he's supporting this bullshit but knows she'd do it anyway, so he might as well babysit.

But it's not babysitting. He's here because he cares. He cares about Lacey. And now he's paying the price. Thinking about her every goddamn second of the day. He can't take much more of this.

They gotta figure this out. Soon.

As she's on her way over to Seth, Lacey pauses in front of Autumn. The glum redhead is snapping commands at a flustered intern who's trying to even out a coffin.

"Excuse me, Autumn," Lacey says, her eyes narrowed, her tone cool. No malice or cattiness in her voice, just a commanding of the room. "If you're going to stand there and complain to Trent that he's doing it wrong, then get down in the shit and help him."

Autumn kind of sags back like she's been expertly filleted, and Seth hides a smirk.

Lacey in her element has got to be the hottest thing he's ever seen. Barking orders. Competent. Confident. It's sexy as hell.

Lacey walks Seth's way, the smile breaking over her face like a gift.

"I gotta admit," he says as Lacey approaches him, her cheeks red and flushed, "it looks terrific, Lace."

She nods, eyes bright. "Thanks. It really does."

Seth scours the crowd. "Your boss here?"

He can't help it. He wants to meet the asshole who's putting Lacey through the wringer. He's not saying he's going to give the guy a piece of his mind, but he ain't exactly going to be friendly.

"No. He only shows up when everything's done." She picks a piece of hay out of her hair. "He trusts me on that at least."

Seth gives her a quick side-eye. Her tone is bitter, her face gloomy. He slings an arm around her shoulder, wanting to cheer her up. "Well, princess. What now?"

She looks up at him and grins. "We get ready."

Upstairs, Lacey and Seth stand outside two majestic suites where their clothes have been brought up. "Fancy," Seth drawls, feeling as if they're in a whole other world. Already the swell of music has begun downstairs. Some synth-pop beat that has Seth internally cringing.

Lacey claps her hands together. She's practically twitching to get into hair and makeup. "Okay, get ready and I'll meet you out here in—"

"Ten."

She quirks a brow, unamused. "I was going to say an hour."

He laughs. "Guess I could splash around in the shower."

She blushes and turns away, but he snags her arm, pulling her close until she's inches from him. "Hey." Their gazes lock. "You did good today."

"I know," she says with a haughty lift of her chin. Then a smile softens her face. "So did you."

Sixty minutes later, after a quick shower and a phone call back home, Seth's sitting on a chaise lounge in the hallway. He's changed into a dark tux. And he doesn't wear tuxes. Not to award shows, not to anything.

He checks the time on his phone. Seven. Lacey's late.

He smears his face in his hands, feeling awkward and antsy. The party's in full swing. He can hear the sounds of conversation, the pop of bottles, the frenetic beat of music.

Music.

He thinks of Luke, of the Brothers Kincaid. They're taking the stage tonight at the Station Inn, their old favorite. A pang of regret hits him that he's missing it. His fiddle. His brother. Someone else in his spotlight. But as he thinks of Lacey, he knows there's no place he'd rather be.

He taps a toe, listening. A beat in his boot, his heart.

He flags down a server carrying a tray of champagne. A napkin and a pen now in his hands, he sits back on the chaise.

The song bubbles within him, like some roiling underground current. He isn't sure if it's the distance from Nashville or the change of scenery, but he's damn sure going to go with it.

Hell, it's easy, ain't it? You just pull out your heart and rub it on the page.

> I was reckless, I was wild
> Been making the same damn mistakes
> Since I was a child
> Beat myself up for half my life
> Left is right, right is wrong
> I've always been someone a little more lost than found

He sits back and evaluates what he's written. Not good, not great, but it's a start.

Seth grins.

Maybe Graham was right. Sometimes you stay still to move forward.

A clearing of a throat has him looking up.

Seth's jaw drops.

Fuck him.

Lacey stands in front of him, wearing an incandescent smile and a diaphanous pearly blue dress. With a sweetheart neckline and delicate ruffles clinging to her toned silhouette, it has her looking as if she's made of ocean, made of waves. A slender bronze thigh peeks through the sky-high slit. Her golden hair waves around her shoulders. And her eyes, lined dark and smoky, are greener than he's ever seen them.

She's beautiful. Absolutely smoking hot and Seth's got to pull himself together before his entire brain short-circuits at the sight of her.

At Seth's silence, Lacey smooths a self-conscious hand down the glossy curve of her hip. Then she frowns. "Don't say I'm late, Seth. I'm not late."

He can't. Can't even have his usual comeback. Seeing her

standing there is like knockout gas. He can't even remember his own damn name.

He stands, his throat tightening unbearably. Hastily, he shoves the napkin in his back pocket. Lacey's eyes widen as she takes in his appearance. A faint pink stains her cheeks. "You, uh . . . look nice."

Seth straightens his cuffs. "Some might say handsome."

She scoffs. "Now I wouldn't go that far." Her lips lift at the corners. "But yeah. You clean up okay." Still staring, she steps forward, the space between them closing in a heady rush. "Can I . . . ?" Her hands flutter, graceful fingers reaching out to straighten his thin tie.

Seth shifts in his boots, a strange nervousness sideswiping every emotion.

Christ, what's wrong with him? He's Seth Kincaid. He doesn't do shit like this. But here he is, fucking tongue-tied over some girl who threatens to have him tossing out everything he knows. Who has him on his knees, who has him ready to do everything in life completely different.

Ready to figure out what happens after this. Because it's driving him goddamn crazy not knowing where they stand.

Just ask her, you idiot.

The thought's tempting as hell. To take her into a suite and figure out what they are to each other. But he can't. It's her party, and she deserves to enjoy it. Seth won't be the asshole taking that away from her.

"There," Lacey says, clearing her throat and making one final adjustment to the tie. She presses a hand against the silk fabric.

Seth swallows hard, swallows down his impatience, and instead flashes her a wild grin. "You ready to roll?" He offers her his arm.

Lacey's eyes clear, shaking herself out of whatever daze held her. "Ready," she says, hooking her arm through his.

Together, they descend the grand staircase. Lacey's eyes glow as she takes in the gothic-fairy-tale-like scene. The party she planned, the mass of people gathering, snapping photos, sampling hors d'oeuvres.

"What do you do now?" Seth asks, honestly curious.

"We relax." Lacey waves a hand around the space, sounding unbothered. "It's mostly about keeping an eye open for any problems."

"If you're askin' me, you already got problems." He wrinkles his nose. "That band you hired needs to be put out of its misery."

Lacey hits him with a glare. "Do not embarrass me tonight, Seth."

He gives her a rueful smile. "Oh, you mean no doing the funky chicken?"

Lacey giggles, swatting him with her clutch. Seth breaks away, pretending to dodge her aim, but when he returns, he notes the way she opens her arm for him again, wanting to be near him, to keep by his side.

At the bottom of the stairs, they follow the path leading to the outdoor garden. Seth can't help but gape. It's like nothing he's ever seen. Twinkle lights in every tree. Servers passing around whipped egg white protein shots. Coffin couches. A scene that could only exist in LA. Jace and Luke would shit themselves.

Seth groans when he sees a llama wearing a flower crown. "Please tell me there's alcohol here."

Lacey tugs him closer to her. She points to a spot across the courtyard where a line is forming. "The kiss and tell bar."

"The what?"

She looks over at him with a sly smile. "The kiss and tell bar. It's an open bar all night, but to get a drink you either have to kiss"—she leans close, her lips grazing his ear, and Seth's heart lurches—"or tell the bartender a secret."

He turns. "What kind of secret?" His eyes land on her lips. Glossy. Plump. Pink.

Fuck.

She shrugs, her green eyes shining. "That's up to you."

"For Christsakes," Seth mutters, his gaze on the signs above the individual bar lines that read: GIRLS / GUYS / TELL ME NO LIES.

All he wants is a drink, all he wants is to hang here with Lacey, not play twenty questions with the bartender for a little tequila.

He spreads his arms, the smile on Lacey's face goading him. "Fine, I'll bite. What do you want? Tequila? Champagne?"

She shrugs, nonchalant. "I was thinking . . . maybe whiskey?"

The out-of-left-field answer has his eyes popping open.

God, this girl. Lacey's full of contradictions. Contradictions he wants more of. She keeps on confusing him, keeps him on his toes, and goddamn that's hot.

"Whiskey, huh?" He considers the words, the look in her eye. Her drink order's telling him something. Something he wants to get to the bottom of. "I'll get a bottle."

Seth takes a bracing breath as he strides away from Lacey and up to the bar. He evaluates the signs above, differentiating each line. Without hesitation, he steps into the line for TELL ME NO LIES.

He's kissing anyone tonight, it's Lacey. He's already made up his damn mind. They're gonna talk and talk right. They've wasted enough precious time. And then . . . he wants to end the night with her in his arms. With his lips on hers, Lacey's tan legs wrapped around his—

"What can I get you, if only you'll tell me a secret true?"

At the chipper voice, Seth shakes himself out of his thoughts. A female bartender, wearing a black lace mask on the right side of her face, leans on the bar top across from him.

Seth sighs and needles his temple. "That means you want a secret, right?"

She lifts her brows to the sign above. "For a drink, you must say what you think."

"Great. Rhymes." Seth glances over his shoulder. Lacey's not where he left her. Instead, she's moved inside the foyer, talking to a group of men who are all wearing black. "See that girl over there . . . the blond . . ." His blood roars in his ears, something warm blooming in his chest as he collects his thoughts. "I like her. I like her a whole damn lot and I don't even think she knows."

"Well, have you told her yet?" The bartender stares at him like this is the most exciting thing she's heard all night.

"No." Seth cringes at the rows of alcohol, wishing he had a shot right now. "I haven't."

The bartender shakes her head in fascination, finally dropping the mysterious act, as her jaw unhinges and her eyes widen. "She's downright gorgeous, dude. What are you thinking staying away from her?"

Gritting his teeth, Seth rips a frustrated hand through his hair. He knows all the right answers. She's his best friend's sister. He's here to take care of her. They don't make sense. Nothing about the last few days makes sense.

Instead, he extends a hand, forcing the words past the rock in his throat. "Can I just get a drink? Whiskey. Two glasses. Please."

"Sure thing." The bartender gives him a judgmental stare and pours out the honey-colored liquid. "You should tell her, you know. Don't be an idiot. Girls hate that."

"Thanks a lot," he mutters.

Ready to get the hell out of there, get back to Lacey and talk, he grabs up the drinks.

Only when he turns around, he runs smack-dab into Autumn. She blocks his path to Lacey. Her lips curve in a malicious smile. "I heard your secret. Want to hear mine?"

Seth groans and lifts his eyes to the sky.

It's just gotta be his goddamn night.

Lacey sips the champagne she's snagged from a serving tray and watches as Prentiss samples a bacon-wrapped date. He had called her over while she was waiting on Seth. Now she's forced to endure the agony that is Prentiss trying to charm Colin.

She knows Colin secretly detests Prentiss. Mostly for his fashion sense.

As conversation swirls around her, Lacey lets her eyes drift. To Seth, standing uncomfortably in the TELL NO LIES line.

Her eyes soften at the sight of him. He looks so handsome, so sexy in his tux. His hair perfectly mussed. That great smile of his. Boyish. Charming. Adorably hot. Hot and distracting.

Lacey scowls.

Ugh.

She can't believe she likes someone who uses three-in-one shower gel. A cowboy. How many variations on a red plaid shirt can he have? And what was she doing ordering whiskey? It was out of her mouth before she could stop it. Some brazen, idiotic way to tell Seth she maybe, kind of feels something for him.

Lacey lowers her lashes and smiles soft.

She knows she does.

Today, Seth showed her what he's all about. A good guy who makes her laugh. Who understands her. Who treats her better than anyone ever has. She wants more. More of that—him in her space, she in his.

Absentmindedly, Lacey smooths a hand down the front of her dress, grimacing as it brushes against her stomach. The spot's tender. Warm. In fact, the entire house is warm. Unusually hot and Lacey resists the urge to fan herself.

"Something wrong, Sutton?"

Her head snaps up. Prentiss stares at her over his glass of merlot. Colin's drifted over to another group and is snapping photos for his Instagram. No doubt trying to lose Prentiss in the crowd.

"Not at all," she says curtly.

"Well, while you're in your own little world, Colin is going to give me a tour of the house." Prentiss lifts a brow. "I trust you'll hold down the fort."

"I have everything under control."

"The party, Sutton . . ." Prentiss's shrewd eyes scour the bustling scene.

Her heart leaps. But she rubs her lips together, playing it cool, waiting for words of praise, of validation that all her hard work paid off. "Yes?"

"It's fine," he says, checking his watch.

She laughs under her breath in disbelief as Prentiss walks away without further comment. *Asshole.*

She doesn't know why she bothers. Why she's working so hard for approval she'll never get. He reminds her of her father. Distant. Narcissistic. Withholding.

Bullshit. It's all bullshit.

With a sigh, Lacey turns her attention to happier sights.

Only the sights aren't happy.

What she sees hits her like a bucket of ice water. Autumn and Seth cozied up in a corner of the courtyard, deep in conversation. Autumn presses up against Seth and he nods, his hand on her hip, his expression riveted. Lacey's breath hitches. Her heart drops like an anchor.

A pang of pain pierces her as she realizes Seth isn't hers. Another pang as she realizes she wants him to be.

She has to get away. From Seth and the sight of him and Autumn. From her heartbeat. Pounding out an SOS signal of want she can't ignore anymore.

Lacey whirls out of the foyer, rushing down a narrow corridor to duck into the library. She bypasses the mahogany built-ins filled with books and moves to the cobblestone patio. The doors are open, showcasing the gentle bubble of a fountain. A grove of arched trees and vines. Idyllic, peaceful, moonlit.

Blinking back tears, she looks out at the sky, at the glittering city lights.

She waited too long. Held back her joy. And what did it get her? Nothing.

"Shame," a deep rumble says, breaking her thoughts. "Can't even see the stars."

Anger flares in her at the sight of Seth, stepping through the patio doors like he doesn't have a care in the world.

"Then go back to Nashville," she snaps.

His eyes widen in confusion at her sudden outburst. "Hey, whoa." He lifts the glasses of whiskey, striding toward her. "I've been lookin' for you. We're drinkin' whiskey tonight, remember?"

Lacey wants to hurl it at him. Instead, she snatches it out of his hand and shoots it down in one quick swallow. She breathes through the burn, ignoring Seth's impressed expression. She crosses her arms. Squares her shoulders. "Have a nice chat with Autumn?"

He frowns. Then grins. "Why, you jealous?"

She wants to hit him. "Shut up, Seth."

His smile grows wider. "You think I like her?"

"I don't know. Maybe. No." She reddens. "I mean, I don't want you to."

Seth's face softens. "Relax, princess. That girl's drunk as a skunk. Couldn't even stand up straight."

"I didn't like seeing that," she admits before she can chicken out. She's trying to play it cool, but she can't. Not anymore. The last three days have been some of the best she's had, and now they feel like a cheat. "Any of that. You and her. And it's stupid because I have no right to be jealous because you're not . . . you're not mine."

There. She's said it. Every honest thing she's wanted to say finally out in one long ramble at the worst possible time. Colin's party. Not to mention, she's sweating too. Nerves have her so hot, she's practically soaking through her dress.

Seth stares at her, the faint smile on his face unreadable.

Embarrassed by her public display—she might as well have carved out her dumb heart and slapped it on a platter—Lacey tosses her hair and turns on her heel. "I'm done. I don't want to talk about this anymore."

"Hell, I don't fuckin' think so."

A hand wraps around her arm, Seth whirling her back toward him.

He stands in front of her, his face creased. "We're talkin' about it. *Now*. I ain't wastin' another damn second wonderin.'"

Tilting her face up, she forces herself to ask, forces hope back down to her toes. "Wondering what?"

"Wonderin' why we ain't doin' us." His gaze turns heavy-lidded. His voice a ragged husk. "Wonderin' why I ain't kissin' you."

Heat blooms across her cheeks. She props her hands on her hips. "Well?" A dare. A challenge. A damn plea.

Seth pulls her closer, his blue-eyed gaze tracking hers. Bracing a hand on the small of her back, he presses her into him, lowers his face to hers. "If I'm wrong, then stop me." His hand captures a long strand of her hair, tucking it behind her ear. He leans down. Closer. "Last warning."

She closes her eyes. Sparks spiral inside of her, and she is a hundred airborne embers drifting to Seth, to his lips, his kiss. "Seth, I—"

The next thing she knows, Seth's kiss lands like a grenade as he hauls her against him. His hands cup her face, his hands in her hair. His lips are cool, sucking in her breath, her every protest, her next words.

Lacey whimpers like it's an unlocking, something deep inside of her coming alive, melting at his touch.

She grips Seth's tie and yanks him closer, not letting him loose. She parts her lips, inhaling his tongue, savoring his kiss. Wishing she could hook it to her veins. She's never felt anything like it. That slow warming down below. A deep need to be sated, but knowing that under Seth's touch, she never will be. She'll want it more. Always. Again and again and again.

Knowing that this kiss will change everything.

And it doesn't scare her. She wants it to be different. Wants to break all the rules. Wants him with such a fierce need it scares her and thrills her all at the same time.

Lacey breaks the kiss and Seth makes a kind of strangled sound at the loss of her lips on his.

"Let's go home," she says, breathless.

"Yeah?" Seth's eyes spark.

She nods, gulps. "Yeah."

Her part in the party's done. She's ready to let responsibilities slide, take Seth back to her place, get him in bed.

Seth grins. His lean hand cups the nape of her neck, ready to bring her in once more to his lips.

But he doesn't.

He freezes. Stares, dumbfounded. "You're hot as hell, Lace."

"Thank you," she says, happiness flooding her. "So are you."

"No." His eyes, dark with concern, sweep over her. He brushes her hair away from her face, but when he does, instead of falling away, it sticks to her brow. "You're burnin' up, Lacey."

She opens her mouth to tell him he's an idiot, when a sudden stabbing pain, like the sting of a bee, has her gasping.

Dizziness crashes over her like a wave. Lacey clutches at the side of her stomach and feels a strange wetness there.

When she pulls her hand away, she stares in horror. Blood, sticky and warm, coats her entire palm.

chapter
FOURTEEN

SETH'S EYES DRIFT, TURNING WIDE AND HORRIFIED AS HE stares down at a dark red patch spreading across the front of Lacey's dress. One minute he was kissing her, holding her in his arms like the best kind of dream, thinking of the quickest way to get her home and take her to bed, to show her what he's been feeling and then some, and now . . .

Now, she's hot enough to fucking cook on.

"Oh, Jesus," he breathes.

Lacey, her face ghastly pale but her cheeks flushed with color, looks right at him, says, "I don't feel good," and then pitches forward.

Seth surges for her and catches her in his arms like a lover, like a slow dip. She lies listlessly, staring up at him. Her fierce green eyes fading, losing focus.

A little laugh bubbles out of Lacey. "I like you, Seth."

"I like you too." His voice has gone dry and desperate. "In fact, I like you so much, we're goin' to the hospital."

She laughs, and it's the no-fight, the way her hair sticks to her face, the way her body's burning up in his arms that scares him shitless. Fear settles like a lead weight in his gut.

"Unbelievable," a clipped voice snarls.

With effort, Lacey turns her face toward the source of the voice. Seth follows suit.

A stocky man stands in the doorway, glaring in suspicion at Lacey and Seth like he's caught them in an illicit lover's embrace.

"I've been looking for you everywhere. You're supposed to

be picking up new contacts, engaging with Colin, and instead you're in here with the help." The man snorts. "I expected more from you, Sutton."

Weakly, Lacey pushes herself up. Seth wraps an arm around her waist, steadying her against him. "Prentiss, this is Seth . . . he's—"

"Getting her out of here," Seth finishes impatiently.

Prentiss's eyes fly open, his face ruddy from anger. "You're leaving?"

"I have to," Lacey whispers, her hand clutching hard at Seth's forearm. "I'm sick, Prentiss. I—"

"Absolutely not." He blocks the exit, his body trembling in rage. "Sutton, this is the most important night of the year. I pay you well. Get back out there. Now."

Fuck that.

Seth can't hold his tongue anymore. Still curling Lacey against him, he steps toward her boss. "Not gonna happen," he growls, authority in his tone. Already he wants to hit the guy. "Lacey's sick. She ain't got time for your bullshit."

"Prentiss, I can't—" Lacey's glassy eyes flutter and she goes limp, collapsing against Seth.

Gently, Seth scoops her up in his arms, a fresh wave of panic hitting him when she gasps and clutches at her stomach.

Prentiss's eyes widen, as if the idiot's finally realizing the gravity of the situation.

Lacey groans, her eyes fluttering closed. Her head lolls between Seth's shoulder and neck, and he has to bite back a curse. It feels like he's holding the molten core of planet Earth in his arms.

"All right, Lace," he whispers, pressing a kiss to her hot brow. "We're gettin' out of here."

And then he looks at Prentiss. The idiot stands in the doorway, blocking the exit. Which is a bad mistake. The worst fucking mistake.

Rage rolls through Seth. Red and blinding.

He could kill the guy. But Lacey, lying still and limp in his arms, is the only thing stopping Seth from going fucking feral and launching the prick off the staircase.

"Move," Seth commands, his jaw flexing. His voice deadly. "Now."

Prentiss gulps and steps aside.

Then Seth's moving, rushing out the door, the mad pump of his heart like a ticking time bomb, a frantic reminder of everything he can lose.

Hands in his pockets, Seth paces outside Lacey's hospital room. A caged animal. Lost. Tortured.

He's thinking the worst, his brain going to a million awful dark places. All the bad parts of Seth Kincaid. A mental fucking pity party he's content to wallow in.

This is his goddamn fault.

He should have been taking better care of her. If he wasn't thinking with his dick, if he wasn't so damned focused on talking about *them*, he would have been able to see what was happening right in front of his face. She was sick. And he let it happen.

He let her down. All of them.

Because now he has to call Sal and tell her Lacey's in the hospital. Again.

Seth squeezes his eyes shut.

Fuck. Let her be okay. Please Christ.

He doesn't pray, he and Luke lost religion a long time ago, but he'll get down on his knees right here and now if it means Lacey's okay.

And where the fuck is the damn doctor? Seth's ready to go ballistic. After a terrifying car ride to the hospital, where Lacey lay ashen and listless in the passenger seat, the nurses took Lacey from his arms the second he slammed through the door of the hospital. He can still feel the hot singe of her cheek against his skin. Since then, there's been no word.

His mind keeps replaying it. When she could have gotten sick. What he didn't see. But there's nothing. Aside from Lacey saying she was tired, she never let on that she was hurting. And that's on Seth. Because he had one job—take care of her—and he's a worthless piece of shit who wasn't paying attention.

The sound of footsteps jolts Seth from his dark headspace.

He grabs the wall for support when he sees the doctor. "How is she?"

"She's resting. Ms. Sutton's sutures opened up, causing an infection in the wound. Her fever spiked, but fortunately you got her here in time for us to treat it."

Seth shakes his head, numb. It's still not the answer he needs. "So, she'll be okay?"

"She'll be fine. We're giving her a course of IV antibiotics and fluids tonight and then will send her home with a seven-day course of antibiotics to clear up the infection." The doctor pauses, says, "You getting her here as fast as you did saved her life. Otherwise, it could've taken a dark turn pretty fast."

He swallows. A cinder block's in his throat, stomping down his air.

The doctor turns to go. "You can see her whenever you're ready."

Seth manages a brief nod.

And then he's moving. Running.

Only it's not toward Lacey's room. It's in the direction of the restroom. He slams into the neon-lit space to brace the sink, to gulp cool air, to chase away a warm wave of nausea.

He grips the sink, his chest tightening.

Fuck. He can't breathe . . . his heart . . . he's having a heart attack . . .

With a strangled gasp, Seth rips off his tie and throws it in the sink.

Smearing a shaky hand through his hair, he squeezes his eyes shut and tries to breathe evenly. Tries to use every ounce of strength not to break in fucking half.

He could have lost her. Before he ever had her. A world without Lacey? Unthinkable.

What would Sal do without her?

What would he do?

Because Lacey's not just Sal's sister. Or a fling. Or a friend. She's his. The woman he—

The thought takes him down like a bullet.

"Fuck."

His voice, his curse sounds like it's been dragged over sandpaper.

Slowly, he lifts his face to stare at his haggard reflection in the mirror.

He can't. He absolutely cannot. But he knows it's true. The night of that searing kiss cemented it.

He closes his eyes, finally breathing steadily.

He loves her.

He loves Lacey.

Lacey lies listless in the hospital bed, her fingers tracing the line of her IV. Already, she can feel the drugs working their magic, antibiotics chasing away the fever. She closes her eyes, replaying what the doctor said.

She could have died. Lucky, lucky, Lord she's lucky.

The words sting. Have her revisiting the last few days of her life.

Earlier this week, all she wanted to do was get rid of Seth. Deny her feelings, bury them, ice herself over like she's always done. But now, her scare, Prentiss's true asshole turn, has her realizing how pointless everything's been. Her job. Her ice queen act. No friends. Guarding her heart. Keeping life at arm's length.

She put her health, her dignity, her time on the line and for what? A promotion she doesn't even know if she's going to get. A prick of a boss who doesn't care if she lives or dies.

She's been trying to chase Seth away because she doesn't think he'll stay. Because loss runs in her veins. But now, she knows she's the one making herself all alone. Not her father. Or her stepmother. Or Sal. She's doing it now. And she has to stop.

Life's a risk, and all she's been doing is denying the things she really needs.

Like kissing Seth.

She scowls at the ceiling.

Ugh, she's been an idiot. If tonight ruined things, if she wasted her chance, scared Seth off, she'll never forgive herself.

The soft sound of an opening door has her rolling her head across the pillow.

Seth stands in the doorway, tie undone, looking rumpled and uncertain.

Lacey's lips part. "Some party, huh?"

"Been to better," he says, trying for flippancy, but the joke falls flat. His eyes jump to the machines she's hooked up to, the IV in her hand. "How are you feelin'?"

"I'm okay. Thanks to you."

He swallows hard, frozen in the doorway. Like he's afraid to come any closer. Then he shakes his head, guilt and agony etched across his handsome face. "Don't thank me. I shoulda seen it. I shoulda—"

"Seth."

She gives him a look that says he's being stupid. She's one hundred percent positive he sat in that waiting room torturing himself. "I'm pretty sure everything that happened is my fault. You can't blame yourself. Now will you come here?"

Lacey stretches out an arm, fluttering fingertips to beckon him closer. She feels Seth-starved. Desperate for his hand. His steady touch.

He hesitates for a moment and then crosses the floor to her. He sits on the edge of the bed, his eyes misty. Seth's hand closes around hers. He lifts it gently to his lips, pressing a kiss to her knuckles.

His mouth works the words over and then he says, "Lace, if something had happened . . ." But he can't finish the sentence. His voice splinters, and he sucks in a deep breath.

"I'm okay," she says, determined to make him hear her. His eyes look so haunted. "It's all okay. And it's not your fault."

Seth sighs, some of the guilt leaving his tense expression. He brushes a lock of hair from her face. "I want you to get some rest, you hear me?"

Worry stakes her heart. Sharp. Panicky.

She stares at Seth, searching his eyes almost frantically to see if the feelings from tonight are still there.

And they are. But they're different. Changed. A myriad of emotions she can't place. Worry. Pain. Nerves. Emotions that have hot tears springing to her eyes.

She grabs his hand. "Don't go," she whispers. "I need you, Seth."

"I ain't leavin' you, Lace. I'm here." His crystal-blue eyes burn. "I'm yours."

The words, the promise, comes out ragged.

And then Seth dips his head, sweeping the sweetest of kisses over her lips. Lacey cries out in relief and clutches him tighter, pulling him onto the bed with her. Together, they lie there, forehead to forehead, Seth's arm wrapped protectively around her waist.

Lacey closes her eyes.

It's what she wants. This. Them.

Her and Seth.

SETH ENTERS THE BEDROOM, A GLASS OF WATER IN HIS hand, his eyes on Lacey sunk deep into the pillows, looking as golden as the sunlight streaming through the blinds.

His gut twists. She looks soft and fragile in the morning light. But her color's better. Her green eyes clear, not clouded by fever.

"You need anything else?" he asks, setting her antibiotics and water on the nightstand.

"A new career," she says, waving her phone. She's just texted Prentiss that she's taking a week off work, no question.

Seth chuckles.

After a night in the hospital, the drugs out of her system, she's back to being her haughty, feisty pain-in-the-ass self. And he couldn't love it more.

"Ugh, it's so embarrassing." She bites her lower lip, frustration etched across her pretty face. "Everyone's going to talk about it."

He grins. "What? The dashin' cowboy, carrying you out in his arms?"

"Seth, stop," Lacey groan-laughs. She clutches her stomach. "It hurts."

Seth sits beside her on the bed. "I don't want you worryin' about Prentiss." He reaches for her hand, giving it a firm squeeze. "Or Colin. I don't want you worryin' about anything. You're restin'."

A pang of guilt lands like a dart. What she should have been doing in the first place.

"Prentiss won't understand," she huffs, tossing her phone into the pile of blankets as if she can block out his response.

Seth's eyes follow the phone. That guy so much as hassles Lacey about time off, Seth will hunt him down and gladly introduce his face to Seth's fist.

"I don't give a shit about Prentiss. I give a shit about you. And gettin' you better." Seth's smile falls away. "Besides, he don't deserve you. All you been doin'—he don't give two shits."

She frowns and cocks her head. "What're you talkin' about?"

He grimaces, not wanting to upset her, but knowing she has to know. He takes a deep breath. "That's what I was talkin' to Autumn about at the party. You ain't gonna get that promotion, Lace. I'm so damn sorry, princess. He's givin' it to someone else."

Her mouth falls open. Hot tears fill her eyes. "Asshole," she hisses. Blinking back tears, she looks at Seth. "Who is it? I bet it's Tatum. She never could—"

"Uh-uh, you ain't doin' this." He gives her a look that means business. "I know you're gonna hate it. I know it's gonna drive you crazy, but this time, no work. No anything unless you're relaxin'. I mean it," he says when Lacey flattens her lips. "Do it for me. For Sal. For that baby you gotta see."

Her expression softens.

He smiles and thumbs a lock of hair out of her eyes. "You're on house arrest, twenty-four-hour scheduled surveillance for the next week."

Lacey angles her head, a faint smile tugging at her lips. "You're staying?"

He is. He called Luke and Sal early this morning to tell them what had happened. It left him feeling like the biggest asshole around. Every time he calls home, he only makes Sal cry.

"Yeah." He drags a hand through his hair. "Luke's got Beau for three more weeks, so one more week don't matter."

"Are you sure?"

Something primal clenches at him. "I ain't leavin' you." He can't. And he damn well knows it. "You're stuck with me."

"Good." Lacey links her fingers through this. Her green eyes sparkle in the sunlight. "I like you around, Seth. I like you always around."

Christ. He closes his eyes, his heart twisting. Her sweet words are enough to have him coming unhinged.

"Seth . . ." He glances up at Lacey, who's staring down at her blanketed lap. "About last night—"

"We don't have to do this right now."

"No, I want to." She tilts her chin. "If we don't do it now, then when?"

Seth grips her hand tight. He doesn't deserve this. He doesn't deserve her. Not when she's vulnerable as hell, recovering from being hospitalized for an infection that could have killed her, and still wanting to talk about them.

"I just . . . after last night . . . I . . . like . . ." Seth runs a hand over his mouth, trying to hide a smirk. He can see it's hard for her to get out the words. An inhale. An exhale. And then— "I like you, Seth. I like you more than . . . than what we've been doing in Nashville." Her eyes narrow, snagging on Seth's grin. "Are you laughing at me?"

"No, I—ow!" He rubs his arm where she's socked him in the bicep.

She gives him a look, her face flustered. "This is hard for me."

His face turns serious. "It's pretty damn easy for me."

Lacey sighs. "Then what is this? What do you want?"

He knows. After last night, he damn sure does.

No more drunken Nashville nights. He wants more with Lacey. Dates, holidays, Sunday Suppers. He wants to call her his girl, introduce her to his parents, get her on that red carpet, show her off, take her on tour. But most of all, he wants to make it official. Make it a life.

Their life.

Because she is someone he needs. She burns just like him. Found, but still lost, grappling for that purpose in life. The conversations they've shared, the way she understands him, has been there for him, he's never found somebody else like her.

He's never felt this way about anyone. He doesn't want to pass up this chance.

But he doesn't want to scare her by moving too fast. He can see this is hard for her, letting her heart out. It wouldn't take much to wall it back up. But he wants her to see that they ain't gonna know what they are unless they try it.

"You, Lace," Seth says, and her green eyes widen. "You. You're who I want."

And then he's drawing her beautiful face into his hands and kissing her cool lips, kissing her like she's his only one because she is. Seth shuts his eyes against the hunger, the curl of heat charging up between them.

Lacey drags her hand through his hair, her touch like velvet. She lets out a small gasp and pulls him closer, stroking her tongue over his. It's her answer. She wants to do this as much as he does.

With a hungry groan, Seth cups the back of her neck, sliding his hands into all her silky hair, pulling her against him, loving the way she fits in his arms, like she's always belonged there.

He can't get enough. She's gonna set him on fire they keep doing this.

When they finally draw away, their breaths are harsh explosions in the small space between them.

"Why?" Lacey's question comes out wobbly, tears shining in her eyes. She grips his shoulders, trembling against him.

He cups the arc of her cheekbone. "Why, what?"

"You kiss me like you're running out of time."

He grins, stroking a thumb across her cheek. "Why the hell not? We wasted too much time already."

She drops her gaze. Seth stiffens as he feels the creep of her hand up his shirt, her graceful fingers fanning out over his stomach.

"We got time for that too, Lace," he says with a laugh, which earns him a disgruntled growl from Lacey.

But he understands. He's impatient, not to mention hard as hell. He wants a night with her. As soon as her stitches heal up, he's taking that girl to bed.

Seth's phone buzzes. Lacey's pings.

They pull away from each other, check their phones, then look up at each other and laugh.

Lacey lets out a long breath, flushing. "It's Sal."

Seth raises his eyebrows, his phone. "It's Luke." He groans. "Son of a bitch."

No doubt inadvertent payback for all the times he and Lacey cramped Luke and Sal's time together. With a slow chuckle, Seth pushes off the bed, adjusting himself. He leans down and kisses the top of her head. "I'll let y'all talk."

Lacey bites her lip, her face full of lust, her fingers curling against his. "Come back," she whispers.

The needy tone in her voice makes him smile. Because he's there as well. Ready, willing, and able to haul her against his chest and kiss her until her knees give out.

He crosses the room and pauses in the doorway, listening to Sal and Lacey talk. The sound of Lacey, laughing, happy and alive, has his heart clenching. A contentedness stirring deep in his soul.

Today, lines were crossed, boundaries blurred, declarations made.

There are still things to figure out, like how to tell Sal, but for now, Seth doesn't want to worry about any of that. He's got Lacey, and that's all that matters.

Now he just better not fuck it up. Like everything else in his life.

The next week has Lacey and Seth falling into a rhythm: eating cereal in bed, naps at noon, bad horror movies at night, kissing each other like idiots. Sometimes she'll find herself staring at Seth in half-curiosity and half-wonder. She heard him loud and clear, but it still doesn't seem real. The look in his eyes was fierce. Raw and undeniable. He knew what he wanted, and he wanted her.

It terrifies and thrills her all at once. There are so many what-ifs scattered between them, and still, they're doing it. Doing them. It feels normal, natural, like they've already been together for such a long time, and maybe they have been, just without a label to define them.

Seth fits in her space.

Like today.

They lie on Lacey's bed. Seth, propped up by a pillow, holds a dirty and tattered book between his calloused fingertips. His tan feet dangle over the edge of the bed, his brow furrowed in concentration. She can't tear her eyes from Seth. A hot, handsome man who reads. There's nothing sexier.

But what isn't sexy is what they've been doing. Nothing. And that includes the sexy. Seth's been busy fussing over her, changing her bandages, making sure she's okay, instead of making sure she's naked.

Not to mention Lacey's bored. Anxious. She can't take much more of this sitting around and resting schtick. Not working means her mind wanders to the night of the mugging. She can't get the image of the mugger, smirking, tearing the locket from her throat.

She has to do something. Can't stay cooped up another minute.

She sighs long and loud. Peeks over at Seth through her lashes to see if he's heard her.

Nothing.

She wiggles over to him, sticking her phone under her pillow. So far all she's heard from Prentiss about her time off was a curt text that said, "One week, Sutton."

Prick.

Rolling onto her side, she lays her head on Seth's pillow and stretches her arms up and in front of his book.

Finally, he tosses an arm over her waist, trapping her to him.

Still staring at his book, he says, "Somethin' you wanna tell me, princess?"

"I'm bored."

Not having it, he flips a page. "And?"

"Ugh, you're heartless." Lacey glares at the smirk on his face, then asks, "What're you reading?"

"A book about the history of country music." Seth closes it, sweeps a broad palm down the dusty cover in an almost tender manner. He chuckles wryly. "You look surprised."

"No," she says, her eyes widening. Leaning up on her shoulder, she presses a hand against his chest, not wanting him to be insulted. "I never pegged you for a reader." She flushes. "I'm sorry, that's an asshole thing to say. I just . . . I didn't know that," she finishes lamely.

He gives her a no-hard-feelings grin. "Yeah," he says, lighting up. "I love all that shit. The old west. Cowboys. History. Anytime we're on tour, I try to hit up a museum. Drag Luke or Sal along if I can."

"That's cool," she says, flopping onto her back to smile softly at the ceiling. She likes learning the little things about Seth. She turns her head to glance at him. "You know . . . we have museums in LA too."

"Nice try." He leans over to kiss her. "But no."

She scowls. "I bet you've never been this still in your life."

She feels an arrow of guilt that Seth's still there. He needs to be on the road with Luke, but when she thinks about him leaving, it's like someone cut out her heart and flung it into the sun.

"You know what, I haven't." His eyes dare her to argue with him. "But it's for a good cause, ain't it? Bossin' you around."

"Please," she sniffs. Then she sits up and crawls onto his lap to straddle him. Her gaze pinned on his, she says, "Let's go out. I can't stay cooped up any longer."

Wariness creases his face. The book bobs in his hands.

"Pleeeeease." She palms her hands together in a pleading

prayer. "The stitches are closed. I'm off antibiotics. I feel good. I want to go out."

Seth's blue eyes cloud with uncertainty, the memory of her ripped stitches fresh in his mind. He runs a hand over the back of his head. "I ain't so sure, Lace..."

She swallows, anxiety twisting her stomach. "Please, Seth. I need to go to the beach."

Her happy place. That's what she needs.

His mouth opens, then closes. He must see something in her eyes, her face, because he relents. He stares at her and then nods. "Alright. Let's go."

Lacey walks along the shore beside Seth, watching the waves roll out, her mind going, going, gone with them. This is what she needed. A way to get clear, to calm that panicky racing sensation behind her ribs. To get that motherfucker out of her mind. Prentiss or the mugger, she isn't sure.

Maybe both.

"Lace?"

She turns, blinking away her daze. "Yeah?"

Seth peers at her, his crystal-blue eyes searching. "You tell me if you get tired."

She tilts her head, pressing her lips together to hide a smile. "Seth, you're fussing."

He grunts. "And I ain't gonna stop."

With that, she grabs Seth's hand, lacing her fingers with his. He smiles and pulls her in close, tucking her against him. His hand warm in hers, warmer than the sun above.

As if reading her mind, Seth glances up and whistles. "Unreal," he drawls. "How damn nice it is. It's goddamn December and I ain't never seen nothin' like this in my life."

"You should come out here more often," she says, squeezing his hand.

The invite lies between them. Casts an uncomfortable silence.

No one's talked about what happens when Seth leaves.

Three more days and he's gone. *Gone.* The very thought has Lacey sick to her stomach.

"You know," Seth says, picking up the dropped conversation. His gaze drifts to the ocean. "I still remember the first time I saw you on a board. Out in North Carolina, when we went for that show." His smile looks vaguely like pride. "You sure can surf the shit out of a wave."

"I wish I could surf now." She casts a wistful look out at the ocean. As stormy as her heart.

"In the winter?"

"Oh yeah. That's the best time."

"What about bein' cold?"

"Best kind of rush. It's like a shock, but you breathe through it and you beat it."

"Hell, Lace, I don't know," Seth drawls. "What else you been keepin' from me?"

She smiles at the awe in Seth's voice.

"I can hold my breath for four minutes."

He looks at her quick, his eyebrows lifting. Then busts out a laugh. "Bullshit."

"I can." She pokes him in the side. "I used to practice with Sal. She never could do it, but I did."

Seth glances at the waves. "Your mom surfed."

"Yeah. Sal taught me her moves." Lacey shivers, her hair whipped wild by the breeze. "Coming out here always makes me feel closer to her." She leans into Seth as he wraps an arm around her shoulders to keep her warm. "I don't even have memories; I was so little when she died. It was always Sal's job to remember our mom. When Sal lost her memory, I felt like I lost my mom all over again, because Sal's the one who had all the stories, and then suddenly she didn't." She shakes her head. "I know it's selfish. Sal went through so much awful shit, and here I am worrying about—"

"Nah, that ain't selfish." Seth stops, turning her to stare into her face. "I never thought about it like that, Lace. That's rough."

"It is what it is." Lacey lets go of Seth's hand and drifts up the beach to the blanket they have spread out across the sand. "It's about Sal. Protecting her. And what she does and doesn't remember."

"Like what?" Seth asks, following her.

Lacey drops to the towel, pulling her legs beneath her. Seth drops beside her, shoving the sleeves of his Henley up to expose lean, tan forearms. "Like our father for one. A cheating asshole." Seth winces. "Like why I lived with them in college. She doesn't need to know dumb stuff like that."

Seth's frowning. "You know, I still don't know why you lived with them for those two years. Why you left San Diego. All I remember is you had that bedroom with all the pink."

He chuckles. But she can't.

Her heart's a drumbeat. A countdown.

She gives him a quick look. "You really don't know?"

He lifts his eyebrows. "No."

Luke promised he wouldn't tell anyone, and he kept his word. Seth doesn't know.

She waves a dismissive hand, like she can chase away her heart. Hammering fast against her ribs. "You don't want to hear the story, Seth."

"I really do, Lace."

"It was a long time ago."

His eyes fish around hers. "Yeah, but it's your long time ago," he says, flashing a smile. "And I wanna know it."

Seth's sweet words stall out her heart. Normally, she'd duck and dodge. Evade. Control. But not anymore, and not with Seth. Because he's asking, caring about her story, and Lacey finds herself wanting to tell him. Wanting him to know this part about her past. Even if it sucks.

She's quiet for a long minute, keeping her eyes on the waves to ground her. Then she inhales a breath, steeling herself, gathering courage.

"So, after Sal moved to Nashville, I lived with my stepmother, you knew that, right?" she asks, glancing Seth's way briefly, and he nods. "I was in high school and I felt like I had no one. I've always felt like that. That I'm left behind. That everyone leaves." She holds up a hand when Seth opens his mouth. "I know it's not like that, but . . . our dad was always deployed or sneaking around with Vivian when he was home. Then mom died. Then Sal left for college and I was stuck in that house with that . . . that witch woman. And it's so stupid, but I felt like here I was, and everyone I loved was halfway across the world or just gone."

Lacey hugs her legs to her chest, resting her chin on her knees. "I didn't know what to do. I felt lost. Alone. And my stepmother was awful. I hated her so much, Seth. And I was so angry, so sad all the time." She closes her eyes. "I started doing things to myself. To my body."

Beside her, she feels Seth tense. "What kind of things?" he asks, worry in his voice.

Her gaze settles on Seth—his frown deepening—and then moves back to the ocean.

"I . . . I was bulimic. It wasn't a lot of the time or all the time. It was only when things in that house got out of control and I felt anxious." She blows out a breath, remembering. Remembering how when she stuck her fist down her throat, she had a feeling of control she'd never felt before. "I know it sounds weird, but it comforted me. It made me feel less alone."

Heat builds behind her eyes. "It got bad in San Diego. One night, I passed out in the shower. I spent five hours in a hospital with a drip in my arm, and all my stepmother could do was tell me I should have learned how to hide it better."

"Shit, Lacey . . ." Seth looks like someone hit him across the face with a two-by-four. "*Fuck*. That's fuckin' messed up."

Lacey sighs, a tear slipping down her cheek. "That's why I went and lived with Sal and Luke those two years when they first got married. I had to get out of that house. In Nashville, I went to outpatient treatment during the day and community college at night. Like some kind of weird double life." She chuckles sardonically. "Sal and Luke—they gave me a home and got me help. They saved me. I couldn't have made it without them.

"I'm okay now. I went to therapy. Lots and lots of therapy. I have the beach. I'll probably always have a weird relationship with food, but no one really gets over their things, right?"

A wince crosses Seth's face.

She gives him a thin smile. "But I'm good. Healthier. I got help. I don't have those urges anymore." She shakes her head. "Sal doesn't remember. Luke thought it was okay to tell her, but . . . I don't want her to know. It doesn't matter. It's not important."

"It does matter," Seth says in a low voice. "You matter, Lace. I think you should tell her. She would wanna know."

Hot tears run down Lacey's cheek. She looks at the trio of scars on her knuckles, rubbing a thumb across the white moons. Her hands shake. It feels like she's split her chest wide open.

"I can't. I can't tell her again. It was too hard the first time." Lacey's voice breaks at the memory. "I don't want her to feel guilty for not remembering or for leaving. She doesn't deserve that. Not now."

She wipes a tear away from her face and then drops her face into her hands. She can't face Seth yet, face his reaction. Too many emotions all at once. Relief her story's out. Worry that Seth will think the worst of her. And, as always, that furious rush of old shame.

Seth's deep rumble shakes out. "Lace . . ." There's an emotional edge to his voice.

"Don't look at me, Seth," Lacey moans into her hands. "Oh God, I'm so embarrassed. You must think I'm so messed up."

A soft chuckle.

And then, there's a rustle of movement as Seth scoots close and gathers her in his arms. He hugs her tight, pressing a kiss to her temple. He shifts, unfurling her from his arms, tipping her face up to him. "I don't think you're messed up."

"You don't?" She stares at him in wonder, nothing but tenderness and understanding on his face.

"No." He smiles. "I think you're brave. I think you're strong." His voice cracks. "Tellin' me all that—you're amazing. And you shouldn't be embarrassed or ashamed. That's the last thing you should feel. You should be proud of yourself, because I am."

Lacey closes her eyes, almost unable to believe. She'd held a brief flutter of fear that when Seth heard her past, her secrets, he'd run. Not wanting the burden, the darkness she carried for so long. But here he is, telling her he'll carry it too.

"What can I do?"

She blinks. "What?"

"To help you." Seth peers at her, his kind eyes searching.

The question means everything. It slices through her anxiety, steals her breath.

Her heart.

"This." She rests her head against his shoulder, slipping his hand into hers. She smiles, her soul surging in a great, big rush of happy. "This right here helps."

Seth wraps an arm around the curve of her hip and pulls her closer. "I'm glad you're okay," he whispers, holding her tight like she could leave at any second.

She closes her eyes, leans into his strength. "Thanks. I'm glad I am too."

They sit there, curled into each other, watching the sun sinking down into the water in a fiery golden glow.

Finally, the ping of Lacey's phone breaks the silence.

She groans, scrambling to dig her phone out of the bag. "It's Prentiss, I know it."

"I have one question," Seth says, scowling. "How soon can I hurt him?"

Her eyes go wide. "Shit. It's a text from Colin." Lacey bites her lip. Her fingers itch to reply. "Oh, shit," she says as her phone lights up. "He's calling me."

A sharp growl from Seth.

A flare of courage goes through her. Another risk to take. Another wave to break through.

She swallows hard. Then, with one long inhale of breath, she answers. "I am sorry, Colin. I cannot help you right now. I am hurt. And I am tired. And I am . . . on a break. Goodbye."

She hangs up and turns to Seth, who's grinning. "Holy shit. What did I do?"

His expression's sympathetic, but pleased. "Tough?"

"Incredibly." She exhales. A weight lifted. Free. It feels fucking fantastic. She looks at Seth and claps her hands together, energized. "What next?"

He grins. "I got a place we could go."

She arches a suspicious brow. "You know a place in LA?"

"I do." Seth presses his lips to hers and Lacey winds her arms around his neck. "It's got great tap water."

The laugh she lets out shakes them both.

chapter
SIXTEEN

SETH'S STOPPED AT THE DOOR OF THE BLUE COWBOY BY a surly hostess wearing black eyeliner and a necklace made of blinking Christmas lights. "You're on the list," she says, snapping a bubble and holding out a stop-right-there palm.

Seth cackles. "The what? The naughty list?"

She doesn't laugh. Instead, she glances over her shoulder. "Greasy Graham," she calls out.

Beside him, Lacey gives him a look, an eyebrow raise. "Greasy?"

He squeezes her tight. "Just go with it."

"Seth," Lacey says under her breath. She grips his bicep, and he clinches it to keep her close. "It smells like a stable in here."

A minute later, Graham's sauntering over, gnarled thumbs hooked through his belt loops. "You came back, kid." His attention flicks to Lacey. Approval shines in his milky old eyes. "And who's this pretty lady?"

"This is Lacey," Seth says, extending a hand. "Lacey, this is Graham. He's a mean old son of a bitch."

Lacey gives a mock gasp at his rudeness. She clasps Graham's hand, a warm smile spreading on her face. "Nice to meet you. Please don't kick me out of here because of Seth's despicable manners."

Graham sputters with laughter. "Don't listen to him. And not to worry, sweetheart. Any friend of Seth's a friend of mine." Still gripping Lacey's hand, Graham pulls her across the floor with him. Seth follows at a slow lope, enjoying Lacey in his element.

She flashes him a goofy, wide-eyed *what's happening?* smile over her shoulder but lets the old man show her to a booth.

"Best seat in the house," Graham says when they've gotten settled. He turns to Seth. "You came back with a girl, kid. Now how 'bout a song?"

"Oh, man," Seth says, nerves tightening his chest at the mention of getting onstage. "I ain't got nothin' to play. No instrument either."

But Lacey's eyes have lit up. "You should, Seth."

"See?" Graham wheedles. "Pretty lady knows what she's talkin' 'bout."

Seth lifts his hands, helpless. "I ain't got the song, Graham."

"You will." Graham gives a barely sly glance to Lacey, and Seth rolls his eyes. *Smooth, man.* Clearing his throat, Graham claps Seth on the shoulder. "We'll cover Hank, then. I'll play with ya. We'll get you warmed up first." He wanders off, searching the rowdy bar. "Stella! Whiskey!"

Lacey laughs, her sea-green gaze moving to Seth. "He's a riot."

"Thanks a lot," he drawls.

"Why not?" she says with a coy shrug. "I think you need a little practice."

"Oh, now you're an expert on country music?" He lifts a brow. "Who's Hank, then? Last name and decade."

She wrinkles her nose, thinking about it. "Hank Rogers?"

"Pathetic." She bursts into a laugh. Seth shakes his head. "You do know I'm gonna learn you on country music if it takes the rest of my life."

Rest of my life.

Lacey flushes pink.

The words float between them. Honest and raw.

The truth, Seth thinks. *That's for damn sure.*

The bartender breaks the quiet silence, dropping a bottle of Blanton's, a Mason jar full of water, and two glasses. "There you go, princess. Tap water and whiskey." Seth eyes the bottle. It's expensive. It's also Graham's way of saying he approves.

"I'm so ready for this," Lacey says, eagerly reaching for the whiskey. She wiggles her eyebrows, her bright smile launching fireworks in Seth's stomach. "I'm off antibiotics, this is a celebration."

Seth laughs, watching as Lacey measures out the drinks, her long blond hair tousled from the wind on the beach, her green eyes sparkling and lively as they rove around the rowdy bar.

Talk about a goddamn great day. Even with the heaviness of earlier on the beach.

His stomach flips over. Seth knows all about keeping secrets, but he never imagined Lacey had one hell of her own. Back then, he had been so caught up in his own shit he hadn't remembered the reason, the excuse Sal and Luke had given as to why Lacey was living with them. Bad grades, bad school, she missed her sister. But now he realizes what she was really going through.

It hurts him. It hurts him that she went through that, that he never knew, that she still feels alone. But he knows now. And he'll damn sure be there for her, whatever she needs.

He saw it on her face, clear as day. She thought he'd walk away hearing the truth about her past habits. Well, it's the exact opposite. It only has him loving her even more. He's never seen her so brave, so vulnerable. The strength in her words. The fragility of her past. Lacey opening up to him is a damn honor, and he's thankful she trusted him enough to do that.

Thankful that she's healthy and she's here and she's his.

"Seth?"

He glances up to see Lacey beaming, holding out a glass of whiskey. The white slouchy sweater she wears hangs loose over one shoulder, showcasing bronze skin. Her pink lips parted in a smile.

He's overcome. Overcome by everything that is Lacey. Her heart, her beauty—a head rush he can't get enough of. Ignoring the whiskey, he sweeps her into his arms and kisses her deeply. Lacey tenses at the public display but then melts into him, a needy whimper in her throat. Her heart pounds against his chest; he can feel her heartbeat syncing with his.

Slowly, Lacey pulls away, her expression heavy-lidded. Bewildered. "What was that for?"

He stares into her eyes. "Just because."

"Mmm," she whispers, smiling. "I like just-because."

His throat works the words out. "Lace . . . I—"

A crackle on the speaker sideswipes his confession. "We got a treat for you tonight, folks. Seth Kincaid, one-third of the Brothers Kincaid, is in town and gonna bust a string on his fiddle. Seth, get your ass up here!"

The moment broken, Seth reluctantly lets Lacey loose. She presses a palm against his chest. "Go, Seth."

Giving Lacey a hangdog look, he swigs his whiskey down, slides out of the booth, and scales the stage like a pro.

"That California girl, she yours?" Graham asks, handing Seth a fiddle and a bow.

Seth takes a bracing breath. "Yeah."

Graham evaluates Lacey with an appreciative eye. "She's a keeper if I ever saw one."

Seth laughs. He feels antsy, high on tonight, on Lacey and the stage. "Fuck, man, enough with the romance." He runs his bow along a string. "Let's play."

With that, he kicks off with his fiddle, launching into a wild-twanged rendition of "I Saw the Light" that sets the crowd on fire.

When he whips around, Lacey lifts her drink in the air.

To Seth.

Straight to his heart.

Lacey claps her hands together as Seth and his fiddle ignite the crowd, weaving a frenetic tune with Graham, who's on his guitar. Seth plays like he's dipped his fingers in fire. Manic, freewheeling, frenzied.

The floor pounds beneath her feet, a couple two-steps across the room, laughter bubbles on her lips. She likes this feeling, ears ringing, throats raw, hurling fingers to the heavens. But what she likes best is the look on Seth's face. He's happy. His smile is killer, the one he probably gives all the girls in the bar, at shows, but tonight, his eyes tell her, that smile is hers.

So damn sexy. So damn talented.

She's seen the Brothers Kincaid play before, but she never realized how hard Seth works, how amazingly good he is. He has a charm that radiates. An energy that draws others in. His voice is like nothing she's ever heard before—a deep rumble compared to the more mellow twangs of Luke and Jace. Seth just shines. Alone or with his band, he always sings like he's pouring his heart out.

It's all she can do not to climb onto the stage and take his lower lip between her teeth.

Wild applause breaks out as Seth finishes his song. He thanks the crowd, giving Lacey a grin that curls her toes. As he climbs offstage, he's crowded by fans. Lacey smiles and slips out of the booth. But she bypasses him, letting him enjoy the spotlight and heads to the bar for a drink.

"Excuse me," she says, pushing through the swarming crowd. Hot with body heat, thick with conversation. Her world seesaws, telling Lacey she's just the perfect amount of buzzed.

"You wanna dance, baby?" A burly, red-faced cowboy's giving her a once-over.

She waves a dismissive hand, angling her face to the bartender. "No, I don't."

The man steps up. "Just a little two-step. You're lookin' lost in this bar, Blondie." Before she knows it, one of the man's meaty hands snakes around her elbow, and she's being pushed up against a hard wall.

"No," she says, frantic. She looks around for Seth, but she can't make him out in the throng of bodies. She struggles against the man's grip. "Stop."

Terror flips her stomach. His touch is heavy, threatening, rough.

And she feels him. The mugger. It's like he's there with her, in her space. On her body, pressing her up against that red brick wall, his foul breath, his stench. Her purse hitting the concrete. The snap of her necklace as it was torn from her throat. The sick suck of the knife into her stomach.

Lacey closes her eyes, trying to brace herself against the wall, only to sway on her feet. Her skin goes hot and cold, clammy, as the air's squeezed from her lungs.

The cowboy gives her arm a yank, trying to drag her toward the dance floor.

And then Lacey opens her mouth, finds her lungs, and screams.

The terrified scream rips through the bar, tearing Seth away from the group of people gathered around him. "What the hell?" Graham cranes his head, a confused look on his weathered face.

Lacey.

She screams again, panicked and high-pitched.

Seth bites back a curse and spins around, his eyes frantically searching out the direction of the sound. And then he sees it. A blond woman huddled against the bar. A man with his hand wrapped around her arm.

Fury flashes hot through him.

Seth moves so fast he has the guy pinned against the bar before he knows what's hit him. Lacey cringes and cowers back against the wall, terror all over her face.

"Back the fuck off," Seth snarls.

"Hey, man!" the guy bleats, his eyes wide as saucers. "What's your fucking problem?" He tries to look past Seth to Lacey. "She's the one freaking the fuck out!"

Seth clenches a fist and advances. "I said back off and shut the fuck up."

Then there's a hand on his shirt, on his shoulder, tugging

him away. Lacey's soft voice saying, pleading, "Don't fight. Please don't fight."

Seth wants to hit the guy. Bad. But then he remembers Luke, the slash of the beer bottle, the blood, Sal's scream. And he's blinking. He blinking away that rage to focus on Lacey.

Lacey, who's shaking and terrified.

Lacey who needs him.

He immediately turns to her, sweeping his eyes over her, checking her condition.

He doesn't like what he sees. She's trembling, her arms wrapped around herself, her face drained of color, her lips bloodless.

"Hey, hey," he says, putting a hand out. He keeps his voice gentle and takes a step toward her. "It's okay, Lace. Do you hear me? You're safe."

Her face twists up, tears rolling down her cheeks. "I saw him out there, Seth," she says, her breath coming in small panicked puffs. She shakes her head, squeezing her eyes shut. "I don't want to see him. I can't see him anymore . . . I can't, I can't . . ."

He grabs her up right before she breaks down. He locks her body to his, holding her tight, and Lacey hides her face in his shirt, clinging to him. His palm comes up to cradle her face against her chest, to shield her from the silent bar, the people gawking with questions.

"Seth," she cries. Her slender frame shakes in his arms, her voice barely above a whisper. "I want to go home."

He kisses the top of her blond head, wraps his arms around her tighter. "Shhh, I got you," he whispers, his voice choked by emotion. "I got you, Lace."

chapter
SEVENTEEN

LACEY ENTERS HER APARTMENT ON STEADY LEGS, EYES clocking the shadows as Seth flips on all the lights. By now, she's stopped shaking, but she still can't get what's happened out of her head. She thought the mugger was there with her in that bar. Not to mention she turned into a puddle of a hot mess in front of everybody.

God, she's such a basket case.

"How are you doin'?" Seth asks, his voice low and soft.

Lacey turns, holding her elbows. She swallows, hoping to stop her voice from wobbling. "I'm okay. I'm sorry, though."

He frowns. "What for?"

"For freaking out like that." She makes a face. "I saw him there and I couldn't stop it."

"Don't be sorry," Seth says, chasing away her apology. "Never be sorry for that, Lace. You were mugged. You get to freak out. That asshole cornerin' you . . ." His handsome face twists. He walks to the hallway, setting the car keys on the small entry table. "If anything, I'm the one who should be sorry."

Now it's her turn to frown. She follows him. "For what?"

"I shouldn't have taken you there." Anger stains his voice. He thrusts a hand through his hair, twisting it. "The bar was too rough. I shoulda known that."

"No." She steps close to him. The warmth of his body radiates, and she aches to press herself against him. Lifting her face, she stares up into his crystal-blue eyes. "No, I'm glad. I've never seen you play like that. You're so good, Seth. You just shine."

He closes his eyes, pained. Like the compliment is too much. Like he doesn't deserve it. "Lace."

She shivers.

Lace. Just the way he says it, in that low rumble. More intimate than just a nickname. Raw. Ragged. He says her name like he means it.

Lacey wets her lips. "You do." Her hand finds his chest, tracking upward to cup his chiseled jaw. "I've had the best day. I always have the best time with you."

Their gazes lock and Seth tenses. She feels him down below, hard, resisting and wanting all at once.

She tilts her head, their lips inches apart. "What do you think?"

Ping.

He lowers his head, smiling. "You sure you don't need to get that?"

She tosses her purse on the couch. "No way."

She needs his kiss, needs to get naked, or she's going to combust. There's no more waiting, no more dancing around it. They're together, they're something, and she wants this thing they're doing.

She wants Seth.

Now.

Leaning in, her body arcing, Lacey presses her lips to Seth's. No hesitation.

Seth pulls her against him, capturing her mouth just as fiercely. Desire curls in her belly. It's perfect. The perfect kiss. His kiss like gasoline. Fueling. Fiery. Wanting more, Lacey curls her hands around his lean shoulders and digs her nails in.

"Christ, your nails," Seth hisses, breaking away roughly.

Lacey grins. "Don't like them?"

"Love 'em."

He captures her mouth again, cleaving her in his arms, and backs her down the hall to the bedroom.

Their kisses turn frantic and fevered, like they might never get another chance. Like they waited too damn long. Seth covers her throat with kisses, shaking as he inhales her hair, her scent. "Fuck," he says, trembling against her. "Fuck, you feel good."

They stumble inside the bedroom, slamming back against the wall. Greedily, Lacey thrusts her hands under his T-shirt, her hands roaming over his lean, muscled body. She loves the way he feels. Solid. Strong.

At her touch, Seth moans into her mouth and then yanks away with a gasp. He stares at her, his grin hangdog and devilish. "It's about goddamn time," he says, kicking off his boots, shedding his jacket. His eyes blaze with lust. "I can't fuckin' wait anymore."

She grabs the hem of his T-shirt, dragging it over his head, wanting the million-dollar view of his tan, toned body.

Every part of her body has begun to smoke. She is lust shooting down the telephone wires, a living torch.

To her surprise, Seth doesn't let her get him naked. Instead, he backs her up against the bed. "Sit down," he commands.

Numbly, she does.

Seth gets on his knees in front of her. Warm desire, primal lust, flickers in his eyes. He grips her bare thighs, the veins rising in his tan, muscular arms as he slides her skirt up around her hips. "Lie back."

Her heart pounds in her ears. They've never done this before. It's always been straight sex with Seth. Wham bam and then she's gone. No staying over, no conversation, just sheer pleasure, feeling good, breaking one bad habit with another.

No, this is intimate.

This is something different. Just like today. She's done things she's never done before. Taking risks. Telling secrets. Having meltdowns in public. Tonight will be different too. With Seth.

She knows it. Deep inside, she's unraveling. She likes him. More than like, but she can't say it. She won't.

Not yet.

Inhaling a breath, she slowly reclines against the bed.

Seth looks up and grins, cocky, like he can't wait to show

her what she's missing, and then he curls a finger around her lace panties and drags them off. Slow. Teasing.

Impatient, Lacey groans. Raises her head to give him a scowl. "You're insufferable."

"You love it."

Sighing in contentment, she lies back down. She does love it. Loves how at ease she feels with Seth. She's never let a man be so free down there, never let herself feel okay with being on display, so open and receptive to what Seth is offering.

Seth parts her thighs. With the softest of lips, he presses a kiss to her knees, her stomach, a gentle kiss to her healed stitches, her scar, and then she gasps.

Seth's long fingers find her pulse down below, deft like when he's on his fiddle. They dip in and out of her, gently, testing, and her groin tightens with pleasure. Seth sucks in a pleased breath as she clamps tight around his finger.

And then, just like a song, he's changing the melody. He's down below, entering her, swallowing her up with his mouth. Hot. Deep.

She hisses out a breath, gripping the sheet in the small balls of her hands. And it's like he's lifting, commanding her body with his tongue. She arcs upward, her body straining for more, her eyes rolling to the ceiling at the unbelievable pressure building within.

Seth maps her, his tongue exploring the shape of her, the taste.

Breathless, Lacey closes her eyes. She's never felt anything like this, something so damn good, something meant all for her.

The sensation intensifies when Seth drags his tongue over her clit.

Lacey whimpers, her head lolling from side to side. Gold and yellow crackle in her vision as his tongue, his lips, work her over, and then Lacey's on a mountain, sliding down with ever-increasing speed, and she can't stop. Can't do anything but—

"Oh, Seth . . . oh!"

She's shooting off that mountain, plunging into that pool of yellow, into gold, far gone and far out.

She lies there for a few seconds, breathing heavily. Letting the rush of Seth's breath, his touch sweep over her. When her shivers subside, she sits up, swaying unsteadily.

Seth half-stands, bracing himself on the edge of the bed. His eyes bore into hers, wondering. Intent. "Was that okay?"

She nods, so dazed, so euphoric, a coherent sentence can't make it past her lips.

Lacey's eyes roam the room. The clothes scattered on the floor, her heart up in the air. She looks at Seth and she smiles. "More."

His grin matches hers.

And then Seth grabs her around the waist and scoops her up, Lacey squealing in delight as they both hit the bed.

Seth can't think. All he can do is stare at the woman beside him on the bed, losing himself in her face, her eyes, her curves. He's trying to get a hold of himself and his cock, tell it down boy, but it ain't got no chance. Especially with Lacey at the helm.

Any rational thought tonight is DOA. Because she's gorgeous and glowing and crawling onto his lap with all the eager ferocity of a tiger.

He's been so damn hungry for her all this time. Impatient as a goddamn teenager. He'd been happy to wait, but now that she's healthy and healed he's going to give her everything that makes her feel good.

Lacey straddles him and leans down. He captures her mouth with his, his hands plunging into the curtain of silky blond hair. Her lips a massive dose of exactly what he needs. Sweet and sultry.

As Lacey pulls away, all Seth can do is stare like a fool. Her hair's tangled, her sweater hanging off one slender shoulder, her eyes glittering. Lacey looks like some sun-kissed bronze ocean goddess. Seth cups her supple ass, keeping her as close as he can, wanting to have fifty goddamn hands so he can feel every part of her all at once.

"Christ." His exhale is sharp. "How are you so damn beautiful?"

Her turquoise eyes narrow as she smiles. Feline-like. Appreciative of the compliment.

"I'm gettin' you naked," Seth says, gripping the hem of her sweater to bare her slim waist. "I want to see you. All of you."

She tosses her hair. Haughty. Hot. A faint blush blooms across her cheeks. "Seth. You've already seen me naked."

Not like this. Not when it's the right time. Their own damn time. For once, they're not in mourning or drunk. Tonight, it's him and Lacey. And she's getting all his damn attention.

A hard shudder goes through him as he drags her sweater, then bra, off completely, exposing the most perfect breasts he's ever seen: small, taut, her nipples hard, pink buds of beauty.

With a wild grin, his hands palm her back and then he's sitting up. Lacey lets out a giggle as he flips her onto her back and hovers over her.

He wants to lick her. To kiss every inch of her. His lips, his tongue a soft sweep across the curve of her breast, her collarbones. He goes lower. Her hip bones, her stomach. *God.* He keeps saying that. *God.* Because this, tonight, is too good to be fucking true. It's damn near heaven.

Seth lets loose an agonized moan. How is she so tan? So fucking soft. So goddamn sweet.

His dick strains, pulsing with pleasure, wanting inside her.

But not yet. He has other places to be.

He feels the arch of her body as he takes her breast in his mouth and sucks. She trembles, moaning softly as she lengthens beneath him. His fingertips find her down below, sweeping gently over her clit. "Oh . . ." Lacey's eyes roll, her lashes flutter. "Oh . . ."

"You like it this way?" he asks against her ear.

A breathless whisper. "Uh-huh."

He logs it away. Everything he's doing, because he damn sure plans on doing it again. And every time he wants to get it right. For her.

"Seth!"

Her desperate gasp of his name has his dick flexing. He looks down. Lacey's face is flushed, her eyes dark with desire. "Fuck me," she says, her voice ragged. "Fast, Seth. I need you inside of me. Now."

Seth lets loose a canine growl.

He can't get enough of Lacey. Her banter. Her brazen want for him. Her command of her sex, and his. Goddamn. He's a goner. Absolutely goddamn done.

Their breaths pulse hot between them as Seth slides his boxer briefs off. There's no need for a condom because Seth knows she's on birth control. Knows, somewhat innately, that they both haven't been with anyone else. Haven't wanted to be with anyone else. An unspoken agreement, unspoken trust.

Leaning over her, Seth braces his hands on either side of her. Lacey smiles up at him. Her hands grip his shoulders, her eyes urging him on.

Finally, he slides into her. A loud aching groan rises in Seth. She's slick, as sticky and as warm as honey.

He'll never get over the feel of her. The way they fit so good together, the way she moves under him, bucking like a bronco, fierce and wild and feisty as fuck.

Lacey's eyes, her mouth go wide as he thrusts deeper. "Yes," she whispers.

She rotates her hips rhythmically; Seth drives forward and soon the entire bed's rocking. Lacey cries out, arching as her eyes slam shut.

He's going to come fast. He can feel it. Hell, there's been no one else for him but Lacey.

A savage cry builds in Seth and then he's hammering hard, hips pumping, thrusting deeper into her, deeper than he's ever gone. Lacey cries out. Worried that he's hurt her, he opens his eyes.

She's smiling. She's with him.

And then Seth shuts his own eyes and gives one last thrust. His release happens lightning quick, numbing his brain as he spills into her. Seconds later, Lacey is tensing beneath him, letting out her own needy moan.

Seth sinks forward, draping himself over Lacey's limp form. Together, they stay like that, Seth buried deep inside her, Lacey softly breathing.

He sighs a satisfied sigh. Smiling, she moves her mouth to kiss him, her fingers slipping into his hair to brush damp strands from his brow. "You need a haircut."

He laughs. "Nothin' I need 'cept you."

She smirks. "Charmer."

Not wanting to crush her any longer, he rolls off her into the pillows, taking Lacey with him. Noticing goose bumps on her arms, Seth leans off the bed to swipe the quilt, which has taken a tumble. In fact, everything's taken a tumble, he thinks, taking in the room with amused eyes. Clothes scattered everywhere, the bed nearly rocked off the frame, but nothing's ever felt more right.

Seth pulls the quilt up to drape it around her, then cleaves Lacey close. She curls into him soft, raising her face to look up at him. "That was better than Nashville."

He cups her face, brushing a thumb against the high arc of her cheekbone. "No damn doubt about that."

Lacey smiles, but her eyes are cloudy. A little line appears between her brow.

"What is it?" he asks, scanning her face.

"I like you, Seth," she says, fanning her thin fingers across his chest. "I like you a lot."

"I like you too, Lace."

The words are rough in his throat, knowing he could say more. He could tell her everything. He almost tried tonight in the bar, but he hadn't been able to get the words out. Lacey deserves better than dropping the I-love-you bomb on her in some dirty dive bar. She deserves the right place and the right time.

The perfect time.

She stares up at him, lines of worry bracketing her mouth. "And you leave soon."

The unwelcome reminder knocks him off-balance. He pulls her closer, his chest tightening. He ain't ready for this to end. Not by a long shot. "I know."

He wants to ask if she'll be okay without him, but fuck, he won't be okay without her.

When he thinks about returning to Nashville without her, he can't get air. It's like someone punched him in the stomach and ripped out his heart. It ain't happening.

These last two weeks, she's helped him as much as he's tried to help her. Being here with Lacey, being around the music tonight, he feels like his old self again. The song he wrote, the steady hand he's felt, is a sign he's ready to get back to his life. To fess up to Luke.

Graham was right. He was standing still, spinning his wheels all this time, waiting for something that hadn't happened yet. But he wasn't running away, he was running forward.

To Lacey.

She's given him so much and she still doesn't know about his past. She's showed her true self to Seth these last two weeks, and he wants to do the same. Give her back everything she's given him. Honesty. Love. Acceptance. The truth.

He swallows. "Listen, Lace. I gotta tell you somethin.'"

She props herself up on the pillows to look at him. Her hair swirls around her, making her look wild, vixen-like and venomous. "What is it?"

She reaches out and takes his hand. He wishes she wouldn't do that. Make it harder.

Seth takes a deep breath to steady his nerves. "When you were out in Nashville last, when you came to my apartment and saw . . . well, that wasn't the first time."

She tilts her head. "What do you mean?"

Even now, a hot swirl of old shame flushes through Seth. "Ten years ago . . . I . . . I did what I was tryin' to do that night." He clears his throat. Lacey's eyes are on his, intent, listening. "It wasn't for very long. Just six months. But I was young and dumb and didn't know when to stop. I didn't think it was anything to worry about. After the Brothers Kincaid started goin' places, gettin' up there, I didn't know how to handle everything. It let me feel comfortable onstage, let me fit in, go numb if I needed it. But then . . ." He swallows. "One night, after a show, I overdosed."

Lacey's fingertips fly to her mouth. "Oh my God, Seth."

He stares at Lacey, who's gone still beside him. "Sal found me and saved my life. I never touched the stuff since—since that night."

"Sal never told me that," Lacey whispers. Her eyes shimmer with tears.

"They weren't supposed to." Seth shakes his head. "Sal and Luke—they saved my ass. That's why it matters so much to Luke. That's why I've been so goddamn worried." He closes his eyes in disgust. "I lied. I broke a promise to my brother that I'd never touch the stuff again. And I did. I'm a goddamn coward."

The admission stings like a son of a bitch, but he wants Lacey to know. Wants nothing but honesty between them in this new start.

When he opens his eyes, Lacey scoots close, taking him in her arms. She palms his chin, forcing his gaze to hers. Nothing but understanding in her eyes. "Oh, Seth," she says, kissing him lightly. "You're so hard on yourself. You're such a beautiful person. You worry about everyone but yourself." She smiles sadly. "You made a mistake. We all make mistakes. I don't think any less of you."

He stares at her, his lungs contracting. "You don't?"

The edges of her lips crest. "No. I never would."

Seth closes his eyes. Her fierce belief in him has him coming undone. Straight up has his heart shooting off to the moon. He's never had anything like this before. Not with a girl he loves, someone who accepts the good, the bad, and everything in between.

Fuck. She's too perfect. What is he doing with her? What is she doing with him?

"Luke will forgive you," Lacey says. Then she chuckles. "He forgave me for acting like a raging bitch and demanding that he declare his wife dead, so yeah." She looks him in the eyes. "Tell him, Seth."

Seth nods, knowing he will. All he's gotta do is scrounge up the courage.

Lacey lies against him, resting her head on his shoulder. "Thank you for telling me."

He kisses her forehead, clutching her tight in his arms. So fucking thankful for her.

"Listen," he says, intense, urgent. "You gotta know somethin' else too."

Her eyes flicker in worry. "What?"

"Sal didn't ask me to come out here."

"She didn't?"

He cups her face. "No. I wanted to," he says, watching her eyes soften. "And I want you to come home with me for Christmas."

For a second, she says nothing, then sighs. "Seth, I want to, but my job . . ." She smiles, forced, and leans up on her elbow to kiss him. To end the conversation. "We still have three days."

"Right."

Something sharp twists inside of him.

Time's running out.

"I**T'S TOO EARLY TO BE MORNING**," L**ACEY GROANS**, pressing a hand against her face to block out the sunlight. Seth grunts and responds by wrapping an arm around her stomach. He drags her into him, kissing her cheek. "Lucky for us, we ain't gotta do shit today." She feels his smile against his ear. "'Cept go back for round three."

She rolls over into the crook of Seth's arm, resting her head on his shoulder. His sleepy blue eyes stare back at her. She traces a finger across his jaw. "I think it's round four."

He laughs. "Won't argue with that."

She smiles at the memory of last night. Her and Seth staying up until three a.m. talking about everything under the sun. When they weren't talking, they were going back for round two. And then round three. And then the best sleep of her life. Seth beside her, holding her close like nothing would ever change.

But it is changing.

A ripple of worry shoots through her. Their time together is limited. In three days, Seth will be on a plane back to Nashville, their worlds torn apart once again, and the thought strangles her heart. What was she thinking getting serious? She can't even keep a plant alive.

Missing nothing, Seth traces her lips where her smile has faded. "Hey, what is it?"

"Nothing. I just—"

Lacey freezes at a hard knock hammering on the front door. Insistent. Grating.

Seth scowls at the interruption. "The fuck?"

Slipping out of bed, she grabs the nearest article of clothing and tosses it on. As she's yanking on a pair of yoga pants, she catches Seth's grin.

She looks down. She's wearing an oversized Brothers Kincaid T-shirt.

Seeing his warm, pleased stare, she flushes. "Sorry, should I—"

"No," he says. "It looks good on you. It's yours."

She bites her lip.

I'm yours.

But she keeps the thought to herself. The worst kind of intrusive thought—forever.

The knocking becomes more insistent. "Jesus," Lacey swears, storming out of the bedroom and swiping her phone off couch.

Her guts toss themselves. "Shit," she whispers, staring at her phone. Thirty missed calls.

She smooths her hair back, hoping she looks at least elegantly disheveled. And then she answers the door, swinging it open to stare into the very red, very unhappy face of Prentiss Scott.

"Prentiss, hi, I'm just—"

He steps inside without waiting for an invitation, the lens of his dark glasses fogged over from the cold outside. "You're just blowing off my calls, shirking your responsibilities, and alienating our clients?"

She clenches her jaw and shuts the door behind him. "What're you talking about?"

He paces into her living room. She doesn't miss the disgusted once-over he gives her apartment. "I got a call last night from Colin Cane. He is very upset and disappointed, Sutton."

She crosses her arms, trying to keep her voice even. "He called me to run an errand. In case you've forgotten, I'm a party planner, not a personal assistant." When he says nothing, instead staring at her without sympathy, she says, "I am off, Prentiss. That means not working."

"Your time off nearly lost us the Colin Cane account. The client doesn't wait, you know that." He sucks his teeth, contempt in his eyes. "You're lucky I could smooth things over."

He shakes his head like he's scolding a child and Lacey bristles. It reminds her of her father, how he'd talk down to her and Sal, gaslight them into thinking he was so busy with work, when really he was fucking Vivian in a Super 8.

"You are going to have to do a lot of making up for this," Colin continues. "Overtime. Weekends. Holidays."

A sick feeling settles in her stomach. There goes her time with Sal and the baby. Already gone before she even had it.

She sits on the edge of her couch, bracing herself, weak-kneed. "I already work double hours, Prentiss, and you know that."

"Well, of course you do." He frowns like there's no other option. "This job's your life, Sutton. Your entire world. Your family. You live it and breathe it."

The grim thought has her stalling out, freezing. God. He's right. Prentiss is absolutely right. Who is she? Is this what she wants for the rest of her life? Stuck working for Prentiss at a soul-sucking job, stuck in this shitty apartment, missing her sister so much it hurts, when her family, her *real* family, is off living their life without her?

"Get your phone," he commands.

Lacey blinks herself out of her daze. "What?"

"Get your phone, call Colin, and apologize. It's the only way to remedy this situation."

"Prentiss, I—"

"Prediction." Seth's deep rumble rings out, and she and Prentiss both turn to see him strolling out of the bedroom. His hands in the pockets of his jeans, plaid shirt unbuttoned, a lazy grin on his face. "Lacey ain't apologizin' for shit."

Lacey hides a smile, watching as Seth casually leans up against the wall, his eyes tracking between the two of them. Giving her the space to handle this, yet backing her up if needed.

Prentiss sneers. "I thought you were sick."

Her teeth clench. She crosses her arms, juts her chin. "Seth's right. I'm not apologizing to Colin. And I don't have to explain myself to you."

Prentiss stares daggers. "I want you back in the office today. You started this mess, you fix it."

Lacey curls her fingers, her long nails digging into the heel of her hand. Anger crests over her in a warm wave. She's never been one to speak up, always a perfectionist at work, an *I can do anything*, a *yes sir* girl. Going above and beyond. Always.

But for what?

Here she is busting her ass for some ingrate asshole who'll never give her that promotion. It was just a carrot dangled to keep her in line. It's all bullshit, is what it is.

"Do you hear me, Sutton?" Prentiss snaps. "Pick up the phone and move your ass."

A sharp inhale of breath from Seth.

Lacey pushes herself to standing, her spine like a rose stem. Straight, ready to prick. "No."

Prentiss frowns. "What?"

She exhales. Hard. "You heard me. No."

Prentiss peacock-puffs up his chest. "Who the fuck do you think you are?"

"Watch it," Seth snarls.

How do you swim a wave if you're drowning, Lacey? You break through it. You break it.

Lacey steps up. "I think I'm smart enough not to put up with your bullshit another minute. I think . . ." She smiles, props hands on her hips. "I think I quit, Prentiss."

He stands stunned for a long minute.

Then he chuckles, a smug sound that makes Lacey want to stick a nail file in his neck.

"Please. You and I both know you'll come crawling back."

"Oh, fuck you, Prentiss." Lacey points at the door. "And get the hell out of my house."

"You heard her." Seth pushes off the wall, crossing his arms. A thread of warning in his voice to listen, or else. "Leave. Now."

Red-faced, Prentiss turns on his heel and stiffly walks out, slamming the door shut behind him.

Lacey stands frozen, the words blinking in her head like a gigantic neon sign of doom.

I QUIT. I QUIT. I QUIT.

Zero promotion, zero commitments, zero money.

She gave it all up.

"Oh my God, Seth," she moans, pressing a hand to her head. "What did I do?"

A chuckle comes from behind her. Seth's warm arms slide around her waist. Lacey twists, turning into him. Awe flashes in his eyes. "You did good, Lace. I'm proud of you."

She moan-laughs again, resting her forehead against Seth's chest. She takes a steadying breath, inhaling his reassuring scent before she panics her way into a spiral. "Tell me I'm not an idiot."

A wry chuckle. "You ain't an idiot."

She looks up at him shyly, sliding a hand up his chest. "So now that I'm unemployed . . . it looks like I'm coming for Christmas." She gives a casual shrug. "If you still want me to."

Joy, straight-up joy, overtakes Seth's handsome face. He grins. "Hell yeah, I do."

With a wild hoot, he kisses her, then picks her up and spins her around and around. Laughing, Lacey winds her arms around his neck. No doubts, no anxiety, no worry about where this is going or how long it'll last.

Right now, freaking out is not in her cards. That comes later.

For the first time in her life, she feels like she just won everything.

chapter
NINETEEN

S ETH BLOWS DOWN THE DUSTY BACK ROAD, HAPPY TO finally be freewheeling and not stuck on a damn plane. He and Lacey flew into Nashville last night, picked up his ATV and his fiddle, and are now making the scenic three-hour drive to the Smoky Mountains to meet Sal and Luke.

Christmas in the country. He'd say there was nothing better, except . . .

Beside him, Lacey sticks a long tan arm out the window, fluttering her fingers in the breeze. After a few seconds, she pulls her arm back in and rolls up the window. She makes a *brrr* face at Seth and shivers. "It's chilly out there."

He looks over at her, trying to hide a smile at the lightweight lavender hoodie and thin moto leggings she wears. "I ain't even askin' if you got enough clothes. You got three bags back there. I just hope you brought warm ones."

She sniffs and crosses her arms. "I did." Then a sly smile tugs at her lips. "Although, if you're so concerned about me being cold, maybe I'll just forget about the very sheer, very thin article of clothing I packed."

He side-eyes her, half-tempted to pull the Bronco over and kiss her like crazy. That flirty smile's a goddamn dare he can't say no to.

"You're killin' me," he says.

She laughs and reaches for her coffee in the console. Her green eyes on the window take in the scenery.

Seth watches her for a beat, then turns back to the road.

Nothing looks better than Lacey beside him in the cab of his Bronco. Hell, everything feels a lot better with her along. She gets him out of his own head, gives him the strength to tell Luke, makes him want to be a better man.

Bringing her back with him is the best damn gift he could get. Lacey quitting her job was a surprise, but he knows she made the right call. The way that asshole was talking to her . . .

Even now, Seth scowls at the memory. He ain't a vengeful guy, but if Prentiss accidentally tripped into a chain saw, he wouldn't be super upset. No one talks to Lacey like that. But she handled it like a pro. Seth's never seen something so hot. Her putting the guy in his place.

All the same, he knows she's worrying about what comes after. Lacey was born in motion, won't slow down for anything, and while he's proud of her, he also wants her to rest and relax.

He eases on the gas, taking a right onto another thin stick of a road, and then glances her way. The wrinkle in her forehead tells him she's worrying.

"You thinkin' about your job?" Seth asks.

"No," she says, looking his way with a smile. She slides over to him. "I'm happy, Seth." A little shrug. "Although, I still don't know what I'm going to do when I get back to LA. I should have applied for jobs before we left."

His stomach flips, reality threatening to sideswipe his contentment. "The only thing you need to worry about is rememberin' how to have fun."

He reaches for her hand and Lacey threads her fingers through his. She looks down, curious, tracing her fingertips over his. "Your fingers aren't calloused anymore."

"Time off," he quips.

"You miss it?"

"Yeah. I do. Especially playin' with Luke."

One thing he's learned in all his time away—he misses his brother. Playing without Luke is like cutting off his right arm. He can't do it. He won't.

"We're recordin' a new album after the new year," he says, checking the directions on his phone. On the side of the road is a sign for Hawk's Hideaway. He takes a left, then adds, "And I fuckin' suck, so I gotta sneak some practice in."

"Hmm, well, I love these fingers." Lacey's lips curve, bringing up his hand to kiss each fingertip. "They do many beautiful things."

His body tenses, heat rocketing through all regions of his body—lower included. If they weren't so close to the cabin, he'd pull over right now.

Instead, Seth blows out a breath and directs his gaze to the window, to the familiar scenery. Everything looks the same. The craggy mountains, the clouds hanging like fog, the quiet country. When he and Luke were kids, they'd visit the Smokies every summer with their parents. It's still Seth's favorite place in the world.

"Seth?" Lacey's voice, quiet, concerned, fills up the small space. "What are we telling Sal? About us?"

His eyes flick to hers, a slight current of worry that she won't feel the same way. "We're . . . together. That okay?"

A smile lights up her face. "Yeah. That's perfect." She bites her lip, her expression turning thoughtful. "When do we tell her?"

Seth swallows. "I don't know."

"I don't either. It's just . . ." Lacey frowns, hesitates. "It's so much."

He knows what she means. Hell, he's still grappling with how to tell Sal. Because what does he say? That he went out to LA and fucked her sister when he was supposed to be taking care of her? That they've been doing this sneaking around business for the last three years? That they're together? That he loves her?

He's got no clue how Sal will react. Back in LA, all he was worrying about was what Lacey felt for him, and now he's worrying about what Sal will think. He remembers her always teasing him about his casual indifference to relationships. Girls he picked up after shows, in bars. It never lasted. Even Sal knew that. So, he doesn't know how she'll take the fact that he's with her baby sister. If she'll believe it's serious.

His bond with Sal is deep, and the last thing he wants to do is ruin it.

The Bronco rumbles down a steep incline. Seth swears, checking quick over his shoulder to see how the ATV's holding up. It was an impulse purchase, a blowout from a nice check, and here, out in the country, he'll finally get the chance to use it right.

"Whoa," Seth says when he sees a glittering lake surrounded by Fraser firs. Through the thick trees, he spies a house, but the sharp curve of a road has him losing the sight. "Luke's really got us out in the middle of fuckin' nowhere, don't he?"

Excitement lining her pretty face, Lacey straightens up. A little gasp puffs out of her mouth when they round the corner and the cabin comes into full view. It rises up like something unreal, perched high above the Smoky Mountains, a massive three-story mahogany chalet with decks on every level and floor-to-ceiling windows showcasing mountain views.

"Jesus," Seth says, gawking himself as he steers them down the landscaped pathway.

Luke got Sal a goddamn mansion. And why wouldn't he? It's his and Sal's last getaway before the kid comes. A quiet Christmas for Sal without the press around.

Lacey's smiling, her face a bright beam of joy. "This is unbelievable," she breathes.

Seth glances at her quick, the sudden urge to give her everything overwhelming in its intensity and need.

"We can't tell Sal," Lacey blurts as he arcs around the driveway, throwing the Bronco in park next to Luke's truck. "Not yet. Not right away. She's here to relax. We can't show up and spring it on her."

Seth stares. She's right. He knows they have to go about this the right way. He wasn't exactly going to come out of the gate swinging, but still . . .

He rubs the back of his head. "How long you thinkin'?"

"I don't know." Lacey's biting her lip. "After Christmas?"

Seth cocks a brow and exhales. "You're tellin' me I gotta keep my hands off you for four damn days?"

He ain't happy about that. Especially right now. Lacey's looking so damn beautiful he's got a bone-deep ache. They barely started this thing, made it official, and now . . . he's gotta play hands-off?

Lacey leans into him, pressing her breasts against his chest. "Not hands-off, just out of sight." She nibbles his earlobe and Seth goes hard. "Who knows, it could be fun?"

"Yeah, for fuckin' you," Seth growls, reaching to take her in his arms, but then Lacey's quickly scooting back to the passenger-side door. He follows her gaze.

The front door of the cabin opens to reveal Sal and Luke, and a barking Winston. Lacey squeals, giving Seth a bright smile before bolting for her sister. Chuckling, Seth climbs out of the Bronco. Instantly, he's hit with a high of fresh mountain air and a fierce bear hug from his brother.

Seth's throat tightens, and he hugs Luke back just as hard. "Hey, man, good to see you."

"Good to have you home," Luke says, pulling away after a moment. He looks Seth over, gripping him hard by the shoulder, his dark eyes serious and soft. "'Bout damn time too."

Seth's nerves ease a bit seeing Luke's face. His brother's grin is bright, no trace of worry or concern on his face.

They turn toward Sal and Lacey. The sisters are in their own little world, as they tend to do when they're together. Sal's eyes on Lacey, Lacey's eyes on Sal.

"Oh my God, Sal," Lacey says, untangling from Sal's embrace to look down. Her cheeks flush with happiness as she presses palms against Sal's budding stomach. "You're still so tiny."

Sal laughs. "Oh, there's a baby in there alright. A tiny kickboxer who beats me up on a daily basis."

"And your boobs." Lacey gasps. "They look so good."

"Amen, amen," Luke drawls, waggling a devilish brow.

Sal gives Lacey and Luke a wry grin before turning her

attention to Seth. She drifts toward him, her arms outstretched. "How much do I love you?" she says, her green eyes sparkling. "For taking such good care of my sister. For convincing her to come." She hugs him. "Thank you, Seth. It's the best present you could give me."

He squeezes her tight, leaning back to take her and her belly in. "I don't know how much convincin' I did."

"Yeah, having no job tends to make travel real easy," Lacey quips, pulling out of Luke's embrace.

"Well, you two didn't kill each other, so I'd say it was a success," Luke drawls, slinging his arm around Lacey's shoulder.

Lacey crosses her arms, jutting her chin at Seth. "He only did about seven or eight annoying things."

Seth raises an eyebrow, a tendril of desire flexing his cock at the bantering tone in Lacey's voice. He gives her an *it's gonna be like this?* look, and she shrugs, a faint teasing smile on her face.

He grits his teeth. Reminding himself to behave is going to be a bitch.

Sal links her arm through Seth's, stretches out her other to take Lacey's. "C'mon, let's go see everyone."

"Who's everyone?" Seth asks.

As if in answer, a shout rings out from the second-floor balcony.

He almost groans when he sees Griff Greyson and Alabama Forester. Griff's raising up a cold one, Alabama waving a hand. While he likes Alabama alright, Griff's still a sore subject. Seth can't get over Griff calling Luke names in the press, trying to start a damn fight in a bar down in Texas.

He knows it's not a competition for Luke's friendship, his brother never made it one, but Seth still can't help going back to when they were kids. When he was in some petty rivalry with Jace for Luke's attention. Luckily, he and Jace have a decent friendship now ever since they had to come together for Luke after Sal went missing.

He hides a smile when he sees Lacey's irritated expression.

She's never been a fan of Alabama, especially after she crashed Sal's birthday party. A cardinal sin in Lacey's world.

Sal sees the expression on Lacey's face too and laughs. Points a finger. "The two of you, play nice."

Lacey looks outright offended. "I will be cordial, Sal."

Luke and Seth snort.

"Emmy Lou and Jace here?" Seth asks as they walk up to the cabin.

"Yep." Sal hesitates. "And Beau should be here tomorrow night."

Seth stops. Frowns. "Why's he comin'?"

Sal's eyes flicker, uncertainty there. She glances over her shoulder at Luke, who's grabbing the bags from the car. Lowers her voice. "I think Bobby invited him on behalf of the Brothers Kincaid. Luke isn't happy about it."

"What's he like?" Seth tries not to feel resentment toward the poor son of a bitch who took his place. It's not like it's permanent. Hell, the mere fact that he's jealous tells him that leaving the band is not what he wants.

At all.

A long pause. "I haven't met him yet. Luke hasn't brought him by. I think he missed you too much." Sal laughs. "It's like all those girls you never bring home because you don't want 'em to last—"

"Sal . . ." Seth cuts her off by slinging an arm around her shoulder. "You're fuckin' hilarious."

As they climb the stairs, Lacey leans back behind Sal to give Seth an *oh really?* look.

Seth wants to bury his head in his hands and groan.

Vacation's off to a perfect fucking start.

Lacey gasps as Sal cracks open the front door, revealing the inside of the cabin with a flourish.

Instantly, she's hit with the scent of cedar, of fire. Rising up from the center of the foyer is a circular wrought-iron staircase. To the right is the living room, where an enormous antler chandelier hangs, a floor-to-ceiling fireplace, a buttery leather couch made for at least fifteen people, and a Christmas tree buried in gifts. Majestic windows offer a grand view of the mountains, the setting sun.

Colin Cane would kill to have an event here. Hell, she'd kill to plan one. A pang goes through her at the thought of her job, but she shakes it out of her head and follows Sal inside.

"This is unreal," Lacey says, clutching at Seth's arm, and then quickly tears herself away from him like she's been burned.

Shit.

He gives her a look like he's planning on devouring her later.

A slight thrill of adrenaline goes through her. They haven't been in cahoots like this since they both worked together to take down Mort. It's hot.

Sal turns, just missing their contact. "Everyone already got a bedroom." Her smile's apologetic. "Lace, I saved you one upstairs. Seth, you're downstairs."

Lacey sneaks a peek at Seth. He's frowning. Probably already plotting a way up to her room. Because she is too.

"We set up a studio on the bottom floor," Luke drawls, his eyes on Seth. "We'll get some practice in."

"This way," Sal says. Winston skitters past her, a happy woof rumbling out of him. "Everyone's in the kitchen."

Lacey can hear them. Voices chattering, boisterous laughter. They pass the living room, a deck, a dining area, and then they're in the kitchen. A large expansive space, warm and smelling of cookies. At the round breakfast bar, perched on a stool—Alabama Forester, wearing a cream sweater dress and thigh-high boots.

Thankfully, Lacey's saved from the awkward interaction by Emmy Lou. The chipper blond, clad in a frilly apron, perks up as all four of them step inside the kitchen. "Well, lookie who the cat dragged in!" She lifts her hands. "I'd hug y'all but I'm wrist-deep in cookie dough."

"Hey, man!" Jace pounds across the floor to Seth. They shake hands, clap shoulders. "You're just in time for happy hour."

"You happy to see me, Jace?" Seth laughs, a ghost of a smile curling his lips.

"Hell yeah, I am." Jace lifts his rusty brows. "We got shit to talk about." His kind hazel eyes land on Lacey. Sympathy on his face, but he won't bring up the mugging. Not wanting to risk a subject she doesn't want to talk about. He squeezes her arm. "How are you, Lace?"

"I'm good," she says, smiling. "Thanks."

"Hi, Lacey." The voice comes from Alabama. Her gray eyes hesitant. "Nice to see you again."

She manages a nod. "Hello."

Lacey fights to keep a neutral face. The last time she saw Alabama was when she kicked her out of Sal's birthday party for crashing it. She still can't believe her sister is friends with a woman who kissed Luke. Who set him up for Mort Stein.

Sal, smiling broadly, glances between them, then extends a hand at the blond guy crossing the floor. "Griff, this is my sister, Lacey."

"Hey, nice to meet you," Griff drawls, shaking her hand with gusto. His tawny eyes study her close. "California girl."

"That's right," Lacey says, eyeing Griff warily. His lank chin-length blond hair, his tattooed biceps, his scruffy beard. She knows all about this rough cowboy, Alabama's husband, but Sal seems to love him. "Los Angeles."

"I'm still trying to get her to move to Nashville." Sal hip-checks Lacey, her green eyes hopeful. "Maybe now I have a chance."

At the words, Lacey stiffens, feeling Seth's blue eyes on her, feeling his warm palm subtly graze the small of her back as he strides across the floor with Luke and Jace to examine the beer situation. As the conversation goes on around her, she smiles, content to watch Seth.

He's that happy, relaxed, sunny Seth she knows and loves. Her heart takes a dip. She hopes Seth knows he's so loved. Luke's like a puppy dog now that his brother is back. Pride and love in his eyes as he catches up with Seth. The two of them can't get along without each other. It's ridiculously adorable.

Lacey's attention drifts as Griff busts out a laugh, him, Sal and Alabama in an animated discussion. Luke swings by, pressing a kiss to Sal's brow, then steals a cookie from Emmy Lou. The kitchen is loud as bustling. Laughter rings out, drinks poured, conversation chaotic.

Only Lacey's quiet, an awkward out-of-sorts sensation settling around her. That old, anxious feeling of not belonging rears its ugly head. Here, in the presence of Sal and Luke's friends, she's out of her element and failing to swim.

She knows she's seen as cold, closed off. A talent that helped her in her career, but not with making friends. It's how she protected herself all those long years without Sal, with her stepmother and her father. But she doesn't want to be like that anymore. Especially here.

She craves that group of close friends, wants to belong, wants to let her guard down, but it's hard. She doesn't know how to thaw that icy shell she's cloaked herself in for so long.

Lacey leans back against the counter, wishing for Seth. For a warm hug from him, the comforting hold of his arms. She knows she was the one who laid down the rules, rules Seth wasn't too happy with, knows all they have to do is tell Sal, but Lacey's hesitant. Her sister just got off bed rest. She's finally back to normal. What if she takes the news bad? If Lacey ruins Sal's Christmas, she'll never forgive herself.

For comfort, Lacey's hand unconsciously moves to her locket. Not finding it there, remembering it's gone, is like a punch to the gut, a harsh reminder of her reality.

Lacey bites her lip. Her eyes, hot with tears, slide to Seth.

Maybe it was a mistake. Coming here.

THE SUN'S SINKING LOW IN THE SKY OVER THE SMOKY Mountains when Jace and Seth gather around the bar nook. "So, what'd I miss?" Seth asks, hooking his thumbs around his belt loops.

Jace laughs. "Damn near everything." His lips twitch as he locates Luke, who's across the kitchen, out of earshot. "Luke hates Beau. But Beau's in a contract for three more weeks."

Seth blinks at the words as they settle. Hates? Luke's cool and calm. It takes a lot to piss him off. "No shit?"

"No shit."

"Well, hell." Seth frowns, wishing everyone would stop being so damn cryptic. "What'd he do to rile up Luke?"

Jace hesitates. "He keeps talkin' about you not comin' back. Thinks he's gunnin' for your spot." He rolls his eyes. "Long story short, he suffers from assholeitis."

Seth cocks a brow. "Worse than Griff?"

"Griff's a saint compared to this guy." Jace strokes a finger down a rusty sideburn. "I don't know how Beau was doin' things before, but Luke ain't havin' it. But Beau ain't gettin' it either." He gives Seth a *just wait* look. "You'll meet him tomorrow."

"How's he play?"

"He's okay. He ain't you."

"Hell, I'm touched, Jace."

"Just make sure you buy me dinner later."

Seth gives him a shit-eating grin. It feels good. Being with his band. His family.

Before he can say anything else, Luke steps up, a bottle of whiskey in his hands. He nods at the window. At Seth's ATV. "You know I'm drivin' that into the lake tonight."

Seth laughs. His brother's hatred for his ATV knows no bounds. "Hey, I gotta put ol' June to use one of these days."

Griff glances over, latching onto the conversation. "Luke's got a doctor parked down in the guest house, so feel free to take a swim."

"That lake's cold as shit," Jace says.

Seth grins, too amused to be annoyed with Griff. He stares at his brother. Luke's pouring out generous shots of whiskey. "You ain't serious."

Sal floats to his side. Her smile mischievous. "Oh, he is."

"First daddy jitters," Emmy Lou chimes in from her spot at the counter, where she's cutting Christmas cookies into star shapes.

A nod from Luke, his eyes on Sal's belly. "We're out in the fuckin' boonies. You think I'm takin' chances?" He swears finding himself short on glasses and strides away to grab another.

Under her breath, so Luke can't hear, Sal says to Seth, "Watch this."

She presses a hand against her stomach. Pulls her beautiful face into a neutral expression. And stands there. Waiting.

Jace snorts.

Alabama clicks her tongue. "She's been doin' this the last two days."

Instantly, Luke hustles back over, his face an intent frown, the whiskey glass forgotten. "Sal, darlin', you okay?"

"I'm fine, Luke. Just heartburn."

He splays his lean hand across the curve of her stomach. His long fingers fanned out protectively. "You sure?"

"Uh-huh."

Trying to hide a smirk, Seth crosses his arms, watching in amusement as his scatterbrained brother strides back to the counter, clumsily dodging Winston, who's winding through his legs, looking for a handout. Leaning into Sal, he says, "You know you're gonna give him a heart attack, right?"

Sal, her face, her eyes, adoring as she watches Luke, says, "I swear, he won't stop fussing. He gets what he gets."

Seth laughs, emotion overwhelming him. Sal and Luke—they're happy. They're gonna have a goddamn kid. Hell, he's gonna be an uncle. Everything about tonight is too damn perfect.

As the group gathers, deciding to do happy hour on the patio, Seth realizes someone's missing.

Lacey.

The sight of her hits him like a fist to the face. She hangs back against the counter, looking beautiful with her loose braid trailing down her shoulder. But her face is sad, her eyes far and away.

Fuck.

He's the asshole of the century.

So caught up in conversation, he didn't even notice she was all alone. So caught up in trying not to kiss her, he avoided her completely. The last thing he wants is for Lacey to feel alone, left out, or anxious.

He grabs a glass of whiskey, abruptly leaving the conversation, and strides toward her.

"I'm sorry," he says in a low voice.

Her eyes meet his and she smiles, accepting the drink, her fingers brushing briefly against his. "Thank you," she whispers, taking a long sip.

A husky voice breaks their connection. "Since when do you drink whiskey?"

Sal's grinning.

Lacey looks flustered, all eyes on her. "Since . . . since Seth."

Luke raises a glass. "He's learnin' you right out there in LA."

Alabama looks around, says, "Y'all wanna head to the patio?"

A chorus of agreement, people grabbing drinks, bottles of wine, the sliding glass door opening, the kitchen empty, leaving Lacey and Seth alone together.

"Fuck," Seth swears, angry at himself. He braces hands on either side of her. "I'm so damn sorry, Lace."

She shakes her head. "It's not your fault."

His hands drift down to tangle with her fingers. "No, it is. Hell, we're friends," he says, frustrated. "I stayed with you for two damn weeks. We ain't got to avoid each other." He evaluates her, the planes of her beautiful face, still so sad. "What's wrong? What is it?"

"I feel weird here," she admits, staring into the whiskey. "Like I maybe don't belong."

He winces.

The statement carries weight, and Seth's heart hitches. After losing her mom, having an asshole of a father, she never felt like a part of her family, other than with Sal, and he should have done better at making her feel included. He knows Lacey—knows what she's not showing to the others. She's warm. Funny. Kind. A goddamn gift to know, and anyone who doesn't is missing out. Still, she's holding herself back. Protecting herself from getting too close so she doesn't get hurt or left behind.

Seth leans in. "There ain't nothin' maybe about this. You belong here. With me. With Sal."

Lacey stares at him. Seconds later, a faint grin graces her lips. "I wish I could kiss you right now."

Seth grins. Exhales. Wanting to lay her down right there and show her how much he's craving her. "I'm goin' goddamn crazy here."

She gives him a flirty grin. "Maybe tonight I'll show you what you're missing."

Then, she pulls her shoulders back, grabs her whiskey, and heads for the deck.

All Seth can do is growl and follow her out.

If he wasn't dying a slow death already, he is now.

Outside, everyone gathers around the fire pit in a loose circle. Lacey selects a love seat, with Sal curling up beside her. Seth takes a seat in the chair to her right, Luke to Sal's left.

"You okay?" Sal whispers, her eyes alert, worried. She's noticed Lacey's quietness earlier tonight.

"Yeah. I'm great," Lacey whispers back, meaning it. She's already feeling better. Thanks to the relaxing effect of the whiskey, to Seth's bolstering words, to the sight of her sister snuggled next to her.

She's going to enjoy this time. Have fun. Relax.

Sal groans as Emmy Lou uncorks another bottle of wine. She lifts a wineglass filled with clear liquid, her voice droll. "Don't mind me. I'll nurse my sparkling water in sober silence."

Emmy Lou tuts. "Only for a little while longer, sugar."

Lacey giggles. She wraps an arm around Sal and pulls her close. "Don't worry. I'll drink enough for both of us."

Sal laughs, winding a strand of Lacey's blond hair around her finger. "I'll live vicariously through you."

"How many more weeks y'all still have?" Alabama asks, looking to Luke and Sal.

"Due in March." Keeping watch on Sal's face, Luke says, "Couple more months."

Griff slings his arm around Alabama. "What are y'all bettin' on? Boy or girl?"

"Oh, I bet it's a girl," Emmy Lou chimes in. "You're carryin' high."

"I just want a healthy baby in my arms," Sal murmurs, staring into her water, her eyes dim.

And then because Lacey knows Sal hates this conversation, knows they haven't found out the sex because they're trying to brace against another heartbreak, Lacey sniffs and says, "Whatever it is, I just hope it's not ugly."

A round of chuckles lightens the mood.

Sal floats her a grateful glance.

There's a chill in the air and Lacey shivers, tucking her hands between her legs. Seth's right; she should've brought warmer clothes. Although, she'll never tell him that.

But she doesn't need to. He reads her loud and clear, attuned to her needs. Understanding her with one quick, searching glance.

That's the best part of their intimacy. Someone who knows her for her.

Seth stands, slowly dragging a blanket across her lap. "Here you go, princess." To the group, he drawls, "California girl can't hack it." Her eyes narrow in a snappish retort, and then she realizes that's what Seth wants. Their banter. One thing they can do in front of everyone.

"Eat bees, Seth," she bites back.

Griff chokes on his beer, while Jace gives an amused head shake.

Alabama turns to Seth. "Speakin' of California? How was it?"

"Aside from babysittin' this one . . ." Seth jerks a thumb at Lacey and she rolls her eyes. "Was a real blast from the past. Played with Graham Watts."

Luke turns to Seth, his eyes surprised. "No shit. You did?"

"Just a cover. No big deal."

"It was a big deal," Lacey says, determined for Seth to take the spotlight. "He was amazing." Her cheeks warm as Jace raises a brow. The compliment too nice. She shrugs. "For Seth."

Seth smiles into his beer.

"Cool, man," Griff says, awe in his voice. "Graham's a legend."

Seth looks wary at Griff's compliment but concedes, "Yeah, it was pretty damn cool."

"You remember that mixtape we had when we were kids?" Luke asks Seth. His brother's eyes are bright. "What was on it?"

"Jesus," Seth laughs and slaps the leg of his jeans. "Ludacris, Nirvana, Garth and Graham."

"Oh, my word, the variety," Emmy Lou trills.

"One thing that trip did was get the fuckin' press off your back." Jace shakes his head. "Man, that article was some bullshit." His eyes flick to Luke. "Now all that's in the paper is you movin' to California or Beau bein' the next best thing in the Brothers Kincaid."

At the mention of Beau, Luke scowls, raising his beer to his lips and draining it. "As far as I'm concerned, Beau never even happened."

Sal's eyes widen in Luke's direction. Luke being an outright hard-ass is rare.

Lacey takes a sip of her whiskey, stealing a glance at Seth.

But he isn't looking at her. He's looking into his whiskey, his face anguished. Haunted. His shoulders tense. The mention of the article's dragged up his guilt. His mistake. The conversation with Luke he's been dreading.

Her breath stalls in her chest.

Seth losing his smile is like sunshine dropping behind a mountain.

Needing to say something to direct the attention off Seth, Lacey disentangles from Sal and sits up straight. She takes a breath and channels her inner ice bitch. "I'm sure you all heard I got mugged." Lacey crosses her arms as all eyes slide to her. She stares at Alabama. "Out in California."

Alabama flushes red. "I didn't mean—"

Lacey waves a hand. "It's okay. I did get a pretty gnarly scar."

Griff leans forward, tapping his own scar that runs from the corner of his left eye to his mouth. Almost unnoticeable, except in the right light. "Yeah?"

"Here we go." Emmy Lou groans. "Men and their scars."

Griff's mouth curls up. "Well, let's see it, California."

Her eyes narrow.

It's some kind of dare. Like he's trying to egg her on. Or sniff her out. Who she is. Her dislike of Alabama. That or just fuck with her.

And Lacey's never been one to lose a challenge.

She takes a steeling breath, trying to ignore that sharp edge of panic and anxiety. She reminds herself there's no mugger here. She's safe in Nashville with her sister and Seth beside her.

"Fine," she says, with a toss of her hair.

Sal sighs, setting her glass on the edge of the firepit. "You don't have to do that, Lace."

She smiles, mouth dry. "I don't mind. Really."

After daring a glance at Seth, whose face has gone dark, Lacey grabs the hem of her sweater, bracing herself as she pulls it up. She knows what they'll see. A puckered red vertical line right above her hip bone. She used to think it ugly. But now, it's a piece of her. There's power in showing it off, in talking about it.

"Oh, man." Griff whistles. Beside him, Alabama's biting her lip. "Damn, California, you nearly got gutted."

Lacey traces a path down the scar with her finger. "I guess it's my one claim to fame, huh?"

Sal sucks in a ragged breath. "Oh, Lace," she breathes, mild horror on her face. She leans down, her brow knotting as she inspects the damage. And then she bursts into tears.

Everyone freezes, surprised by the unexpected outburst.

Lacey yanks her shirt down. "Sal."

Luke winces, stretching out a hand. "Darlin'—"

Sal covers her face. "I'm sorry," she whispers, shooting to her feet and rushing into the house.

"Nice fuckin' job," Seth snaps in Griff's direction.

"Shit." Griff's shamefaced. He smears a broad hand down his scruffy beard, tawny eyes wide as he stares after Sal. "Kincaid, I didn't mean . . ."

Luke sighs, says quietly, "She's . . . protective." He shoves out of his chair to go to Sal, but Lacey beats him.

"It's okay," she says, cutting a sharp glance at Seth, his face worried, and then to Luke. "I'll go."

She hurries into the house. After a second or two of getting her bearings in the massive space, she finds her sister in the living room.

Sal's curled up on the couch, her face wet with tears. "I'm sorry." She sniffs and wipes her eyes. "I'm so emotional. Damn hormones."

Lacey sits beside her. "It's okay. Although, I think you scared the shit out of Griff Greyson."

Sal lets out a light laugh. "Was I this way with Henry?"

She thinks on it, trying to conjure up Sal's first pregnancy. The baby she lost when she was four months along. "I'm sorry, Sal, I don't remember."

Sal looks down at her lap, picking at a thread in the blanket. "One thing we have in common."

Her sisterly sense tingling, Lacey scoots closer. She gathers Sal's hand in hers. "What is it? What's wrong?"

"I'm so sorry that happened to you, Lacey." Sal's pretty face screws up in frustration. "I'm the one person who should have been there, and I wasn't."

"Yeah, and for good reason." Lacey smiles down at Sal's belly. "You're pregnant and were on bed rest. You physically couldn't be there." She smiles softly. "Besides . . . I wasn't alone. Seth was there, and he took great care of me." Her cheeks are warm.

Very, very great care of me.

"I know. And I'm so grateful to him." Tears fill Sal's eyes again. "But seeing your scar . . . you could have been killed. The thought of me losing you, the baby not knowing you . . ." She blows out a breath. "I'm sorry. I'm so sappy about family these days." She squeezes Lacey's hand. "I was scared, Lacey."

"Well, you shouldn't be. I'm okay."

"I wish you lived closer," Sal says wistfully. "Lately, I've been remembering stuff about us . . ."

Lacey swallows, something hard twisting inside of her. "What kind of stuff?"

"Just little memories. When we were kids. Like me making you breakfast in the morning or taking you to the park. And it makes me sad. It makes me wish I remembered more. It makes me wish you lived closer." Sal sighs. "Sometimes I feel like I just got you back."

"I got *you* back." Lacey pulls Sal into her arms, her sister's rounded belly sweeping against hers.

"You might as well live across the world," Sal whispers, hugging her back just as fiercely.

Lacey's heart cracks open at the sadness in Sal's voice. "Well, who knows. I'm unemployed. Maybe I'll find my way to Nashville one of these days."

Sal sniffs and pulls back to face Lacey. Her smile is wobbly. "Yeah, maybe."

Footsteps.

They both glance over the back of the couch to see Luke, arms crossed, worry dancing in his gunpowder dark eyes. "Everything okay?" His gaze sweeps between the two of them.

Sal stands, heading to Luke. "Everything's great," she says, leaning into his tall frame. "Just being a big baby."

Luke cups the small of her back, her belly, his eyes asking her questions, but Sal smiles.

"I'm going to get cleaned up. I'll meet you back on the deck?"

Luke watches Sal head down the hallway, the crackle of the fire the only sound in the room. When Sal's disappeared upstairs, he turns to Lacey. "Thanks for talkin' to her."

"Of course."

"She's trying to make this vacation perfect for everyone—"

Lacey smiles. "And you just want to make it perfect for her."

"Yeah." He takes a step toward her. "I'm glad you're here, Lacey." He smiles at her with a genuine warmth that hasn't been there in a long time.

She finds it hard to believe that only three years ago she and Luke were at each other's throats, each of them trying to protect Sal in their own way. She's thankful Luke's forgiven her after every awful thing she did. She'd gone off the deep end after Sal disappeared. Trying to force him to declare Sal dead. Accusing him of cheating with Alabama. She's so ashamed of herself. She never wanted to ruin things between Sal and Luke. She just wanted her sister back and went about it very, very wrong.

Lacey clears her throat. "Luke, can I talk to you about something?" Tonight's the night for going all in. Baring her truth like she's bared her scar.

"Sure." He sits across from her, his expression intent. "What's goin' on? You okay?"

Her chest tightens at the kindness of his words. In his eyes, she sees determination to help her, to listen. In that instant, Lacey detests herself. How could she ever think Luke was anything but a good guy? He's Seth's brother, and Seth's the best.

"I was thinking . . ." She glances down at her hands, wired together like a bomb. Then looks up and takes a breath. "I wanted to tell Sal about why I lived with you two in college."

She waits for it, waits for him to tell her it's a bad idea, that Sal doesn't need the stress. Instead, Luke exhales, says, "If you want to tell her, I ain't gonna stop you. I think it'd be good for her. For you too." He gives her a gentle smile, and it's the Luke from the old days. Like none of their issues ever existed.

Luke heads back to the deck and Lacey stares into the fire, piecing together the fluttery feeling in her chest.

Hope.

chapter
TWENTY-ONE

BY ELEVEN O'CLOCK, AFTER A HEARTY DINNER OF STEAKS, cherry pie, and many whiskeys by the fire, Seth goes to his room. Everyone else is off doing their own thing—Sal and Luke to bed. Emmy Lou, Jace, Griff and Alabama in the pool hall on the lower floor. He sits on the edge of the canopy bed, impatient, checking his phone for a text from Lacey. He's crawling out of his skin. Staying away from her is torture. Flat-out torture.

He wants to kiss every square inch of her, fawn over her drop-dead gorgeous body. The strawberry birthmark on her hip bone that looks like a dewdrop, the sprinkle of freckles over the bridge of her nose, her tan sun-kissed legs, and her ocean-green eyes.

Standing, Seth lets out a growl, takes a pace across the room. He checks the time, wondering if he should go to her room, hell, if she's even coming after the way he fucking ditched her tonight, and then—

The crack of the door.

Lacey slips inside, barefoot, clad in a long black silk robe, her blond hair spilling around her shoulder, curled from her braid, looking like the physical embodiment of a goddess.

His heart sparking, Seth shakes his head, grinning as he crosses the room toward Lacey. "Oh man, I am gonna kiss your face off."

"You're vile." She smiles, placing her phone on the night-stand. "But me first."

She's moving and then they're colliding like asteroids. Hot, crushing mouths, his hands in her hair, Lacey's hands palming his face. Her kisses as frantic and as fumbling as his.

He walks her backward, trying to shed his boots, and instead ends up slamming her against the wall.

She gasps and he draws back, thinking he's hurt her. But her green eyes glitter, feline. "Do it again."

Hands shaking, he palms her shoulders and presses her back against the wall.

Hard. Firm.

Pinned.

Her nostrils flare. Her hands drift.

Seth's dick flexes as Lacey peels his T-shirt from him, and then his pants. She cups his erection in her palm and he lets out a long hiss of appreciation.

"Let's see what we got here," Seth says, taking the belt of her robe in his hands. She stands, letting him, watching him heavy-lidded, as he tugs it away.

"Fuck."

His voice—hoarse. Desperate.

She could gut him, the way she's looking right now.

Lacey's got on a shimmering, sheer black bustier top that hugs her toned waist, complete with garters, thigh highs, and a lace thong.

"You tryin' to kill me?" he asks, his voice a growl.

She arcs a sassy brow. "Now who's bitching at me to pack warmer clothes?"

Seth dips down, taking her breast in his mouth, sucking at the hard bud through the lace of her top. He slides the tip of his tongue across her nipple. A needy whimper comes from Lacey. Knees buckling, she sags in his arms at the sensation, her eyelashes fluttering.

Bracing her against the wall, Seth goes lower. He slides a hand up her toned leg, his fingers dipping into her through the edge of her panties. Christ. A low moan rips out of him. She's so wet. And he can feel her down below, slick, warm, her body pulsing out a melody to his touch. The only fucking melody he wants in his life.

Lacey.

Always.

His whole heart is in this.

So why the fuck can't he tell her he loves her?

The shudder of Lacey's body returns his attention to her. Her slender frame trembles, little gasps of air heating the space between them.

He can't wait another damn second. He tears at her underwear, yanking it free.

Lacey gasps and lifts her stunned eyes to him. "That's Givenchy."

"Not anymore."

Seth drags her leg up around him and plunges into her, pinning her against the wall.

Lacey tilts her head back, knocking the wall, her hair tangled up all around her. Her nails dig into the hard muscle of his shoulder. Leaving marks he likes. Territorial. Claiming. Seth's hers and no one else's. And that's how he wants it to stay.

"Goddamn," he growls. "You feel so fuckin' good, Lace. I can't stop thinkin' of you. I want you, no one but you."

She closes her eyes. She writhes restlessly, tightening her leg around him, urging him deeper, faster.

He captures her lips to his, a desperate groan erupting. He's so far gone, over the edge of pleasure. He ain't gonna last. Not tonight.

She clenches around him, hot, soft.

Seth gathers her tighter in his arms and thrusts. There's no more waiting. His hips slam her back into the wall, their bodies melted together, merging like wild atoms. Magnetic. Atomic.

And then, Lacey lets out a cry that's half torment, half pleasure. With a roar, hearing her need finally satiated, Seth spills into her. He buries his face in her neck, panting against her feather-soft hair. "Lacey," he whispers.

Breathing hard, she goes limp against him, and Seth catches her in his arms. He picks her up and carries her to the bed. Gently, he places her on the pillows, grabs a towel for cleanup and then joins her.

He pulls her close. Lacey snuggles in his arms, letting out a content sigh. He kisses her brow, studying the angular planes of her face. Contemplative. Content.

In that moment, his chest aches. She's so fucking beautiful. So unfiltered coming to Seth and showing off her sexy side. That's brazen, ballsy. It takes trust. And they have that. Something he's never had with anyone else.

Lacey twists in his arms to kiss him. "That was fun." She makes a face. "Although my underwear will never be the same."

"Hey, you come in here lookin' like that, I ain't responsible for what happens next."

His hands find her hair, weaving a golden strand between his fingers, the chaos of the day settling around them. "You doin' okay? After tonight?"

"I am. Believe it or not, I had fun." Her face turns wry. "Even with the whole scar debacle."

He scowls. He could kill Greyson for egging Lacey on, for upsetting Sal. The last thing he wanted Lacey to do was relive her mugging in front of everyone. But he knows what she was trying to do—take the attention off him. He's still stunned by the self-lessness of her actions.

"Did you see Sal?" Lacey pushes up, rolling over to face him. "She was really upset, Seth."

"Yeah," he says around the rock in his throat. "She was."

"If she's that upset about a scar . . . what about us?" Lacey's eyes are wide. "What if we tell Sal and she flips? Oh my God, or what if she's so upset, she goes into labor? What—"

He kisses her lips, silencing her. "Lace, you're spiralin'."

She settles back into his embrace, making a sharp sound of frustration. "I hate lying to her." She gives him a look. "Sal hates liars."

Seth flinches. "I know." His low rumble fills the silence. He tucks a lock of hair behind her ear. "We'll find the right time."

Ping.

The soft chime of Lacey's phone breaks the tension. Seth laughs. "Hell, I don't think I've heard that sound since LA." Carefully,

Lacey untangles from his arms. She rolls to the side, to the night-stand. He watches her stiffen as she stares at the phone.

"What is it?" he asks, stroking a hand down the curve of her hip.

"Nothing. Wrong number," she says, her face unreadable as she returns to his arms.

He stares at her, gathering her close. "You missin' your job?"

"Kind of," she says with a little laugh. "I'm trying to enjoy the moment. It scares me not having a job to go back to but . . ." She inhales a determined breath. "That job wasn't my life." She roves her eyes around the room and then meets Seth's gaze. "All this is. I missed out on so much with Sal, and I won't miss out with you."

His throat bobs, her confession so honest it knocks him off-balance.

Her lips hitch up. "Word of warning, though—see how calm I am when you're driving me to the airport in two weeks."

The beat in his chest speeds up at the thought of her leaving. He had overheard the conversation between Griff, Lacey, and Sal earlier. Lacey moving to Nashville—he's got hope for that. Hell, he wants that with every fiber of his being. Still, it's gotta be her decision. He won't push.

He strokes a thumb across her lip, thumbing it out into an adorable pout. "We'll figure somethin' out."

He means it. He knows they haven't talked about what comes next after this. But what he does know is that he wants more than this vacation, more than the memory of LA.

Lacey's smile breaks into a yawn. She closes her eyes, snuggling into him. "Don't let me fall asleep here . . ."

Seth places a protective palm on her waist. His own eyes grow heavy. He should wake her, but he can't stand to tear her beautiful body from his arms. The absence of Lacey is like the absence of air. He learned that this afternoon, far apart, far from each other.

When he falls asleep beside her, he's thinking about the one fact he already knows: the future. He wants that with Lacey.

chapter
TWENTY-TWO

Lacey sits up in bed with a jolt and a gasp. Sunlight streams through the window. The sound of bustling conversation, the clatter of coffee cups filters in from the kitchen. The clock on the nightstand says nine a.m. Her eyes fly open with panic.

Shit. Shit. Shit.

It's not her room.

She glances beside her. Seth's burrowed boyishly into the blankets. Reaching out, she shakes his shoulder. "Seth. *Seth*." He raises his sleepy face. "I fell asleep," she hisses. "In your room."

His eyes widen slightly, and then a sly grin forms on his lips. "Wakin' up next to you ain't nothin' to be sorry about."

She harrumphs, refusing to let herself be charmed by his *aw, shucks* drawl and his big blue eyes. No, definitely not.

She slips out of bed. Seth's gaze goes laser-focused when he sees she's still in her lingerie. "This is serious, Seth. Now how am I going to sneak out of here?" She dips, grabbing up her black robe and cell phone, her mind calculating all the ways she can rejoin the group without attracting attention.

He props himself up on his elbow. His eyes snag on her bare skin. "Hey, Lace, you look goddamn gorgeous and if you put that robe back on, I'm gonna tear it off you."

She snorts. Then she lifts her chin, gives an *I dare you* smile, and slips on the robe. "Come and get me."

A feral hunger enters his face.

Seth lunges off the bed, headed straight for her.

Lacey yelps in delight. Dodging his grab, she snatches a pillow off the chair, launches it at him, and hops up on the bed, latching onto the bedpost for balance. Seth snags her sleeve, dragging one side of her robe off.

The knock on the door freezes them both.

Lacey gasps, shooting Seth a wide-eyed *what do we do?* look.

"Seth?" Luke's drawl floats. "You in there?"

Then Sal's gentler voice saying, "Maybe he went for a walk."

"It's Seth," Luke responds. "He don't do before noon."

Seth rolls his eyes at his big brother's remark, then yanks at the sleeve of her robe, tugging Lacey off the bed and into his arms. "Get in the closet," he whispers, setting her softly on her feet.

She glares at him. "I don't hide in closets, Seth."

He flashes a crooked grin. "You do today, princess." And then he's pushing her backwards, pressing a kiss to her lips and shoving Lacey and her robe into the closet.

"Ugh," she grumbles, hating that he's right. Sal and Luke finding her half-naked in Seth Kincaid's room wouldn't exactly be breaking the news gently.

Lacey presses herself back into the empty space of the closet, watching through the slats as Seth shrugs on a pair of jeans. With a quick hand, he plucks her panties from the floor. Lacey smothers a smile as he looks around and then shoves them in his back pocket. *So smooth.*

Seth swings open the door. "Damn, man," he says, scratching his bare chest. "Can't a guy get some shut-eye?"

Arcing a brow, Luke surveys Seth and scans the trashed room. "Bringin' back the ol' high school vibe?" He doesn't sound impressed.

Seth chuckles. "Got an image to live up to here, you know what I'm sayin'?"

"Yeah, well, while you're livin' it up, we're waitin' on the day …"

Lacey groans silently as the conversation continues. From her vantage point, she sees what Luke does. Spilled sheets, the bed crashed against the wall, Seth's dusty boots strewn across the room, pillows scattered. And oh God. The smell. Can he smell them?

Mortified, Lacey sinks to her feet, half-listening as Seth and Luke make plans. Instead, her eyes are on the phone in her hands. On the text Colin sent her last night. Saying he wanted to talk. What about, who knows? She itches to call him back, but she can't. Not now. Not here. She's got enough to worry about hiding her and Seth's relationship from Sal than get a dressing-down from Colin Cane. She can't deal with the old remnants of her LA life. Can't entertain the what-comes-next when she's trying hard as hell to enjoy the in-the-now.

Her home is in Los Angeles, but her heart's here with Seth. Which is a stupid idea. Because they're not there yet. Are they?

"Good news," Seth says, whipping open the closet door so fast she jumps. "You're goin' shoppin'."

She brightens. "Really?"

"Yep. Go get dressed." He reaches behind her, one hand slipping beneath the robe to cup the curve of her bare ass. "You're leavin' in half an hour."

She gasps. "I can't get ready in thirty minutes, Seth."

"You can today."

She gives him the finger and pushes past him, heading for the door.

"Lace?"

She whirls on him, hisses, "What?"

A warm grin from Seth. "You look really beautiful."

She scowls at him, at that damn smile that has her threatening to melt, and yanks the door open. She peeks her head out of the room.

Alabama Forester turns the corner of the hallway, already dressed for the day in a chunky knit sweater and leather leggings.

Shit.

Alabama freezes at the sight of Lacey in Seth's doorway.

Lacey grimaces and adjusts her robe. She has two options. Retreat or walk.

She walks.

Spine straight, Lacey exits Seth's room, chin held high as she strides down the hall. Fast. For the kitchen.

At the coffee bar, Lacey keeps a straight face as Alabama enters behind her. A tight tension fills the space.

"I reckon we both have the same idea," Alabama drawls, going straight for the coffee mugs.

"I guess so." Lacey pours herself a cup of coffee then steps away from the pot, freeing it up for Alabama. Praying she doesn't bring up what she just saw. She needs coffee first for that conversation, and if Prentiss were here, she'd steal a Xanax.

As she hunts in the fridge for some cream, Alabama's soft drawl floats. "Top left shelf."

Then— "I know you don't like me, Lacey," she says from the other side of the fridge.

Lacey shuts the door to meet Alabama's solemn gaze.

She sniffs. "I don't like what you did to my sister. Or Luke."

"I understand. And I agree with you." She shakes her red head, guilt creasing her pretty features. "Sometimes I still ain't sure how Sal can forgive me."

Lacey dunks a dollop of cream in her coffee, refusing to be swayed. She leans back against the counter. "Because that's Sal." Pride swells in her. "My sister's the best."

"She is." Alabama reaches across her for the cream. "Which is why, even if you don't like me, I hope we can at least get along. For Sal."

Lacey considers the thought. The door held open to something between her and Alabama. At the very least, a defrosting.

Before she can respond, Sal's in the kitchen, dressed in running gear: tennis shoes, leggings and a navy hoodie hugging her belly. Beside her, Winston trots, his nose hoovering across the kitchen floor for scraps. Sal smiles at Alabama, says to Lacey, "Where've you been? I've been looking everywhere for you."

Lacey's throat tightens. She looks down into her coffee like it can give her an answer. "Oh, uh, I—"

"We were checkin' out the pool on the lower level," Alabama offers.

"You were?" Sal looks surprised. Surprised, but pleased.

"You could get lost in this place," Lacey adds weakly, glancing toward Alabama. The woman's face neutral. Betraying nothing.

"I'm going for a run." Sal lifts her brows. "Any takers?"

Alabama laughs. "Good lord, Sal, this is a vacation."

"She's right," Lacey adds. "That's sadistic."

Sal chuckles. "So, I take it that's two no's?" Her eyes land on Lacey. "When I get back, I thought we could go shopping in town. Grab some last-minute gifts, have lunch?"

Lacey perks up. "Sounds great."

"Not me," Alabama says. "I'm draggin' Griff to a spa."

Sal laughs. "I want pictures of that."

Lacey wiggles her fingers at Sal. "Have fun, Rocky."

Sal strides for the deck, Winston click-clacking on her heels. "Go get ready, sleepyhead," she tosses back at Lacey. "I swear, between you and Seth . . ."

Heat rushes up Lacey's neck, but Sal's already gone.

Alabama meets Lacey's stare over her cup of coffee.

"Thanks." It's meager and grudging, but it's all she has.

"For what?" Alabama asks with a shrug and a polite smile.

But Lacey knows she knows. And if she knows, who else does?

chapter
TWENTY-THREE

FROM HIS VANTAGE POINT ON THE BALCONY, SETH watches in silence as two hawks glide through the crisp winter air. Clouds that loom like smoke swirl over the mountains. The sparkling waters of the lake shine bright below.

At the sound of the sliding door, he turns to see Lacey exiting. She shivers at the chill in the air. She's in boots, ripped jeans, and to his amusement, a camo hoodie.

Seth arcs a brow. "Camo?"

She blushes. Then lifts her chin. "Oh, I'm going country. And next time, I'm gonna put on some bluegrass," she drawls in a hokey twang, "while I whip up some peach cobbler."

Seth laughs.

Lacey steps forward in wonder, stopping beside him at the railing, her gaze on the mountains in front of her. "Oh my God, Seth," she breathes.

"Most amazin' place in the world." He grins, unable to tear his eyes from her delighted face. "Call me biased."

She turns to him, angling her body to his. "It is amazing. I love it here."

Her honest reaction has his heart flipping over. He and Lacey—they've both showed each other the places they love best in the world. The beach, the Smoky Mountains. This is what it's about. Learning about each other. Lacey loves the place. And he loves her at this place. In Tennessee.

With him.

His eyes drift to the lake, a thin icy frost coating its surface. "Bet you wish that was the ocean."

"No way." She feigns a shiver but arches a brow. "Bet I could surf it, though."

He chuckles. "Better not."

Lacey groans and he follows her gaze. Down in the backyard, acres and acres of frozen land and firepits, Sal's running up a steep incline next to the lake. "Sal's seven months pregnant and can still scale a hill better than me."

"Which reminds me." Lacey turns to him, her face harried. "We're caught. Alabama, she saw me this morning doing the walk of shame back to my room."

Seth blinks. "That was fast."

Good, he thinks. *It's about damn time.* After last night, he's far from happy keeping their relationship under wraps. He wants to talk about her like Luke talks about Sal, tell everyone she's his, kiss her down by the water without worrying who sees. It's goddamn agony, is what it is.

But he knows they need to tell Sal first. Which is one reason it's taking so long. They're chickenshits. If he hurts Sal . . . if this ruins their relationship . . .

Christ. The thought turns his stomach into a pit.

"We have to amp up the hatred."

Startled out of his thoughts, Seth looks to Lacey. "I never hated you, Lace."

Lacey's green eyes slide away from his. "Well, that makes one of us."

"Wait, what? When?" His grin toys the line between amusement and consternation.

She tucks a lock of hair behind her ear. Gives an Oscar-worthy eye roll. "You were Sal's best friend, and you had fantastic hair and impeccable eyelashes. What's not to hate?"

Seth grins. "I mean, I am kinda a heartthrob."

Lacey rolls her eyes. "Ugh, you are insufferable."

A beat, and then Luke's exiting onto the balcony and—

Lacey slaps him.

It's light, barely a graze, but Seth stands there blinking in confusion.

"And that's for using my La Mer moisturizer without asking," Lacey huffs before whirling on her heel and storming off.

"Fuck," Seth breathes, half-terrified, half-turned on.

Luke sighs at Lacey's retreating form. "What's with her?"

Seth exhales. "Lacey's just being Lacey."

Luke opens his mouth to reply but then swears. He leans over the railing, calling down to Sal, who's making her way up the slick back porch stairs. "Go slow, Sal. I don't want you slippin'." He looks at Seth. "I swear, she's gonna give me a heart attack."

Seth laughs. "She's doin' her job. Keepin' you on your toes."

Luke nods, then says, "We playin' today?"

Seth cracks a grin. "Hell yeah."

"Cool. I think the girls are headed into town, so we got the place to ourselves till the gig tonight."

"Beau comin'?"

Luke's smile fades. "Not yet. Tonight." He steps close to Seth and claps him on the shoulder. In a low voice, he says, "Listen, the guy gets to me, so don't let him get to you. One of us needs to not get arrested for murder."

"Now I can't wait to meet him," Seth says wryly. He can't tell if Luke's joking or not. "What's he do, turn into a gremlin after midnight?"

"Somethin' like that," Luke says, wary.

"You talkin' trash, country boy?" Sal's husky voice hits them both as she makes her way onto the balcony.

Luke's previously tense expression lightens about a thousand watts. "You caught me, darlin.'"

Sal gives Luke a flirty little smile and Luke's expression turns hangdog as he follows her into the house, his tongue practically dragging on the floor.

Seth can't help but laugh. His brother's a damn lovesick fool. Not like he's much better himself when it comes to Lacey.

He's about to join them inside when his phone buzzes. He pulls it from his back pocket. Stares at the screen. An LA number.

Graham, he thinks and picks up. "Hello?"

He listens to the voice on the other end of the line, braces his hand on the back of his neck in disbelief, and then smiles. "How fuckin' fast can you get here?"

An hour later, Seth finds the studio Luke set up. It's on the lower floor, sandwiched between an indoor pool and a game room. The room is massive, filled with a piano, a bar, and a long boardroom-like table.

Scanning the instruments, leaned up gently against the wall, Seth feels a surge of excitement. Another one. He's still high on the phone call from earlier this morning. The pawnshop kid got Lacey's necklace in. Tonight, the guy's on a first-class ticket out here; Seth ain't trusting the mail. He wants to give it to her for Christmas. The pawnshop kid got a look at the guy too, and Seth's hoping it's only a matter of time before Lacey's mugger is caught.

Seth drifts, settling himself at the long table. Notepads, pencils fanned out across it.

Palming a notepad, he slides it his way. It's instinct to write. The song, a song from what seems like so long ago—the night of Lacey's party—held vibrating in his head all this damn time.

Like a vow.

Like some sort of confession.

Seth starts scribbling.

> It always was one hell of a time,
> Till I got a case of them ol' Tennessee blues
> Broken, beat until you stomped across my heart
> With the ice-cold tip of your high-heeled shoe
> But then you leaned down
> Girl, the dip of your lips to mine
> I still don't think I've ever felt more damn alive

> What's the point of this ol' life
> If we don't do it together
> Because, girl, I'm needin' you, needin' you, needin' you now
> Needin' you now and forever

One line, then two. It comes like instinct. Automatic and trancelike. Before he knows it, he has a song. Rough, raw, but it's there.

"Fuck," he swears when he reads it over, realization dawning. It's about Lacey.

He wrote a goddamn song about Lacey.

Of course he did. She put the beat back in his chest. She's got him fucked up, heart on his sleeve, on his knees. Got herself stuck like a damn melody in his head and the only way to get her out is to write.

Groaning, he puts the notepad down and buries his face in his hands. Hell, he's as bad as Luke.

At the crack of the door, Seth glances up. Luke and Jace saunter in, a case of beer in Jace's hand. The lift of their brows tells Seth they're surprised he's already there.

"Seth Kincaid, gettin' a head start on practice," Jace drawls. "Never thought I'd see the day."

"Hey, Luke's the real overachiever," Seth says. "Settin' up a gig while we're on vacation. Damn shame, man."

Luke grins. "Can't get rusty." He strides for his guitar, picking it up and dropping onto a stool. "We gotta crank out the album after the new year." He shakes his head, a hint of irritation sideswiping his cheerful tone. "I hate rushin' it."

Seth swallows as he's hit by a guilty reminder that this is all his fuckin' fault. Recording with famed producer Devlon Block is a gigantic leap for the band, and they wouldn't be behind if he hadn't started that damn bar fight. If he hadn't taken his sweet-ass time out in California.

"We got all the songs," Jace says, ever the steady presence. "We'll get it done, man."

Luke nods, his alert eyes falling on Seth's notepad. "Whatcha got?"

"Nothin', it's—"

But it's too late. Luke's standing, sliding the notepad toward him, his gaze scanning the lyrics as Jace reads over his shoulder.

"It's good," Luke says when he's finished. A smile tugs at his lips. "Who's it for?"

Seth scowls. He should have hidden that damn song the second the two of them walked in. Leave it to Luke to laser in on the whole love angle. "No one. It's just a song."

Jace snorts. "That ain't just a song, man. You don't write a song like that without inspiration." He grins. "You meet someone pretty out in LA, Seth?"

Seth glowers, hating him.

Only Luke's quiet, watching him close, curious.

Seth slaps down a pencil. "We gonna get to work or bust my balls all day?"

Luke's smile reappears. His brother's back. His band's here. "Let's fire it up," he says, strumming a couple chords to kick them off.

The Brothers Kincaid work the rest of the afternoon, furiously pitching album titles, jamming out, scribbling the last few songs they need for the album. Finally, around three p.m. they call it quits.

Luke gives a wild hoot.

Seth grins at his brother. "I think we got it, don't you?"

Leaning back in his chair, Luke stretches his long legs out. "Now all we gotta do is record it."

Seth roves his tired eyes around the scribbled notes and lyrics. The scattered beer cans and instruments. Balancing his fiddle on his knee, he laughs. "Nothin' like makin' it a workin' vacation."

"Yeah, Emmy Lou's thrilled," Jace says dryly.

A look from Luke. "Everything okay with Em?"

Jace's face fills with longing at the mention of his wife. "Better than." He hesitates on saying more, then settles for a sip of his beer. "We really needed this, is all. We're finally gettin' back to it. Back to us."

Luke raises his beer. "Good, man, I'm glad to hear it."

Jace stands, his phone in his hands. "I'm gonna get. Me and Em are tryin' to get some alone time in before we head out tonight."

Luke nods. "Good idea."

Silence falls as Jace makes his way out of the room.

"I'm glad they're doin' better," Luke says, his gaze on the door Jace's just exited.

"Yeah," Seth agrees. Jace and Emmy Lou had been in a tough place after his gambling had almost lost them their farm and horse sanctuary. "Good for them." He gestures at the notepads scribbled with songs. "And good for fuckin' us."

With a tired groan, Luke stands, drumming his hands on the table. He's hesitating, wanting to say something, but worried about how to say it.

Seth sighs, shooting him a look. "I ain't plannin' on leavin' the band, Luke. If that's what you're wonderin.'"

Luke looks surprised but relieved. "What changed?"

"I worked out whatever I had goin' on in California."

Luke nods slowly. "I'm glad, Seth. Playin' without you has been some real bullshit."

Seth laughs, his nerves untensing at his brother's words. "Damn straight."

Luke's dark eyes land on Seth's notepad. "It's a hell of a song."

"Thanks." His grin is a beam. Luke's approval means everything. He still feels like that same young kid playing on the front porch, his big brother beside him, telling him he had never seen someone like Seth on the fiddle.

Luke pauses. Then—

"It about Lacey?"

The question lands between them like a bomb.

Seth blinks at his brother, stunned. Caught. He should have known better than to think he could hide it from Luke. They've been in tune since they were kids—this ain't anything different. Seth blows out a breath. "You know?"

Luke chuckles. "Oh yeah. Lacey would have put a lot more power into that slap."

"Shit." Seth runs a hand through his hair, worried. "Sal?"

"Not her. She's too busy worryin' about Lacey, the baby, wantin' everyone to have fun." He angles his head, his dark eyes on Seth. "How long?"

"The last three years."

Luke's eyes widen.

Seth exhales, his heart tightening. "I love her. I love her so goddamn much, Luke."

Saying the words aloud, admitting them to his brother, feels good. Feels right. So damn right. It's like a weight lifted, an intention made clear. At least it's one more secret he's not keeping from Luke.

This time it's Luke's turn to blink. He rocks back on his boots, processing the news. His little brother, ever the bachelor, in love. A genuine smile crosses his face. "Really?"

"Really."

"She know that?"

"Not yet."

"Okay, then." Luke's smile fades, his face becoming serious. He levels a finger at Seth. "You gotta be the one to tell Sal. Not me."

"I know," he says, trying to rein in his guilt that Luke would think he'd put this on him. "We were waitin' for the right time . . ."

Luke raises dark brows. "Soon, Seth."

"I will." He meets his brother's eyes. "She gonna kill me?"

"Honestly . . ." Luke shakes his head grimly and Seth's stomach sinks. "I ain't sure."

THE SILVER DOLLAR SALOON IS THE LONE BAR CLOSEST to the cabin. But it's been Seth and Luke's hangout joint whenever they came up to this neck of the woods. Down home, familiar, the Brothers Kincaid never pass up a chance to play here. It's low-key, chill, and has them remembering their roots. Dive bars. Honkytonks. Tips in buckets.

The group enters the bar to dueling jukeboxes and buzzing neon lights. A long high-top table awaits, the reserved sign staking their claim. The bartenders wear elf hats and sling drinks with reckless precision.

After getting their instruments settled onstage, the group gathers around the table. Sal, Luke, Griff and Alabama on one side; Lacey, Seth, Jace and Emmy Lou on the other.

"Have we ever been here before?" Sal asks Luke in a low tone as she surveys the bar for familiar surroundings.

Luke's eyes go soft in that way they do whenever he answers one of her questions about the past. "A few times, darlin.'"

"Busy for Christmas Eve Eve," Emmy Lou observes.

"Everyone wants to party," Alabama murmurs.

Griff nuzzles her hair. "We should be doin' that too."

An exaggerated sigh fills the air.

Seth turns.

Lacey, wearing a giant white parka with fur trim on the hood, is trying to slide onto a stool.

"Jesus Christ," Seth says, grinning. "Can you fit behind the table in that thing?"

"Shut it, Seth." With a little harrumph, she gives up the fight and slips off her parka.

Seth's jaw drops, immediately regretting his harassment. Immediately going hard in his pants. He grips the table, his eyes on her tan legs, on her itty-bitty dress. His voice drops to a whisper. "Holy shit. Put the coat back on."

The glint in her narrowed eyes says *baby, it's payback.*

"Here, Sal," Lacey says loudly, reaching across the table just enough so that her dress rides up, exposing toned, tan thigh. "I'll take your jacket."

Sticking her tongue out at Seth without missing a beat, Lacey walks herself over to the coatrack. As Seth slips onto a stool beside Jace, he can't do anything but stare.

He ain't never seen anything hotter. Lacey, her hair teased wild, wears a ruffled denim minidress that doesn't fit the bar, that's out of place, but that's Lacey. That's his Lacey, and he fucking loves it. Hell, he doesn't know how he's gonna control himself tonight. That dress is doing things to his brain. Crazy, overheated things. He's got no patience for keeping his hands off her.

Apparently, no one's got patience. Because he sees them—every cowboy in the bar is tracking Lacey. Their eyes hungry, just like his. Some beautiful, blond, hip-swiveling target. But it don't matter—he ain't jealous, because he's the one who's with her.

He's the one taking her home tonight, and if he has his way, every night after.

A chirp of a voice scatters his thoughts. "Why are you gazin' at Lacey?" Emmy Lou's peering at him, owl-eyed.

He scowls. "I ain't gazin.'"

Jace cocks a brow. "Sure looked like gazin' to me."

"Hey, Jace, shut the fuck up."

Lacey struts back to the table, taking a seat beside Seth. She gives him a satisfied smirk and all he can do is chuckle. "You enjoy that?"

"Very much."

Beneath the table, he slides a hand up her bare thigh. Lacey stiffens slightly, then relaxes, looping her pinkie around his. A soft smile on her pretty face, betraying nothing to Sal, who sits across from her.

A waitress appears, dropping beers and shots of apple pie moonshine on the table.

Luke pounds the table, leaning over to kiss Sal's temple. "Let's get our good time on."

Seth cackles, glad to see his brother so carefree for once. Luke had a few back at the house, they all did, which had everyone buzzy and bright before the driver picked them up. "Think I'm flashin' back to the early years of the Brothers Kincaid," he quips to Jace.

Griff tucks his lank blond hair behind his ears. "Now that's somethin' I'd like to see."

"Picture Jace with a mullet and a PBR and you're golden," Emmy Lou says, and everyone laughs.

"If we're gonna do it," Griff says, his eyes glowing with mischief, "tonight's the night to drink until we're seein' double."

Alabama laughs. "Oh, you're gonna be fun later."

Sal raises her water and smiles. "We should toast."

To Seth's surprise, Lacey leads it, her smile a bright beam of happy. "To drinks, to friends, to damn good times that never end."

Luke's hoot of agreement echoes off the walls around them.

Seth squeezes Lacey's hand beneath the table, and she squeezes back.

Everyone nods, lifting their glasses and clinking sides. Laughter rings out, boisterous as shots are downed and more ordered. That's when Seth sees Luke's face. He ain't laughing. Not anymore.

The table suddenly falls quiet.

Seth glances over his shoulder to see what's soured the mood.

Beau Dallas stands in the doorway, brushing snow off his jean jacket. Seth surveys him. The guy who's taken his place, who has his brother on edge. He's tall and lean, with a jet-black pompadour, a fiddle tattooed on his forearm, and in his hands, he carries a fiddle case.

Jace throws a warning glance at Luke. "We still got three weeks left, man."

Luke takes a bracing breath, turning to Sal, who's staring up at him. A slight frown mars her brow. She's confused by her husband's reaction. Seth gets it. He's never seen Luke this tense.

Beau heads over, hands outstretched. "Oh, Lawdy," he crows, evaluating the company. "Looks like a couple of beautiful women and a couple of assholes. Am I right?"

Lacey rolls her eyes.

Luke nods, his expression dark. "Beau."

Seth hides a smirk. His brother looks like he wants to hunt the guy for sport.

Beau pulls the end seat out between Lacey and Sal but doesn't sit, instead preferring to stand. From the inside of his jacket pocket, he unveils a beer. Luke and Jace are unfazed but alert, telling Seth this isn't the first time he's done this.

"Lemme see, lemme see, lemme see y'all," Beau drawls, setting his beer on the table. His eyes, his finger swivel to Seth. "You're Seth? The one who left the band?"

Luke stiffens.

Seth crosses his arms. He's not giving this asshole a handshake. He keeps his voice cool, casual. "Ain't exactly like that seein' as how you're gone in a couple of weeks, but yeah, I'm Seth."

Beau shakes off the dig. Either uncaring or unnoticed.

"Hey." Beau peers at Sal beside him. "This the wife?" His eyes flick to Luke.

"This is Sal," Luke grits out, wrapping a protective arm around her shoulder.

"'Bout damn time we get to meet!" Beau crows, leaning down on his elbows to survey Sal, whose expression is amused. "How's your brain, beautiful?"

The entire table tenses.

Luke's jaw is tight, his eyes dangerous. Every single one of them ready to protect Sal. Her brain, her injury off-limits, especially to nosy assholes like Beau.

Lacey makes a little sound in the back of her throat, clamping down tight on Seth's hand.

Sal's eyes widen in surprise at the question, and then she recovers. Smooth as only Sal can do. "My brain is fine. What's the matter with your mouth?"

"Oh my fuckin' God," Griff cackles, pounding the table.

Beau's face reddens, but then he's turning his attention to his left. To Lacey.

Seth's teeth clench.

Beau looks like he just struck gold. The guy stares at Lacey. At her breasts. At her lips. He cocks his head. "Why, you're outstandin', angel. What's your name?"

The withering look she gives him could crush an egg. "Lacey."

"Well, Lacey, how 'bout I get that number of yours in my phone?"

Lacey sniffs. Loudly. "I know I'm cute and I have great skin. But I live in LA. It would never last."

Beau grins. "Ain't needin' it to last. Just need it for a night."

That's fuckin' it.

Seth stands, ready to throw down, but he's beat by Sal.

Sal slams her drink on the table and everyone jumps. "Hey, Beau," she says, as icy as Lacey's ever been. "That's my sister, and that's enough."

Her eyes snap to Luke as if to say she will kill this man dead if he keeps talking.

"Whoa, okay. Easy, beautiful." Beau draws back, holding up his hands in defense. His eyes drift down. His lips curl up. "You sure you only got one baby in there?"

"Sweet Jesus," Jace mutters, covering his face with a broad palm.

"Shut the fuck *up,*" Luke snarls.

Lacey rockets up, crossing over to Sal, Beau's eyes following her as she walks. "I am taking my sister and we are getting drinks."

She hooks her arm through Sal's, dragging her out of her seat and across the bar.

"Good idea," Emmy Lou says, giving Beau a nasty glare before following the girls.

"Get him onstage, shut him up," Griff says in a low voice to Luke. "Then get him the fuck out of here."

Luke swallows his beer and stands. "Let's get this thing goin.'" His eyes land on Seth. "You get up there for the last set."

At this, Beau scoffs. "Hey, no way. We have a contract." And then he puts a hand out like he can stop Seth. It's a bad move. One that has Luke's face darkening like a storm cloud. His brother's hard to anger, but when he gets there, he's gone.

"I don't give a good goddamn what we have," Luke snaps, and the table falls silent. Beside Seth, Jace is wincing. Luke's tone is dangerous, clear he's done playing nice. "It's my band, and it's my brother, and he's playin.'"

Beau gives a one-shouldered shrug, says nothing, taking it on the chin as he, Luke and Jace make for the stage. But Seth doesn't miss the look Beau's giving him. A look that says this ain't over.

Griff looses a breath. "Kincaid's scary when he's pissed off."

"It's a real shame," Alabama says, watching as Beau tunes his fiddle. "Pissin' all that talent away."

Seth throws her a lazy smile. "If your first instinct ain't to shoot the guy, you're doin' it wrong."

Griff laughs. "Hell, if that ain't the truth." He scrubs the back of his head. "I don't remember Beau actin' like this before."

"You ever think because you acted just like him?" Alabama ventures gently.

Griff blinks. Seth's surprised when he nods, his scarred face contemplating his reckless past. A past Beau's still living. "Maybe. I reckon."

Alabama slips off her chair, kissing Griff's cheek. "I'm gonna join the girls."

Seth leans back on his stool, watching Beau tune his fiddle. His game face on now that he's onstage.

It's easy to see why Luke has a problem with the guy. In the music business, they've known too many musicians like Beau. Desperate party guys from hell, trying to work their way into the right band when they've been at the grind for years. Only, instead of working hard for it, they treat the music like a frat party.

Griff's languid drawl has Seth glancing over. "He hit on Alabama too, you know."

Seth gapes. "You're married."

"Yeah. And he knows it."

"Fuckin' asshole," Seth says, wrapping a hand around his beer. He never thought he and Greyson would be here, bonding in their shared annoyance of Beau. The guy keeps taking asshole of the year every time he opens his mouth.

"You're doin' an awful job," Griff says, leaning in to rest his tattooed forearms on the table. His expression amused. "You and Lacey—pretendin' you hate each other."

Seth groans, smearing a hand down his face. He's two for two here. "You know?"

"It ain't hard." Griff swallows his beer and grins. "Me and Al . . . we did the same thing, tryin' to hide it."

"And how'd that work out?"

"It's workin' itself out," Griff says with a soft glance at Alabama. "Goddamn perfect. Every damn day."

Seth cuts his eyes toward Lacey, at her beautiful face and laughing smile, the very sight of her soaring through his heart like a song.

"When you find it, hold it tight." Griff gives him a pointed look. "Like real damn tight."

Lacey palms the drink the bartender slides her way, a tequila soda, and shifts her attention to Sal. Her sister stands with arms crossed, her eyes bright with irritation.

It's both amusing and concerning to see her sister so riled up. Sal's usually calm. Lacey's always the basket case.

"Sal?" Lacey wraps an arm around her shoulders. "You okay?"

"That guy is an ass," Sal says, lifting her drink to her lips and taking a big gulp. No doubt wishing it was alcohol.

"Oh, sugar, you're tellin' me." Emmy Lou presses a hand to her heart, her big brown eyes wide. "That was all kinds of awkward."

"Try awful," Alabama adds. She peers closely at Sal's shaking hands. "Don't let him upset you, Sal."

Alabama's fierce worry on her sister's behalf has Lacey's icy heart thawing. It's real—their friendship. She truly cares about Sal, and to Lacey that's all that matters.

Lacey nods. "Alabama's right. That little baby in there needs rest and relaxation."

"I'm fine." Sal lets out a great sigh and places a hand on her stomach. "Beau's not ruining this vacation. I won't let him."

Throughout the bar, the sound of strings and Luke's warm voice ring out. Lacey watches her sister's face soften, the sight of her husband like a balm.

Emmy Lou glances over at Seth and Griff, surprisingly in deep conversation. "Well, look at them, behavin' like civilized adults."

"Good." Alabama plucks the olive out of her martini and eats it. "Let 'em talk. God knows they need it."

The women settle onto barstools as the Brothers Kincaid kick off their first song, "Holy Roller." Lacey's eyes drift to Seth, not wanting him to feel left out of his band, but the easy smile on his face tells her otherwise.

Not even Beau's jackass antics can get her down. She's having a great time, finally fitting in, having fun. For once in her life, letting her guard down and enjoying. And today, she spent the day with her sister. Just the two of them, shopping in town, having lunch. Not to mention she found the perfect Christmas gift for Seth at a small bookshop. She hopes he loves it.

"Whoo, look at Luke, y'all," Emmy Lou drawls. "Playin' angry."

"Think he's imaginin' that guitar's Beau's neck," Alabama murmurs.

Sal snorts. "If only."

They all watch for a beat.

A shrug from Sal. "I have to admit. Beau's good."

"Yeah, onstage," Alabama says. "Too bad he lacks manners, boundaries, social graces everywhere else."

Emmy Lou leans over, eager to make conversation. "How long you in Tennessee, Lacey?"

Lacey, feeling Sal's eyes on her, says, "I'm not sure. I'm pretty much jobless, so I probably should get back on the hunt as soon as I can . . ."

"Shoot," Alabama says, understanding on her face. "That's rough."

"But . . ." Lacey swivels on her barstool, spine straight, an idea suddenly coming to her. "What if I come back to Nashville first?" she asks Sal. "Give you a baby shower while I'm out here."

Sal's eyes light up. "Really?" She clutches Lacey's hand. "God, anything to keep you here a little longer."

Lacey moves her eyes to Alabama. She takes a breath, inhaling courage. Friendliness. "I'm not from Nashville, so if you have time . . ."

Alabama's mouth falls open at the offer. Then she recovers, smiles. "Yeah. I'd love that, Lacey."

Emmy Lou claps her hands together.

The bartender appears with three tequila shots and a pink drink that looks like a Shirley Temple. "Gentleman sent 'em over." He nods at Griff, who's grinning at them wickedly.

Lacey smiles, taking the shot. "Think he wants us to get in trouble."

Alabama smirks. "With Griff, trouble is a given." She shoots back the shot and then grins. "Oh Lord, we got one."

Lacey follows Alabama's finger. A woman in a cowboy hat is doing a slow sway all by herself at the front of the stage.

The women are smiling, in on some inside joke she isn't. Sal, seeing Lacey's confusion, speaks up. "Fans. Groupies." She arches a brow. "Girls."

Emmy Lou downs her tequila. "Think she's 'bout to crawl up Luke's boot any damn second."

But Sal just smiles, content.

A pit grows in Lacey's stomach.

Seth's a country star. She always knew that, but now . . . he's hers. Soon they'll be back in the real world, and he'll be on the road. She should know the drill. But she never considered what she'd be in for if they did this relationship thing.

Lacey scowls. But why is she even worrying about this? They're not permanent. They haven't even discussed how to make this work.

If it'll work.

She tries to ignore the pang of worry rushing through her. Are they too much too soon? Or is she just trying to talk herself out of something good because she fears losing it?

"Lace?"

She startles at the voice, turns to Sal. Her sister's brow is wrinkled. "You okay?"

"Fine. Just . . . embracing the alcohol."

Sal chuckles.

She wishes she could talk to her sister about Seth. To see if she's doing the right thing. Sal's always been her voice of reason, her confidante, and not to tell her this . . . it sucks.

"How do you do it?" Lacey leans in. "All those girls all over Luke? Doesn't it bother you?"

Sal thinks on it. "I never worry. He always comes home to me." Her lips curve up. "And I'm right there with him. On the bus. Or backstage."

Picking up on the conversation, Emmy Lou waves a hand. "Ooo, not me, sugar. I ain't cut out for the bus. Let me tell you, the first couple of years was awful. Jace was travelin' all the time. The press like a mosquito, always buzzin' . . ." Her sympathetic brown eyes land on Sal and Alabama. "You either can't do nothin' right or you gotta play the perfect wife."

Alabama lifts her shot. "Amen."

Lacey looks away, undone. Emmy Lou's words have ripped a hole of doubt in her a mile wide. Her heart pounding against her ribs, she leans back against the bar and orders another round of shots. She needs something to take the edge off. All kinds of vulnerable emotions are surfacing inside, and she doesn't like it. Not one bit.

Lacey looks over at the stage, watching as Seth hops up in time for the finale finish. His back is to her as he talks to his band, all cool confidence and charisma.

She shoots back the shot, breathing through the sting. She aches to feel steady. But there's nothing steady about this at all.

TWENTY-FIVE

STANDING ON A SMALL CORNER OF THE STAGE, SETH tunes his fiddle as Luke steps up to the mic, telling a story in his languid drawl about the last time they played at the Silver Dollar Saloon, and thanking the audience for being great as always.

"I don't know if you can handle this," Beau says from Seth's right. His eyes gleam. "Especially since I've been kickin' ass as the Brothers Kincaid's new fiddle player."

Seth rolls his eyes. The guy's arrogant and an asshole. A combination that annoys him to no end. Listening to this jackass talk makes Seth want to punch himself in the face.

He blows out a breath and focuses on his fiddle. Ignores Beau. He's pissed they're stuck with this guy—the Debbie Downer of the hour. Pissing off Luke, harassing the girls, talking bullshit. He's trying not to let Beau get to him, but it's damn hard.

A wolf whistle from Beau. "Ooh boy, get a load of this."

Seth's spine locks up when he sees where Beau's gaze is lasered. Lacey. Her long, tan legs. She's leaving the bar with Sal, headed to the dance floor.

"She's seein' someone," Seth snaps, irritation and anger curdling in his stomach.

Beau snorts. "That's what they all say. Blah, blah, blah, and then two minutes later you're bangin' 'em." He grins. "Women love when you chase 'em."

A flare of primal protection rolls through Seth. He clenches his fist. He opens his mouth to tell the asshole that the only thing he's going to be chasing is an ice pack, when the strum of Luke's guitar jars him. Seth grits his teeth and pulls his head out of his ass.

He turns to his brother.

Luke's grinning. Their eyes meet, the song passes between them, and then, missing nothing, they each jump in on their part. One of their favorite songs to play, "Never More True" is a fast-paced folk-rock song he and Luke wrote back in their early days on the porch.

Gripping the mic, Luke belts out, "Oh my darlin', howdy do? Because tonight, we're never gonna be more true. Gonna get drunk, a little Jack, a little Jim. It's Saturday night, damn sure might bet on a win."

Seth wheels around onstage. His deep rumble, the frenzied saw of his fiddle, makes the crowd come alive. "Gonna spin you around that hardwood floor, and when the music stops, we'll make some more. Never gonna get more true, baby, me and you. Oh my, darlin', let's swing along and chase away these ol' blues . . ."

With Jace practically splitting the strings on the bass, Seth and Luke's voices blend boisterously. Their groove onstage, their brotherhood, found. Their bond solid. As they play, Beau and his bullshit forgotten, it's just Seth and Luke. Like they're kids again on their front porch. Luke teaching him the chords, Seth eager-eyed and earnest, wanting to make his brother proud. In sync.

Always.

Seth wraps up the song with a frenetic fiddle solo, scanning the crowd in front of him. Lacey dances with Sal, her eyes on him, a bright smile on her face. Laughing and joyful. The only fan he wants.

What should be two more songs turns into five, Griff Greyson joining in during the set, and then the Brothers Kincaid are done. High as hell. Ready to keep the night going.

As they climb offstage, Luke claps Seth on the shoulder. "Think you coulda played that song standin' on your head."

Seth gives him a cocky grin. "I don't know, man. Took some real cardio to keep up with you."

The group converges at the high-top. Emmy Lou and Jace hit the dance floor; so do Alabama and Griff, Luke and Sal. Only Beau hangs back on the sidelines, pounding a beer and scanning the bar with an even expression.

Lacey approaches Seth, almost shyly. "You were wonderful, Seth," she says, staring at him with heavy-lidded eyes. He fights a smile. She's tipsy. Damn near adorable.

"Everyone else is dancin'." Seth holds out a hand. "Might as well."

Lacey scoffs. But her eyes are soft. "Fine."

Taking her hand, Seth spins her on the dance floor. The jukebox cranks out a fast, hip-swiveling number that Lacey is clearly feeling. The hem of her denim dress kicks up as she dances and twirls along with the music. Seth hangs back and just watches. Love-stunned.

Damn, that girl can dance.

And kiss.

And kill him with kindness.

Goddamn.

Seth's heart clenches. Lacey gets him higher than a great song, a cold beer, prime weed. There's something about her he just can't stay away from.

The music switches over to a slow ballad. Slowly, Lacey moves back toward him, her eyes all kinds of *should we do this?*, and yeah, yeah, they should.

Seth takes her in his arms.

"Are you drunk?" he asks, fighting the urge to kiss her.

A cute little half smile lifts her lips. "I don't have to tell you a thing."

"So that's a yes." He pulls her closer, craving the feel of her body in his arms. "A very strong yes."

She looks up at him with big ocean-green eyes, scattering his thoughts. "You were so great onstage, Seth. Here and in LA. You're amazing."

Her words send a jolt of happiness zipping through every

fiber of his being. He's never had this with a woman. Support. Comfort. Friendship.

But before he can say anything, Lacey slants her slender body into him. "I told Sal I'd give her a shower before I head back to Los Angeles. What do you think?"

His body goes cold. Any talk about her returning to LA has him spinning out. Thinking about leaving her, ever losing her, has Seth's heart in a knot.

Christ. How'd he get here? Loving this girl so damn much, his heart aches. Turning into a slavering fool at the very nearness of her.

He's gotta fix this. Gotta do something.

But she's waiting for him to answer her about the shower, so he grins and says, "It's a great idea, Lace. You're gonna give her one hell of a shower."

Lacey wets her lips and slides a hand up around his shoulder. Her graceful touch like tinder, like temptation, lighting up every single cell in his body.

He stares down at her, wondering, impatient.

It would be easy to end it. Everyone already knows. Just kiss Lacey. Right here on the dance floor. Shut down any doubt, be honest about how he feels, really feels, tell the world and everyone watching that she's his.

That he loves her.

But the music's stopped.

And they're still dancing. Lacey curled in his arms, against his chest.

They realize it at the same time.

Seth tenses as Lacey turns to stone in his arms. She glances over his shoulder to find Sal watching them. Her eyes wide, horrified, she rips out of his arms. Her lower lip pushes out, flustered in that cute way that drives him crazy. Worked up as only Lacey can do.

With a gasp, she whirls away from him, breaking their contact.

"I have to use the bathroom," she says, before she turns and rushes off, the click-clack of her heels swallowed up by the next song.

Her dramatic exit makes him smile. Seth heads to the bar to wait when a matter-of-fact voice says, "Held on a little too long."

Seth turns to Beau, who's swaggering up beside him. "You got a problem with that?"

"I don't." Beau shrugs. "Someone might." His eyes move to Sal, at the other end of the bar talking to Alabama.

Motherfucker.

Fire boils Seth's veins. Messing with Sal, messing with Lacey ain't happening.

Seth meets Beau's eyes. Stares him down. "That ain't a smart idea."

Beau's grin is broad, satisfied. "She's a gorgeous girl. You ain't claimin' that out loud, then I can't help what I do, can I?"

It's a threat. Beau's looking to fight, to rile him up.

And it's working.

Seth's teeth clench and he takes a step toward Beau. But it's not jealousy rising up. It's not the realization that he doesn't want anyone else, and he doesn't want Lacey to be with anyone else. That the thought of Lacey kissing some other guy has him fucking sick to his stomach. It's more than all those things combined. Something primal. Protective. Some guy creeping on Lacey after she's been mugged isn't what she needs right now. She needs to feel safe, and Beau ain't safe.

"Everything okay?"

Sal's soft voice jolts Seth out of his staredown with Beau. She's giving the two of them a curious look.

Seth forces a grin. He extends an arm, drawing Sal close to him and away from Beau. "All good here. Beau was just leavin'."

Beau's face darkens at being handed his exit. But instead of saying anything, he slaps his hands on the thighs of his jeans. "I'll be seein' y'all around." He tips an imaginary hat to Sal. "Ma'am."

As Beau heads out, Sal presses a hand against her stomach. "What'd I interrupt? Looked serious."

Seth clears his throat and shakes his head. "Nothin'. Don't think that guy would know how to be serious even if it bit him in the ass." He frowns, curling his arm tighter around Sal's shoulder. "He ain't stayin' with us, is he?"

"No. He's on the other side of the property. Thank God."

A long moment of silence, then Sal glances up at him. "I know what you're doing with Lacey," she says quietly.

Seth freezes. "Sal, I—"

"Steppin' in for a dance, getting her out of there so that creep couldn't bother her all night." Her eyes narrow in the direction of Beau's exit. "Lacey doesn't need that, especially after what she went through. She doesn't need some asshole wrecking her heart."

The words hit him square in the gut. Seth stares. Ice cold. That's Sal. He ain't never seen her this way. Protective. Watching Lacey with a big sister eye as she's snagged by Luke and pulled into a clumsy two-step on the dance floor.

Sal puts a hand on his arm. "I really appreciate it, Seth. You looking out for my sister." She smiles up at him, her green eyes sparkling with tears. "I don't know what I'd do without you."

With that, Sal turns, heading back across the dance floor to Luke and Lacey.

Seth stares after her, his mouth as dry as cotton.

He doesn't deserve Sal's gratitude. Her faith in him. Hell, he's the one lying to her. Sleeping with her sister.

Fuck.

He's the asshole.

Lacey stumbles into her bedroom, head spinning from the shots, and fumbles for the light on the wall. A low rumble of a chuckle sounds from the dark. And then Seth's dimming the light, drawing the blinds.

"Easy, princess," he says, watching in amusement as she tugs off a heel, swaying as she balances and chucks it across the room.

A toss of her hair. "I'm fine, Seth."

She's drunk.

It's about damn time she loosened up. Ever since the bar, since Emmy Lou's words, she's been wound tight. Wondering, worrying about whether she and Seth will even work when they go back to their lives. But her dance with Seth shook off her nervous feeling. Had left her wanting to live in the moment. Take risks.

Seth steps up behind her and wraps his arms around her waist. Steadying her. Pulling her back into him. They sway slow and steady. She smiles as he buries his face in her hair, inhaling her scent. "You have fun tonight?"

"Yeah." She turns around in his arms, staring up into his blue eyes. "Did you?"

"I did." He fiddles with a lock of her hair. Then, a dark look passes over his face. "With the exception of Beau."

"Oh, now look who's jealous," she teases.

"Damn right, I'm jealous," Seth grouses, his handsome face boyish and chagrined. "You lookin' like that. Hot as hell and me not bein' able to touch you. Then we got Beau leerin' at you all night—"

She arcs a brow, amused. "Leering?"

"Leerin'." He scowls, pressing a kiss to her brow. "You don't need that shit."

"Well, don't be jealous. He's obnoxiously harmless, not to mention a nightmare of a human being." They continue to sway. "Besides, look who I'm with." She nuzzles his throat, nipping at his collarbone. "You, Seth. You, you, you."

His arms tighten around her. But he doesn't kiss her. In fact, he doesn't do much of anything except hold her close and brood. She frowns. Ever since they left the bar, he's been quiet, a million miles away from her in some brain space of his own. Yet, that's Seth, working a problem out on his own, torturing himself for probably something he has no control over.

Staring up at him, she asks quietly, "What is it? What's wrong?"

Seth's eyes search hers. "What you said earlier to Beau—that it would never work because you're in LA—you mean that?"

Warily, she shrugs off his hold, drifting to the bed. "I don't know, Seth, it was just something I said." She sheds her dress to stand in her lace bra and panties, wobbling once as a rush of alcohol hits her. She glances over her shoulder. "Is that what's bothering you?"

"Yeah, it is." He rips a hand through his hair. "It's botherin' me a whole goddamn lot."

She angles her head, confused. "Are we still talking about tonight?" Maybe she's still drunk or too tipsy to follow where Seth's going with this.

"No, we ain't. We're talkin' about us." He meets her eyes and swallows. "When we leave here, I don't want this to end, Lace."

His words steal her breath, have her heart beating wildly. Weak-kneed, she sits on the edge of the bed and then raises her gaze to his. "Me neither."

His eyes light up. And then he's crossing the room to kneel in front of her. Leaning in, Seth slides a lean, muscled hand over her bare leg to rest on her thigh. "Then I want to do this. Do us. Anything I gotta do to make it work, I wanna do it."

"Really?"

"Hell, yes."

Her heart tumbles. She's never had a man like this before. So open, so honest. Seth comes to her when she needs him, always making her laugh, feel safe, working hard to be with her. The way he loves her sister, his family—he's just such a good human.

She reaches out and cups his scruffy cheek. The action causing him to go still, to close his eyes for the briefest second. "I want to do this too." But then, just as quick, worry knocks hope out of the running. "But how? I'm in LA and you're . . . all over the place."

Being without Seth for even a minute has her unhappy. She can't imagine doing it long distance.

"Tickets are cheap," he says, his voice eager and resolved.

"We'll meet in the middle. Hell, we'll just schedule more shows in LA."

His determination to make this work fills Lacey up with her own. Has her rejecting the voice in her head that tells her this will end. That Seth will leave. Instead, she gives herself over to hope. Her belly dips. Thinking about a future, a new future with Seth has her feeling vulnerable and brave. She wants to take risks, do things that scare her, do things that feel right.

"Or," she says, gathering courage. "I could, possibly, maybe, think about moving to Nashville? I don't have a job in LA anymore, so . . ." She lets herself trail off, leaving the offer open.

Seth inhales a sharp breath, his expression unreadable.

Panic rolls through her. It's too much, too soon. Oh God, how desperate did she come across?

She tries to backtrack. "But I mean, I don't have to do that if—"

"No." He's grinning. Bright. A beam. "Christ. I want you there. So damn bad. I wasn't gonna ask you that to do that for me but . . ." He exhales a long breath, his face turning serious. "I can't imagine my world movin' without you in it." He gathers up her hand. "I feel found with you, Lacey."

Hot tears spring to her eyes. She knows what he means. Being with Seth feels like her heart is outside of her body. Experiencing everything to the truest.

She closes her eyes and nods. "Me too."

And then Seth presses himself up, his lips meeting hers in the slowest, sweetest kiss she's ever had.

An infinity kiss. Long. Everlasting.

Without breaking their connection, Lacey loops her arms around Seth's neck. Every part of her is electric and buzzing. Seth's fingers sweep over every inch of her skin, her lips, her hair. She arcs at the contact, the heat charging between them, the intensity of his need.

She's never felt so happy, so alive. So much peace. Hope. Love.

No.

Not love. It can't be. She's tried so hard to ward it off, to bury the feelings she has for Seth six feet under.

But it is.

It's love.

Because all she can think about is the next time. All the times like this with Seth. Vacations. Holidays. The good kind of sleepless nights. Waking up next to him and only him. Screaming her joy all over the stage as he plays. Being the one he goes home to after a show.

Life. Their life.

Lacey trembles, making a needy moan in the back of her throat as Seth lays her down on the bed. Hovering over her, he aligns his lean muscled form to hers. His blue eyes stare down into hers, intent, soft. A gorgeous smile on his handsome face.

Overcome with emotion, she reaches up to cup his strong jaw, the words on the tip of her tongue. "Seth, I—"

"What?" His eyes, heavy-lidded, pupils blitzed, stare back at her.

Her mouth opens. Closes. "Nothing."

Instead, she kisses him.

She can't say it first. Absolutely not.

Seth dips his head. Her name rolls off his lips, a reverent plea, a grateful gasp.

Lacey sighs, tilting her head back as his broad hand parts her thighs. His fingers find her pulse down below. Warmth flows through her. Graceful, gorgeous fingers that work her over better than any string. But she wants more. She wants him. She reaches down, stilling him, and brings his gaze to hers. "I need you, Seth. Please."

A lovestruck look crosses his face. And then he smiles, knowing exactly what she wants. Straightening up, he yanks off his T-shirt, unzips the fly of his jeans.

Lacey hooks her legs around his waist and he slips into her. A hungry, guttural groan rolls out of him. She closes her eyes, letting Seth drug her with his very touch.

Because this time, it's different. A connection, a commitment. If it's meant to be, they'll make it work.

Seth's words have quelled her worries from tonight. Have her rejecting that voice in her head that tells her this will end. That she isn't being some dreamy lovesick fool. That hope has a place in her head and heart.

She can see the future so bright.

Her and Seth.

Happy.

TWENTY-SIX

CHRISTMAS EVE AND THE MOUTHWATERING SCENT OF barbeque wafts through the air. Crisp air and pine tree scent. A thin frost of snow covers the ground. The sun, shining bright through the clouds, takes away the chill of the winter afternoon.

Seth sips his beer and roves his eyes around the sprawling backyard. The group circles the fire pit, Luke stoking the flames. It's been an afternoon of backyard shenanigans. Corn hole, bocci ball, running Seth's ATV across the frozen field. Laughter. Beer. Music. The best kind of day. Everyone happy. Celebrating together.

Seth can't believe that only three years ago this wouldn't even have been an option. Sal was gone. Luke off his fucking goddamn rocker. The Brothers Kincaid lower than low. And now—he's got his brother, his best friend, his band back.

He can't stop being so goddamn grateful.

But best of all, now he's got Lacey.

He watches as Lacey exits the house, two bottles of champagne in her hands. She stops by Emmy Lou, pouring her a glass, then heads to Sal's side. The sound of her laugh launches his heart into the sky.

Goddamn, last night ruined him.

A promise of her being in Nashville . . .

It's more than he could ever hope for.

Because he's over the moon, he's in. He's finally experiencing that full-tilt, no-holds-barred, howl-at-the-moon kind of love that Luke and Sal have, and goddamn if he doesn't want to hook that to his veins.

Now all he's gotta do is say it. I love you. Just three little words. How fucking hard can it be?

Apparently pretty damn hard because it's got him shaking in his boots. He's never been in love before. Never said it. What if he fucks it up? What if she's not ready?

Alabama, bundled in a black puffer jacket, backs away from the roaring fire. "Good Lord, Luke. You're gonna char us all."

"Don't listen to her." Emmy Lou makes a *praise Jesus* motion with her hands. "More fire, Luke, I think I'm about half frozen."

A loud bark echoes across the lawn.

Sal rises from her chair, shielding her eyes against the sun to watch Winston skirt the edge of the choppy lake, which sits fifty yards away. She turns to Luke, her pretty face worried. "He's getting too close to the water."

"He's fine, darlin'," Luke says, his amused eyes flicking to Seth.

Seth smothers a smile. Sal loves that damn dog.

"It ain't iced over," Jace says, taking a sip of his beer. He juggles a beanbag in his hand. He and Griff have been engaged in an epic beanbag battle for the last hour. "Not yet at least."

Sal bites her lip. "It's cold, though." She takes a step forward, only to be stopped by Luke.

"You ain't goin' anywhere near that water," he says, eyeing Sal. She's off-balance with her stomach. Something that doesn't sit well with Luke, not when she can slip and fall.

Seth slaps his hands on his jeans. "I'll get him." Relief fills Sal's face. Seth's eyes land on Lacey. "You wanna take a ride on ol' June, princess?" Taking a chance to be alone with Lacey, he jerks his head toward the ATV.

She downs her champagne and stands, her posture haughty. Her cheeks a faint pink. "Ugh, let's get this over with."

A snort from Griff.

They hop onto the ATV. Seth gives her a wicked grin and then he guns it. Lacey lets out a squeal, bracing herself on the frame as he zips them down to the edge of the lake. He throws it in park. And then Lacey laughs, like some brilliant sun lighting up his world.

He grins at her. She's as damn adventurous as he is. Her little wild streak showing itself more and more these days. Everything he's discovering about her a better surprise than the last. "You like that?"

"I do." She looks amazed at herself. "That is fucking fun, Seth."

"Yeah, well, try tellin' Luke that," he grumbles.

His brother had been a stick in his ass all morning as he raced the ATV around the backyard. Luke worries too much. Still thinks of him as that wild, reckless kid, when all Seth wants to do is let loose and have a little fun.

Lacey slides close to him. They're still in eyeshot of the group, so she slips a covert hand into his. The feel of her skin on his has him shivering. He leans in. "I'd give anything to fuckin' kiss you right now."

"Yeah, well, you should have stuck around longer this morning." She tosses her hair, her narrowed green eyes curious. "You were gone when I woke up. Where'd you go?"

"Sneakin' out before we got caught."

It's a lie. A white one, though. He had snuck off to pick up Lacey's locket. He met the pawnshop guy in town at a diner. Gave him a thousand bucks and a weekend stay in Nashville for his trouble. It also let Seth do some last-minute Christmas shopping. Usually, he and Luke traded six-packs on Christmas Day, but he's never shopped like this before. But hell if he ain't gonna learn. Especially for Lacey.

Tomorrow, he'll give her the locket. But not in front of everyone. It's a sensitive topic with the mugging, and he wants to make sure she has space to process it.

"Well, I'll be damned," he teases. "You tryin' to say you missed me?"

She scoffs. "Hardly."

He laughs, then turns an eye to the lake. Winston's dipping a toe in, his paws and nose covered in mud. Seth gives a sharp whistle and the dog's head snaps up. "C'mon," he shouts. "Let's go."

Lacey frowns, seeing the mud. "Seth, if that dog—"

But it's too late. Winston bounds into the ATV, rocking it like a boat, and lands right on Lacey's lap.

She punches Seth's arm. "You asshole," she groans, but she's laughing, wiping at her white puffball of a jacket. Mud streaks her dark leggings. "I'm never gonna get this out."

Seth waggles his eyebrows. "I'll help you clean you up later."

Her eyes spark. "You wish."

With a wild whoop, he takes off, heading back to the house.

The ATV parked, Lacey and Seth cross the yard. Winston bounds over to a grateful Sal, who herds him into the house.

"Hell of a time, Kincaid," Griff hoots, taking a swallow of his beer. "My kind of day when I'm winnin' against Taylor." He extends a broad hand. "Pony up, man."

"Yeah, yeah," Jace grumbles, handing Griff a twenty-dollar bill. "Another round?"

"Good Lord almighty, ain't you had enough?" Griff raises a brow. "How much you lost now?"

Emmy Lou takes a step toward Jace, her eyes troubled. "Jace."

Seth frowns, catching the tail end of the conversation.

What the hell is Jace doing? Sure, it's a bet between friends, but Jace shouldn't be betting. Two years ago, he came close to losing the farm. Luke bailed him out. But now . . .

Luke, holding Sal on his lap, his hand fanned out over her stomach, meets Seth's gaze. And he's opening his mouth, to say what, Seth doesn't know, when an engine cuts the lazy haze of the afternoon.

Seth's ears prick in the familiar rumble.

They all turn to see a dark Polaris fishtailing across the dusty makeshift road. It parks itself next to Seth's ATV and then out of it comes Beau Dallas.

Seth groans. "That's it. I'm sellin' June." Anything that invites comparison to this guy ain't happening.

Luke chuckles, but his eyes are hard, his wary gaze on Beau.

"Hey, y'all!" Beau calls out, swaggering over. "Thought I'd mosey on over and see what all the ruckus is about!"

The group gathers in front of the fire, and instantly, the atmosphere is charged. As taut as the men's fists. Luke grasps the back of his neck. He looks like a headache's coming on and that headache's Beau Dallas.

Emmy Lou whispers, "What on earth is he still doin' here?"

"He didn't have anywhere to go," Sal murmurs.

"Probably because he's an asshole," Alabama snipes. Griff drifts to her side and wraps a protective arm around her.

"I've already run him over in my head three times by now," Seth mutters.

"Just three?" Lacey asks with a faint smile.

"Hey, Luke, how's it hangin'?" Beau asks when he finally makes it to the group. He looks like he just woke up. Bloodshot eyes, disheveled hair.

"What're you doin' here, Beau?" Luke asks, his jaw clenched.

Seth and Jace exchange a tense glance. Luke's trying to play nice because that's Luke, but Seth knows his brother and knows this is the last straw. Coming here uninvited, rude as hell, ain't winning Beau any fans.

"Relax, Kincaid," Beau drawls. "I'll play nice. I came to pick up my fiddle. I left it at the bar last night. But now that I'm here . . ." He cocks an investigative brow. "Y'all havin' a party. How come I ain't invited?"

"You know why," Griff growls.

He shrugs. "Seems borin' anyway." Beau lasers his gaze to Lacey. "You wanna cut out of here, angel? Go have some fun?"

She faces him squarely, undeterred. "Not in this lifetime."

"Icy," Beau laughs, then, ballsy as all hell, he reaches out. Traces a finger down the line of her arm. "I like that. More fun to defrost."

A chorus of objection sounds around the group.

"Hey, man." Seth gets between Lacey and Beau. His hands

spread, open, out, because if he makes a fist, he'll deck the guy. "Don't fuckin' touch her."

"Pig," Lacey snaps in Beau's direction. Sal steps close, drawing her sister to her side.

Griff shakes his head. "Beau, me and you go way back, but you gotta get the hell out of here." His fists are clenched, and Seth doesn't miss Alabama slipping a hand through his arm to hold him back.

Beau's eyebrows shoot up. "Shit, who knew you were such a square, Greyson? We used to raise hell, burn guitars, chase those girls." He sucks his lip. "Married life, takin' up with Kincaid changed you, man." He looks at Seth. "Now, I heard you're the fun one." Seth stiffens. Beau keeps talking. "All those papers say you're gettin' wild these days, ain't ya? Although I'm surprised to see it. The Brothers Kincaid keepin' a junkie in their band. Damn shame."

Seth freezes, hating how that one callout threatens to take him down.

Not surprisingly, Luke starts. His expression dangerous, his tone lethal, he steps forward. "What'd you say to my brother?"

"You heard me," Beau says evenly, holding Luke's deadly gaze.

"Beau," Jace groans. "Stop talkin.'"

Seth's gut clenches as Sal moves close to Luke's side. Her pale face says it all. Her green eyes worried, her body slanted forward, as if she'll leap between the two of them. Seth knows she's thinking of Luke's injury. The bar fight. Luke on the ground, bleeding, unmoving.

"Listen, you helped us out when we needed it and we appreciate it," Luke says, his voice authoritative. "But you won't disrespect my wife and my family. You take your bullshit somewhere else because I ain't havin' it here." Luke's words are cold, his face cement. A man who's pissed. A man who will go absolutely ballistic if this trouble touches his family.

A muscle in Beau's cheek twitches. "And if I don't?"

Seth tenses, anger flaring inside of him. Bright red. Hot.

This is bullshit. This asshole sticks around long enough to

piss everyone off, to ruin their good time, and then leaves them in the wreckage. And Luke's taking it on like always. Taking it on for *him*. The mess Seth made because he couldn't deal with his goddamn problems, and now, they're stuck in a contract with the guy for three more god-awful weeks.

As Seth scans the yard, wracking his brain for what to do instead of straight-up decking the guy, his eyes land on the ATVs, neck and neck, just like him and Beau. Just like they've been this entire goddamn time.

The idea hits him like lighting.

He's the one who got them into this mess. He's fixing it. The only language Beau speaks right now. Asshole.

"Tell you what," Seth says, and all eyes swerve to him. He nods at the ATVs, looks at Beau. "You like playin' fast and loose—what about a race?"

"Seth, knock it off," Luke snaps, the big brother in him kicking in.

But Seth ignores him. "If I win, you pack your shit and get out of here. You don't bother finishin' out your time with the band."

Beau's eyes flash with interest. "A wager. Interestin'. But what do I get?"

"A song."

Now, all eyes swivel to Griff. Seth's included. "I'll put you on my next album." He doesn't look at Alabama, who's wincing beside him.

"Ain't such a bad deal." Jace arcs an eyebrow. Pretends to closely evaluate the ATVs. "Although, I don't know. Think Seth's rig might have you beat."

"Jace." Luke's warning is sharp.

"No," Beau interjects. He grins, the challenge irresistible. Better yet, the fact that it pisses off Luke. "I dig that. We race."

They shake on it.

Griff exhales. "Hell, yes."

Lacey frowns, not bothering to keep the tremble out of her voice. "You're being stupid, Seth."

"Lacey's right," Sal says, linking her arm through her sister's.

The women stare at him, their brows wrinkled with worry.

Luke twists to face him. "You ain't doin' this," he says to Seth, his voice low, deadly serious.

"You're outvoted, Kincaid," Griff says, taking Seth's side.

Luke's jaw clenches. Irritation flashes furious in his eyes. Seth knows it's killing Luke that he doesn't have a say in this.

Griff meets Seth's eyes. He's just as eager to get rid of Beau as Seth is. Crossing his arms, his tattooed biceps bulging, he lifts his voice so both Beau and Seth can hear. "You race from the end of the lake . . ." His tawny eyes scour the snowy horizon. "To the old stop sign there. You stay in your lane, you aim straight. First one through wins."

Seth clocks the track Griff's detailed. About seventy yards away. A clear, icy shot.

"Fine by me," Seth drawls.

"Let's do it," Beau says with an almost smile. Then he turns on his heel and strides for his ATV.

Jace drifts to Seth's side and squeezes his shoulder. "You got this," he tells him.

Seth gives Luke a lopsided grin, wanting to reassure him. "Relax, Luke. This is what the country is for, ain't it?" He swaggers, brushing past his brother. "Raisin' hell?"

Luke relents, but the worry on his face doesn't.

"Oh Lord, I don't know if I can watch this," Emmy Lou moans as the women gather in a loose huddle. Alabama and Lacey wear the same scowl. Fierce. Unhappy.

Before he can climb into his ATV, Griff pulls him aside, his expression grim. "You win this, but you don't get hurt either." A gruff edge stains his voice. "Keep it straight to the stop sign, no turns, no tiltin', you hear me? Because you're gonna go fast."

Seth grins. "Fast as fuck."

Griff's eyes swivel to Beau. "Kick his fuckin' ass."

Seth's gut twists as he climbs into June. He props his feet on the pegs, eyes ahead. He knows what he's doing is stupid as hell, but if it'll get Beau out of the contract, sign his fool self up. Even if he is going to get his ass chewed out later. He saw the group as he passed them by. Luke stone-faced. Lacey's glare so fierce she's going to light him up on the snowbank when he's done.

Beau, behind the wheel, flips a wave, an unlit cigarette in his mouth. "Good luck, kid."

"Good luck." Seth faces forward, pulling on his helmet. "Asshole."

Griff steps in front of them, raises his arm, and then they're off.

Tires squeal. Rock and wet snow crank out as Seth pushes the ATV, throttling clutch, keeping his elbows loose. Adrenaline has him in a viselike grip. He doesn't look over to see where Beau is, because fuck Beau Dallas. And fuck himself for not telling Luke the truth.

Tonight. He tells his brother tonight.

Seth punches the gas.

Faster.

Up ahead, he can see the stop sign. A minute out, thirty seconds, the finish line.

So close.

It's a straight shot.

He can't lose.

He doesn't.

Seth whips over the finish line and lets out a rip of a howl. Only out of nowhere, Beau crosses the center line, sideswiping his rig.

The ATV jerks, jarring Seth.

And then it flips, his brain whiplashing in his skull, warm blood filling his mouth, his world spinning into blackness.

Lacey watches in horror as Seth's ATV sways to the side and then flips. For an impossible second, it does a slow roll of a hurtle through the air before landing hard upside down on the frozen earth.

A cry of dismay goes up in the group.

Sal gasps. "Oh my God."

"*Seth!*" Luke screams, strangling over his brother's name. He's up and running, charging for the wreck, staggering and falling in his haste to make it over the frozen incline of the road.

Griff and Jace on his heels, rush to help. Sal, too.

Only Lacey stands frozen on the porch, terrified, covering her mouth with her hand, her brain struggling to process the scene. She can't breathe, her vision tunneling. Her heart threatens to bash itself out of her chest.

Not Seth. Please, no. Not him.

Luke hits the side of his shoulder against the ATV, trying to roll it off his brother.

"Get it off! Get it off him! *Now!*" The sharp snap, the torment in Luke's voice, shakes Lacey out of her daze. Shakes her awake.

This time, she's the one running, leaping off the porch up the ice-covered grass to where the men grunt, straining to move the ATV.

Lacey joins the half-circle of Emmy Lou and Alabama. She feels faint as she watches. All the blood rushing from her face, her body drifting somewhere else, far away.

Silence. Deathly silence.

Only the faint sound of a dying engine as Beau exits his ATV.

"Fuck, fuck, fuck." Luke's voice is a chant, and all Lacey can do is stare. He can't catch his breath. He's shaking. Full-body tremors that have Lacey's kegs threatening to give out. Because if Luke, the leader, their steadfast calm, their easygoing presence, is scared, then they're all scared.

Finally, they roll the ATV off Seth. He lies still and immobile on the ground.

Lacey lets out an anguished cry.

Luke, his face white with fear, collapses back and crashes to his knees beside his brother.

Sal's there, beside him, reaching, seeing what he's about to do. "Luke, you can't . . . you need to—"

But Luke, his eyes wild and unstrung, doesn't hear her warning. It's instinct, Seth's his brother, he's panicking and he can't be stopped.

Luke rips Seth's helmet off.

Seth's eyes are closed. A tendril of blood streams from his ear down his neck.

Griff swears, a muscle jerking in his jaw.

Emmy Lou whimpers, bringing her hands up to cover her eyes.

"No, Seth," Luke moans, his face twisting up in the worst expression Lacey's ever seen. He shakes his head, *no no no*, his body a ball of pain.

"No," Lacey whispers. An echo to Luke. That's when there's a warm hand in hers. She looks over in surprise.

Alabama.

Hot tears fill her eyes. She's never been so grateful for the contact, for something to keep her upright when all she wants to do is collapse. Alabama gives her hand a squeeze, and together, they watch as Sal checks Seth over.

Lacey closes her eyes, resisting the sight of Seth lying there, so still, so unlike Seth. The thought has her swaying on her feet. It feels like her world is over. Like her life is ending. She can't lose him. She absolutely cannot.

"He's breathing," Sal announces, leaning over Seth, and Lacey's eyes flash open. A relieved cry goes up. Low swears. Muted sobs from the sidelines.

Then, as if to prove Sal's point, Seth groans.

Lacey's heart hitches.

Luke, kneeling by Seth's side, grips his brother's hand. His eyes flicker, tears and worry shining in their dark depths.

And then Seth laughs. A full-bodied laugh that has everyone letting out their held breaths.

Seth's eyes open to stare at the blue sky above. "Oh man," he groans, pressing a hand to his head. "Who turned out the fuckin' lights?"

Lacey's heart jump-starts, her legs threatening to give out, if it weren't for Alabama keeping her up.

Sal, her eyes shiny with tears, presses a hand against Seth's chest. "Stay still."

But Seth isn't having any of it. With help from Luke, he sits up. He flinches at the movement, swaying for a second and then steadies. Surveys them all, his gaze aware, clearheaded.

Luke stifles a sob as he grips his brother's shoulder. He cups Seth's face, making Seth look at him, clocking his pupils, the blood at his temple.

"I'm okay, man," Seth says softly to Luke.

"You sure? 'Cause I ain't." Luke holds his eyes. His hand still on Seth's shoulder, squeezing tight.

Seth chuckles, rolls out his neck. "I'm a little bruised up. But I'm alright."

Lacey's mind, her heart, overheats. Gripped by the notion that's Seth's okay, but she's not. Regret curdles her stomach, balls her fist. She could have lost him. The man she loves, and he doesn't even know it. Next comes a wave of rage. Stupid men and their stupid games. He could have been hurt, could have died, and all he's doing is playing it off.

Seth grins up at Griff and Jace. "Well, what about it? Did I win?"

Griff exhales. "Yeah, you won alright."

Jace just shakes his head, studying Seth.

A snort from left field. "Barely." Beau stands there, unfazed, arms crossed, no hint of concern on his face. "Think you forgot how brakes work."

All eyes snap to Beau, forgotten about in the chaos of tending to Seth.

Luke whips his head up, nostrils flaring, but he stays by his brother's side. "You fuckin' idiot!" he yells at Beau, hot anger in his voice. "You hit him with your goddamn wheels!"

Beau rolls his eyes and kicks a rock with his boot. "Whatever, man."

Luke looks at Jace. "Get him outta here before I kill him."

A growl from Griff. "I'm gonna boot this motherfucker all the way out of town," he says, stalking over to a retreating Beau.

"Asshole," Seth mutters, shaking his head and pushing upward. Luke and Jace are there, each taking an arm to gently hoist him up.

For an instant, Luke locks eyes with Lacey. A shared look passes between them, relief, terror. A joining, a connection of their love for Seth.

Sal stands in front of Seth, her hands shaking as she palms his chest. "I want to get you inside and check you over."

"I'm fine, Sal."

"Don't you *I'm fine* me." Sal's eyes glitter with tears. "You could have been seriously hurt, Seth."

In small, halting movements, Lacey approaches Seth, her gut churning, her heart heavy. All the fear in her has been replaced by something else. Relief. Regret. Anger.

Anger that she's not by Seth's side, comforting him, openly worrying about him. And why? Because they're being stupid idiots hiding this thing. Because Sal still doesn't know. Because she's so stubborn, so icy, so scared of letting herself go all the way with Seth.

She's in front of him, so close, her heart blazing, her hands trembling, when Seth lasers his gaze to her. His grin tired, but still cocky, still all confidence. "What'd you think, princess?"

All she can do is press a hand to her mouth, letting out a small sob.

Seth's blue eyes flicker with concern. His expression softens. He stretches out a hand. "Lace—"

A flare of anger. "You asshole."

She hits him. She hits him again. Lacey beats her fists on his chest, little lashing fuck-yous of rage.

His eyes widening, Seth tries to take her in his arms to calm her, but she rips away, ignoring the perplexed expression on her sister's face.

"Fuck you, Seth," Lacey flings back and storms for the house.

chapter
TWENTY-SEVEN

SETH SITS IN THE OFFICE ON THE SECOND FLOOR, HIS LEG jumping impatiently as Sal hovers over him, cleaning the gash on his brow. Her med kit lies open on the desk beside her. Luke leans in the doorway, his brow furrowed, watching in silence.

It's the last place he wants to be. What he wants to be doing is finding Lacey. But before he could go after her, Sal and Luke corralled him, wanting him to get checked over.

Seth wasn't about to put up a fight. He's got enough people mad at him.

Lacey included.

The *get fucked* swings she took at him out on the lawn tell him he's got some serious groveling to do. She's pissed. Really pissed. For taking on Beau. For playing it off. Hell, if she had been in his same position, he would have lost his goddamn mind. He saw the fear in her green eyes, and he feels like the worst kind of asshole for scaring her.

As soon as this is over with, he has to find her and apologize.

Sal affixes a butterfly bandage to his brow. She leans back and evaluates him. "Well, I think it's a Christmas Eve miracle, because nothing's broken." She bites her lip, trying not to cry.

"You're lucky, you know that."

His heart clenches. "Sal, don't—ow! Jesus." He stares at her, blinking in surprise. She's just socked him in the arm.

She frowns up at him. "That's for acting like an idiot. And for scaring me to death." Then, just as quick as she hit him, she hugs him tight. "You can't do that to us. We need you around, okay?"

The sad stare she's giving him cuts him down. He swallows. "Yeah. Sure."

She turns her gaze to Luke. "Your turn."

Seth groans, looking at his brother warily.

Sal chuckles, but her expression turns serious. She gives the two of them one last look and exits the room.

Luke pushes off the wall, his dark eyes intent. "You sure you're okay?"

Seth slips off the chair and stands. "You heard Sal. No concussion, no broken bones. Just luck." He grins. "I'm still pretty spry, man."

Only Luke doesn't grin back. He stares at Seth a long moment, then says, "Today . . . I didn't like today, Seth. It had me flashin' back to . . ." Luke shakes his head, letting the words hang unfinished.

Seth's stomach plummets. He licks his lips, squeezes his eyes shut for the briefest second. "Luke . . ."

But Luke continues. Has to continue. "I still see you . . . you know? In that bathtub. Thinkin' you were gone and . . ."

Seth hangs his head. The past, the trauma never far from his brother's mind. And why wouldn't it be? He'd terrified Luke and Sal both. Had them thinking he was dying. He brought drugs into the band, around Sal. Put them through hell. Luke has the right to worry.

"You gotta be careful, Seth." Luke grips Seth by the shoulder, and Seth lifts his eyes. His brother's voice is raw, honest. "I got Sal, but without you, I ain't got my family. You hear me?"

Seth nods, choked up by his brother's fierce love. "Yeah. I hear ya."

He should tell him. Now. Here.

Seth clears his throat, swallows the boulder. "Listen. Luke. I—"

But he's cut off before he can get the confession out. Luke

moves closer, his face a mess of hard anger. "What Beau was sayin' today, callin' you that bullshit." His fingers dig into Seth's shoulder and he lowers his voice. "Don't let it bother you. You ain't back there no more. He don't know shit and he don't know you. I do."

Seth pales, his resolve frayed.

What Luke means is that he's got faith in him, and it's that faith that has Seth clamming up. He pulls the trigger on the truth, and what happens? Luke's already upset by his dumbass stunt to challenge Beau, how's he gonna handle this?

"Seth?"

Luke's staring at him, waiting.

To chase away his nerves, Seth runs a hand through his hair, exhales. "I oughta go find Lacey."

"That's probably a good idea," Luke says with a wry chuckle.

Seth gathers himself, willing himself not to wince in front of Luke, because his hip's sore as hell, and exits the room.

On his way down the stairs and through the back hall, he runs into Griff and Jace in the lounge. They're bellied up to the small bar, the jukebox cranking out Guy Clark, the neon BEER sign aglow.

Seeing Seth, Jace lifts a rusty brow, waving him into the room. "Hey, man. How you feelin'?"

"Ain't doin' too bad." He nods at the bottle of Johnnie Walker parked between Jace and Griff. "Drinkin' alone?"

Jace lifts his glass in salute. "The way today's goin' we're gonna be eatin' alone too."

Seth grimaces. "The girls—"

"Are fuckin' pissed," Griff finishes. He pours Seth a drink, sliding it across the slick bar top. "Alabama already gave me an earful. That woman's spittin' fire." His tawny eyes, crinkling into a squint, scour Seth. "Anything broken?"

Seth sips the whiskey, thinking of Lacey. "Not yet."

Griff, his face contrite, says, "Hell, I'm sorry, man."

Seth's brow furrows, and he looks questioningly at Griff. "For what?"

"That was a bad scene out there. And I'm goddamn responsible. I recommended the guy to Luke, and he brings all this shit here." Griff twists a ring on his pinkie, regret in his expression. "Y'all are like family. And when someone fucks with my family, they fuck with me."

Seth takes a second to appreciate Griff, what he did out there. Putting himself, his reputation, on the line to help Seth out, to get Beau gone for the Brothers Kincaid, for Luke's sake. The guy ain't so bad.

"Nah," Seth says with a slow shake of his head. "That ain't your fault. Where is he anyway?"

"Outside," Jace volunteers. "Freezin' to death, hopefully."

Seth snorts.

Griff sits back on the stool and growls. "I don't know what his fuckin' problem is. It's like he's sniffin' goddamn glue."

Seth stiffens as the words land like a lit stick of dynamite.

Fuck.

How in the hell has it taken him this long to figure it out? Maybe because he was too focused on Lacey. Maybe he blocked revisiting that painful part of his past. But all the signs are there. Hyped up. Controlling it onstage. Wild and reckless to the point of annoyance.

Seth should've known. Hell, if he had, he never would have challenged the guy.

Seth swipes a hand through his hair. "He's on somethin.'"

Jace's eyes widen. "Booze?"

"Maybe. Maybe somethin' else."

A curse blasts from Griff's lips. "Fuck." He looks guilt-stricken.

Seth smears a hand down his face, leans in the doorway, evaluating the long corridor.

"Lookin' for Lacey?" Jace's lips twitch.

He sighs. "Yeah."

"Good luck."

"Right." He slugs down the rest of his whiskey and steps out of the lounge.

Seth checks the living room, the kitchen, even his own bedroom. No Lacey.

Seth swears to himself, steps out farther into the hall, when a dark figure at one of the front windows catches his eye.

Seth pushes out the heavy double doors to find the last person on earth he wants to talk to. Beau. He's leaning up against the wooden post beneath the awning, smoking a cigarette, his fiddle case in his hand. White clouds of smoke hover in the icy night air.

With a backward glance at Seth, Beau returns his stare to the gravel driveway. "Looks like you survived," he quips, his voice a flat drawl.

Seth scowls, makes a move to go back inside.

Then he hesitates.

He may want to run the guy's face into his fucking fiddle, but the least he can do is point him in the right direction.

Because Seth knows what it's like. Being in the grip of something so tight, nothing can pull you out. Hiding it. Hurting everyone around him. Beau's Seth. Ten years ago, minus the whole asshole part. And he knows what a difference it can make, someone offering help, making you listen, and in Sal's case, not leaving his side until he was steady.

With a sigh, Seth turns back around. "Listen, man . . . I don't know what you think you're doin' actin' like an asshole, but whatever it is, if you're on somethin', if you need help—"

A ragged laugh escapes Beau. He staggers around, his cocky posture from earlier flattened. The spark in his eye diminished. "Man, spare me the bullshit pity speech. You got what you wanted. Fair and square, right? I'm gone." He tosses his cigarette, barely missing the tips of Seth's boots. A dark sneer twists his face. "Fuck the Brothers Kincaid and fuck you."

With that, Beau turns on his boot heel and heads into the night, the harsh wind whipping his dark hair as he cuts across the frozen grass for the guest house.

"Jesus," Seth mutters, adrenaline hammering in his veins.

He tried.

Fuck Beau Dallas.

Now he's got to find the one person who matters.

Lacey.

Lacey dips the plate in the sink full of bubbles and absentmindedly runs a washrag over it. She rinses and places it in the rack. The air hangs heavy with the scent of pine from the Christmas tree and tonight's dinner. She had volunteered to do the dishes since she was MIA for most of dinner prep, having claimed a headache. Even though today was a shitshow, dinner was salvaged after opening a couple of bottles of wine. The men all doing their damnedest to behave.

She still hasn't spoken to Seth. All night, she kept close to Sal. Her sister was like her shield, warding off Seth, his ridiculously hangdog blue eyes, and their impending conversation.

She sighs. She's washed the same dish twice. She dries her hands on a towel and reaches for her wineglass, resisting the urge to chug it all down in one gulp.

No matter how much wine she drinks, she can't get the image of Seth out of her head. Lying still on the ground, unmoving. Luke's scream, the torment in his face an echo of hers.

Footsteps sound behind her.

Lacey steels herself, expecting Seth, but when she turns, it's Sal. Her sister looks relaxed, changed into a gray velvet dress, her dark hair loose around her shoulders.

"How's your headache?" Sal asks softly, crossing the kitchen. She sets her cell phone on the counter and leans back. Her eyes intently scouring Lacey's face.

"It's good. It's gone now."

"Are you sure, Lace? You were so quiet at dinner."

Lacey flicks a soap bubble at Sal. "Stop worrying. I feel better. Really."

"Okay . . . ," Sal says like she doesn't believe her. She places a hand on the moon of her stomach. "We're all going to play pool downstairs." A wry grin graces her face. "Not sure how I'll reach the table, but you should come. Spot me."

"I will." Lacey picks up the rag. "I'll finish up and meet you down there." She attempts a weak smile. "These dishes won't wash themselves."

Sal squeezes her arm and heads out.

Lacey turns back to the sink, hot tears pricking her eyes. She was hoping it was Seth. Only he's not here because she fucked it up by acting like an idiot earlier today.

Falling for Seth has her doing things she's never wanted to do. Getting too close. Taking risks. Falling in love. Being left.

She inhales, blinking fast to chase away the emotion.

It all feels the same.

It fucking sucks.

She continues to wash, moving onto the utensils, her gaze drifting to the window. To the dark, to the cold outside where fat white flakes of snow fall. *Perfect. Right in time for Christmas*, she thinks and shivers at the thought.

"You cold, princess?"

Her heart seizes, and she closes her eyes.

The rumble of Seth's voice warms her like a blanket.

Not like she'd tell him that.

Slowly, she dries her hands on a towel. Then she turns around to face him.

Seth stands in the kitchen, hands in his pockets, a sheepish expression on his handsome face.

"No," Lacey huffs, crossing her arms. "I'm perfectly fine, in fact."

He arches a brow at her words, then his face darkens. "Well, I ain't fine. I'm a long way from fine." Taking a step closer, he whisks his long fingers together. He looks halfway agonized. "I've been tryin' to talk to you all night, Lace."

She lifts her chin, stares straight at him. "Then talk."

It's a Herculean effort to stay away from him. To not throw

herself into his arms and hold him tight. Hold him like she'll never let go. Because she doesn't want to let go. Deep down, she knows.

It's Seth.

All the way.

He runs a hand through his sandy-blond hair.

"About today . . . hell, I'm sorry, Lace. It got out of hand. I acted like—"

"An idiot."

He stares at her. Nods. "An idiot. I wasn't thinkin' about how it would turn out. All I was thinkin' about was gettin' that asshole out of there." He takes a step closer. "The last thing I wanted was for him to ruin this trip for Luke and Sal." He pins his eyes to hers. "For you."

Another step.

Lacey braces herself against the counter.

"And I know I scared you."

"Scared?" Her mouth flattens into a white line. "You terrified me, Seth. I was so afraid you were hurt. If you had . . ."

She breaks off, not wanting to cry, but unable to stop herself. She places a hand on her mouth to smother a sob.

Seth's right there beside her, concern in his eyes.

"And it's so stupid, but I couldn't be there, I couldn't worry about you because we're stupid and keeping us a secret, and it made me so angry." She squeezes her eyes shut, letting the words tumble out. "I don't even know what we're doing anymore, all I know is that I don't want to lose you." She shakes her head, the tears falling freely now. "I can't lose you, Seth, anyone else, I can't . . . I can't do it . . ."

She's crumbling, losing it, but before she can weep a puddle, Seth's there.

He gathers her in his lean, muscular arms, pulling him to her. Lacey gives herself over to her emotions, to Seth's comforting hug. She clings to him, pressing her cheek against his shoulder.

"I'm sorry," he whispers, kissing the top of her head. "I'm so damn sorry, Lace."

"No, I'm sorry," she murmurs into his shirt. "I'm acting crazy. I'm rambling. I don't know what I'm saying."

"No." He shifts her gently out of his arms so he can look at her. "You ain't crazy. I know exactly what you're sayin.'"

"You do?"

"I do. I'm crazy about you, Lacey." He leans in, sweeping his lips softly over hers. "I wanna go back to Nashville, and you're comin' with me, and honestly, that has me over the goddamn moon."

His words melt her. Sniffling, she scans his handsome face, reaching up to touch the butterfly bandage on his eyebrow. "Does it hurt?"

"Nah. I'm tough." He runs a finger across her cheek and hits her with a grin. "You wanna talk about what hurt? How about those right hooks you were throwin' out there on that lawn?"

Lacey smiles. "You deserved it."

He chuckles. Then, his face softens into an expression she's never seen before. "Lace, I—"

Before he can get the words out, Lacey throws her arms around his neck and kisses him back, kisses him deep, and that's how they're caught when Sal walks in the back door.

TWENTY-EIGHT

ONE MINUTE SETH WAS KISSING LACEY, HIS BRAIN blitzing out and switching off so completely nothing registered. Not where they were or who was around. All that mattered was Lacey and making sure she knew she was the most important thing in his orbit. Making sure he didn't fuck up the best thing that ever happened to him. Ready to give her the goddamn best *forgive me* kiss of her life and finding he was dangerously close. Close to saying it.

I love you.

Only she had kissed him first. And he was gone.

Then, from left field, the softest of gasps.

Seth freezes.

Lacey stiffens in his hold. She turns her face, Seth's lips sliding from her lips to her cheek. Her eyes flash wide, a small yelp leaps out of her mouth as she leaps out of his arms and stares over his shoulder.

Let it be Luke, he thinks. *Let it be Emmy Lou.* Anyone but Sal catching them in the act. Not with Seth's lips on her little sister's mouth.

He stares at Lacey, hoping against hope, but the horrified look on his face tells him everything he needs to know.

They're caught.

By Sal.

Seth grimaces and turns around to face the firing squad.

Sal and Luke stand there in the opening of the sliding door. Sal's gaze jumps between Seth and Lacey, her brow crinkled. But

Luke hangs back, his solemn expression telling Seth to handle this. And handle it right.

Sal's the first to speak.

"I, uh, forgot my phone," she says, stepping around them to grab her cell off the counter. She stands there, studying them, confusion written all over her pretty features.

She looks at Seth first. "You and Lacey?" A bad sign because that means she's blaming him. Or she's trusting him. He doesn't know which is worse.

All he can do is nod.

Sal tilts her dark head, wondering. "She's my sister, Seth."

"I know."

"How?"

He grins. "Well, the whole thing started with alcohol."

Lacey elbows him. "Seth," she hisses.

Sal meets his eyes with a steely stare.

His smile, the joke, fades.

They're best friends. They've stood by each other. Kept secrets. Told jokes. But Sal's face says no more joking. Not now. Not tonight. There's only her sister and Seth and if what they're doing means anything.

Seth swallows and steps up. He owes her that. "Sal, listen—"

Sal lifts a hand, closes her eyes. "Don't talk to me, Seth."

He snaps his mouth shut, braces his arms back against the counter to hold himself up.

Inside, Seth's dying a slow death. Christ, if he ruins things between him and Sal. If he loses her . . . he'll never forgive himself.

Briefly, he chances a glance at Luke. His brother's content to stay out of it, keeping to a corner of the room, his dark eyes on the trio.

Sal cuts her eyes to Lacey. "You tell me."

Lacey nods, stepping forward, her hands on her heart. "It happened after the plane crash, when you were missing." Sal's eyes widen at the lengthy time span. Lacey continues. "I needed someone and Seth was there. After that, it was kind of ongoing whenever we were together and now . . . now it's something."

Sal's eyes fill with tears. "When were you going to tell me?"

Fuck. Sal's flashing back to the past. When Luke kept secrets from her to protect her. Seth knows she hates that. Knows she worked hard to keep the truth in her life.

Seth can't stand it any longer. He's being eaten up by guilt. By Sal's watery eyes, her trembling hands. She looks fragile and making her cry—making her cry while *pregnant*—he's an asshole. Pushing off the counter, he says, "Sal, you gotta know we didn't want you to find out like this."

"We wanted to wait until there was a right time," Lacey adds. "And you've been worrying about the baby and the vacation and then there was Beau and you were getting protective and Seth crashed his ATV because he's an idiot and—"

Seth needles his brow. "Lace, you're ramblin."

Lacey lets loose a giant sigh. "We all didn't want to risk upsetting you."

It's the *we all* that gets her.

Sal whirls on Luke. "Did *you* know?"

Luke's mouth falls open, his eyes flashing with worry. He straightens up, clearing his throat. "Darlin' . . ."

She turns away from Luke, giving his brother the coldest cold shoulder Seth's ever seen. Luke, pained, leans back against the wall, tossing Seth a thanks-a-lot glare.

Sal stands there, processing the news, while Lacey and Seth wait, frozen.

Finally, Sal turns to them. She inhales a breath, places both hands on her belly, and asks, "Is it serious?"

Seth reaches for Lacey's hand. "It is," he says. The only thing he can do to prove to Sal that he's serious. "Lacey, she's . . ."

He wants to say more. Say that he loves her desperately, stupidly, but he can't. It's like the words stick. Like letting his guard down in front of everyone, like finally owning it, will have him failing all over again. Fucking things up like he always does.

And he can't ruin this. Not this.

Lacey squeezes his hand, and he looks over at her, almost startled, the simple action spurring Seth forward. She's there for him. Just like she's always been. Giving him strength, making him better, holding his heart.

"She's perfect," he finishes. "She's my everything. I care about her so damn much, Sal."

Lacey, her own eyes glittering with tears, says, "We're going to try and make it work in Nashville."

Something like life comes into Sal's pale face. "You are?"

Seth draws Lacey into him. "We are."

Lacey's got a death grip on his hand as they wait for Sal's response.

Sal takes a breath and raises her eyes to the ceiling as if debating with herself. And then she lets out a great burst of a sob. Seth's heart plummets. They all take a step toward her and stop.

She's laughing.

Holding her stomach and rolling with full-throttle laughter.

Lacey tilts her blond head, perplexed. "Sal?"

Sal covers her mouth, reins back the laugh, and says, "This is the best news ever."

Lacey squeaks. "Wait, what?"

"Hell, I'm fuckin' confused," Seth says. He peers at her. "Sal, you okay?"

"Of course." Her smile softens in wonder and she looks at Seth. "I'm so happy for you two." She arches a mischievous brow. "I had to feel you out first. It is my sister after all."

"Jesus Christ." Seth laughs, ripping a hand through his hair. His nerves off the charts. "You're officially cut off from playing bad cop. You goddamn terrified me."

Lacey floats him a look of relief as she brings Sal in for a hug. Their happy squeals fill the kitchen, a rush of contentment nearly knocking Seth over.

Sal knows. It's out.

Lacey's coming back to Nashville.

Now all he's gotta do is tell her he loves her.

It should be easy.

So why is he waiting?

Seth exits Lacey's room, descending the stairs with a groan. The day feels longer than long, and he's sore as hell, not like he'd tell Luke that, but there's one thing he's gotta do first.

Talk to Sal one-on-one. Talk honest. Make sure she's okay. Really okay.

He loves that Lacey understands his and Sal's friendship. That the only thing she's jealous about is Sal liking Seth more than her. He chuckles to himself. That he can deal with.

He finds her in the living room. It's late, the fire's still going and so is Sal, apparently. Her back to him, he watches in amusement as Sal balances herself on the lip of the fireplace. A bag of gifts in her hands, she stretches out on tiptoes to reach the stockings that hang high on the mantel.

He goes to her side. "You know, I'm tall and I'm also not pregnant."

She blinks down at him and smiles. "Tomorrow's Christmas. Just playing Santa."

"Yeah, I can see that, and so will Luke if he walks in here anytime soon." He takes the bag from her, helps her onto solid ground. "I got the rest."

Sal perches her slight frame on the couch. When Seth finishes stuffing stockings, he sits beside her. "I wanted to make sure you're okay." He gives her a look. "That we're okay."

She nods. "We are."

But her lip is trembling, tears pooling in her emerald eyes.

He scoots close. "Sal, what is it?"

She wipes at her face. "Nothing."

"It's somethin'. You're in here cryin' and I know it's not over bad Christmas presents." He chances a glance over his shoulder.

The last thing he wants is Luke walking in here and finding Sal weeping a river because of Seth. This time, his brother really will kill him.

She shakes her head. "It's just . . . I'm scared."

He frowns. "Of what?"

She gestures around her. "Of everything changing." She cradles her stomach. Lowers her voice. "Of something happening to the baby."

Sighing, Seth takes her slender hand. "Ain't nothing goin' to happen to you or that baby. I won't let it. And Luke sure as hell won't. You hear me?"

"What if I'm an awful mother? I mean, I can't even cook. What if we're not ready?"

Seth chuckles. "Sal, there is no way you'd be a bad mother. You're the most selfless person I know. You and Luke are gonna be great parents. I mean, hell, bossin' people around is Luke's business."

Sal laughs, her eyes shiny with tears.

"What else?" he asks. "Give it to me now."

She nods. Biting her lip, she raises her eyes to meet his dead-on. "I'm scared of you and Lacey," she whispers. "I'm so happy for you, but . . . if you break up . . . if that changes, we change. I can't lose either of you."

His heart twists. "You ain't losin' me. You're my best friend, Sal. Nothing's gonna change that. And Lacey . . . you don't gotta worry about that either." He exhales. "She's a massive pain in my ass, but . . . I love her more than anything."

Sal sniffs, smiling up at him. "You do?"

"I do."

"Does she know that?"

"Not yet."

She peers at him, confused. "Seth, why not?"

He swallows at the gentle admonition, meets her eyes. "I don't want to fuck it up." Though the admittance is hard, it feels good to talk to Sal, to confide in her. He missed that. "I've never said it to anyone before. What if she ain't there?"

"She's there. And you won't fuck it up, Seth." She squeezes his arm. "Back in the kitchen, you were talking serious. I've never heard that from you before."

"Yeah. It's pretty damn serious." His chest tightens thinking about it. "I want to give her everything. A fuckin' house, hundreds of shoes if she wants 'em."

Sal laughs, then her face turns stern and solemn. "I love that you love her. So much. Just . . . my sister has a soft heart, Seth. Don't break it."

Her words cut him, make him realize the seriousness of the situation. He needs to make it count, make it work. Otherwise, it's not just Lacey he'd lose. He'd lose his best friend too.

Swallowing down the boulder in his throat, he reaches out and pulls Sal in for a tight hug. "I won't." They stay there like that, watching the crackling fire, Seth's heart a wild drumbeat in his ears.

Because he fucking hopes, prays, he didn't just lie to Sal.

TWENTY-NINE

LACEY WAKES TO SUNLIGHT, TO SETH BESIDE HER. SHE lies there for a second, listening to the world outside the bedroom. Laughter, the clink of dishes, the smell of freshly brewed coffee.

"Merry Christmas."

Seth's deep rumble has her smiling. As does the very sight of him. He's grinning, his hair tousled, his eyes sleepy as he leans up on one elbow to kiss her.

Sweet. Soft. Warm.

She pulls away, cupping his cheek in her hand. "Merry Christmas."

Seth groans as a loud whoop fills the hallway outside. "No one's got kids yet," he grumbles, wrapping a lean arm around her shoulder to loop her into him. "Why the hell is everyone up so early?"

Lacey laughs at Seth's bah humbug attitude. "Uh, presents?"

"Stayin' here with you all day . . ." He wiggles his brows. "Now that's the present."

She rolls her eyes at Seth's all-the-time charm, but secretly, she loves it. With a sigh, she snuggles deeper into his arms.

"Last night . . . ," she hedges, looking up at him. "I think it went okay, don't you?"

He hugs her a little tighter. "Better than."

She closes her eyes. Seth's right. Despite their awkward start, the talk with Sal went better than she had hoped. She couldn't survive if Sal wasn't okay with their relationship, and she knows

Seth couldn't either. The stricken look on his face when Sal had caught them kissing said it all. But they're okay, they're all okay, and now it's out, and Lacey's free to savor every moment with Seth. To kiss him in public if she damn well chooses.

Another wild whoop blasts through the door.

"Jesus, we get it." Seth drops a kiss on top of her head. "C'mon," he says. "Let's get out there before Luke starts bitchin.'"

They slip out of bed, changing quick. Lacey shrugs on a robe, Seth, gray sweatpants and a T-shirt.

He grabs her hand as they exit the room together, drifting down the hall and into the living room, where everyone's gathered. Christmas tree lights twinkle, the fireplace roars, a pile of presents ready to be ripped open. Through the tall windows, snow falls, fat, white flakes of powder.

Emmy Lou, Alabama, and Griff are curled up on the couch, a fuzzy blanket on top of them. Sal's perched on the lip of the fireplace, content and beautiful in ruby-colored silk pajamas.

Griff and Alabama's mischievous eyes dance between Lacey and Seth. Alabama grins in Lacey's direction. A tilt of her red head. "So, it's out?"

Lacey laughs. "Oh, it's out. In the very worst way it could be out."

Emmy Lou and Alabama gasp as one. "Lord, say it ain't so," Emmy Lou drawls. "You got caught."

"Big-time busted," Seth adds, floating Sal a smile.

Griff snickers. "'Bout time you two idiots got out of your own damn way."

Sal makes a face of consternation. "So everyone else knew but me?" she asks, eyeing Lacey sternly as best a big sister can.

Emmy Lou smirks. "You don't hit someone like that unless you care, sugar."

Lacey grins at her sister and goes to sit beside her. "Sal is growing a life," she cajoles, side-hugging Sal. She grabs up a stray bow and sticks it on Sal's belly. "She can't worry about ours."

Sal laughs, her eyes glowing with happiness.

Luke and Jace crash through the back door, their faces flushed red from the cold, loads of firewood in their hands. "Hell, we got a white Christmas out there," Luke hoots, walking backwards through the living room. "Damn near snowed in."

From there it's commotion. Emmy Lou pours Irish cream into cups of coffee. Lacey plucks the presents from the tree and passes them around. Luke pulls Sal onto his lap and she giggles at whatever he whispers into her ear. Lacey and Seth sit on the floor together, curled up against the back of the couch.

Everyone settles in for presents. The soft rustling of wrapping paper, of exclamations, of laughter, of thank-yous.

Lacey, her eyes bright, is content to watch. The awkwardness that had been there so early in the trip is gone. Everything is right. Perfect. These people are her family, her friends. She's never been so thankful.

"Oh Lord, Griff," Alabama drawls, raising her hands to reveal a pair of star-shaped diamond earrings. "You're spoilin' me."

"Always, sweetheart," Griff says back, giving his wife a big, broad grin as everyone oohs and ahhs.

Sal bends to pick up a gift wrapped in pearly white paper. She turns to Lacey, pressing it into her hands. "This is for you."

Smiling, Lacey lifts away the wrapping to pull out an exquisite silk scarf with a faint pink paisley pattern.

Sal peers close. "I hope you like it."

"Sal," Lacey breathes. "It's beautiful. I love it. Thank you."

When she looks down, another present has settled in her lap. A small, messily wrapped square about the size of a Post-it. Seth's grinning at her, his blue eyes bright, eager.

She narrows her gaze. "When did you get this?"

He shrugs. "I have my ways."

"Sneak," she hisses. She turns the present over in her hand, having no idea what to expect. Though they spent many Christmases together, they never exchanged serious gifts. She gave him something practical, like a hairbrush for his unruly hair, and Seth usually gave her some gag gift that had her blushing in embarrassment.

She opens the present, wondering, and gasps at what it reveals. Her favorite place in the world—pocket-sized. A small painting of the ocean. A stunning abstract square of blue, white and green depicting the graceful roll of waves.

"Oh, Seth," Lacey whispers, running the tips of her fingers along the side of the painting.

"I found it at an art gallery in town," he says, his voice husky. "For when you need to take the ocean with you."

She looks at him, feeling like the sun is charging up inside her heart. "It's too much."

"Not for you." He leans in, his breath a whisper against her hair. "I got another one for you, but you gotta wait till later."

She smiles, delighted, but before she can pry, a laugh rolls out of Luke. He's holding up a six-pack of beer called Hillbilly Stout. "Think this is the name of our next album."

"Can't stop tradition now," Seth counters with a wicked grin.

Lacey turns to Seth. He has an assortment of gifts at his feet, but she pulls hers from the pile. "Open mine next."

"Should I be worried?" He grins, his eyes on hers, his long fingers pulling back a corner of the wrapping paper. "It ain't another toothbrush, is it?"

"Maybe," Lacey teases, eyeing him as he unwraps it.

Suddenly, the tight twist of her stomach has her in knots. What if he doesn't like it? What if it's not Seth? What if—

"Oh man." Seth's staring at the leather-bound book in his hands. He looks up at her, his throat working. "Where'd you find this?"

Her face heats at the warm stare he's giving her. But she settles for a one-shouldered shrug. "At a bookstore in town." She reaches out, tracing the gold-leaf cowboy on the front cover. "It's about the gunfight at the O.K. Corral. I thought you'd like it."

"This is . . . amazin', Lace." Holding the book like it's some precious artifact she personally dug up from the earth, Seth flips through it, then lifts his gaze to her. His eyes crinkle as he smiles. "I goddamn love it."

He leans in to kiss her, sweeping his mouth against hers.

Silence falls, only the sound of the crackling fire.

Wrapping his arm around her, Seth chuckles, kisses her quick, and then growls at the room. "Y'all wanna take a damn picture?"

Her cheeks warming, Lacey laughs and buries her face in his chest.

Luke, thankfully, stands and hands Sal her present, taking the attention away from Lacey and Seth.

Untangling from Seth, Lacey leans against him, watching as Sal opens her present from Luke, a loopy in-love smile on her face. "Oh, Luke," she sighs as she unveils a pair of tiny ear protectors for the baby to wear at future concerts.

"Get him started early," Seth crows with a proud chuckle.

"*Her*," Lacey shoots back, and a laugh goes up around the room.

Lacey looks to the mountain peaks, the lake glittering through the great windows, Seth's laughter lighting her very soul on fire.

Everyone she loves all in one place.

Her eyes settle on Seth as he tears open a gift from Sal.

Now he just needs to know that.

After a hearty breakfast of homemade buttermilk biscuits, sausage gravy and blackberry jam, everyone breaks to get ready for the day. Lacey goes back to her room, showers and changes into a ruby-red gown with a deep V-neck and a full, sweeping maxi skirt. She's Christmas with ruffles. Standing in front of the mirror, she combs her glossy hair. She can hear commotion going downstairs. Doors slamming. Griff's bark of a laugh. Alabama and Emmy Lou in the kitchen preparing Christmas dinner. Lacey chuckles. She and Seth have strict instructions to keep Sal out.

A knock on the door has her turning.

Seth.

He whistles, low, wolf-style, and presses a hand to his heart. "Good Lord almighty. You're lookin' fine as hell, Lace."

She flushes. His appreciative grin, the drop of his jaw, has her toes curling. Not to mention Seth himself. The entire room started spinning the second he walked in. In black faded jeans and a classic plaid shirt with the cuffs rolled up to expose corded tan muscles, he looks smooth as hell.

She gives a quick spin, flashing her teeth, her dress. "Oh, this old thing?"

"Yeah, right," he says back with a grin. "We both know that cost you an arm and a leg."

She laughs, loving how he knows her. "It's Christmas. I have to be unreasonably glamorous."

He walks over, hooking his hands around her waist and kissing her. "Well, I ain't complain'. You look beautiful."

"Thank you," she says, taking his handsome face in her hands. "You don't look so bad yourself."

"So, listen," he begins, his expression turning anxious. Serious. "I got you somethin' else. It ain't a present exactly, and I wanted to give it to you without everyone gawkin.'"

"Okaaaay," she says carefully, curious.

From out of his back pocket, Seth brings an elongated box. Unwrapped. "Jewelry?" she asks, tilting her head.

He holds it out to her. "You'll see."

Lacey takes it, Seth watching closely as she snaps open the case.

"Oh my God," she breathes. "My locket."

Almost hesitantly, like it's some kind of mirage, Lacey runs a finger over the heart-shaped charm. The gold polished shiny. She sticks a nail into the groove and it opens. Inside are her and Sal's names in cursive script. Eyes brimming with tears, she stares up at Seth. "Where did you get this?"

"I went to a pawnshop back in LA," Seth says, his eyes locked to hers. "I talked to a kid, told him what to look for in case it came in, and it did." His voice goes husky. "I wanted to get it back to you. I know how much you loved it."

Lacey stares at Seth, amazed. Thankful. She has no words for this. Seth found her locket, brought her back her most precious belonging—the memory of her mother. The necklace, the lengths he went to to get it, has her heart aglow.

A lone tear slips down her cheek. "Thank you. I . . ." She stares at the necklace. Her voice wobbles. "This means so much to me. You don't even know."

"Here," he says, reaching for the necklace. Gently, he untangles it from the box and Lacey turns to face the mirror. He slips it around her neck and fastens it. With a smile, Seth wraps his arms around her waist, leaning down to press a kiss to her cheek. She reaches up, covering the locket with her palm.

Lacey stares at them in the mirror, her heart burning in her chest, love swelling in her. Bravery, too.

She spins around to face him, his arms still holding her tight around the waist. She presses into him, to cup his cheek, to meet his eyes. "Thank you so much, Seth." She bites her lip. "You're such a good man, a good person. Whenever I need you, you're there. You keep me together." Tears sparkle in her eyes. "I just . . . I—" An inhale. "I love you. I really love you."

He freezes, his expression going stunned. Caught off guard.

A heartbeat of silence passes.

She swallows. Her heart hammers behind her ribs.

Oh God. Oh no.

It's too early. What did she do?

She's a fool, panicking, looking for the nearest exit, but then Seth grins the most beautiful grin and says, "I love you too."

Lacey blinks. "You do?"

"I do." Inhaling a deep breath, Seth steps closer. His hand cups her face, his calloused thumb skimming her cheekbone. "I've been wantin' to say it for so damn long now. Since the night of the party." Her eyes widen in surprise at the admission. "But I didn't want to scare you off. I wanted to wait for the perfect time. And this is it."

She closes her eyes, hope and love and longing swelling inside her. "Seth . . ."

But he's not done. "And now I'm sayin' it. I love that you are messy and wild and dramatic as hell and make me fuckin' insane. But you're also silly and kind and so goddamn beautiful inside and out. And I love that about you." His eyes, his voice soften. "I love you beyond reason, Lacey."

She shudders at his words, her heart pumping so fast it could fly out of her chest. Hot tears roll down her cheeks. "I love you so much, Seth."

Eyes sparking, his trembling fingers reach for her face, taking it in his hands to bring her lips to his. Seth kisses her hard. A sob works its way out of both of them. Lacey lets out a happy sigh, curling her arms around Seth's neck as he gathers her in his arms.

She has Seth's I-love-you. A note she'll forever live by. Locked tight in her heart like the most perfect song she's ever heard.

chapter THIRTY

Day five of vacation has Seth ambling up the snowy driveway to the cabin. Winston bounds ahead of him, barking at nonexistent birds. He's volunteered to take him on a walk for Sal. The first of many babysitting duties, he's sure.

He glances up, a grin on his face. Through the big windows he can see Lacey. She looks beautiful. Happy.

His heart tightens. Christ. He feels love-stoned. His life changed out of the blue when Lacey told him she loved him. And he said it back. No hesitation. The perfect time to tell her what she meant to him.

For once in his life, he didn't fuck up. He did something right, and he's gonna hang onto it.

He's got that once-in-a-lifetime kind of love. He's finally where he wants to be with Lacey. And the thing that really has his heart skipping all kinds of beats is that they have the rest of their lives to do *them*. He's ready. Ready to give this all he's got and then some. Put a rock on her hand, give her everything, keep her safe, make her wildest dreams come true.

Striding up the bank to the front door, Seth gives a sharp whistle. But Winston bolts. Damn dog. Seth shakes his head, ruefully watching as the scruffy mutt buries his nose in the snow beside a dead rosebush. Since Christmas Day, the snow's been coming down fast and furious, leaving the entire group housebound.

As he gets closer to the house, Seth hears a voice.

It's Jace. Standing beneath the awning of the house, away from the snow. Cell phone held to his ear.

"Listen, I don't know who the fuck you are, but don't call here anymore. You understand me? I ain't got your damn money."

Seth goes numb, not believing what he's hearing.

Fuck. His hunch from Christmas Eve was right. Jace is gambling again. Two years ago, his money troubles were what prompted Luke to come back to the Brothers Kincaid. He and Luke thought he had gotten straight, especially after Jace sat them down a few months ago and explained why he had done what he had, but apparently not.

As Seth stands there, debating whether or not to make himself known, Winston decides for him.

The scruffy terrier bounds up to Seth, barking, alerting Jace.

"Hey, man," Jace says, stepping out from the eave. He lowers the phone, his expression uncertain.

"Hey," Seth says, shifting his stance on the threshold to open the front door and let Winston in the house. "How's it goin'?"

"Oh, you know. It's goin'."

"Where's Emmy Lou?"

"She's out ridin'."

"Why ain't you out there with her?" When Jace is quiet, his hazel eyes hitting the ground, Seth expels a long breath. "You're doin' this again, man?"

Jace wears a look of discomfort at being caught. "It ain't what you're thinkin', Seth."

"You sure about that?" Seth arches a brow. "You remember the farm, Jace? Because I remember the farm."

Jace turns away and cups a hand on the back of his neck. He looks angry at himself. "Listen, I don't wanna drag you into my mess."

Seth takes a step closer. "If it's your mess, it's our mess." He means it. He and Jace haven't been close in the past, but they're brothers. They take it together, they fix it.

Jace meets his eyes. Nods his thanks. Exhales and explains.

"The last three days, someone keeps callin' me, sayin' I owe them money."

"Well, do you?"

Jace looks insulted. "No. I paid my loan two damn years ago. You fuckin' know that."

"Then who is it?"

"It's gotta be the *Star* fishin' around for another front-page story." Jace drags a tired hand down his face. "Either way, I haven't gambled since I got myself into this mess and that's how it's gonna stay. I ain't goin' back there again." A shake of his head. "That thing with Griff the other day, I saw y'all's faces . . . I was havin' fun. It wasn't anything to be worried about."

A grin breaks out on Seth's face. "Jace . . . that's great, man." He opens his hands, relieved. Relieved Jace wasn't doing what he thought. Relieved Luke ain't gonna put a boot up his best friend's ass.

This is Jace they're talking about. Steady, easygoing, serious Jace. He fucked up. He learned his lesson. He's fixing it. He ain't like Seth. Or Beau and his bullshit.

It hits Seth then that they haven't seen Beau in a couple of days. With any luck, the guy tucked tail back to Nashville.

"And listen. Emmy Lou doesn't know about the phone calls, so don't go tellin' her."

Seth jerks his head up. "Why the hell not?"

Jace makes a sound of disgust. "She finally trusts me again. We're back to where we were before everything happened with Luke. Before I got our farm in trouble." Jace grimaces. Seth feels for the guy. He knows Jace doesn't like to talk about the painful parts of his past. "I don't want her to think I can't keep it together."

Seth's throat tightens. "You should tell her, Jace. Keepin' secrets . . . that ain't no way to live."

He's a fine one to talk. He can't even tell his own brother the truth.

Jace gives him a frown, picking up on his mood. "*You* okay?"

A halfhearted shrug. "Still workin' on it sometimes."

Jace nods, then laughs. "Good to know we're both fuckin' messes."

Seth cracks a grin. "Same shit, different day."

The front door swings open. Luke stands in the doorway.

Jace swallows like he's caught, his gaze dropping on the ground.

"Seth," Luke says, his expression grim. "Lacey needs you."

Inside, the living room's quiet. The mood somber. The group gathers around the crackling fire, listening. From Seth's periphery, Griff and Alabama lean back against the wall. Luke and Jace at the fireplace. But Seth only has eyes for Lacey.

She stands in the middle of the room, phone pressed to her ear. Her grip tight. Her eyes are closed, as if bricking away whatever is being said.

Stomach dipping, Seth goes to stand next to Sal. "Who is it?" he whispers, his eyes on Lacey.

"The police," Sal says quietly. Her brow's drawn in concern.

His spine stiffens. Shit.

Seth aches to go to Lacey but forces himself to stay put. She has to handle this. Lacey's strong. A fighter. Capable of so damn much and whatever the news is, he's got her.

"Yes. I understand." A bob of Lacey's blond head. She swallows. "Okay. Thank you."

She ends the call and stares at the phone.

And then she looks up. Tears glisten in her eyes.

Every breath in the room is held.

"Lace," Seth says carefully, taking a tentative step toward her. He reaches a hand out. Waiting. Worrying.

"They caught him," Lacey announces, her face dazed. Her voice trembles. "They caught the mugger." She smiles at Seth and then turns that dazzling smile to the room. "He confessed. He's in jail."

A joyous cry escapes Sal, and she launches herself at Lacey and embraces her.

Luke lets out a hoot, pounding a palm against the fireplace mantel. Together, the room erupts as one. Comes alive. Whoops of relief, rejoicing. Griff growls, "Glory fuckin' hallelujah," and squeezes Lacey up in a big bear hug. A jubilee right in the middle of the living room.

And then, though the room is abuzz with excitement, Lacey finds Seth at last. Her turquoise eyes fixed on him. "Seth," she says, and it's all she needs to say.

For a long moment, he stares at her. Wrecked. Relieved.

He sees Lacey then. Steady. Safe. Strong.

"Hey, princess," he says, his voice hoarse. "Looks like things just keep gettin' better and better."

"Yeah," she says, smiling through her tears. "They do."

Seth takes Lacey in his arms. She leans into him, fragile and fierce all at once. She throws her arms around his neck right before he dips his head and kisses her.

His love undimming.

The hell, the pain she endured this last month is over.

Their future endless.

He's got Lacey. She's safe. She's his. And they've got nothing but time.

THE NEXT AFTERNOON, SAL UNCORKS A BOTTLE OF WINE and then hands it over to Alabama. With flourish, Alabama pulls a stack of red Solo cups from a cabinet and then a box of long matches from a drawer.

Lacey takes a seat across from Sal at the round breakfast bar, watching as the women work in sync. Something that, only months ago, would have had her jealous or protective but now only has her curious. "What's happening?"

Beside her, Emmy Lou doesn't look up from her puzzle. Her pink mouth purses. "We're doin' a bonfire, sugar."

"On the patio," Sal amends.

"Firepit," Alabama adds.

"Tradition," Luke drawls as he sweeps into the kitchen, guitar in his hand. He dips to press a kiss to Sal's temple. "Sing some tunes. Drink some drinks. Make some fire."

"Please, Lord, Luke, do not burn this cabin down," Emmy Lou murmurs. "I am minutes away from this kickin' this puzzle's ass." With a victorious squeal, she snatches up her needed puzzle piece.

A wild cackle. Seth appears, fiddle case in hand. Leaning into her, he runs a smooth hand down the back of her long antique-white eyelet dress. With small buttons down the front and tight sleeves, it's a dress as romantic as she feels. "Hey, good-lookin'," he murmurs against her ear.

"Hey, yourself," Lacey says, twisting into his golden touch.

"Another million-dollar outfit?"

She flashes a smile. "You know it."

Seth kisses her lazily, like they've been at it all afternoon, then pulls back to look at her. "You gonna stick around for the show?" he asks, his eyes lasered on hers.

"Guess I could make an appearance," she teases. She scans his face. There's something strange in his eyes. An eagerness, an earnestness she's never seen before.

Seth laughs and kisses her once more before loping off toward his brother.

Lacey leans back on the barstool. She swerves her eyes around the cabin, taking in everything before her. The afternoon sun sinking behind the mountains. The men tuning instruments, trading ball-busting banter as they prep for their jam session. The room's warm with fire, with friendship. Everything so perfect. She's never felt so lucky.

Her mugger's been caught. There's so much relief in knowing he's off the streets. A strength in knowing that if she survived that, she can survive anything. And in another week, it'll be a new year. A new chapter, transformative, just like Lacey herself.

Beneath heavy lashes, she steals a look at Seth. Her heart thunders as she glimpses his handsome, boyish face. He wears his black Henley from LA, his blue eyes as crystal as the ocean. Lacey flushes. Ugh, she feels like a frazzled mess of lovesick blues. She laughs softly to herself. God, she's turning into a bad country song. But her heart warms at the thought. Warms at what he's done for her.

Lacey reaches up to finger her locket.

He'd never take credit, of course, but Seth, not the cops, caught her mugger. If he hadn't tracked down her necklace at that pawnshop, it never would have happened. She has him to thank.

"You okay, Em?" Sal's husky voice jolts Lacey from her reverie.

Lacey turns from Seth to look at Emmy Lou. The sunny blond's scanning the room, her pretty face creased in irritation.

"Oh, you know. Just lookin' for Jace." Emmy Lou scowls, her

tone bitter. "Other than my husband bein' on the phone the entire damn day, everything's just peachy."

Sal's jaw drops.

Lacey slides her eyes to Alabama's, Her own surprise reflected in the redhead's gray depths. It's the first time she's ever seen Emmy Lou drop her prim and proper facade. An admission of the trouble brewing under the picture-perfect surface.

Emmy Lou scowls, a puzzle piece strangled in her hand. Her voice a hushed whisper. "I swear, if he's steppin' out on me with some hillbilly harlot, I'm gonna . . ." She lets out a frustrated growl, but Lacey sees the pain on her face. The worry.

Sal rushes to reassure, placing her small hand over Emmy Lou's. "Oh, Em. Jace would never."

Alabama tuts. "I'm sure that isn't it."

Lacey knows it isn't.

Yesterday, Seth had confided in her about his and Jace's conversation. Still, despite knowing the facts, she'd never say anything to Emmy Lou. That's Jace's business. She can only hope he owns up to whatever he's gotten himself into. Otherwise, Emmy Lou looks on the verge of taking a frying pan to her husband's face.

Before any of the women can say anything further, a ping from Lacey's phone.

An LA number. Name unknown.

With one quick slide, she answers. "Hello?"

"You're a hard woman to track down, darling. To think I had to resort to buying a burner phone just to get the drop on you."

At the sound of Colin's familiar voice, Lacey sits up straight and lets out a squeak.

Shit. Shit. Shit.

"Lace?" Sal's deep green eyes pin her down.

"Tell me, what have you been doing? Other than ignoring my calls."

Lacey flinches, thinking of all the calls from Colin she's denied. "Give me one second," she says into the receiver. Then—

"I have to take this," Lacey says to the women, slipping off the stool to stand and grabbing her parka from the hallway coat hook. "I'll be right back."

A wave of guilt hits her as she sneaks right past Seth and out the back door, wanting to get out of the house before he over-hears and worries.

Time to face Colin like she's faced this last month. With strength. With resolve. Not to mention a little bit of stone-cold fear.

Outside, Lacey picks up the conversation. "Colin, hi," she says, trudging through the fresh snow. The cold cuts like a knife. Tucking the phone against her ear, she zips up her parka, her eyes scouring the clouds above. It's only three p.m. and the sky is gray and fat with snow. "I know I've been off the grid. I'm in Tennessee. I needed a vacation. I was—"

"Mugged."

She stops. "How did you know?"

"My darling, Autumn told me. Had I known . . ." He lets out a huff of a sigh. "I acted atrociously. And so did Prentiss. As I'm sure you've heard, they are no longer my agency of rep."

"I hadn't. I kind of tuned out the world these days." Hair whip-ping around her face, Lacey moves in the direction of the dock. "Colin, why are you calling?"

"I want you to come work for me." Though his voice is tinny over the line, she hears him loud and clear.

Her mouth drops. "Excuse me?"

"Directly. I want you to be my personal party planner. All the parties. You'll have carte blanche. A credit card. The guest house out back if you want to live there." Colin's melodic voice sings. "You're the one Prentiss needs, not the other way around."

"Colin. That's an amazing offer, but—"

"And I swear, no more dead-of-night errands. Unless it in-volves Prentiss and a hit-and-run."

Lacey chokes on a laugh.

"What do you say, darling?" Colin asks, his voice cajoling. "Don't make me plan my parties without my right-hand woman."

A thrill of excitement zips through her. Holy shit. Her dream job offered to her on a silver platter. All her worries about what comes next instantly solved.

But what about Seth? The thought of leaving him has her soul slowly disintegrating.

She glances back at the house, softening. Resolved to finally do what's in her heart.

"Colin, I'm sorry, but I'm happy. I have a life here now." Stepping onto the dock, she walks its length down to the railing to overlook the water. Steeling herself, she inhales a sharp breath. "Thank you, but I can't accept. I—"

The line sizzles with static.

"Darling . . . no for an answer . . ."

"Colin, I can't hear you. What—"

" . . . the offer is open . . . no one else . . ."

She keeps her tone firm, no room for bullshit. "Colin, no. I meant what I said." She frowns when there's silence. "Hello? Colin, you there?" she says into the phone, but all that greets her is crackling static. "Ugh."

"Can't get service, angel?" a dry voice says from behind her. "Join the club."

Lacey turns, shoving the phone into the pocket of her parka. Surprised he's still here, she sighs as she takes in Beau's haggard form. He wears a thin jacket and an even expression. "You shouldn't be here, Beau."

He lifts a flask. "Lot of things I shouldn't be doin'."

She crosses her arms. "Luke's inside. If he finds you here . . ."

"Yeah, yeah, I'll run fast." He swaggers closer to her. "Came to see if I could use the house phone. I'm gettin' snowed in over there. I ain't got no service and I want to get the hell out of here, y'all bein' so accomodatin' and all."

Lacey rolls her eyes and turns back to the water. Too distracted by her conversation with Colin to tell him to get lost.

Her mind running wild, she stares out at the choppy lake. The current's fast, churning out whitecaps and foam. A thin shell of frost crusts its glittering surface. Lacey shivers. It's cold out on the dock, but it's nothing compared to how she feels after her conversation with Colin.

Beau settles beside her. Lacey makes a face. He reeks of booze. "You wanna get out of here? Go get a drink?"

"You're already drinking," she says, threading her hand through her snarled hair and giving a defiant chin lift. "Besides, I'm with Seth."

"You sure?" He peers at her, a sly smile on his face. "One night with me, I'm bettin' I could persuade you otherwise."

Lacey avoids his gaze, instead glancing over her shoulder at the cabin. The warm glow of the lights. The chimney puffing up white smoke to the gray sky. The people inside, laughter, love, music. And where is she? Out here, freezing her ass off and talking to the slime of the earth.

Suddenly, a contentedness like she's never known settles over her. Even though her brain, her irritatingly obnoxious type A brain, is screaming at her to be a responsible adult, to choose stability over romance, her heart tells her she made the right decision about Colin's offer.

She's in love with Seth. They have a plan, a future.

She closes her eyes and breathes.

A forever.

She turns around fully to face Beau. "I'm going back to the house. I'll ask Luke about the phone."

"Ah, c'mon now," he says, taking a step backward to block her path. "We just got started talkin.'"

She stares at the man who ran Seth off the road, who's been an asshole to her sister and her friends, and she balls a fist. "I'm not talking to you."

Beau's eyes go flat, a sadness, a strange something shining in their depths. Then, as quick as it came, it's gone, and he grins at her. He reaches out, his eyes lighting, his hand lifting for her throat. For an excuse to touch her. Sweeping a thumb over the locket, he says, "Hey now, this is pretty."

The words rip through her like a wave.

His words. The man. The mugger from the alley.

He may be off the streets, caught, gone, but his memory isn't.

Lacey's hands fly up to clasp the necklace around her neck protectively. She backs up on the dock. Wanting to get away. Needing to get away.

How do you swim a wave if you're drowning, Lacey?

"Leave me alone." Her voice is a raw whisper. "Don't touch me."

You break through it.

Fear swarms her, cutting off her senses. She doesn't know what to do. All she knows she has to get out of there.

Beau's bloodshot eyes go wide, as if realizing he's finally crossed the line. "Shit. Hey, listen, I didn't—" He staggers forward, too fast, too close, stumbling and knocking Lacey off-balance. Knocking her back hard against the wooden railing.

You break it.

A crack. A creak.

The railing snaps.

Her hands fly up and she tries to grab onto something, anything. But Beau's hitting his knees, dazed, swaying, too drunk to help as he throws up violently on the side of the dock.

Lacey's world tilts.

And then she hits cold water.

Seth, chewing on a Red Vine, steps into the kitchen, groaning at what he finds there. Everyone but Lacey. This goddamn maze of a house. He fucking hates it.

"You see Lace?" he asks Luke. The Brothers Kincaid, Griff, they're set up. They're ready to play and Seth's itching to find Lacey. To tell her he's got a song for her. It's a risky move, a heart-on-his-sleeve gesture playing it in front of everyone, but nothing's ever felt more right. He wants Lacey to hear it, wants everyone to know what he feels for her.

"No," Luke replies as he's tossing Griff a beer. "Sal might've." He nods at the big window where Sal and Alabama are outside stoking the fire pit.

Blowing out a breath, Seth pushes through the sliding door and steps out onto the deck. "Hey," he says, sidling next to Sal.

"Hey." She reaches up and steals the Red Vine from his mouth and pops it into her own.

Seth gives her a crooked grin. "That baby's turnin' you into a bum."

"What can I say? It's a lawless land out here in the country."

A chuckle rolls out of him. "You seen Lace?" he asks, whisking his hands together. His breath comes in white puffs. "Can't find her anywhere."

"Last I saw her, she said she had a phone call she had to take." Sal steps away from the fire, thinking on it. "Maybe fifteen minutes ago."

"She's out on the dock," Alabama offers, a glass of wine in her hands. She swivels her red head to the choppy waters of the lake. Her lips purse. "That's funny . . ."

Sal tilts her head. "What is?"

"She was just there . . ." Alabama frowns, her gray eyes narrowing.

Puzzled, taking a few steps to the railing, Sal scans the backyard, then the choppy waters of the lake. Seth follows suit. Slanted sunlight casts its shadows. A hunched figure on the dock.

A harsh gasp whitens Sal's face. "Oh my God." Horror rises up in the green depths of her eyes. "Oh my God, she's in the water."

Seth almost laughs, almost tells Sal she's nuts, but then the hunched-over figure straightens up, and he sees that it's Beau, hanging over the edge of the dock, trying to grab at something and failing.

Seth's heart stops.

Sal's right.

Someone's screaming, the sound like a siren, shouting for Luke, for Griff, but Seth doesn't hear any of it.

He's already off and running, his chest heaving, picking up speed as he tears down the steps and across the lawn.

Lacey Lacey Lacey.

Her name's the heartbeat in his ears, the blood in his veins, as he explodes across the frozen earth.

He's only vaguely aware of the world beside him. Luke by-passing Sal to grab her high around the waist and slam her back into Griff. Sal struggles in Griff's tight grasp, letting out a sob, cursing him, as Griff drags her back. Because she'd be the next one in that water right after Seth.

Finally, he makes it to the dock.

Beau's up and staggering. Seth grabs him by the collar, shoving him back toward the splintered railing, ready to kill. "Where is she?" he shouts. "Where the fuck is she?"

"She's in the lake," Beau stutters, his eyes wet and terrified. "She fell—I tried to grab her, but—"

A harsh gasp wrenches out of Seth and he shoves Beau away. He falls to his knees at the edge of the dock. His eyes scan the dark water, the rushing current, his soul ripping in half. "*Lacey!*" He screams her name into the wind, his throat raw, ragged.

Nothing. Silence.

He's going in. After her. To the goddamn bottom if he has to.

Seth braces himself on the dock, preparing to push off when a strong hand grips his shoulder.

"I'll get her," Luke says, his eyes terrified—for Seth and Lacey both.

"Fuck you, man," Seth grits out. "Let me go." He struggles against his brother's tight hold, frantic, desperate to shake Luke loose when there's a sharp explosion from the water.

Lacey.

She's gasping for air, shooting to the surface, reaching out with a faint cry. Seth, whip-quick, lurches for her. The fastest he's ever moved. By some miracle, he manages to grab her wrist. With all his strength, he pulls her up onto the dock, where she collapses, facedown, her matted hair pooling around her face.

She's still. Too still.

A burst of fear, of clawing panic, has him scrambling.

And then Lacey moans in pain. Harsh coughs wrack her body as she chokes up water.

Relief sucker punches Seth. She's breathing, her cough the most beautiful sound he's ever heard.

"Thank God," he says hoarsely. He rolls her over, gathering her slender frame in his arms, sucking in a breath at the shock of cold, at the harsh tremble of her body. Her white dress, now sheer, clings to her skin, her nipples dark through the gauze.

Luke drops to his knees, ripping off his jacket and draping it around her.

She lets out a small moan but lies there, eyes closed. The stillness of her body in his arms, the blue of her lips, has Seth scared shitless. "Open your eyes, princess," he urges, sweeping hair away from her pale face. "Please open your eyes. Talk to me, Lacey."

With effort, she does. Her lashes flutter as she meets Seth's gaze. "S-Seth," she whispers.

"I'm here." Anguish wrecks Seth's voice. "I'm here, Lace."

"C-c-cold," she rasps, her voice weak. Her teeth chatter.

"I know you are," he says, fighting the knot in his throat. "We're gonna get you warm, okay? You're gonna be okay."

Closing in on Lacey's other side is Sal, having somehow made it out of Griff's arms. Her face tense, her eyes scouring her sister intently, she places fingers on Lacey's neck to check for a pulse. Her eyes snap up to Beau. "How long was she in?"

Only Beau stands frozen, staring down at Lacey.

Seth's jaw tightens. If it weren't for Lacey freezing to death in his arms, he'd kill him. Beau would be in that fucking lake.

Getting no answer, Sal shouts over at him, *"How long, Beau?"*

"T-t-two minutes," he stutters, squeezing his eyes shut. "Maybe three."

A small groan escapes Lacey, hitting Seth hard like a bullet in the chest. Clutching her tight in his arms, he leans in close. "Breathe," he whispers, willing her breaths less ragged. "Breathe for me."

The dock vibrates with movement. Seth looks over. Jace and Griff come skidding to a stop, their faces tense and worried.

"Should we take her to the hospital?" Griff asks, staring down at Lacey, both hands on the back of his head like he wants to start pacing then and there.

Sal, taking her concentration from Lacey, says, "It's quicker to get the doctor. It's a two-hour drive to Gatlinburg." She turns back, wiping hair from her sister's face. "She's breathing. We just have to get her warm."

"I'll go," Luke says. His eyes wild, he hustles off the dock, followed by Jace.

Sal glances sideways at Seth, tears bright in her eyes. "We have to get her inside. Fast."

The urgency in Sal's voice has Seth's gut churning.

Seth curls his arms underneath Lacey, lifting her up. He sucks in ragged breaths, fights back tears as he runs for the house. His heart near to bursting. He's holding his entire world in his arms and he doesn't know what he'll do if he loses it.

Lacey's world tilts as she's cradled in strong arms against a hard chest. Seth's moving fast, his arms so tight around her, and she wants to tell him to slow down, he's making her dizzy, but she doesn't think she has the strength to make that happen.

She's cold. So cold. Freezing.

The soothing rumble of Seth's voice vibrates through her. "Be okay," he says. "Be okay. Please, Christ, you're gonna be okay." His voice a whisper, a chant, like some desperate plea to someone far away, up above.

Lacey strains to look up at him. The hard set of his jaw, the fierce worry in his blue eyes.

But soon, the cold gives way to warmth.

Lacey opens her eyes to see a crackling fire. A pile of blankets. The concerned faces of Emmy Lou and Alabama.

"Oh no," Emmy Lou squeaks, her hands together as if in prayer.

"Start a warm bath," Sal instructs Emmy Lou. "Make some tea. Not too hot," she tells Alabama. Both women scatter.

Lacey's eyes close again as she's settled somewhere soft. The floor. The rug. In front of the fire. Seth shifts as she's propped up in his arms. Her world feels blurry, like she's still underwater. In that cold, dark lake, fighting her way up to the surface.

She shivers. She can't stop. She lies limply against Seth, his body steady and strong as he presses her tight against him, trying to give her all his heat.

"Lacey." Sal's husky voice sounds. "We're going to get you out of these clothes."

She stares up at Seth, who's frantically trying to unbutton the tiny buttons on the front of her dress. It would be funny if his handsome face wasn't so serious. If she weren't so damn cold.

"Mmm, you're always trying to get me naked," she says sleepily.

Seth smiles at that and kisses the top of her head, but his eyes are misty, his hands shaking as his fingers find a rhythm.

And then she's undressed and Lacey lets them, uncaring of her modesty because they move fast. Carefully, her arms are raised, her soaked dress peeled away from her body. Her nipples pucker from the air and she whimpers as goose bumps cover her skin. Socks are slipped on, blankets are wrapped around her, swaddled tight so she can't move. Sal starts towel-drying Lacey's long hair in swift, whisking motions.

Still, she shivers. She's so cold, she shakes violently.

Seth hoists her higher in his arms. He takes her hand, turning it over in his, rubbing her palm, trying to keep her warm. "She won't stop shakin', Sal."

"She will." But her sister sounds worried. "Here." Sal lifts a mug of warm tea to Lacey's lips. "Drink this."

The steam feels good on her face. She sips. Chamomile. The warm liquid shoots through her, a good kind of heat rising in her chest.

"Good," she whispers, rolling her head to Alabama, who's suddenly appeared on her knees beside her. Lacey swallows, her throat burning, but says, "Thank you."

Alabama smiles. "You're welcome."

"I'm sorry I was a bitch to you."

Alabama laughs, her eyes wet as she gives Lacey another sip. "Oh Lord, don't even worry about it."

Sal settles close. Once she's confident Lacey's warm and bundled, she says, "Lace, I'm gonna ask you some questions, okay?"

"Okay," Lacey says faintly.

"Do you know where we are?"

"Tennessee. At the cabin. F-f-for Christmas."

"Okay, good." Her eyes flick to Seth. Back to Lacey. "What was your favorite Christmas present?" When there's silence, Sal presses. "Do you remember?"

"My necklace." Her brow crinkles as she thinks on it, and then she gasps. Her eyes fly open, panic filling her. "Where is it?" She goes to reach for it, but she's held tight by the swaddled blanket. "No," she moans, devastated. "It's gone."

"Easy," Seth soothes. "You still got it." A flash of gold, Seth's fingers bringing the locket up to her eyeline. He kisses the side of her temple. "It's right here, Lace."

That calms her, but the effort's exhausting and she sinks lower into Seth's arms, her head sliding to the side.

Sal's hushed voice. "What happened on the dock, Lacey?"

"Beau," Lacey murmurs, and it's as if the air leaves the room. Sal lifts her eyes to Seth's. Lacey feels Seth's arms tighten around her. He's so still, she wonders if he's even breathing.

"Oh no," Alabama whispers. A harsh curse blasts from some-where across the room. *Griff*, Lacey thinks.

"He knocked me in the water." She closes her eyes, her mind a confused mess. "He tried to take my locket, and I got scared. I thought . . . he was the mugger. He was there . . . but then he wasn't."

Sal lowers her head, a sob finally working her way out of her.

She's not making sense, she knows that. Everything's fuzzy, almost disembodied. A strange, weightless, floating feeling.

Sleep. She wants to sleep. She's warm here in Seth's arms, her mind too murky to puzzle out anything else.

She hears her sister's voice, wobbly, urgent. "Don't go to sleep, Lacey."

She sags lower in Seth's arms, her eyes fluttering as the room blinks in and out around her.

"Lacey?" Seth says brokenly. "Lace, baby, you gotta stay with me. You hear me? I need you here."

She wants to listen, but she's tired. So tired. The haze in her mind keeps growing. Swallowing her down just like the blackness of that lake.

But she has to do something first.

Seth. She needs Seth.

She needs to tell him she loves him, that he's her favorite person in the world, but her lips are frozen and her eyes are anchors. Heavy. Falling. The dark looks nice, welcoming, and so she gives up.

She gives in to the dark.

Seth sits on the couch in the living room, forehead against his clasped hands, staring into the crackling fire.

Thirty minutes ago, Luke and Jace returned with the doctor. Now, upstairs, Lacey's getting checked over. It seems like he's been waiting an eternity. Fear, god-awful fear has him paralyzed. He's unraveling not knowing how she is.

Tears burning his eyelids, Seth buries his face in his hands. Lets guilt drag him down into the abyss.

Lacey's words haunt him. What Beau did. Cornering her, scaring her like that, and Seth has no one to blame but himself. He knew the guy was bad news, had tried to cut him a break, but it was the worst mistake he could have made. It made Lacey vulnerable. Hell, it made all of his friends and family vulnerable.

He hates that he wasn't there for Lacey in her worst moment, hates that he failed to protect her like he promised he would.

Regret washes over him.

Fuck. He and Lacey—they just got to this place he's been wanting to get to, and now . . .

Now he could lose her.

The thought so staggering, so damn awful he can barely breathe.

Christ, let her be okay.

She can't leave him. Not when he's finally found who he's been needing all his life.

Jolted from his thoughts, Seth blinks as a warm blanket covers his shoulders. He looks up in surprise at Alabama, tucking a quilt around him. "You got cold clothes," she drawls, sympathy etched all over her pretty face.

Seth presses fingers into his wet eyes, nods his thanks.

"He don't need a blanket, sweetheart, he needs a drink." Griff stands over him, his arm draped around his wife.

When Seth hesitates, Griff jerks his head. "Five minutes."

Seth pushes up and drags himself over to the bar, a hollow feeling inside his chest.

Jace and Luke, speaking in low tones at the other end of the hall, fall silent and follow.

At the bar, Seth stares, numb, as Griff shows him a bottle of Jack. With an uncaring shake of his head, Seth says, "Bourbon or whiskey or fuckin' arsenic, I don't give a damn."

A look of concern passes between Luke and Jace.

Griff pours out a shot for Seth, takes one for himself. He breathes through the sting, turns to Seth. Sympathy creases his rugged face. "Lacey fought like hell to get back up," he says gruffly, reaching out to clasp Seth's shoulder. "She's strong. She'll be okay, Seth."

At Griff's words, fresh tears prick his eyes. Seth swallows down the honey-colored liquid, thanking Christ Lacey is a strong swimmer. That her body's conditioned to the cold. Otherwise . . . she might not have survived the current.

When he glances up, he meets Luke's stare. His brother looks just as agonized as he does. "It's gonna work out, Seth," Luke says quietly. "Lacey's breathin'. They're just gettin' her warm."

"I need to be with her," he croaks.

"I know you do. But you can't."

Seth squeezes his eyes shut. His own damn fault he can't be with her. A flash of memory, of earlier, of Lacey passing out in his arms. Her head lolling, the way she went limp, too still and too quiet for Lacey, had Seth thinking the worst. He had lost his damn mind, was beside himself, and effectively got himself banned from her bedroom by the doctor and Sal.

Now he waits. He'll never forgive himself if she wakes up, needing him, and he isn't there because of his own idiot actions.

Seth nods, his throat convulsing. "What if she's not okay?" He forces the words out, his voice thick with grief. "What if—fuck—"

He breaks off, tears blurring his vision.

A firm hand on his shoulder. Luke steps up and pulls him away from the group.

"Don't be doin' that," Luke says calmly, sliding his hands over Seth's shoulders. "Griff's right. Lacey's strong. She'll make it." Luke's dark, worried eyes search his. "No matter what happens, I got you."

Before Seth can break down into a blubbering mess, Luke pulls him into a fierce hug. Seth hugs his brother back, tears burning his eyelids. Thank Christ for Luke keeping his cool. For being the source of calm when all Seth wants to do is lose it.

Pulling back, Seth clears his throat. "Thanks." He lets out a shaky sigh. "I'm goin' damn close to crazy here."

The creak of a door.

All heads snap up.

Seth turns toward the sound, to the stairs, thinking it's Sal and the doctor.

That's when he sees Luke. His brother's face is hard, staring over his shoulder at the front door.

Seth turns.

It's Beau. His expression haggard, his eyes bloodshot. "Is she okay?" asks hoarsely.

Seth stares.

And then he lunges for him.

"You motherfucker."

The living room erupts into chaos. Luke leaps between his brother and Beau, while Jace and Griff each grab Seth's arm, holding him back. Emmy Lou covers her mouth with her palms.

Alabama props her hands on her hips, her face white with rage. "I know y'all ain't fightin' right now."

All Beau does is stand there, looking like he'd relish a fist to his face, anything to make him forget. "I'm sorry," he says, his lips trembling. "I'm so sorry."

"She almost died, and that's what you have to say," Seth seethes. "*I'm sorry*? Fuck you, Beau. You did this to her. This is on you."

This time, he can't find forgiveness. Or pity. Not with what Beau did to Lacey. Not when Seth gave him a chance, and he fucked it up. Hurt the woman he loves.

No sympathy. Not anymore.

Beau stares at Seth, vacant-eyed. "I didn't mean to hurt her."

The words light a fire, send fury boiling through his veins, and Seth lunges for Beau again. Jace and Griff slash forward to catch him, Luke thundering a warning to calm the hell down, but a soft gasp from Alabama has them all freezing.

Sal and the doctor stand at the bottom of the staircase.

Everyone quiets. Quickly.

Seth's mouth goes dry. "How is she?" he asks anxiously.

The doctor surveys the room, transferring his bag to his other hand. "I treated Lacey for a case of mild hypothermia. Her lungs are clear of water and her core temperature has come back up. She's stable and will make a full recovery. Right now, the most important thing is to keep her warm and monitor her throughout the next few days." He looks down at Sal. "It would be a good idea if someone stayed with her tonight."

Sal nods. "Thank you."

Seth lets out a breath, relief nearly capsizing him.

Luke steps forward, keeping a wary eye on Seth and Beau as he shakes hands with the doctor. "Thank you, sir. I really appreciate it."

A long beat of silence as the doctor exits the house. Then Seth turns to Beau. His clenched fists ache to do damage. But he ain't gonna do it here. Not now. Not with Lacey needing him. "If you come near Lacey again, if you fucking set foot in the same room as her," Seth says, taking a step toward Beau, "I'll kill you."

Beau nods, his Adam's apple bobbing. Helplessly, he looks around at the group, his haunted eyes finally settling on Sal. "Will you tell her I'm sorry?"

Fire flares in Sal's eyes. "Get him out of here, Luke." Her voice stays steady. Her heart hard, she has no intention of easing Beau's guilt. "Get him away from me. Now."

Beau flinches. All the blood drains from his face.

Jace steps forward, his arm out. "C'mon, man. We're gonna have a talk." With that, he walks Beau down the hall to the exit.

And then Luke's right there beside Sal, pulling her to him. Sal, her eyes cloudy with tears, her hands on the swell of the belly, leans into Luke.

"Sal, you're exhausted, mama," Alabama prods gently.

When Sal starts to protest, Luke shakes his head, wrapping his arms around her. "Alabama's right. You've been on your feet all day. I want you restin' now darlin'."

"I'm fine," Sal says, her smile tired, but relieved. "Lacey's okay. That's all that matters."

Seth's throat knots in gratefulness. Sal's done so much for Lacey. For him, too. Because he never would have survived this without her. He owes Lacey's life to Sal. Hell, he owes his own life to Sal.

As if sensing his very thoughts, Sal looks at Seth. He walks over to take her into his arms, hugging her fiercely, preciously. As they hang onto each other, that old friendship, that familiar love passes between them.

"Thank you," he whispers into her ear.

She pulls away to stare at him. "Lacey's asleep, but she was asking for you," she urges, squeezing his hand.

He nods. "I'll stay with her tonight."

After a second glance at Sal, making sure she's okay, he lets go of her hand and starts for the stairs.

chapter

THIRTY-THREE

Lacey's bedroom is dim and warm. A space heater kicks out hot air in a corner of the room. As Seth crosses the floor, his entire focus is on the small ball curled up in the middle of the bed.

His chest tightens when he sees Lacey close up. She's cocooned in blankets. A silky heap of blond hair spilled across the pillows. Her lashes dark against the white pallor of her skin. Her breathing steady and even. Alive. So goddamn alive and infinitely precious to him.

He should have protected her from Beau, and he didn't.

He had his chance, and he fucked up.

Like so many times before.

Not touching that cocaine, the first time around.

Stepping away from that redneck before Luke became collateral damage.

Staying with Sal at the hospital when she needed him.

Catching Lacey's fever before it even started.

Seth exhales, fighting his demons.

He wouldn't blame her for blaming him. For calling it quits.

Not like it matters anymore. The only thing he wants is for her to be okay. Then to tell her he's so damn sorry. That he'll love her every single day for the rest of his life if she'll still let him.

Seth crawls onto the bed beside Lacey, needing to feel her against him. Needing the contact after being kept apart from her. She's radiating warmth, warmth she desperately needs. He scoots beneath the covers, pulling more blankets around them to keep the heat in. His hands tremble as he reaches out to touch her. He places a palm against her cold cheek, smoothing a finger across the arc of her cheekbone. The bluish tinge to her lips scares him. A reminder of how close she came.

How close he came to losing his entire world.

Tears burn his eyelids and he squeezes his eyes shut tight. He can't fall apart now. Not when Lacey needs him.

She's been so goddamn strong. Fierce as hell. Cracking jokes trying to make him feel better when she was the one who damn near died.

Lacey moans, a soft whimper that has his heart caving in. Then, like she can see him in her sleep, her hands flutter restlessly, reaching out to clutch his shirt. Her slender form curls into him. Her voice a breathless whisper. "Seth."

His name on her lips threatens to break him. Has Seth closing his eyes to the wave of emotion billowing over him.

"I'm here, Lace," he chokes out, instinctively pulling her closer. Into his warmth, his strength. "I'm here and I ain't goin' nowhere." He scoops up her slack hand and presses a kiss to her knuckles.

Christ. She's cold. Still so damn cold.

Again, she moans, her brow crinkling in pain.

Seth tucks her against him, carefully taking her hand to warm her cold and clammy fingers in his. Lacey stirs slightly and Seth rests his forehead against hers. He listens to her breathe, in and out, steady and strong, and then he's palming her cheek, hot tears are filling his eyes and he's the one who can't breathe.

"I love you," he whispers. "I love you so much, Lacey."

He hopes she can hear him.

But most of all, he hopes she forgives him.

Lacey opens her eyes, and the first thing she feels is warmth. Warmth from the sun, shining bright through the windows.

Warmth from the twenty tons of blankets she's been covered with, stacked so heavy she can barely move. And most important—warmth from the body pressed close to hers, cleaving her close and tender.

Seth.

He holds her tight against him. One arm draped protectively over the curve of her hip, the other up and on top, his broad hand palming the crown of her blond head.

She smiles, content to take in Seth as he sleeps. He looks exhausted, still dressed in his clothes. His hair mussed, his eyes red-rimmed and raw.

And that's when she remembers.

The phone call from Colin. Sneaking away from Seth. The dock. Beau. Hitting that icy lake, the water like knives, threatening to take her down, to steal her under. But she fought. Fought her way past the rushing current up to the surface, shedding her boots, her jacket, telling herself it was just surfing. Like winter in the Pacific. The coldest wave she ever dropped. Then there was Seth, pulling her out of the lake, coming for her like she knew he would.

Overwhelmed, she closes her eyes against the rush of memories.

Thank God for Seth. She never would have made it without him.

When she opens her eyes, Seth's staring back at her. She blinks, chasing away a cloud of head fog. "Seth," she whispers.

"You okay, princess?"

His rumble of a drawl has Lacey shivering.

Carefully, she wiggles her arm free, reaching up to touch Seth's stubbled cheek. "I'm okay."

Seth leans up on his elbow, his gaze intense as he studies her. "How you feelin'?"

Her brow furrows. "I don't know." She lies still to take in the sensations of her body. Her head aches, but she's clearheaded. Her warm edges tinged by a chill. "I feel cold."

He runs a hand down her arm. "We'll get you warm."

She rolls her head across the pillow to look around the room. "What day is it?"

"Three days after Christmas," he says in a low voice. "Do you remember yesterday?"

"Ugh, don't remind me." She cringes, embarrassment rolling through her. She presses a hand to her eyes, remembering. "I ruined the bonfire. And my dress." She groans. "I had the best makeup too."

Seth smiles. But his voice is serious. "No one was worryin' about the makeup, Lace."

Worry. Lacey's brain lights on Sal. Her sister had been there beside her, taking care of her all night. "Is Sal okay?"

Seth smooths a long strand of hair away from her cheek. "Sal's fine."

Lacey sighs at the gentle, soothing motion, the tips of her toes curling at Seth's touch. So damn unfair. Then her eyes go wide as another thought occurs to her. The person who got her into this mess in the first place.

"What about Beau, what happened?"

Seth's lips pull tight, a ripple of anger passing across his handsome face. "I don't want you worryin' about him either."

She narrows her eyes. "He's not dead, is he?"

Seth chuckles, but there's no humor in it. "Close," he says, his voice deadly. "It was real damn close."

Lacey leans up on her elbows, trying to wriggle free from the tightly tucked-in blankets. Seth moves to sit at the edge of the bed, his eyes amused as he watches her struggle.

"I can't . . . move," she huffs, pushing weakly at the blankets. She looks at Seth. "A little help?"

The corners of his mouth twitch. "Nope. You're restin'."

"I am not." Stubbornly, she wrenches an arm free. She wants out of bed. She wants to move, to see her sister. She sits up straighter, finally twisting free of the covers, scowling down at the boxy flannel shirt and oversized sweatpants she's been dressed in.

With gusto, she kicks away the covers and rolls off the edge of the bed. Her feet hit the floor, the solid contact like another reminder she's alive.

Needling his brow, Seth sighs, long and pained. "Goddamnit, get back here. You ain't ready to be up."

She waves him away, her gaze leading her toward a pair of luxurious silk pajamas. "Seth, it's fine, I—"

As soon as she says it, a wave of lightheadedness hits her. All the blood rushes from her face. She sways on her feet, her eyes fluttering.

The world tilts, but Seth's there to catch her. He swears at her, scooping her into his arms and carrying her back to the bed. All her strength sapped, she sags into the pillows. Seth sits beside her, dragging the mound of blankets back up over her. He stares down at her, his blue eyes tender, serious. "And that's why you ain't movin' from this bed till tomorrow."

A rush of love hits her square in the chest. She closes her eyes, overcome by his concern. Overcome by the fierce determination in his voice. A determination to take away her pain. To keep her safe and protected, always.

"Lace?"

"Thank you," she whispers, opening her eyes and lifting her gaze to his.

Seth tenses and looks away from her. His throat bobs with emotion. "Don't. Don't do that."

She stares up at him, questions rising in her at the haunted look on his face. A look she's seen before. After Luke and the bar fight. After Colin's party.

Of course.

He's blaming himself. She can see Seth's pain, the hard clench of his body as if to ward off her sympathy completely.

She touches his arm. "It's not your fault, Seth."

He looks away at her gentle admonishment, closing his eyes, making a tortured noise in the back of his throat. After a second, he composes his emotions and turns toward her.

"It is." He reaches for her hand, then hesitates. "I knew Beau was on something and I did shit-all to protect you." A muscle twitches in his jaw, tears in his eyes. "I let you down, Lacey. And I'm so goddamn sorry."

"No, you're wrong," she says simply. "You saved me, Seth. You came for me. I never would have made it back up on that dock if it weren't for you." She swallows and lifts her chin to stare at him. "Everything's okay. I'm okay."

"I ain't okay," he chokes out. When she reaches to touch his arm, he closes his eyes like it's too much for him. "What would I have done without you, huh? If I lost you, I never would have forgiven myself."

He gathers her hand in his. His very touch—warm, steady—has her trembling. Seth kisses her fingers, her wrist where her pulse pumps, her damp brow. "Christ, I would lose my fucking mind if something happened to you."

Shivering at the savagery in his voice, Lacey sits up and presses a palm against his chest. "I'm here, Seth. I'm here and I'm yours and I love you."

"I love you," he says hoarsely, his blue eyes shiny with tears. "I love you so fuckin' much, Lacey."

Their gazes lock, hunger, love and loss passing between them, and then Seth's pulling her into his arms. He holds her tight, his strength like a shield, and kisses her. His lips sweet and hot on hers. Lacey tastes his salty tears and clings to him, determined to savor every moment in this new future she has with Seth.

THIRTY-FOUR

LACEY COZIES INTO THE COUCH IN THE LIVING ROOM IN front of the crackling fire, flipping through her notebook to the right page.

"Cakes or cupcakes?" Alabama asks, pressing a pen down into her own notebook.

"Definitely cupcakes. Easier cleanup." She leans back, taking in the view of the snow-covered mountains through the grand windows. "They should be cute. Petite." She grins, excitement curling her stomach. "Just like Sal's baby."

"There's a great little bakery in Nashville. Bluegrass Bakery," Alabama drawls. "I can call them tomorrow."

"Make sure they're pink and blue. It's a strict theme."

Alabama laughs lightly, sending a smile her way. "I really appreciate you lettin' me help plan Sal's shower, Lacey."

Lacey waves her pencil in the air. "You're helping me. It's a quick turnaround. Besides, I don't know Nashville."

"You will soon, though."

Lacey smiles, even as a flutter of nervousness passes through her at the thought of going back to Nashville tomorrow.

The remaining two days of vacation at the cabin have passed slow. No drama. No sightings of Beau. Now, even though Lacey started the vacation anxious and out of sorts, she feels at home with these friends she's made. The memories, the time with Sal, with Seth, she wouldn't trade it for anything.

Well, minus the whole near-drowning experience.

She shivers, unable to help it. Even two days after her accident, she still feels cold. Like she can't get enough warmth.

As if in answer to her thoughts, a soft blanket is dropped around her shoulders.

Lacey blinks up at Seth. "Thank you," she says with a smile.

He stares down at her, his face creased with worry. His eyes asking if she's okay. She gives a nod, the conversation passing unspoken between them.

"Look at you," Alabama drawls, "bein' the charmin' man of the century."

Seth grins and raises his fiddle case. "Gotta do country music proud."

A soft shuffle of footsteps. Sal and Luke entering the living room along with Emmy Lou, Jace and Griff.

"Oh no," Lacey says, making the sign of a cross with her pencils. "You can't be here."

"We're plannin' your shower, Sal," Alabama adds a little less dramatically.

Sal looks delighted.

Lacey narrows her gaze at her sister. "Let me ask you this, are you opposed to a crown and a throne?"

Sal lifts a brow.

Emmy Lou laughs. "That might be a bit much, Lacey."

Lacey meets Luke's eyes. "Not for Sal."

Sal chuckles. "Fine. If I'm not wanted, I'll go groupie it up with the boys."

Luke hoots and wraps an arm around Sal's shoulders.

Jace's eyes sweep to Seth. "You gonna sing us that love song you wrote, Seth?"

Seth shakes his head, glowering. "I fuckin' hate you, man."

Lacey tilts her head, wondering. Seth drops a kiss on the top of her head. "I'll tell you later," he says against her ear.

With that, Seth, Luke, Sal and Jace disappear down to the studio, leaving Lacey with Emmy Lou, Alabama and Griff.

Griff lingers, cupping the curve of Alabama's shoulder as he stands over her. "'Bout ready to go, sweetheart?"

"In a second," she says, giving Griff a smile. "We're just finishin' up here."

Emmy Lou settles beside Alabama, her brown eyes going to Lacey's planner. "Oh, it's so excitin' you're givin' Sal a shower."

"It is," Lacey says. "It's going to be perfect."

What feels perfect is Lacey settling back into party-planner mode. She hasn't realized how much she's missed it.

"Are you stayin' in Nashville, Lacey?" Emmy Lou asks.

"I think so."

"Movin' in with Seth?"

"I don't—" Her mouth opens. Closes. That's when she realizes she doesn't know. They haven't planned that far ahead.

Emmy Lou flaps a hand. "Well, I'm glad you got some time in with Seth while you can. Once the new year hits, with that album they're recordin', they're flat booked."

Griff grunts, his tawny eyes sliding to Lacey. "Don't worry 'bout it, California. I'm sure Seth's already got a place for you on that bus."

Lacey smiles at him, but her emotions are taking a turn for the overwhelming. She and Seth haven't discussed it. What happens when the Brothers Kincaid tour. If Lacey goes with him. She wants to be the girl who's on the bus with Seth, but what if he hasn't brought it up because he doesn't want her cramping his style?

Emmy Lou leans in, her elbow on her knee, her chin in her palm. "What about work? Have you—"

"I think Lacey's plannin' to take it easy and figure it out back in Nashville," Alabama says, interrupting Emmy Lou's assault of questions. Griff huffs a *goddamn* under his breath and shoots Lacey a sympathetic glance before stalking out of the room.

"Now, about that shower . . . ," Alabama says, kindly redirecting the conversation away from Lacey and back to one she can handle.

As Alabama and Emmy Lou chatter about babies and boppies,

Lacey's mind whirls. Absentmindedly, she fiddles with the locket on her throat, tuning out the conversation and tuning in to all the things she hasn't planned. A job. Living arrangements. Her future.

Reality.

Tomorrow, she's going back to Nashville. But she can't stop the doubt from creeping in. Back to what?

A smile spreads across Seth's face when he finds Lacey in the kitchen humming a song and swaying as she cuts into an onion.

For a second, he's content to watch her. She's barefoot in a long flowered dress, wearing a loose fawn-colored cardigan embroidered with GOOD VIBES on the back.

He stares, speechless. Two days ago, he held her body limp in his arms, praying she'd be okay. And now here she is. Alive. Beautiful.

His.

Finally, he can't stand it any longer. The temptation to touch her too strong. He sets his fiddle case on the counter and goes to her, wrapping his arms around her waist. Lacey makes a little purr of contentment and leans back into him.

"Now call me crazy," he says against her ear. "But someone said they'd be restin' later." He eyes the messy kitchen. Black rice. Scallops. Butter. "Not cookin' up a gourmet meal."

His eyes scan her with worry. The doctor said pneumonia could surface days later. He ain't taking any chances.

Lacey tucks away an exasperated sigh. "Seth, I'm fine." She twists, turning to face him, but stays in his arms. "It's our last night. Stop fussing. I want us to have a good time."

Seth blinks. "Everyone's gone?"

"And then there were four," Lacey teases.

He laughs. "You and that spooky shit." With a grin, he leans in. Kisses her slow. "Can't say it's so bad. Got you all to myself."

A laugh from the sidelines. Sal and Luke cautiously entering the kitchen.

"Still getting used to this," Sal quips, smiling, waving a finger between Lacey and Seth. "The two of you . . ."

"Just like high school," Luke drawls. "Walkin' in and findin' Seth with girls in the kitchen."

Seth rolls his eyes.

Lacey laughs. She looks at Seth and Luke. "How was practice?"

"Practice was a hell of a time," Luke says, looping his arm around Sal. "Ready to get in the studio and finally record this damn album."

Seth nods, echoing his brother's sentiment.

Today felt like he found his groove again. Like he belongs.

Seth rubs his hands together, eager for one last night of vacation. "Well, what's on the agenda tonight? Hot tub? Pool?" He chuckles at Sal, who stands leaning tiredly against Luke. "Although, I ain't so sure this one'll make it."

Lacey peers at her sister. "Sal, you look half-asleep."

Luke cups Sal's shoulders. "I've been tryin' to tell her that all day."

Sal scowls. "Everyone stop." She swivels a finger across the group. "When I have this baby, it's all over for you. I'm kickin all of y'all's asses."

Ping.

Everyone looks around, looks at Lacey, but she shakes her head. "Don't look at me. My phone's at the bottom of the lake."

Sal, staring at her phone in her hands, sucks in a harsh breath.

"Darlin'?" Luke takes a step forward, his eyes on her stomach.

A flash of Sal's phone. The front page of the *Nashville Star* screams: *Country Singer Beau Dallas Checks into Rehab for Alcohol and Drug Abuse.*

The headline has them all stunned, the lighthearted atmosphere suddenly somber.

"I feel bad for him," Sal says gently. Then her eyes land on Lacey. "Almost."

Seth stares at Lacey, understanding what Sal means. Lacey almost died. Beau could have killed her. He'll never forgive the guy. But he's glad Beau's getting help. It's the best thing he could do.

Luke grunts, sliding a hand over the back of his head. "I could give a sliver of a fuck about Beau after what he did to Lacey, but it's about damn time that guy's bein' honest with himself."

The words hit Seth in the chest, hard.

Honesty.

That's what Luke wants.

It's what Seth needs.

Time to get in front of the past. Face it. Confess. No matter how painful, no matter what happens. He owes Luke the truth.

Because, in another life, he could have been Beau. But he isn't. Not anymore.

Steeling himself, Seth exhales a hard breath. "Y'all, I gotta tell you somethin.'"

Picking up on his mood, Lacey drifts to his side. She slips her hand into his. Her long fingers twin with his, linking, squeezing. Seth closes his eyes for a beat; he's never been so thankful for her support. Her strength.

Luke's brow furrows. He leans down, resting his elbows on the counter to meet his brother's gaze. "It about Beau?"

"It ain't about Beau. It's about me." Luke and Sal lock eyes, surprised. "It's about that article that came out last month . . ."

Luke's back straightens. "I told you, we took care of it."

A sharp edge stains Luke's voice, one that's bracing himself against Seth's next words, hoping against hope it's not what he thinks.

"That's the thing. You shouldn't have." His throat convulses, but he gets the words out. "I fucked up, Luke."

All the blood drains from Luke's face. He closes his eyes in disbelief. "When?" The crack of his voice is like a gunshot.

Seth flinches and clears his throat. "The night you got hurt.

I left the hospital, and I went and got wasted at some bar on Broadway. And . . . I got somethin' to get me through it." He squeezes his eyes shut, feeling himself come apart all over again at the memory. "I got you hurt. I couldn't take it. If you weren't okay . . . I didn't want to be."

A small sob escapes Sal.

Seth watches a tear roll down her cheek, his heart twisting at her pain. He hates himself for hurting her, but he owes them this. The truth, no matter the consequences.

Taking a breath, he continues. "I took it back to my apartment. But I didn't—I never touched the stuff. I swear. I fuckin' swear it."

Seth's gut clenches. Luke looks agonized. Beside him, Lacey's green eyes glow with tears. A match to her sister's.

"I was so fuckin' scared to tell you. I know you said if I touched the stuff again, you'd never forgive me. But you shouldn't have been defendin' me in the press. Y'all have done enough for me." He looks at Sal, at his brother, these two people who mean the world to him.

"I'm so damn sorry. I let you down. I ain't no better than Beau. And I should have owned up to it."

For a heartbeat, Luke stands still. Silent and stone-faced, his jaw clenched as he stares at Seth.

Seth braces himself, expecting the worst.

Instead, Luke's suddenly moving, crushing him in a fierce hug. "I'm so sorry. I'm so goddamn sorry."

Seth clings to his brother, a shaky sob ripping out of him.

"You're my little brother," Luke chokes out when he pulls away. Silver shines in his dark eyes. "I should have done better to listen to you." He palms Seth's face with both hands. "And you didn't fuck up. You stopped yourself. You gotta forgive yourself, Seth. You did your best back then, and you're doin' your best now."

Seth stares at Luke, the fear he felt melting away to be replaced by relief. His brother's unwavering support knocking him over like a sledgehammer. It's better than he imagined. It's hope.

It's like coming out the other end of the blackest tunnel and finding light. Finding his family.

"I'm proud of you," Luke says in a steady voice. "I love you. And I'll always be here for you."

Seth shoves him away, not wanting to break down into a sniveling mess. "Goddamn, man, quit it." His eyes drift to Sal. She's watching him, hands on her stomach. He grins. "I suppose you want a hug too."

"I do," Sal says, smiling through her tears.

He reaches for her, pulling her petite frame into his arms, the curve of her belly hitting him in the stomach. "I'm so glad you're okay," she murmurs as Seth squeezes her tight. "You're so important to me, Seth." Her eyes fill again as she stares up at him, her expression fierce and full of love and understanding. "To all of us."

Lacey, who's been standing silently all this time, smiles at him. Pride shines in her eyes. Ambling forward, Seth loops an arm around her and hugs her close. "I couldn't have done it without you," he whispers.

Love in the air. All around them.

It's a goddamn great feeling.

He did one of the hardest things he's ever had to do. But he did it. He took the long road home. Now he's back and here to stay. With his brother and his band and the best part of this new life of his—Lacey.

L ACEY ADJUSTS THE BALLOON ARCH, EXCITEMENT burbling in her stomach. Nerves, too. Even though it's only been a few weeks since she quit her job, planning a party feels weird. Like it's so far away from herself. Still, it's nice. Normal. Not to mention, she misses it. The logistics, being bossy, barking orders. It's what she was good at.

She lets her gaze drift around the old farmhouse that is Wild Antler Farm. Now, currently decorated in a country chic theme. But back then, it was her oasis those two years she lived with Luke and Sal. Her oasis now. It's been a week since she and Seth came back to Nashville.

New year. New phone. And soon, a new baby.

Lacey gasps when Sal enters the living room, followed by a loping Seth. She scowls at him. "You had one job. Keep her out."

Seth raises an amused brow and sneaks around Sal to give Lacey a kiss. "Kinda hard seein' as she lives here and all."

Sal laughs, pretending to shield her eyes from the gigantic throne set up in the corner of the room. "I'm so sorry, Lace, but I needed—" She breaks off. Her sister has a wince on her pretty face, her hands rubbing slow circles on her stomach.

"You okay, Sal?" Lacey ventures.

She turns, her face clearing. "Yeah." She exhales. "Baby is squirming."

Lacey moves close, her hand out. "Can I?"

Sal smiles. "Of course."

Lacey palms Sal's belly, feeling the motion inside. "Oh my gosh," she giggles. "She's so wiggly."

"Don't you mean he?" Seth's grinning.

"Absolutely not. Boys as a species are overrated." Lacey arcs a brow at Luke, who's stepping inside the living room. "No offense."

He laughs, looks at Seth. Pride evident in his eyes. "You ready to get?"

Seth raises his fiddle case, swaggers. "Down to clown, man."

Luke crosses the room to kiss Sal. His broad hand slips over her stomach. "We'll be recordin' all day. You'll be okay?"

Sal shakes her dark head, amusement dancing in her eyes. "I'll be fine, Luke." Lacey smothers a smile. She's never seen Luke so nervous.

"I'll take good care of her," Lacey reassures. "We'll pamper her."

"Relax, man, it's a shower," Seth quips. "Not delivery day." Then he slips Lacey's hand into his and leads her out into the hall.

She stops in front of him, bracing a hand against his chest. "I'll miss you." She sounds all of a lovesick girl, but she hasn't been without Seth in over a month.

"Hell," he says, his gaze heavy-lidded, "I'm already goin' crazy."

She yanks him into her, kissing him hard. Seth growls, his hands going to her hair, the front of his pants stiffening against her.

A clearing of the throat.

With a sigh, Seth pulls away. Tosses a grin over his shoulder. "I don't s'pose we can be late?"

Luke snorts. "Nice try."

Turning back to Lacey, Seth sweeps a finger under her chin. He leans down, giving her one last kiss. "I love you. You're gonna kill it," he tells her.

She nods, his confidence in her a comfort. "You too."

Lacey smiles and follows them out onto the porch into the chilly morning air. She watches them leave, taking in Seth's relaxed lope. Ever since he confessed the truth to Luke, he looks lighter. Sunnier. Like a weight's been lifted from him.

Then, Luke's truck is spinning out dirt and snow as it winds down the snakey road to the highway.

The sight has her stomach plummeting to her feet.

Seth's back. But what about her?

She thinks of Colin's phone call, the offer she turned down, and is struck by a wave of regret. Only she shakes it off. Tucks it in the back of her mind. This is what she wants. Right?

At the ping of her phone—Alabama asking if she should pick up ice—Lacey puts on a brave face and turns back inside.

She's got a party to host.

The music fades out with a slow, weltering warble, Luke letting out a wild hoot when Seth lays down his bow.

"Fuckin' finally," Seth says, shooting Jace a wide-eyed look.

Shellshocked. That's what they all are. Their new producer, Devlon Block, is kicking their asses. They've been in the studio, playing live and recording all day, and all they've got done is two songs. It feels more like a music boot camp than having fun with the band. Devlon wants them to take their time, grow into their sound. Whatever the hell that means.

"Ain't so bad," Luke drawls, and Seth and Jace snort. Luke's loving this. The torture that comes with making a new album. The turtle-like crawl and analysis of every song. Hell, at this point, their new album, *Assembly*, won't be out until next Christmas.

The crack of a door. Bobby Mazon, their manager, pokes his head into the room. "Let's break. We got lunch on the way."

Groaning, Seth slips off his chair, stretching his legs. He grins, watching his brother check his phone.

"How's Sal?"

Luke grunts. "Fine."

"Still got a way to go."

"Couple of months."

"You nervous?" Seth grins. "I get the cool job. Gonna be an

uncle." The best damn uncle he can be. He already loves that kid, and Luke's gonna be one hell of a father.

A goofy smile breaks out on Luke's face. Seth smirks, ready to give him shit, when a low curse from Jace catches his attention.

"Hey, y'all," Jace interjects, phone in his hand. "Don't wanna interrupt, but . . ." His hazel eyes land on Seth. "You see the *Star*?"

"Shit," Luke swears. "What now?" His eyes are worried, his mind on Seth and that article. Only Seth's calm. He and Luke and Sal have already talked about it. If it resurfaces, he'll own it.

But the article's not about Seth. It's about Lacey.

A snap of her exiting the Bronco, her hair in a messy bun, her hand tangled up in Seth's. The headline: *Seth Kincaid: Bachelor No More? Why Is Our Country Grit Taking up With California Glitz?*

Motherfuckers. Seth's hands ball into fists.

The asshole headline deliberately meant to fuck with Seth. The *Star* saying they're still pissed at Luke for killing their story and now it's payback. He should know the drill with the tabloids by now, but Lacey being on the receiving end has his teeth clenching.

That's the last thing she needs.

Jace, his eyes scanning the article, says, "*Star* don't like it. She ain't country enough."

Luke snorts. "They said the same thing about Sal. Now look at them. They can't get enough damn pictures."

Seth bristles at the disgustingly obvious attempt to paint Lacey as unsuitable for Seth. "They don't have to like it."

Jace grins. "Tell 'em that on the red carpet."

Seth gives a slight smile. "Damn straight." And then some. He'll laugh right in their faces and tell them to move right the fuck along.

The door opens, people bustling in, voices hushed as lunch is set up. A spread of food. BBQ. Potato salad. Cornbread. PBR.

"Speakin' of Lacey, while we're on the subject . . ." Luke grins, arches a brow. "You two thinkin' of livin' at the farm or . . ."

Seth chuckles, some of the tension easing out of him. "Okay,

okay, I get it." He drags a hand through his hair, squeezing the back of his neck. The last thing Sal and Luke need are two kids taking up residence when they got one on the way. "Nah. I don't know what we're gonna do, but she and I gotta talk."

Luke arcs a brow. "Yeah?"

Jace laughs, a red Solo cup in his hand. "Shit, I know that look."

All Seth can do is grin. He blows out a breath, then laughs. Letting it all out, his heart, his thoughts, his plans. "I wanna buy her a ring, man. A house. I wanna do every goddamn thing I called you an idiot for." He softens. "Before Sal."

Luke nods. Smiles. "You wrote her a song."

"Yeah, I did."

Luke studies him for a long moment. "You should put it on the album."

Seth blinks at him. "Hell, I should." He grins, his stomach doing a happy flip. "I gotta play it for her first. Fuck. It scares the hell out of me."

Luke tosses him a shit-eating grin. "That's how you know you're doin' it right."

Lacey groans as she enters the nursery, hefting the stack of diapers on top of the changing table. "There," she says, exhaling and dusting her hands. "That's the last trip."

"And now," Sal says as she slowly lowers herself into the cream-colored rocker, "to never move again." A tired but happy smile spreads across her full lips. "I live here now. I will become one with the chair."

Lacey laughs and fans a quilt over the edge of the crib.

Lifting her eyes, Lacey scans the familiar room. The nursery used to be her old bedroom. But now it's fit for a baby. Sal and Luke's baby. With a dusty terra cotta accent wall, a cowskin rug, and framed pictures of musical instruments, it's adorably countrified.

Glancing toward the window as she crosses the room, the farm looks endless, covered in glossy snow and deer tracks.

"Tell me you had fun," Lacey says, kicking off her heels to sink onto the cushion in the bay window. Tucking her legs beneath her, her eyes skim Sal. A tiara on her head, her belly riding high on her petite frame.

Finally. Finally, Sal gets to have this.

"I had a blast. It was amazing," Sal says, her eyes full of admiration. "I don't know how you pulled it together so fast."

It *was* amazing. The shower was a success. Four hours of friends and family oohing and ahhing over baby clothes and pampering Sal senseless. Alabama had been a great help. And the best part is, thanks to the cleaners she's hired, no cleanup.

Lacey smirks and flips her hair, her old confidence having found her during the day. "That's what I do. Party planner extraordinaire. At least once upon a time," she says wryly.

Sal gives her a droll look. Then a look of frustration crosses her face. "I wish I knew more about your life in LA. Or your life in general."

"Sal, that's not your fault."

"I know. But I still feel like I missed out on you. And us."

Sal's words are an opening. A moment to share her past with her sister. She thinks of Seth and the courage he gathered to tell Luke. Lacey wants to do the same. Tell the truth. Even if it's hard. If it hurts. Because Sal's strong, she can take it.

And so can Lacey.

Inhaling a breath, Lacey looks at Sal. "Did you know this used to be my bedroom when I lived with you and Luke?"

Sal's eyes widen and then she smiles. "No, I didn't."

"Yep." She points to the wall behind the crib. "That wall was pink. Like Pepto-Bismol pink. Luke hated it, said it blocked his creative flow." Sal laughs. "And at night, you would pick a book and we would read. Like we would do when we were little."

Sal's gaze holds on Lacey, a content look there. The glimpse of information like a cool drink of water after a drought.

Lacey pulls a pillow into her lap, wrapping her hands tight around its side. "I have to tell you something else. About why I lived with you and Luke back then. But I don't want you to be sad or feel bad for not remembering. It's just part of me and I think you should know it."

"Okay," Sal says softly. Her brow furrows as she gives all her attention to Lacey.

And Lacey talks, telling her sister her story. What she told Seth about her past. Her stepmother. Her bulimia. Her gratefulness to Sal and Luke for getting her out of that house, for getting her help.

When Lacey's finished, wiping at wet eyes with a shaky hand, Sal pushes out of the rocker, crosses the room and sits beside her.

"I knew there was something," Sal whispers, her eyes glistening. She scoots close, gathering Lacey in her arms. "The way you talked when I first met you . . ." She breaks off, her voice catching, but composes herself. "I'm so sorry you went through that, Lacey." Sal smiles, her proud look seeping through Lacey like the warmest sunlight. "But I'm so glad I know. Thank you for telling me."

Lacey smiles and squeezes Sal back. "You're welcome."

Later that night, Lacey slides into bed, phone in her hands. Scowling, she hides the *Nashville Star* article Emmy Lou had texted her earlier and turns her gaze toward the window. Fat snowflakes glitter across the night sky. The full moon hangs like a shiny dime.

Despite how great today went, she can't help but feel lonely. Listless. Uninspired.

Sal's party is over. What now?

The free time she enjoyed over Christmas, then strange and wonderful, is now scary and stale. It has her default mode switching on. Doubt. Worry. Anxiety. Colin's job offer like a beacon of salvation. A way to fix her panic. Her life.

Shit.

She's too alone with her thoughts.

But before they can spiral, the bedroom door opens and there stands Seth. A crooked grin on his face, his hair disheveled.

Lacey perks up. The sight of him like a shot of caffeine to her bloodstream, chasing away her doubts, ramping up her pulse.

"Sorry I'm late," he says, kicking off his boots. In one quick flash, he's crawling across the bed to softly kiss her lips. "Tired?"

"No." Lacey cups his jaw. "How was your day?"

"Goddamn great." Adjusting his position, Seth flops next to her. He pulls her close, curling her into his shoulder. "How 'bout you?"

"Fabulous." She nuzzles his neck, relaxing into him. "The shower was perfect. Sal loved it." She bites her lip. "Also, I told her about why I lived with her and Luke."

Seth's eyes widen. "Shit, Lace. How'd it go?" He watches her with interest, with worry.

"It went so good, Seth. I'm glad I did it."

He exhales, reaching out to take her hand. "I'm proud of you."

They lie in silence for a few minutes, Seth twirling a golden strand of her hair around his finger. Finally, his gaze on her, he drawls, "Ready for a little good news, bad news?"

She frowns. "What?"

"We're gettin' evicted." He nods solemnly when she arches a brow. "Yep. Luke's givin' us the ol' heave-ho."

Shit.

Seth meant the news to be lighthearted, but suddenly, her mind cartwheels with worry. Regret soaks through her like a cold rain. What the hell has she been doing the last two weeks?

Pulling away from Seth, she grabs up her phone.

Seth runs a hand down the curve of her hip. "What're you doin'?"

"I need a job."

Flopping back in bed, she stares at the phone, overwhelmed by the prospect of suddenly starting over in Nashville. No reputation. No clients.

Once again, she thinks of Colin. Ugh, she's an idiot. She could have a job right now. Stability. Money. Los Angeles. The beach.

Seth groans, realizing his mistake. "Hell, I didn't tell you that to scare you."

"Well, it did," she shoots back, frazzled. She chews a nail. An ice-cold dose of the real world getting dropped on her head. She should have been a realist about her situation, not some idealist romantic.

She turns her eyes toward him. Sick to her stomach. "I'm nervous, Seth. I don't have a job or an apartment. I still have bills to pay back in LA."

"You were on vacation. Plus, did you forget the fact that you nearly drowned?" His face twists up. "Because I sure as hell didn't."

She flashes her phone. The *Nashville Star* tab. Seth's lips tighten in anger. "Not to mention, everyone hates me." She picks out the line she wants to firebomb, reads it aloud in her most sarcastic voice. "Country crooner Seth Kincaid taking up with a California Diva? In this case, we hardly think opposites attract, and we hope that the youngest (and only unmarried) member of the Brothers Kincaid keeps his hunky bachelor status."

Seth closes his eyes, cursing softly under his breath.

"Listen to me, princess," he says, his expression softening. "I don't want to you worryin'. About anything."

Easy for him to say. He's the one with a job.

With a life.

Her chest tightens.

"I get it," Seth says, taking her gently in his arms. "It's scary. Nashville ain't LA. We ain't got no beach. But you're gonna kill it here. And whatever you need, I'm gonna bust my ass to help you get it." His concerned eyes stare back at her. "Okay? Alright?"

Though his words take the edge off, nerves still fray her edges. But she nods, wanting to believe him.

"Come with me to the studio tomorrow." She tilts her head. He licks his lips. His voice goes husky. "I wrote you a song, Lace."

Her eyes widen, her breath catching in her throat. "You did?"

"Yeah." He traces a finger over her lips. "I wanna play it for you tomorrow."

"Seth, I . . ." She cups his cheek, her heart flickering like an ember. "I can't wait to hear it."

"Lace," Seth breathes, leaning into her.

And then his hands are in her hair, their clothes are off, her worries forgotten.

Until tomorrow, at least.

chapter
THIRTY-SIX

SETH PICKS UP HIS FIDDLE AND STEADIES HIS BOW. HE'S ready and wired to play. Nervous like nothing else. Luke always writes the music. Or they write it together. But this. This is his song. His heart slapped on a piece of paper, ready to be sucked through a microphone to be pumped out on the radio. Christ.

He looks up as Luke pushes through the door, guitar in his hands. "You nervous?" his brother asks.

He sighs. Luke's got him pegged. Still, he floats him a lop-sided grin. "It's just a damn song, man."

But as soon as he says it and looks up, his words cut off. Lacey stands in the booth, watching him through the window. Her big green eyes locked on him like they'll never let him loose.

It's more than a song. It's her. One he'll sing again and again. For the rest of his life, if he can.

He wants to make everything better for her. She'd understandably freaked out last night when he mentioned moving out of the farmhouse. But that's Lacey. Type A. A planner. He understands, loves that about her, but wishes she wouldn't panic. They'll figure it out. Together. And the first thing on Seth's agenda is an apartment. One with a big-as-hell bathroom.

Luke bellies up to the microphone. "You ready?"

Seth grins. Just his fiddle, Luke's guitar and their voices.

Just like the good old days.

"Ready."

Seth clears his throat. He opens his mouth and he sings.

I was reckless, I was wild
Been making the same damn mistakes
Since I was a child
Beat myself up for half my life
Left is right, right is wrong
I've always been someone a little more lost than found . . .

It always was one hell of a time,
till I got a case of them ol' Tennessee blues
Broken, beat up until you stomped across my heart
With the ice-cold tip of your high-heeled shoe
But then you leaned down
Girl, the dip of your lips to mine
I still don't think I've ever felt more damn alive
What's the point of this ol' life
If we don't do it together?
Because, girl, I'm needin' you, needin' you, needin' you
now
Needin' you now and forever . . .

Tears fill Lacey's eyes as Seth's deep rumble wraps her up in its velvety smoothness. He's singing to her. He's inside the song, holding it close like a heartbeat, his fiddle a low warble of wonder. Not to mention the way he's looking at her. Like she's his sheet music.

She's the song.

Beside her, the Brothers Kincaid's producer, Devlon Block, taps a toe, his eyes closed, swaying like a shaman.

Lacey does the same. Listening. Letting the words stun her like a spell.

I always ran too fast
Down that lost highway
But I found my way back
When I found someone worth makin' me stay
You're every piece of me

The good, the easy, the wild and free
Yeah, this ol' world may go 'round
But doin' it with you makes me feel a little less lost
And a little more found
What's the point of this ol' life
If we don't do it together?
Because, girl, I'm needin' you, needin' you, needin' you now
Needin' you now and forever . . .

When Seth's finished, he looks to her, his smile hitting her like a blazing sunbeam. Tears in her eyes, she stares at him, her hands clasped to her chest. She's so proud of him, so in love, and she takes a step to enter the studio to tell him exactly that. To kiss him senseless. But there's commotion all around her. Luke and Jace and Bobby and Devon Block are crowding in to whoop wild with congratulations.

Lacey freezes on the sidelines.

An ache of sadness wells up in her. A desolate realization. A fact she can't ignore anymore. She's in their world. Not hers. Everyone has their own lives. Even Sal's at the hospital right now, filling in for a friend. And her? She's a planner with nothing to plan. No Pavlovian ping to let her deal with someone else's life instead of hers.

Lacey's hand goes to her throat, twisting her locket. She's an anxiety ball, bouncing from nerve to nerve, from problem to problem. Her worries from last night now tenfold. Her eyes drift to the window. Here in Nashville, all she has is doubt. Seth won't always be around to be the bright, sunny voice talking her down from the ledge of panic.

Needing a breather, she slips out of the room, walking fast down the hallway to exit the front of the old stone church that is Ocean Way Studios. Light flurries dot the air. Lacey holds her elbows, hugging herself tight, trying to wrangle her emotions back into the icy box of her heart.

Seth's song echoes in her head.

The most beautiful thing she's ever heard. It also scares the shit out of her.

She doesn't have it together. Seth doesn't need her stupid neuroses in his life. Because Seth loves her too hard, because she needs him too bad. And sooner or later...

Seth's the guy she'll love too much. Go through pain and hurt for. And for what? Eventually, she'll mess it up, and he'll leave her when he realizes she's a disaster. She'll lose him. Just like she lost her mother and Sal. That means she loses herself. That means she never gets over him. And then she'll be stuck in this new, unfamiliar life.

They rushed it too fast. It was fun to pretend in LA, at the cabin, but now she's back in the real world. And she's scared. It's selfish of her to expect Seth to deal with all her bullshit. He's famous. He's touring. He's recording an album. She can't ask him to put his life on hold for her.

Suddenly, going back to LA seems so easy. In control and safe. That world is hers. The glitz, the drama, the hustle and the stress. Colin's offer is too good to refuse. She'd be a fool to pass it up.

Her eyes drift to the recording studio, her heart like a ticking time bomb in her chest. Seth has his life. Sal too. Why shouldn't she have hers?

Lacey slips out her cell phone and stares at it for a long minute.

And then she dials and lifts it to her ear.

Seth sets his fiddle case in a corner of the living room and straightens up. Automatically, his eyes find Lacey. She's in front of the window, arms crossed over her chest, watching the glow of the sunset disappear into the horizon. The snow's coming down outside Wild Antler Farm, casting the world in a gray hue of gloom.

She looks beautiful. Sad, but beautiful. A thread of worry tugs at him.

Something's wrong.

Lacey returned to the studio, quiet, her green eyes far away. He asked her what was wrong, but she played it off, putting on a happy act as they went out to lunch, had drinks on Broadway. Now, after unloading the instruments, a bottle of wine uncorked, Luke and Sal are in the kitchen tossing together a salad to go with the pizza they ordered.

But Seth knows better. Something's bothering Lacey, and he ain't letting her be upset for one minute longer.

Seth sets his whiskey on the coffee table. The knock of glass on metal has Lacey turning. Seeing Seth, her eyes soften, but not before he catches that river of sadness welling up behind her green depths. "It's really coming down out there," she murmurs. "I've never driven in the snow before."

"Now is that what's botherin' you?" he asks softly. "The snow?"

She meets his eyes, shaking her blond head. "No, it's not that."

"Then what is it?" He peers at her close. "Was it the song? You didn't like it?"

"Oh, Seth, no. I loved it. I . . ." She swallows. "We need to talk about Nashville. What we're doing."

He grins, stepping up to hold her by the arms. "We damn sure do. How 'bout you come stay at my place?" Her eyes flash warily, and Seth amends his offer. "Or we get you a place of your own. Or we could get a place together."

She drops her gaze. "I called Colin today."

The news catches Seth off guard. "Colin from LA?" When she nods, he lets out a breath. "For what?"

She bites her lip. "Back at the cabin, he offered me a job. A really great job, Seth. One I can't turn down."

"But you did, right?"

"No," she says, shamefaced. "I didn't. I go back to LA tomorrow night."

He shakes his head like there's water in his ears. Her news like an atom bomb that's been dropped on his heart. Every conversation they've had has been about the future, about him and Lacey doing them, and now he's confused as hell. "I don't understand," he says. "I'm serious about you, Lace. I thought that's what we've been talkin' about. Us."

She tosses her hair. "Talk is all. We've been on vacation. Of course things seemed easy and fun. But now we have to be realistic, Seth. This is real life."

He stares, hurt. Her words skewer him.

Lacey lifts her arms, lets them drop to her side. "I thought I was ready to walk away from LA, but . . . I don't belong here. You have your band and you're going to be on the road and I have nothing. I'm in the way."

"Goddamnit, no, you ain't," Seth says, desperate to make her understand. "You belong here. You belong with me. We'll make it work, whatever we gotta do."

"You can't fix everything."

"The hell I can't. You don't want me to."

She scoffs. "We're not in love like a country song, Seth."

He closes his eyes. "Don't do that."

"There's no ocean in Nashville."

"North Carolina's hours away."

"I can't drive in the snow. No one likes me because I'm not country."

"Who gives a shit? I'll get you a limo, kick anybody's ass who says otherwise—you're just lookin' for damn excuses." He scoffs, takes a pace around the floor, then faces her. "Hell, I don't know why I'm surprised. You've been fightin' us ever since you got back here."

She bristles, her defenses going up. "That's not fair."

"Isn't it?" He gives her a doubtful look. "I don't know what you're goin' back to, Lace. A shitty job that works you to death."

"You'll be on the road and I'll be stuck here." A stubborn lift of her chin. "I can't give up my life for you."

Seth winces like he's been slapped. "And you want me to?"

"No, I never asked you to do that." She reaches for him. "I love you, Seth. But, it's . . . it's not the right time for us. For any of this."

He rips a hand through his hair. "This is all so fuckin' stupid. We love each other and you're runnin' away?"

She flinches.

Anger wells in him. He's frustrated. Agonized. He's watching everything he loves slip away. "Well, when is gonna be the right time for us?" he says, his tone hard. "Maybe when you get promoted in LA? Or you decide your job didn't work out like it should?"

Tears fill her eyes. "You're being awful."

"I love you, Lacey. I want to take the risk, I want to do us, but there's no way in hell it just ain't the right time for us. It's always been us and you damn well know it." He stares at her and then shakes his head, resigned. "If it's this easy for you to walk away, then maybe I was wrong about everything."

"It's not easy," she whispers, wounded. "None of this is easy." A sob rips out of her, one that tears at his heart. But before he can respond, she rushes past him, disappearing upstairs.

"Fuck," Seth says to the ceiling.

When he turns around, he freezes.

Nothing has him feeling worse than Sal, standing in the doorway, having overheard everything. Her forlorn eyes meet his.

He sighs, not in the mood for a lengthy analysis of what the fuck just happened. Or a lecture. It feels like he just went fifty rounds in the ring with a bull. "Don't look at me like that."

Sal's frowning. "So what? It's over?"

He scrubs a hand down his face. "What do you want me to do, Sal? Make her stay?"

"Yes, Seth, that's exactly what I want you to do. Scale the plane and fight Colin to the death." Sal's voice drops an octave. "I don't know. I don't know, Seth, but *make* her stay. You two are perfect together and you're both just stubborn idiots who can't see it."

He stares, numb. Sal's right, he should do more, but all he can do is just shake his head.

"Come on," Sal urges. "You're letting her go too easy. And you know it."

"She's better off without me."

The excuse lands lame, weak, between them.

"Oh, fuck you, Seth," Sal snaps with enough venom that he stiffens.

Tears in her eyes, Sal turns on her heel and heads for the stairs after her sister.

Gritting his teeth, Seth walks fast for the front door, blinking back tears, ready to get the hell out of the house. He meets Luke's eyes as he goes, his brother's face a mess of sympathy, but Seth opens the front door and walks out without looking back.

chapter

THIRTY-SEVEN

THE NEXT MORNING, LACEY STANDS LISTLESSLY IN HER bedroom, her luggage arranged on the bed. Her eyes sweep the room. The unmade bed. The glass of wine, or three, she had last night to drown her sorrows. The phone she didn't use to call and apologize to Seth. It takes all she has to resist burying her nose in the sheets. The sheets where she and Seth have been sleeping for the last week.

Despair swirls around her and fresh tears jump into her eyes. She sniffles, wishing she was already back in LA. Wishing she could forget. But she knows it will never be that easy, because she left her apartment with remnants of Seth too.

With a sigh, she grabs up a pair of moto leggings and tosses them into the suitcase.

A light rap on the door has her turning.

Sal stands in the doorway, concern on her face. "How are you doing?"

"I'm fine." Lacey sinks to the edge of the bed, reaching out to ruffle Winston, who's hopped next to her. He does three quick turns and settles beside her. At the warmth of his snout on her thigh, tears hit her eyes again. He's sandy and scruffy just like Seth.

"Lace . . ." Sal's green eyes are full of sympathy. "You're not fine."

"Fine." Her lower lip pushes out. Her emotions beg to be released, to let someone in, let someone help. "I'm not fine. I'm awful."

Sal sits beside her and puts an arm around her. "I know you are." Lacey closes her eyes and lets her sister hug her.

"I just want to get back to LA."

"Then why are you still staring at your suitcase?" Sal asks gently. "If you're leaving?"

Lacey swallows, trying to hold herself together. To tell her sister a lie. But she can't. She doesn't want to leave. All she wants to do is take back last night.

"Ugh, I hate that you know me so well," Lacey grouses.

Sal laughs. Then her face clears out. Genuine curiosity in her expression. Her full lips a half smile. "Why did you agree to go? You love Seth."

"Because I'm stupid." Lacey scrubs at her face, her makeup ruined. "I didn't want to say goodbye. We're so different and I thought . . . it wouldn't work out. He'd leave. Somewhere along the way I'd lose him."

Lacey drops her face to cry into Winston's fur. He's soft, and he licks away her salty tears, which only makes her sob harder.

Sal rubs calming circles across her back. "Oh, Lace."

Lacey wipes her eyes and raises her face. "I don't know how you do it, Sal. You and Luke." She stares at her sister, needing an answer. Some sort of truth to get her through this. "You came so close to losing each other so many times. How does that not scare the hell out of you? How do you do it? Why?"

Sal smiles, her entire face aglow at the mention of Luke. She looks at Lacey. "It does scare me. All the time. But I've never regretted any of it because I'd never do this life with anyone else. Luke's it."

Her chest squeezing tight, Lacey looks to the window, to the morning. Snow falls, soft and delicate. She thinks about her sister's words. Like sunlight chasing away a shadow. Hope sneaking in through the cracks in her heart. Love goes through it, but the risk is worth it. For the right person, and that person is Seth.

Everything she didn't know she needed, she found in Seth. He changed her for the better. Showed her a kindness, a strength she never thought possible. Never made her feel hard to love. Made her laugh in a way no one ever could. Constantly backing her up and supporting her when she asked—and when she didn't. She never had to sacrifice any part of herself to be with him. Instead, she showed him all the pieces of her—ugly, sad, bad—and he took it on. Asked for more. Loved her.

Memories of the last month together spark in her mind. Caring for her when she needed him in LA. The two of them slow-dancing at the Silver Dollar. At the cabin, that strange, beautiful calm right before he told her he loved her. The beautiful song he wrote her.

Suddenly her fears, her job, their fight, all the rest of it, doesn't matter.

What matters is Seth.

The only risk. The best risk.

Lacey inhales a deep breath and sits up straight, resolute. Determined. "I'm going to call him."

It's not too late. She's in control. This is her life, and while she isn't sure about what comes next, what she knows is that she's going to give it her all with Seth.

If she still can.

Sal nods, her lips curving up. "Good."

But then Lacey groans, remembering last night. She covers her face with both her hands, peering through slitted fingers at Sal. "Oh my God, I can't. I was such a bitch to him."

Sal chuckles. "He adores you, Lacey. He'll forgive you."

Lacey doesn't know about that.

She saw it on Seth's face last night. She had hurt him. Horribly. While he was fighting for them, she was channeling that ice-cold chill that let her walk away from things she got too close to.

Anguish twists her heart. She should have talked with him about her fears instead of springing the news on him. She should have done a lot of things differently. He had left so abruptly, racing his Bronco out of the drive. She doesn't even know where he is or what he's doing. He left alone and hurt and angry. And she did that.

Sal's soft voice rouses her. "Take it from me. It's never too late."

Lacey chews a nail. "I don't know, Sal."

"I'm selfish. I want you here in Nashville," Sal says with a mischievous grin that soon sobers. "But Seth needs you. He loves you, Lacey." Her sister floats her a smile. "Think about it."

Sal stands, moving to the door as Lacey weighs the options—packing a bag or picking up the phone. Both have her chickening out all over again.

A harsh gasp cuts the silence of the room.

Lacey glances over her shoulder to see Sal gripping the doorknob tight. Her eyes slammed shut. Winston bounds off the bed.

Lacey's brow lifts in suspicion. "Very funny, Sal." She stands, balling up a shirt and tossing it into a suitcase. "Luke isn't here. So take your jokes somewhere else."

Suddenly, Sal doubles over, letting out a sharp cry. Her hands cradle the high swell of her belly.

Lacey hurries to Sal, panic turning her stomach. "Sal? What is it?"

Sal sags against the wall, lifting her wide-eyed gaze to Lacey. But Lacey's looking down.

"Oh no," she whispers, horrified. The entire front of Sal's dress is stained with blood. "No."

Seth bypasses the bartender as she's flipping the Tonk's sign from Closed to Open. She arcs a brow, turning to watch him sit on a stool in the empty bar. "Early mornin.'"

"Bad mornin,'" Seth groans, leaning on his elbows to dip his face in his hands.

He slept like hell last night. After he left the farm, he drove around Nashville wanting to rip up the town, to wreck himself, but he decided that's what got him in trouble in the first place.

Instead, he went back to his apartment, cranked on his records as loud as they could go, screened every call from Luke, and passed out after his fifth glass of whiskey.

"Somethin' I can get you?" the bartender asks, pushing a napkin square his way.

"A beer. Tomato juice."

"You got it." She moves down to the other side of the bar, flipping on the neon above the bar.

Seth swivels his eyes around the familiar surroundings. The cheap wood paneling, the neon lights, the corner jukebox. He's a sick son of a bitch coming to Tonk's. He considered it his and Lacey's bar. But then again, it's a fitting spot to mourn. To pour one out to whatever the fuck happened last night.

Even though it's the last thing he wants to do.

The bartender drops the drinks, and he grips the beer tight. His knuckles wrapped white around the glass. He stares into the foamy liquid, wishing it had all the answers instead of just a bad headache waiting for him at the end of it.

But hell, he doesn't need a crystal ball or a beer to tell him what went wrong.

He knows.

He went wrong.

Last night, he had been believing Lacey was done, thought she was saying she didn't care for him. But now, in the clear light of morning, he's seeing differently. Replaying that conversation over and over in his mind. And what she was really saying was that she scared *for* them.

She was getting out first before she got hurt.

Losing her mom, losing Sal, had taught her that.

When she started talking about Los Angeles and her job, he made her sound selfish and heartless, when all she was was scared. He should've seen it. Lacey was a planner. She needed control. Of course, her being out of her element would scare her. And what did he do? He acted like an asshole. Great job, Seth.

He swallows a gulp of his beer.

Because she was uprooting her life for him while he was re-cording an album and planning a tour, and just assuming she'd be there, because hell, he wanted her there more than anything in the world—but did he ask her to come? Or did he just let that slip through the cracks like everything else?

He should have compromised. They could have done long distance for a few months. Hell, he could have offered to move there. Anything to make it work.

Sal pegged him right.

He let her go too easy. Sal knew it was a cop-out, knew Seth was blaming himself for not being good enough, and she called him on his bullshit.

Now he's got the two women he loves most in the world pissed as hell at him.

He and Sal have never fought before. At least not like that. The way she looked at him, pain and betrayal in her eyes, it was like a fucking knife to his heart.

And Lacey . . .

They've barely been apart twelve hours, but already he feels like he has some great sucking wound in his chest. A void that needs her. Because despite everything, no matter how they left things, he never wanted it to end like it did. He still loves her. So goddamned much.

He's gotta call her. Fight for her. Apologize. He did her wrong. Real fucking wrong. The last thing he wants her to do is leave be-lieving that they ain't got a chance. Because they do. And Seth's gotta make her see that. See that there's no one else in the world he'd rather be with.

Holdin' someone new? Fuck that. And fuck him.

Seth groans at the buzz of his phone. No doubt it's Luke. If he keeps screening his brother's calls, he's in for a real ass-chew-ing the next time he sees him.

"Okay, okay," he mutters, pulling his phone out of his back pocket. Only when he sees Lacey's name on the screen, his heart sparks with hope. With reconciliation.

Quick, he swipes it up and answers. "Lace."

"Seth?"

He tenses. Instantly, he can tell this isn't the conversation he wanted. Something's wrong. Her voice is shaky like she's been crying. "Princess, what is it? Are you okay?"

"It's Sal." Her voice comes high-pitched and panicked. "She's in labor."

Seth's stomach plummets. It's too damn early for that baby to come. He rips a hand through his hair. "You ain't serious."

"Oh, I am very serious, Seth," she hisses. "We're on our way to the hospital, but I can't find Luke. He's not answering his phone."

"Shit." Seth rockets off his stool and tosses down a twenty-dollar bill.

"You have to find him." Lacey's voice drops, a hushed whisper, trying not to scare Sal. "Sal's bleeding. Something's wrong."

Christ, no.

He closes his eyes, opens them. "I'm on my way." He pauses. "It'll be okay, Lacey."

She lets out a shaky breath. "Hurry. Please."

Seconds later, Seth's in his car dialing Luke. No answer. Next up is Jace.

"You seen Luke?" he demands as soon as Jace answers.

"No. He might've been headed to the studio to meet Bobby, but I ain't sure."

Fuck. Where the hell is his brother? He's been a damn helicopter husband this entire pregnancy and now when Sal needs him, he's MIA.

"Listen, Sal's in labor and he ain't answerin' his phone."

"Christ," Jace exhales. "I'll find him."

"Find him fast, man."

White-knuckling the wheel, Seth punches the gas. He drives like hell on the way to the hospital, his nerves frayed by frustration and worry. By the time he gets there, Luke's voice mail is full and Seth's cursing his brother something fierce.

Upstairs, Seth makes his way to labor and delivery right when

Sal's getting wheeled down the hall on a gurney. Lacey follows behind her. Briefly, Seth meets her eyes but goes to Sal.

As he nears, the strong scent of copper hits his nostrils, turning his stomach. Blood seeps through the sheet covering the lower half of her body. "This can't happen," Sal moans, capturing Seth's hand. Fear and anxiety cloud her pale face. "It's too early."

"You're gonna be okay," Seth says, hustling to stay by her side. He doesn't know if it's true or not, but he has to say it. He has to believe it. It can't go any other way. "The both of you."

Sal, her pallor ghost white, nods. She stares at Seth, tears in her eyes. "I'm sorry we fought," she pants. "What I said—"

"Don't worry about that. We're good." He squeezes her hand, his gaze pinning to hers. "We're always good, you hear me?" He gives her a grin. "'Sides, you got more important things to worry about now."

A tiny smile graces her face. But her breaths are coming short and shallow. "Find Luke," she begs. "Please, Seth. I can't do this without him."

Seth smooths her hair. "I'll find him, Sal. Don't—"

"I'm sorry, sir, you'll have to move." The nurse shoves the gurney, breaking their connection. "We need to get her to delivery."

And then Sal's gone, sweeping through the double doors and disappearing down the long hallway.

"Fuck!" Seth's curse is loud and he tears a frustrated hand through his hair. His heart pounds in his chest. If something happens to Sal—to that baby—Luke's a goner.

They all are.

A small sound gets his attention. Lacey, standing in the hall, looking frightened and fragile, hits him in the gut. "Hey," he says, pulling himself together and going to her. "We'll get through this."

Her green eyes brim with tears. "I just want Sal to be okay. And the baby. If anything happens . . ."

"We ain't thinkin' like that. You hear me?" He reaches out to take her hand. She doesn't resist. The feel of her fingers in his—warm, slender—is like a centering calm. His breath steadies, and so does Lacey's.

Seth gives her hand a squeeze. "You okay?"

Her inhale's a shudder. "It was scary. Sal was bleeding, and I didn't know what to do, but I did it. I had to."

"You did good. You got her here." He chuckles. "Hell, princess, you drove in the snow."

Lacey laughs, but it's cut short, her gaze jumping to a point over Seth's shoulder.

He turns, anticipating Luke, but it's Sal's obstetrician, Dr. McKibbon.

"Sal's already dilated to six," she says by way of a greeting. Her wary eyes land on Seth's. "We're moving her to delivery. I'm going to need a daddy to appear soon."

Seth grits his teeth. "Yeah, me fuckin' too."

"It's early," Lacey says in a no-nonsense tone, her hands propped on her hips. "What are you doing to help my sister and her baby? Nothing can happen to them—do you understand me?"

Seth side-eyes Lacey with pride. Any panic that was there is gone. Instead, Lacey stands there, determined to be strong for Sal.

McKibbon nods. "Thirty-four weeks is soon, but ninety-nine percent of babies born this early survive." Her eyes flick to Seth. "I'd be more worried about Luke." She smiles gently and moves in the direction of the double doors. "I'll keep you updated."

Lacey grips Seth's arm, her eyes enormous. "Where is he?"

"I don't know." Seth laces his hands behind his head and paces, trying to chase away the panic. The restless energy building. "Luke, goddamnit," he mutters. "I'm gonna kill you if you miss this."

Lacey peers behind Seth as he paces, keeping watch on the entrances and exits for Luke.

Closing his eyes, Seth hurls a positive thought out into the universe. All the positive goddamn thoughts for his brother and Sal. *Please, Christ, let that baby be okay. It's got a family to join. The best parents in the world to meet.*

Anything else ain't happening. Anything else is unimaginable.

One minute.

Two minutes.

Thirty minutes pass.

Then—

The hard sound of frantic bootsteps in the hall hit Seth's ear.

He whips around, Lacey gasps, and then Luke's rounding the corner, wild-eyed and crazed.

Seth's chest expands in relief at the sight of his brother.

Thank Christ.

Seth lifts his arms. "It's about goddamn time, man."

"I left my damn phone in the truck," Luke shoots back, not slowing his stride as he rushes down the hall. "Where is she?"

Seth points at the double doors. "She's in there. Go," he says. "Go, man. Go take care of Sal."

Luke barely has time to give Seth a grateful glance before he slams through the doors and disappears.

Seth lets out a steadying breath, turning his gaze to Lacey.

For the last half hour, she's been tense and alert. Now, her shoulders sag. Every ounce of adrenaline drains out of her as reality settles in. Her beautiful face crumples and she bursts into a heartbreaking sob. "I can't do this," she whispers.

"C'mere." Seth grabs her hand, gathering her into his arms, the pump of her heart quickening against his. "I got you."

THIRTY-EIGHT

LACEY SITS IN A CHURCH PEW OF THE HOSPITAL CHAPEL, watching the candles flicker. It's dim and empty inside. A quiet respite away from the harsh hospital lights. She's grateful to Seth. She felt like imploding and he got her out of there before she broke down completely. All she could think about was the blood. So much blood this last month. Her blood, Sal's blood, God forbid, the baby's.

Wiping her face, she watches as Seth settles beside her. "I didn't know you went to church," she says.

He laughs. "I don't. Hell, Luke and I haven't been back since we were kids. He had the bright idea of tryin' to vault the church pews every Sunday mornin.'"

She arcs a brow. "Uh-huh. I'm sure that was Luke's idea." Seth chuckles. Then she clears her throat. "Thank you. For coming when I needed you."

His gaze jumps to hers. "You're welcome."

"I just want them to be okay." Tears swim in her eyes at the memory of Sal's anguished face in her mind.

"I know. I do too."

Seth's deep rumble hangs heavy between them. It's then that Lacey takes a closer look at him. His handsome face is tired. He's still in yesterday's clothes. And then she sniffs. Her nose wrinkles, as she says, "You smell like alcohol."

"What can I say? Was cryin' in my beer this mornin.'"

Lacey sighs. She straightens up, gathering strength. "I owe you an apology, Seth."

He shakes his head. "You don't, though."

"I do. I never meant to hurt you. Ever." She looks down, ashamed. "I've spent my whole life avoiding things, not taking risks. When Colin offered me that job, the first time, I turned it down. But when things got hard, I panicked. I saw a way out. A way not to get hurt, and I took it." She shakes her head. "It seemed so easy to go back to the job I knew, instead of starting something new with you."

"I know," Seth says, and she looks up, blinking in surprise. "I spent last night thinkin' you didn't love me, or maybe it was all bullshit between us—"

"Seth, no," she whispers, hating that he thought that.

"But this mornin' I realized that what you were doing was protectin' yourself. I didn't give you much of a chance to explain." Seth shifts, and so does Lacey, their bodies turning toward each other as if on instinct. Their hands automatically finding each other's. "I acted like an asshole and I'm so damn sorry, Lace."

"We both acted like assholes." She pulls his hand into her lap, squeezing it.

"And I'm the one who's sorry," she says, frustration entering her tone. "I got scared. I have a bad habit of running away when life gets too close. I worry too much and that's my fault. I can't use you to reassure me all the time."

A fierce look crosses his face. "But you should have. Hell, this is all new for you, Lace. Nashville is new. I shoulda been there more for you than I was."

A tear slips down her face. "No, you have a career."

"And you got one too. I coulda compromised." He runs a thumb over her knuckles. His voice turns tender. "I ain't perfect, Lace, I know that, but I wanna be a good man for you."

"You are, Seth. You're perfect for me. I'm the one who's a gigantic mess. I don't even know where I'm going or what I'm doing," she says hotly, glancing away at the flickering candles.

She sweeps a hand over the tears running down her cheeks. "I don't even know why you put up with me."

"Look at me," Seth says in a soft voice. Gently, he tilts her chin up to stare her in the eyes. "I love you, Lacey. I love your dumb, gorgeous face and I can't imagine my world without you in it. Hell, I can't stand bein' without you."

A sob-laugh bursts out of her, warmth glowing inside her chest like a million fluttering fireflies.

Reaching out, he swipes away a tear from her cheek with his thumb. "I don't care if we gotta do this thing long distance or if I have to move to Los Angeles or if we shack up on goddamn Jupiter. I want to do it. I want you."

She lifts her eyes, staring at him beneath lowered eyelashes. Her heart like a drumbeat inside her chest. "I love you too," she says, and Seth closes his eyes, relief and hope etched across his features. "I still want us. I want our chance. Even if you are excruciatingly annoying."

Seth's laugh tumbles out of him in a bright burst of joy.

And then he's pulling her into his arms, cupping her face and lowering his lips to hers. A quiet heat between them, a trembling of hands, of words. "I love you," Seth whispers, and Lacey curls her arms around his neck, keeping him close, savoring Seth finally back in her arms.

When they pull away, she curls up against Seth's chest. A shaky sigh whooshes out of him, his lean body untensing. His relief, his love, so powerful that she closes her eyes against the rush of emotions.

They stay there like that in the soft flicker of the candlelight until Seth kisses her brow.

"What about your job?" he asks, his voice soft.

"I'll figure something out," she whispers, reaching up to palm his jaw.

He gathers her tighter against him. "We will."

Quiet silence drifts over them, and for a few brief minutes, the outside world forgotten, everything is perfect.

Seth stretches out in the waiting room chair, careful not to disturb Lacey. He's dog-tired and worry for Sal and the baby eats at him. Everything in the world right now feels so precious.

Only Lacey, tucked contentedly in his arms, offers him any relief. She sleeps off and on, worn out from everything that's happened today. He holds her tight against him. A reminder of what he's gotten back.

He closes his eyes.

Losing her again ain't an option.

They're gonna work it out. It's the damn surest thing he knows. Whatever he's gotta do, he'll do it. For the rest of her life, Lacey will know what she means to him. She won't ever wonder if she's safe or loved because he'll show her every day how much his heart beats for her.

Leaning down, he presses a kiss to the top of her blond head.

Lacey lets out a small moan, stirring in his arms. She raises her head and stares at him sleepily. "What time is it?"

"A little after four," he says in a low voice.

"Anything?"

He shakes his head. "No."

She sighs.

He knows the feeling. They've been at the hospital for hours with no word from Luke. He doesn't want to think the worst. Hell, he can't think the worst. Because the worst ain't happening. Not to Sal and not to Luke.

Seth sits up, exhaling a long breath. "Hell, I gotta do somethin.'" He rubs his palms on the thighs of his jeans and looks to Lacey. "You want a coffee or—"

A small squeak cuts him off, Lacey's eyes wide and wondering.

Seth follows her gaze. Luke's striding down the corridor, looking like the luckiest son of a bitch in the world.

"He's smiling." Lacey turns to Seth, a grin on her own gorgeous face. "Luke's smiling." She grabs his hand so hard he winces. "That's good, right?"

"That's goddamn great," Seth says, and then they're standing, meeting Luke in the middle of the hall.

"Well?" Seth says, rubbing his clammy palms together. Nerves damn near got him beat. "What's the word?"

"Are they okay?" Lacey blurts, tears already welling in her eyes.

"Sal's okay, the baby's okay," Luke says with a shaky exhale. He looks almost shellshocked at his good luck. "She lost some blood, but it ain't nothin' serious."

Seth blows out a relieved breath. "Thank Christ."

"Well?" Lacey jumps up and down, her hands clasped together. "Don't keep us in suspense. What is it?"

Luke grins. "A boy." His voice snags on the words, choked by emotion. "He's tiny, but he's perfect." Luke's eyes turn misty. "Cash. We named him Cash."

Seth grins and squeezes his brother's shoulder. "Damn, man," he says, his own voice cracking. "Congrats."

Lacey emits an earsplitting squeal. "Oh my God!" She latches onto Seth, shaking him so hard his teeth rattle. Luke's next. She throws herself into his arms, hugging him and then hugging Seth until they're all jumping around the hallway laughing so hard, they're crying.

Luke laughs and runs a hand through his hair. "You want to see them?"

With that, they follow Luke down the hall to the large private room where Sal is.

Once inside the room, Seth's hit by a wave of emotion.

Just like that—his brother and Sal are mom and dad.

It's too goddamn great for words.

Sal's propped up in bed, a small bundle wrapped tight in her arms. She looks luminous with joy. Seeing Lacey and Seth, her face lights up. "You both stayed!"

Lacey, her squeal on a low simmer, rushes to Sal's side.

Seth affects a casual shrug. "Hey, someone had to stay to make sure Luke kept it together."

A snort from Luke.

Seth evaluates at Sal. She looks tired but happy. "You doin' okay?"

"Oh, we're great," Sal whispers and smiles. "You want to meet your nephew?"

"Yeah." Seth says, choked up. "I do."

His heart's in his throat as he approaches the bed.

Carefully, Sal removes the blanket to give him a good look at the swaddled baby. "This is Cash." She stares up at Seth, her face one of wonder and joy. "Want to hold him before they take him to the NICU?"

Not trusting himself to talk, Seth nods. With help from Lacey, he gets Cash settled in his arms. His chest tightens as he takes in the tiny baby Sal and Luke worked so hard to have.

"Oh my God, Sal," Lacey whispers, edging in. Together, he and Lacey peer down at the baby. "He's so beautiful."

He is. Small and quiet, Cash peeks up and out of the safety of the blanket. The baby has Sal's dark hair and Luke's dark eyes. Cash stares at Seth, head cocked as if he's ready to listen to it all. "Hey, kid," Seth says, around the lump in his throat. "You're pretty cute, even if you caused all of us enough stress to have a heart attack."

It's then Seth makes the kid a vow that he will always be there for him. The way his brother was for him. Sal and Luke's son will always be safe and protected. For as long as he lives, that kid will have him as backup. No matter what.

A small squawk from Cash has Lacey giggling.

"Great," Seth says and stares at the baby in awe, his eyes wet. "Another loudmouth in the family."

Luke laughs. "Learnin' how to sing already."

"You're terrifying him, Seth," Lacey says, smiling. With a gentle ease, she steals away the baby, fawning over his dark, wispy hair and adorable yawns.

All Seth can do is watch. A warmth, a tightness, grows in his chest, overwhelming him in the best possible way. He doesn't want kids, not now, not for a long time, but goddamn does he want Lacey to be the mother of his children.

Seth meets Lacey's soft green eyes as she passes Cash back to Sal. While Sal takes her son into her arms, Lacey drifts to his side, lacing her fingers through his.

"Wait," Sal says, catching Lacey and Seth curled into one another. Happiness shines bright in her eyes. "Really?"

"You know, if I didn't know any better, I'd think you planned this." Lacey laughs, tilting her face up to Seth's to give him a dazzling smile. "But, yes, really."

Seth grins, looping an arm around Lacey's shoulders. "Just next time, go easy on the whole goin'-into-labor-early thing."

Luke groan-laughs, going to his wife's side. He puts an arm around her, looking down on her and his son in wonder. The new lights of his world.

As quiet laughter and conversation fills the room, Seth takes in his family, a contentedness filling him up inside like nothing he's ever known. He's finally where he needs to be. With his family. No secrets between him and his brother. Sal and Luke have their second chance with Cash.

He and Lacey get their second chance too. And he's going to make every second, every damn minute count.

Lacey snaps the latches on her suitcase and gives her hair one final brush in the mirror. She smiles, picking a milky-white clump from her black velvet sweater. Baby spit. As gross as it is, it's been her new accessory for the last two weeks.

Suitcase, duffel bag and purse in her hands, Lacey exits her bedroom and enters the hall. Instantly, she's hit by the faint smell of baby powder. Stale reheated coffee. The thump of a guitar. Wild Antler Farm is still the same house she lived in so many years ago, but now it's louder, more chaotic, filled with so much love she could burst.

Only now it's time for her to go.

After Sal had Cash, Lacey called Colin and told him her decision to stay in Nashville. He had been unhappy, but understanding, and somehow talked her into planning one last event for him. So, she's going back to Los Angeles for four months. To help him with one final party, to get her stuff in order, and then she'll be back.

Lacey wobbles at the top of the stairs, her bags obscuring her vision, when there's a deep rumble from in front of her. "Careful, princess, you take a tumble I ain't gonna be too happy."

Lacey looks up, warmth tracking through her as Seth's handsome face comes into view. She tosses her hair. "It'd keep me here, wouldn't it?"

He chuckles and reaches for her bags. "Let's think of somethin' a little less drastic than hurlin' yourself down the stairs." He leans in and kisses her, his blue-eyed gaze taking her in. "You ready to go?"

"Ugh, no," she says reluctantly but lets Seth take her hand and lead her downstairs into the living room. What she sees has her smiling, her heart expanding. Sal on the couch with Cash cradled in her arms. The baby is healthy and his lungs are strong, only needing a week's stay in the NICU for jaundice until Sal and Luke were able to bring him home.

Lacey heads straight for them and sits beside her sister. She dips down to kiss Cash's downy head, inhaling velvet baby skin and milk. "He's going to be such a heartbreaker," she coos, tickling a chunky baby thigh.

"Takes after his uncle," Seth drawls, leaning in the doorway.

Lacey rolls her eyes.

Sal laughs.

"I'm going to miss him so much," she tells Sal. "He'll be so big the next time I see him."

Luke, in the corner chair, his guitar on his lap, yawns. "Hopefully, he's sleepin' through the night by then."

"Hopefully, we all will be," Sal murmurs, smiling. She stays on the couch, pinned by the sleeping baby, but stretches out a hand to take Lacey's. "I love you. I'll see you soon."

Lacey pulls her shoulders back, swallowing the constriction in her throat. "I love you more." She gives Luke a look. "Take care of my sister."

He grins and gives her a wave. "Always."

Shouldering her bags, Seth ushers Lacey out onto the front porch. But when she sees his vintage Bronco in the drive waiting to take her to the airport, tears hit her eyes. She's going to miss this world she made for herself. The snow, the country, the farm and her family. And Seth. Him most of all.

"I'm going to cry," she moans. "And I promised myself I wouldn't."

Seth sets down the bags and pulls her up close to him. She buries her face against his chest, sliding her arms around his waist. "I can stay."

"No. You're goin'." He tips up her chin to press a resolute kiss to her lips. "Every two weeks," he reminds her. His Adam's apple bobs. "I'll be out there."

She sniffles. "I can do two weeks."

"Do not work yourself to death, you hear me? I want you back in one piece."

A smile graces her lips. "I can do that too."

Seth inhales a long breath and cups her cheek. His voice thickens. "I love you, Lace."

She curls her arms around her neck and leans against him. "I love you."

As Seth draws her back in for another sweet kiss, Lacey savors it. Savors everything about this moment. Out of everything she could have ever planned for herself, she never pictured this. Her life's never been more out of whack, but she can't imagine anything more perfect.

And even though in a few short hours, she'll be in LA, on the other side of the world, her heart's already back here with the man she loves, planning their future.

The sweetest one she's ever imagined.

epilogue

Four Months Later

SETH TOSSES THE RAG INTO THE SINK AND PIVOTS TO place the bottle of white wine in the fridge. His favorite Bob Dylan album plays on full blast, the music as loud as the bright May sunlight outside. He checks the vase of pink tulips, the steaks marinating on the countertop.

He thanks Christ Luke isn't around to see this. His brother's already called him a lovesick son of a bitch one too many times this last week. Not like he has any room to talk. Luke's practically tripping over his own feet to make it home to Sal and Cash these days.

Grabbing up his phone, Seth shakes his head in disgust at the latest *Nashville Star* headline to hit his text notifications. *Brothers Kincaid Bassist Jace Taylor Involved with Other Woman?* The accompanying photo shows a suspicious-looking Jace ducked into a hallway, a cell phone pressed tight against his ear.

Poor bastard, Seth thinks. Apparently, the *Star* just won't move on from trying to crucify the Brothers Kincaid. *Fuckers.*

Seth shakes off his worry for his friend, trying his best to focus on Lacey. As his eye snags on the time, he curses. He's late. Or he's going to be if he doesn't get the hell out the door. He's got about fifteen minutes to make Lacey's plane.

A surge of excitement hits him at the thought of seeing her again. After four months of doing long distance, of late-night phone calls and quick weekend trips, they're making it official.

She's moving in.

But she doesn't know Seth plans to do more than that.

Tonight's the goddamn night. He's getting down on one knee and asking the question he's been dying to ask ever since she left.

Because it's been too damn long without Lacey. Ever since she went away, he's been going crazy. Counting the days until he gets her back. Each day apart has been brutal, but it's been worth it. They've only gotten stronger. Better.

He's more in love with her than he's ever been.

"Shit." Seth, harried, pats his pockets to make sure everything's right where it should be. Satisfied, he stomps across his apartment, grabs his keys and strides for the door.

What he sees when he whips it open has him freezing.

Lacey.

She stands there, luggage at her feet, her green eyes big and wide. Seeing Seth, she does a little ta-da motion with her hands. "Surprise!"

His stomach flips over at the sight of her, every atom in his body coming alive, charging up. "What the hell are you doin' here?"

She looks indignant, pretending to turn away. "Fine, if you don't want me—"

"No fuckin' way," he growls, grabbing her arm and spinning her into him.

She laughs, looping her arms around his neck. "I took an earlier flight. I wanted to surprise you."

A smile breaks over his face. "This is the best damn surprise." Then he's kissing her, holding her tight against him, his hands sliding into all that silky blond hair. God, she tastes good. Like that first drink of water when you've been parched for days.

When they pull away, they're silent. They run their hands over each other, mapping each other, as if they weren't together just four weeks ago. Seth's gaze travels over her low-cut floral blazer and short velvet shorts. Her long tan legs and flash of cleavage are heart-stopping.

Lacey leans in and kisses him again, running gentle fingers through his hair. "You need a haircut."

He chuckles. "I was on my way to get you."

"Lucky for you, I planned ahead," she says with a triumphant toss of her hair.

Seth stares at her, the rock in his throat expanding. "Lucky me."

He is. He's so damn lucky.

He never expected this to be real. Him and Lacey, they were supposed to be a one-time thing, an accident, a fling. Both of them living in that same stale, flat key. Lonely, lost. And then she found him that night. Rock bottom, ready to throw it all away, only she was there, pulling him up, rescuing him before he got too far gone. Because of her, he's a better man. Because of her, he finally knows what true love is.

There's a rock in his throat as he stares at her. At this woman he loves more than life itself.

Tearing his eyes from her, he grabs up a bag, grabs her hand and leads her inside.

Lacey looks around the familiar space. Her observant eyes take it all in. The recent cleaning, the vase of tulips on the counter, the bottle of wine. She's been here before, it's still the same old place, but now it's different. Because it's theirs.

"It smells good in here," she says, a look of appreciation crossing her face. "You cooked?"

"And cleaned." Seth leans back, bracing his hands against the countertop. "You get packed up okay?"

"I did." She kicks off her heels, immediately sinking four inches. "Everything should be here next week."

Seth brushes his eyes around the small apartment. "I ain't even askin' if it'll fit."

She sniffs. "I pared down."

"Bullshit. Leavin' a pair of shoes behind don't count."

"I did, Seth." She laughs, crossing the room to palm the

pink bud of a tulip. "Oh, get this. Colin asked if I'd plan his summer camp party virtually."

He rolls his eyes at the theme but grins at Lacey. "Let me guess, your mind instantly went to Camp Crystal Lake."

"Maybe," she says with a smug little shrug. Her green eyes gleam. "I turned him down, though."

"You did? Why?"

"Because." She bites her lip. "I told him I might be busy on tour with you."

Seth's mouth falls open. "Really?" It's what he's been wanting for such a long time. Lacey on the tour bus with him and his family. The Brothers Kincaid have a monthlong tour starting in three weeks, and Lacey being there would be the cherry on top.

"Really." Lacey flushes. "Work can wait for a few months."

"Hell yeah, it can." Seth grins. He's already put the good word out on the street about Lacey, using his music industry connections to talk her up. She's going to kick ass in Nashville, and Seth will be beside her for whatever she needs.

"I want to go with you, Seth," Lacey says, almost shyly as she closes the gap between them.

He tugs on the lapel of her jacket, getting an eyeful of sun-kissed cleavage. "What if I told you you had to pack light?"

She gasps. "Monster." Then smiles. "I'd say you're stuck with me anyway."

A surge of excitement sweeps through him. He lets out a bright laugh and sweeps her up in his arms to twirl her around the living room. She squeals and peppers his face with soft kisses.

"I'm so goddamn happy, Lace," he says, kissing her hard and setting her on her feet. "Goin' with me on the road, hell, it means fuckin' everything."

She smiles bright, her excitement a match to his. "No work. No parties. Just us."

"Now I don't know about that." At the quirk of her brow,

he goes on. "I'm thinkin' you might have to plan a party on the road."

"Whose?"

In answer, he lowers himself down on one knee.

She gasps and takes a step backward. "What're you doing?"

Seth reaches up to take her hand and Lacey's eyes widen like she's finally put it together. His heart thrums in his chest, nerves threatening to take him out. "Askin' you to marry me, but if you're gonna be all difficult about it . . ." From his pocket, he pulls out a shiny pink diamond solitaire. He clears his swollen throat. "I love you, Lacey. I want to start our life together and I can't wait another damn second."

Lacey stares, tears tracking down her cheeks, her hands clutched to her chest.

"What do you say, princess?" He holds the ring up to her, tears filling his eyes. "Will you marry me? Will you wreck my bathroom in the worst possible way?"

A choked sob tumbles out of Lacey's mouth. And then she's grabbing Seth's arms, pulling him up and into her. With shaky hands, she palms his jaw. Her kisses, her tears, land hot on his face. "Yes," she sob-laughs. "Yes, yes, yes!" Squealing, she flings her arms around his neck, nearly knocking him off his feet.

"Gotta make this official," Seth says, pulling away. He grins, his heart like a melody in his chest, finally finding the right tune. With trembling hands, he slips the glittering ring on her finger. "It looks damn good on you, princess."

Lacey evaluates the ring, a happy flush blooming across her cheeks. She leans back against the counter, tugging Seth against her. Her green eyes are wicked. "*You* look good on me."

The front of his pants is suddenly tight. Leaning in, he kisses down the curve of her neck, his hand slipping down the waist of her shorts.

A whimper rolls out of Lacey. "Seth . . ." She tilts her neck and bares her teeth in that ferocious way he loves. Because

Lacey's got all the power. Got him by the balls. Got him on his knees. Got him forever.

"C'mere, princess, we gotta do this right."

Lacey gasps as Seth's long fingers dip into her. She's on a high. From Seth's kiss. The ring on her finger. Their reunion. And now his hands. Roaming every part of her body like it's a map to heaven. Into his ear, she whispers, "Is this the part where we christen the apartment?"

"Startin' with the livin' room," Seth says, closing his eyes as she cups the front of his jeans. Just the heat of him, the length has her shivering.

"It might take a while."

A roguish smile breaks out on Seth's face. "Now ain't that a straight-up shame."

Lacey lets Seth dance her back to the couch. Her jacket, her shorts removed with clever fingers. He groans when he sees her strappy bodysuit. "Anyone ever tell you you're a pain in my ass, princess?"

"You hate it," Lacey breathes.

He dips his head to her breast, his look ravenous. "I do, but you're also the love of my life, so it looks like I'm stuck with you."

Her stomach, her toes curl as Seth tugs the strap of her bodysuit down to take her breast in his mouth. His tongue laps at her nipple, stroking it to a hardened bud. Hungry, so hungry, Lacey cups his scruffy jaw, bringing Seth's mouth to her lips. She pulses down below at his fevered kiss. A kiss that says they've been apart too long. That it'll never happen again.

Curling an arm around her waist, Seth gently lowers Lacey onto the couch. He sheds his jeans, his shirt, and then he's lowering himself onto her, lengthening with her. "Christ," he says, shaking as he inhales her scent. "You're too fuckin' perfect."

Moaning, Lacey arches her body up into him. Begging. Seth is doing dangerous, impatient things to her body. It's been so long without him, she can't wait anymore. She's going to burst. Hands curling against the lean muscles of his back, she says, "Please, Seth. I need you."

His eyes flash at her words. Their calling card for so long. Only now, it's everlasting. No longer a bad habit or a fling.

A forever.

Grinning, Seth lowers his hand, unsnapping her bodysuit. His dick jumps to attention and then he slips into her with a pained sound. A gentle gasp from Lacey, the flutter of her eyes, and she's tilting her head back. Every second like that first taste.

Lacey wraps her legs around Seth's waist, clamping him tight against her.

Together, they rock. The feel of Seth finally inside of her, his throaty rumble, tears through Lacey like fire. Her body is feral. "Faster," she breathes. Her nails dig into his shoulder. Seth gasps. Thrusts. Her head falls back and Lacey closes her eyes. Curves her body higher, pressing her breasts against his chest.

"*Lace . . .*" Her name's a moan and then Seth's thrusting, picking up speed, curling fingers in her hair. Lacey writhes, her body igniting into warmth, into stars, and then Seth's right behind her. His entire body stiff as he spills into her. His lean body pulses with shivers, a grunt of satisfaction echoing out of him to fill the apartment.

Chuckling, Seth lowers himself beside her on the couch, tucking her against his side. His warm breath tickles her ear as he presses a kiss to her neck. "Have I told you how much I god-damn love you?"

"Mmm." Lacey smiles up at him. "I could hear it again."

A low rumble of a laugh. "Well, I do. I love you," he says, reaching back to grab a blanket from the back of the couch, pulling it over the both of them.

Lacey sweeps her eyes across the living room. "Looks like the living room's accomplished."

Seth chuckles. "One room down, four to go."

And then she sighs, long and content, letting where she is wash over her. Like the best kind of dream. She flops on her back and stretches out her arm, finally taking the time to drink in the gorgeous ring on her finger.

"You like it?" Seth hedges, his eyes on her face.

"I love it." She cups his jaw. "So much."

The ring's perfect. It's everything she could want. Beautiful, big, sparkly. Pink. But none of that truly matters. Seth could give her a rubber band and she'd wear it. She has love in Seth, no ring can top that.

"I still don't believe this," Lacey says, sitting up on her elbows. Her gaze narrows in on Seth. "When did you have time to buy a ring?"

He grins at her, his handsome face so calm, so steadying it feels like home. "Started lookin' at rings the day you went back to LA." His shrug's sly. "Sal may or may not have had a hand in it." He eases down, pressing a kiss to her lips.

She smiles. "Of course she did."

Seth takes her tight in his arms, resting his chin against the crown of her head as they burrow back down on the couch. "I'm glad you're home, Lacey."

She closes her eyes, reaching up to palm his cheek, the ring glittering bright on her finger. "Me too."

Home was never LA or her job or being alone or controlling her perfect world, no matter how miserable she was.

Home is here. With Seth.

She's not alone anymore. She never was. She always had Seth, but now she has Seth and their story. A world they get to make just for them. Something beautiful and bright and filled with family and friends and love and music. Touring with Seth, building her own business in Nashville, seeing Sal and her nephew every day if she wants to.

Her life.

And she'll live it with the man she wants to be with forever.

The only person who can call her on her bullshit, whose banter sets her heart aflame. The man who came to her when she needed him and led her through the dark times and into the light.

The best kind of love.

An always-and-forever country song.

Here's a special sneak peek of *Bring You Back,*
the fourth book in the Nashville Star series!

chapter
ONE

THIS ISN'T JACE TAYLOR'S GODDAMN DAY. OR NIGHT.
In fact, the last six months haven't been his goddamn life.

He's tried to hide the mess he's in. Tried to fix it. Now there isn't anything to do but own it and try to make sense of the last twenty-four hours. Because he's got to figure out just what in the hell to do next.

His mantra.

Figure it out. Fix it. Always fix it. Get it the fuck together.

Sweat beading his brow, Jace groans, dragging his sorry ass up the staircase of the rustic apartment overlooking the river. It's late, nearing midnight, the humid summer August night remind-ing him of all the better things he could be doing right now if he were a better man. Like relaxing in his own bed, a stiff drink in his hand, his wife curled tight in his arms. Instead, all he's got is a black eye, a headache, and the coldest shoulder Emmy Lou's ever given him.

He pauses on the dark stairwell, clenching his teeth at the radiating pain pulsing through every inch of his body. Hissing a breath, he tucks his right hand against his ribs. Then, stomach knotting, he raises a fist—his good fist—and knocks.

He fucked up royally. He can't go home. He's got nowhere to go. Nowhere except—

The door swings open.

Seth Kincaid, fiddle player of the Brothers Kincaid, stands blinking in the doorway of his apartment, his sandy-blond hair standing on end.

"Damn, man," Seth says, his voice rumbling out in his signature baritone drawl. "We waited for you after practice. Luke damn near drank up all of Tootsie's. Think he's still on a high from signin' that contract."

Luke should be on a high. Earlier today, the Brothers Kincaid closed a deal that landed them a residency in Vegas. Big deal star status. Three months. Quarter million dollars a show. And Jace should have been right there beside his best friend celebrating, only he wasn't because he was too busy getting his ass beat in the parking garage at Six String.

Seth cocks his head, squinting in the dim light. "Where you been?"

"I've been screwin' up." Without waiting for an invitation, Jace pushes his way past Seth and steps inside the apartment. "Can I get some water?" he rasps, licking dry lips.

"Sure, you can get some water, but what—"

The sunny grin drops off Seth's face.

In the light of the apartment, Seth's blue eyes widen as his gaze takes full stock of Jace. "Holy fuck." He draws back horrified. "You got a damn hole in your mouth, man."

Wincing, Jace sits on a leather stool. He swears at the blood dripping onto the white countertop and sticks a tongue through his busted lip. Then he unveils his hand. Bloodied, knuckles busted, crumpled like a piece of paper.

Seth swears and rips a hand through his hair, standing it on end. "Shit. It's broken."

Jace waves him off, flexing each swollen finger one-by-one. They all work. "It ain't broken. It's busted as shit, but it ain't broken." He tries to grin. The motion hurts, feels exactly the way Jace does right now.

Numb.

There's a flurry of commotion as Seth, bypassing a vase of tulips and a fat stack of wedding magazines, grabs a rag from the sink, wets it, and tosses it to Jace. Jace catches it without looking up, in sync now as much as they are when they're on stage.

As Seth steps around the counter to hand Jace an icepack there's a harsh suck of air. They both turn to see Lacey coming around the corner.

Seth swears.

Lacey freezes in her tracks, drawing her short black robe tight around her. Her big green eyes are as wide as saucers as she stares at Jace.

Jace stiffens. *Shit.*

Lacey tilts her head, her long blond hair falling over one slender shoulder. She takes a step toward him. Her pretty brow a frown. "Jace, what happened?"

"I'm fine, honey," he says good-naturedly, not wanting to scare her. He breaks off, glancing around the apartment, feeling his asshole-status skyrocketing. Music blasts from the back bedroom. Two glasses of red wine sit forgotten on the counter. Lacey's stilettos strewn across the living room.

Jace internally groans. He's a shithead, coming here unannounced, interrupting their night.

Curious, confused, Lacey drifts toward Jace, but Seth's quick. He intercepts, scooping her up protectively in his arms, like he doesn't want whatever is touching Jace around his girl.

"Emmy Lou's got a mean right hook," Seth jokes, but Jace can see Lacey doesn't buy it.

"He's bleeding all over the counter, Seth." She peers at Jace. "Should I call Sal?"

"Nah." Jace lifts a hand. "It's just a bar fight."

She arches a brow. *Bullshit* her stubborn gaze says.

Seth leans in close, touching Lacey's cheek. "I got this, princess."

Lacey gives Seth a doubtful look, but kisses him, then disappears into the back bedroom.

When he's sure Lacey's out of earshot, Seth turns to Jace. "What the hell happened?" The kid's voice, more serious than Jace has ever heard it, has him grimacing. "I've seen a bar fight. This ain't a bar fight."

Jace buries his face in his battered hand, wondering where to fucking start.

Coming Fall 2022

books by
AVA HUNTER

The Nashville Star Series

Know You More – a Prequel

Sing You Home

Find You Again

Love You Always – a Novella

Need You Now

Bring You Back

acknowledgments

Thank you for reading *Need You Now*! Seth and Lacey hold a very special place in my heart and I hope you loved them as much as I do. Thank you to Eliza Dee for the edits and Sarah Hansen for the gorgeous cover. Thank you to my beta readers. Thank you to Eve Kasey and Anna P. for being fabulous sounding boards and blurb masters. Thank you to the Trauma Fiction group for their amazing help with all the medical issues my poor characters go through. Thank you to the wonderful bloggers and bookstagrammers and readers who have shouted the word about the Nashville Star series this last year. I appreciate you so much. And as always, thank you to my family for your support.

about the
AUTHOR

Ava Hunter is a strong believer in black coffee, red wine, and the there's-only-one-bed trope. She writes contemporary romance with healthy amounts of angst, where the damsels are never quite damsels, but the men they love (good, bad and rugged) are always there for them. Her first series, Nashville Star, centers on sexy country singers and their honky-tonk drama-filled lives. When Ava isn't parked in front of the computer writing, she is mom-ing, reading, traveling, drinking wine, baking and watching good TV. She writes from her home in Arizona, where she lives with her husband, daughter, and a very chonky cat.

Don't miss out on Ava Hunter's upcoming books!
Subscribe to her newsletter:
www.authoravahunter.com